Justin turned the *Centurion* south and hurried through the low brush. He squeezed his 'Mech between some tight tree stands, then loped out onto the low ground. The groundskeepers had provided a sandy river-bed to break up the area between large islands of greenery. *A perfect place to play hide and seek,* Justin thought, with a knowing smile.

Suddenly, his sensors exploded and burned the *Rifleman*'s yellow silhouette onto his forward screen. The 'Mech sprang from behind a hillock and leveled its arms at Justin. The large laser on the *Rifleman*'s right arm bathed the *Centurion*'s right arm with its scarlet fire. Armor boiled and melted on *Yen-lo-wang*'s limb, but held even as the *Rifleman*'s autocannon ripped chunks of armor away from the same arm.

Justin, ignoring the medium laser that flashed at him and missed, brought up his autocannon. He dropped his jaw and opened a radio line to Wolfson. "It's all over, Billy. At this range, you're history." Justin tightened his finger on the autocannon's trigger.

But nothing happened…

THE WARRIOR TRILOGY

WARRIOR: EN GARDE

VOLUME ONE

Other BattleTech Novels:

The Gray Death Legion Saga
by William H. Keith, Jr.

   Decision at Thunder Rift
   Mercenary's Star
   The Price of Glory

The Sword and the Dagger
by Ardath Mayhar

THE WARRIOR TRILOGY

WARRIOR: EN GARDE

VOLUME ONE

by

Michael A. Stackpole

To Liz,
for absolutely everything
and then some...

FASA Corporation
P.O. Box 6930
Chicago, IL 60680

Cover Art: David English
Cover Design: Jeff Laubenstein

Prologue

ComStar First Circuit Compound
Hilton Head Island, North America, Terra

1 June 3022

Myndo Waterly, the Precentor of Dieron, tried to slip into the Primus's chambers silently. So fluid was her gait that she made it all the way to the golden star symbol inlaid in the floor without so much as a whisper of her silken robes to announce her approach. Taking a deep breath, she stopped there and let the hood of her red robe slip back from her fair hair. In the half-second she allowed herself to recall the starting point of her argument, the Primus utterly shattered her strategy.

Standing stock-still and with his back to her, the voice of Primus Julian Tiepolo suddenly rang out. "The Peace of Blake be with you, Precentor Dieron."

How could he know I was here? Mynda thought, momentarily shaken. *The man is unnatural.* "And His wisdom with you, Primus." Though she fought it, a nervous tremor undercut the boldness of

Myndo's riposte. She swallowed and waited as the tall, cadaverously thin leader of ComStar turned slowly to face her. He had been looking out through one of the high oval windows of the chamber, which let in enough of the bright afternoon sun to illuminate the room. His aquiline nose and piercing brown eyes had always made Myndo think of a hawk, but today she reacted differently to his gaunt boniness and bald head. *He's more a vulture*, she thought. Keeping his hands tucked into the broad sleeves of his dun-colored robe, Tiepolo slowly descended the short stairway leading from the window to the main area of his private audience chamber.

He narrowed his eyes slightly. "You rebuke me with your greeting, Precentor. I know better than to spar with you, for you soon become impatient of such games." Tiepolo's gaze flickered toward the wall behind her, where a massive starchart was splashed from floor to ceiling. "How you, with so little tolerance for word play, are able to deal with the Draconis Combine never ceases to amaze me."

Myndo Waterly stiffened and met the Primus's dark gaze with the fierceness of her own. "More than words and honor, House Kurita respects action and wisdom."

Tiepolo pursed his lips and nodded his head slowly. "Again you chasten me." He let his right hand drift back and point toward the window. "As you are not down below witnessing the signing of the treaty between Hanse Davion and Katrina Steiner, shall I assume that is the matter you wish to discuss?"

She nodded curtly. "You've issued orders for me to leave for Dieron immediately. Is this just to be rid of me because I differ with you concerning this alliance?"

"Precentor Dieron, you have made your concerns very clear in the communications you've sent me and during the First Circuit sessions we both attended here on Terra."

Myndo raised herself up to her full height. "You say that as though you have actually *listened* to my arguments and even given them due consideration."

"So I have, Precentor."

"No, Primus, you know that is not true, and now you send me away because I disagree with you." She stabbed a finger at the window. "Down there in the courtyard, Hanse Davion and Katrina Steiner are being allowed to sign a treaty that will forever destroy the balance of power in the Successor States. With Davion's Federated Suns and Steiner's Lyran Commonwealth tied so closely together, we of ComStar lose all hope of maintaining stability. That piece of paper will destroy everything we've worked toward."

Primus Julian Tiepolo tapped his right index finger against his narrow chin. "Will it? You suggest that the treaty will destroy the balance of power between the five Great Houses, but I doubt that. Wolf's Dragoons will switch from the service of the Lyran Commonwealth to your own House Kurita."

"Ha!" Myndo Waterly's barked laugh echoed through the domed wooden chamber like a gunshot. "How dare you use information I supplied you as a means to refute my argument!"

Tiepolo's face revealed no embarrassment. "Ah, you *were* the one who provided the information about *that* mercenary unit. Then you must know as well that the Kell Hounds have accepted a new contract that will return them to the Federated Suns for the short term, though our analysts predict that they will eventually return to Katrina Steiner's service in the Commonwealth. For now, however, the Lyran Commonwealth will be stripped of its two most capable mercenary units."

Myndo shook her head violently. "You know as well as I do that all this has nothing to do with troops—be they crack mercenaries or these new, half-trained units Prince Davion hopes to create. The Lyran Commonwealth is dangerous, and now you've allowed them to become paired with the most advanced of the Successor States."

Tiepolo nodded slowly. "Ah, now I sense the core of your discomfort. You are concerned that for the first time in the 240 years since the blessed Jerome Blake accepted his mission to restore communication among the stars, I have allowed an occurrence that jeopardizes the completion of that sacred mission. Is this what I am hearing you say?"

Myndo nodded quickly. "The Lyran Commonwealth sees us as nothing more than an organization of glorified messengers. Those cursed, money-grubbing Lyran merchants look at us as nothing more than another profit-seeking business enterprise. They do not realize how slender our profits are, much less do they understand that we care more for our mission than we do any profits. There is no way to explain the spiritual to those who see only with their eyes and understand riches only in a worldly sense."

"This is a truth we have long acknowledged, Precentor Dieron."

"Yes, Primus, we have acknowledged it and we agreed, several Council sessions back, to quarantine the Lyran Commonwealth. We wanted to isolate their view of us so that it would not infect the thinking of the other Houses. But in the sixteen months of negotiations for this Davion-Steiner treaty, it seems as though the resolution has been swept away. You've allowed the devil to mate with damnation, and utter chaos will reign because of it."

Tiepolo narrowed his dark eyes, which flashed with anger. "Your analogy, my dear Precentor, suggests that House Davion is worse in some way even than House Steiner..."

Myndo was no less angry than the Primius, but she struggled for calm. "I have explained my reservations about House Davion countless times before, Primus. Prince Hanse Davion's hunger for old Star League technology—what the unwashed have so quaintly labeled *lostech*—will bring him into direct conflict with us. And with the recent advances made by his New Avalon Institute of Science, I believe the conflict will come sooner than later. Quintus Allard and the Counter-Intelligence Division of Davion's Ministry of Intelligence Information and Operations have made it very difficult for us to get our ROM agents anywhere close to the Prince. And may I remind you, Primus, that even you have admitted that the Prince is impossible to read from a distance."

Primus Julian Tiepolo let a smile warp his thin white lips. "The Fox is indeed an enigma."

"'You call him an enigma, but I see Hanse Davion as a dagger pressed against ComStar's throat! You cannot deny that the treaty's confidential clauses surprised even you."

The Primus nodded. "True. I never expected Hanse Davion would ask for, or receive, the hand of Melissa Arthur Steiner in marriage. That could well be an impressive event."

Myndo snorted derisively. "That's not the marriage I fear between Houses Steiner and Davion. No, what I ask you to contemplate is the match between the Lyran Commonwealth's contempt for us and House Davion's technical expertise. The cultural and intellecutal exchanges demanded by this treaty could well be the birth of a service to rival our own."

"Perhaps, Precentor Dieron, perhaps..." A skeletally slender hand waved her objections aside. "I do not see the reality of the Successor States in the same way that you do."

"I know this," Myndo Waterly replied, her tone serious and even. "Indeed, I am prepared to ask the First Circuit to strip you of your Primacy because of it."

Primus Julian Tiepolo froze and studied his subordinate carefully, but she did not flinch beneath his stern gaze. Icy silence hung over the chamber as the Primus sorted through and organized his thoughts. Finally, with a slight nod, he dispelled the mood.

"Very well, Precentor Dieron, you force me to reveal some of my thoughts to you. I do so reluctantly, and only because I sense in you a true concern for the blessed Blake's plan rather than a desire for personal power."

Myndo nodded formally. "I wish only that Blake's will be done."

"Indeed, Precentor Dieron, I believe this is true." Primus Tiepolo pointed toward the enormous star chart on the wall. "Political," he hissed. At his voice command, a computer superimposed a political map over the chart. "You are correct, Precentor, in sensing that Houses Steiner and Davion are the most dangerous to ComStar. My decision—despite the excellent arguments you and other Precentors presented during Council sessions—was to allow the two Houses to come together. It is my belief that a strong alliance between them will solidify the other Houses' opposition to them."

Myndo frowned. "The opposition is not all that strong, Primus." Pointing at a narrow wedge toward the base of the starchart, she said, "House Liao certainly poses a threat to no one. House Marik, positioned between Liao and Steiner, is still recovering from its civil war of six years ago. Meanwhile, Davion's financial backing of insurgents is further keeping the Mariks off-balance."

The Primus shook his head calmly, like a professor about to correct one of his students. "Liao's Capellan Confederation may occupy a relatively small region of space, but it is rich in worlds. And though Liao's forces are not strong enough to attack the Federated Suns, they are enough to repel any Davion incursions. Aside from the continual border raids and an occasional world won or lost, we will see no major shift on that front in our lifetimes."

The Primus pointed toward the purple area representing House Marik's Free Worlds League. "Janos Marik has recovered control of his realm. Let us not forget that his son Thomas is in our service." Tiepolo shifted his attention toward the red area above the Federated Suns and to the right of the Lyran Commonwealth on the map. "Even more important is your own Draconis Combine. With its dreaded Sword of Light Regiments—and now the Wolf's Dragoons, too—it should be more than enough to hold Davion in check."

Myndo shook her head slowly. "This is possible, and we shall soon have the proof of it when Davion begins his Galtor Campaign. I fear, though, that not one of the other Houses could stand alone against the combined might of the Federated Suns and the Lyran Commonwealth."

"That is more true than you know, Precentor, which is why I have ordered you back to Dieron. You will coordinate the meetings between Takashi Kurita, Janos Marik, and Maximilian Liao. The other Houses will not stand alone, Myndo. They will stand together..." Primus Tiepolo raised a hand to forestall further comment. "You should know that Maximilian Liao is attempting to repeat his success at pitting Anton Marik against Janos in the civil war. He is playing on Michael Hasek-Davion's desire to rule the Federated Suns in place of his brother-in-law, and has already provided Duke Michael with reasons to refuse Hanse the use of his Capellan March troops in the Galtor Campaign."

Myndo smiled unconsciously. "And you will exploit Frederick Steiner's desire to supplant his cousin Katrina…"

The Primus nodded. "The current political situation in the Successor States depends upon maintaining a balance. If any Successor Lord believes he or she is powerful enough to conquer a neighbor, humanity will once again be plunged into the maelstrom of war. We must also remember that ComStar is the balance point. If it ever does begin to seem that the union of Houses Steiner and Davion is a threat to us, have no fear that we will move to crush them both and to establish a new balance."

"I see, Primus," Myndo said, head cocked to one side in thought. "The forces do balance. The elements needed to control Davion and Steiner are in place. If those two realms were not headed up by such dynamic leaders, the threat they pose would be minimized. But how can we trigger the necessary internal and external forces? What could set them in motion?"

Tiepolo allowed himself a mirthless smile. "Each and every Successor Lord—Takashi Kurita, Janos Marik, Maximilian Liao, Katrina Steiner, and Hanse Davion—dreams of being the one to establish and reign over a new Star League. Each has an equal claim to that throne, but the marriage of Hanse Davion to Melissa Steiner will change that stand-off of forces. Suddenly, one House will have a stronger claim to the old throne of the Star League. Until the wedding, we will guard the knowledge of that most secret clause of this treaty, but we will not hesitate to use it in laying our own secret plans…"

MAP OF THE SUCCESSOR STATES

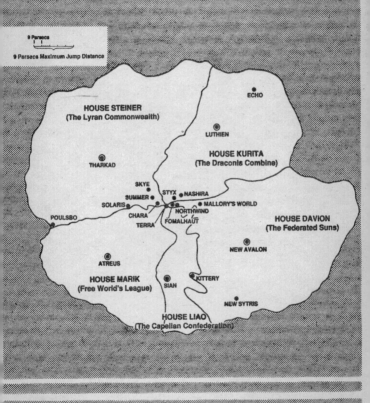

9 Parsecs

9 Parsecs Maximum Jump Distance

ECHO

HOUSE STEINER
(The Lyran Commonwealth)

LUTHIEN

HOUSE KURITA
(The Draconis Combine)

THARKAD

SKYE
SUMMER
STYX   NASHIRA
SOLARIS
MALLORY'S WORLD
NORTHWIND
POULSBO
CHARA   FOMALHAUT
TERRA

HOUSE DAVION
(The Federated Suns)

NEW AVALON

ATREUS

HOUSE MARIK
(Free World's League)

SIAN   KITTERY

NEW SYTRIS

HOUSE LIAO
(The Capellan Confederation)

BOOK
1

1

The loud knock on the plasteel door of Major Justin Allard's office shattered the quiet tranquility he'd been savoring. The slender, dark-haired MechWarrior drew in a deep breath, then exhaled slowly. As he rose from behind his teakwood desk, he straightened his jacket and tried to compose himself.

I hate this part of battalion command. Do well in combat, get a medal pinned to your chest, and they give you a job spending most of your time with discipline or supply problems. Justin shook his head and frowned at the three piles of paper on his desk. *They need an accountant to handle all this nonsense. Then again,* he thought, *this particular problem probably did require a MechWarrior's touch.*

"Enter," he said finally.

A faceless MP opened the door, and Private Robert Craon stepped into the room. The MP waited expectantly at the door because the tall, thickly built Craon towered over Allard. The smaller officer narrowed his almond-shaped eyes and gave a short shake of his head to dismiss the MP. The guard shrugged and closed the door.

"Private Robert Craon reporting for disciplinary action, sir." The younger man's voice, though shot through with nervousness, rang loud and strong. As his gaze flicked around the office, he seemed to recoil in disgust at the sight of the Capellan rice-paper paintings that formed the backdrop for Major Allard's desk.

Justin nodded formally. "At ease, Private." He kept his voice

3

calm, trying to filter out as much anger as possible. When Craon went from standing at attention to a careless slouch, Allard could not help but snap, "I said at ease, Private, not fall apart!"

Craon swallowed and straightened up crisply. "I'm sorry, sir."

Justin snorted and seated himself. "I doubt that, Robert." He quickly typed something on the keyboard at his desk, and bars of light drifted up over his features as information scrolled onto the screen. Justin shook his head once, then looked up. "I want you to understand a couple of things, Robert, and they're matters I expect to go no further than this office. Is that understood?"

Craon nodded solemnly, and the look of sincerity on his face caught Justin by surprise. *Perhaps I can trust him, after all...*

Justin glanced at the screen, then stopped the information flow with an almost casual movement of one long finger. "I want you to know that you're subject to this disciplinary action because of your insubordination, *not* because of your particular actions at the time of the incident." Looking up at Craon, he added, "I don't care that you called me a...Ah, how did you put it?"

A smirk twisted the corners of Craon's mouth, and Justin felt his own anger leap up like a solar flare. "I believe that I called you the half-wit whelp of a Capellan whore forced upon a Davion noble to prevent a war."

Justin studied the computer screen again and nodded. "Almost word for word. You must have practiced." *Since your early years, no doubt. Let's hope your racism has not warped your reason.*

Craon beamed triumphantly. "I aim to be accurate."

"I did not ask for a comment, Private!" Justin snarled. He rose slowly and deliberately. As the two men stared at one another in that instant, both knew that physical size meant nothing in the battle between them. "I don't care that you hate me because my father's first wife was a Capellan whom he met while serving in the Federated Suns embassy on Sian. What you regard as an error in judgement belongs to my father, not me. Your bigoted opinion of me is *not* the reason you will be disciplined."

Justin angrily twisted the screen on his computer to where Craon could see it. "The report indicates that you disobeyed Leftenant Redburn's direct order to return to your watchpost. The report does not mention the altercation that erupted after that, but I assume Leftenant Redburn had his own reasons for not including it."

Craon swallowed again and looked down. He shifted his jaw from side to side and winced as it popped. "Yes, sir."

Justin's stiff posture relaxed slightly. "Believe me, Robert, when I say that I understand your resentment of my dismissing Sergeant

4

Philip Capet. I know he was assigned to your training company after he guided you all through boot camp. I know he's a legend here in the Capellan March. And I know how you all looked up to him."

Craon's head came up fast, color flooding his cheeks. He hesitated a second, then his blond eyebrows narrowed in anger. "He was the goddamn best, Major, and you kicked him out for disagreeing with your policies toward the indigs. He offered to go man-to-man with you, to fight it out, but you just gave him his walking papers. Damn! He won the Gold Sunburst for his actions on Uravan. He wasted bunches of Liao 'Mechs and gave his boys time to get themselves and their wounded comrades out of that ambush. He was a hero, and you spit him out of the corps without a second thought!"

Having spent his long-pent fury, Craon now seemed at a loss for words. His hands, clenched tightly into fists, rose as though to strike, but he made no move toward Justin.

Give him time to recover his wits, Justin thought. *He can be salvaged.* Justin waited silently for the emotion to drain from Craon's body, then he spoke slowly and evenly, measuring his words. "I know what Capet was to you men and of the dreams you all shared. You were to become his new unit to avenge the other boys lost in battle. With you, he would win new awards and would once again become a symbol, a hero, for the Capellan March. With you to lift him up, he would once again dine at Duke Michael Hasek-Davion's right hand."

Justin seated himself again and typed out a new request for information on the keyboard. The computer searched for a moment, then spilled reams of data over the screen. "What you don't know, Robert, is that Capet's men, the ones he saved on Uravan, should never have been in danger in the first place." Craon opened his mouth to protest, but Justin raised a hand to silence him.

"Yes, Robert, a Capellan company did ambush them, but they were ambushed because Sergeant Capet led them into an area where he had no authorization to be. Capet's family lived and, regrettably, died in the village he tried to rescue. His family might still have died in that Liao raid, but if Capet had kept his head about him, a half-dozen MechWarriors would *not* have perished with them."

Justin drew in a deep breath and again forced himself to calmness. He looked up at Craon guilelessly. "All I've just told you is part of a classified report prepared for Hanse Davion to determine if Capet would get his Gold Sunburst. He had become the darling of a holo-drama, and so the High Command hoped that he would also accept an early retirement at the time of the award. When he refused to step down, they gave him a training cadre." Justin lowered his voice and shook his head. "When intelligence sources learned of his plan to hijack a

5

JumpShip to go back and get his revenge on Liao, I refused to let him kill you in such an idiotic scheme."

The color had drained from Craon's face, and his hands had returned to their place at the small of his back. "I appreciate your trust in sharing this information with me, sir. I stand ready to receive whatever punishment you name."

Justin nodded solemnly. "You realize that I could have you dismissed from this training cadre for what you have done?" Craon winced unconsciously. "Yes, I thought you knew that," he added, looking hard at the soldier standing before him. He saw no fear in Craon's blue eyes, only self-loathing at his own stupidity.

You're learning to admit that you can make a mistake. Good. That's the first step toward avoiding them, and the only way to survive as a MechWarrior.

Justin smiled carefully. "You have, in the past, evidenced some leadership ability. As your punishment now, I have decided to let you hone that ability. Until further notice, you will act as shepherd for all of your cadre's exercises. You'll eat everyone else's dust, Robert, and you'll keep them all in line—or it will be *your* career." Justin watched a faint smile come over Craon's lips. "And, you'll help the Techs keep your 'Mech in perfect working order after each exercise."

Craon snapped to attention and saluted smartly. "Yes, sir. Thank you, sir."

Justin stood and returned the salute. "Dismissed."

Craon turned and left the room, but left the door open. Justin smiled at his retreating back, then sat down again to attack some of the paperwork piled on his desk. He initialed a stack of reports and tossed them into a basket for filing. *The sooner the whole of Kittery is tied into the computer system, the easier this job will be.*

He shook his head. *You're not being paid for easy duty, Justin. If you were, they'd not have put you in charge of a local training battalion, especially not on a planet where your Capellan blood makes you a sworn enemy. Prince Hanse Davion put you here because you're half-Capellan and can understand the Capellan natives. Dealing with these sons and daughters of Federated Suns carpetbaggers, on the other hand...*

Justin glanced at the holograph of Hanse Davion and himself that had been taken at the ceremony awarding him the Diamond Sunburst. The tall leader of the Federated Suns towered over then-Captain Allard. As Justin twisted the holograph to examine it closer, he saw that Davion's expression of gratitude and trust was sincere.

In presenting the award, Hanse Davion had said to Justin, "Once again, I find my realm indebted to your family. I hope the Federated

6

Suns is ever worthy of your courage and sacrifice." It was Davion's trust in Justin that had brought this posting to Kittery, for the Prince hoped Justin could help to normalize relations with the newly conquered population. *I only wish that more of his subjects understood that being able to get along with the Capellan natives is not a prelude to giving the Capellan March to Maximilian Liao and his Capellan Confederation*, Justin thought ruefully.

Just then, a smiling man of average height and build paused in the doorway and tapped lightly on the open door. "Major, we've got to get moving."

His musing interrupted, Justin righted the holograph, looked at the time on his watch, and then cursed softly. "Come in, Andy. Close the door behind you." Justin narrowed his eyes suspiciously at the stack of papers the man was carrying. "What are those? I can't deal with anything routine right now. Besides, you know as well as I do that the only reason I can head out with you this afternoon is because the stack of requests you sent through channels is taller than any other mound on this desk."

Leftenant Redburn crossed to Justin's desk and set the papers on top of the computer monitor. Clad in boots, shorts, and a cooling vest that revealed a well-muscled, if somewhat pale, body, the man smiled and ran a hand over his cropped auburn hair. "Forms, filled out in triplicate, for this afternoon's exercise. I've filed an environmental impact statement for every meter of the turf we're to cover today, and the locals have just issued us a 'parade permit.'" He sighed loudly. "Sometimes I wonder why the Duke of New Syrtis just doesn't give this world back to Liao. Michael Hasek-Davion's let so many of them into the government here that he might as well cede the place to Capella."

Justin smiled slyly. "Leftenant Redburn, now you sound like your men when they complain about having a Capellan half-breed as their commanding officer."

Redburn's cheeks immediately flushed red with embarrassment. "Sir, if you think I was saying…"

Justin held up his hand and quieted the young officer. "Easy, Andrew. I understand what you're saying." Justin unbuttoned his jacket and walked to the dressing chamber annexed to his office. His voice echoed through the open doorway. "The idea of turning in a centimeter-by-centimeter description of our line of march doesn't thrill me, either, but there's nothing we can do. This is Michael's domain, and his word is law."

Redburn nodded. "I trust him and his bureaucrats about as far as I can toss Craon."

7

Justin laughed. "Indeed, and just how far is that?"

"What?"

Justin stepped from the dressing chamber in boots, shorts, and open cooling vest. Muscles and veins stood out on a body virtually without fat. "Your report said nothing about the battle I heard about between you and Craon."

The Leftenant shrugged. "Wasn't really a fight. I cracked him a good one on the jaw, then concentrated on his breadbasket." Redburn unconsciously rubbed the ribs on his right side. "He got a couple of punches in, but it ended quickly." He smiled like a child remembering the taste of stolen melon. "Was hardly worth mentioning."

Justin chuckled. "I accept you at your word, Leftenant." Justin nodded at his subordinate. *Thank you for your efforts on my behalf.* Redburn returned the nod, and Justin knew he'd been understood. "I've assigned Craon to be shepherd for this little outing. How many 'Mechs will we have with us?"

Redburn thought for a half-second. "Thirty-two, including us. I have four lances of four and three with five. As usual, I did not assign you to any one lance. I'll be in the *Spider* and I've given you the *Valkyrie* on loan from the Kittery Borderers. You know, those damned regulars said that they were only handing over the 'Mech because you're a real MechWarrior. Everyone else gets a *Stinger*."

Justin nodded. The two men left the office and quickly made their way through the tiled corridors to the massive 'Mech bay that loomed over the smaller Base Command Center. The roof, supported by metal beams and a skeletal framework, arched some fifteen meters over the ferrocrete floor. The translucent plastic used to form and seal the roof let in enough of the gold light from Kittery's F9 sun to illuminate the metal giants housed within the hangar.

Ringing the room like silent tomb-sentinels, BattleMechs gleamed in the sun's bright light. Techs and astechs in green jumpsuits swarmed like insects over units in need of repair, and spare parts dangled from powered winches running on beams above the war machines. Five times the height of the men who worked on them, 'Mechs were objects of fascination rather than fear for the men and women who nursed them back to health. At the moment, these broken giants stood docile and in dire need of the steady hands and diagnostic genius of the Techs before any would again march into battle.

Other 'Mechs, armed and operational, stood waiting with their canopies open. Spilling down their chests like comical ties were rope ladders that allowed men and women to mount the huge machines they would pilot into battle. The *Stinger*s, 20-ton light 'Mechs often used for training MechWarriors, did not look any less deadly than the heavier

'Mechs scattered throughout the bay. The massive medium laser grasped pistol-like in each *Stinger*'s right hand seemed lethal enough for anyone's taste.

As Leftenant Redburn and Major Allard entered the bay, the 1st Kittery Training Battalion, including a hastily arriving Robert Craon, stood at attention in ranks. When Justin nodded approvingly to Sergeant Walter de Mesnil, the one-eyed MechWarrior turned to face his troops. "At ease," he rasped.

Justin cleared his throat. "This afternoon Leftenant Redburn and I will take you through an evaluation exercise. Please bear in mind that your 'Mechs are fully armed and powered. As always, we wish to minimize damage to the surrounding area. Target practice on livestock owned by the natives is discouraged and will be punished by immediate dismissal from the training program." Justin emphasized the word "native" so that his troops would note that he was not using the slang "indig," which most of his trainees preferred. "I know you think I speak of the people here as natives because I am half-Capellan, but you must learn that to accept them is to have them accept you. And that is a major part of our mission on Kittery." He turned to Redburn. "Leftenant."

Redburn nodded and accepted command. "Sergeant de Mesnil… Corporals…form up your lances and conduct them outside." He turned toward three trainees—two men and a woman—and nodded to the largest man. "James, head out after Sergeant de Mesnil and wait for me to join you." He scanned the crowd and caught one Corporal's eye. "Hugh, Private Craon has been assigned shepherd duty, so your lance will run last. Dismissed."

The MechWarriors broke ranks and ran to their 'Mechs while the two officers walked over to where their own 'Mechs waited. Redburn swung up the ladder that hung from a *Spider*. Unlike the *Stinger*, this 30-ton humanoid 'Mech carried no weapons in its hands, but the twin medium laser snouts jutting from the center of its chest left no doubt about its battleworthiness. Reknowned for its speed and the "jumping" abilities that allowed it to range behind enemy lines to wreak havoc, the *Spider* was the perfect 'Mech to ride herd on a company of trainees.

Justin quickly climbed up and into the cockpit of his *Valkyrie*. He strapped himself into the pilot seat and punched a button that reeled in his ladder and slowly closed the polarized canopy. As it shut, the cockpit became pressurized and Justin had to open his mouth wide to equalize the pressure in his ears.

He laced up his cooling vest and plugged the power cord into the socket to the right side of his command chair. After carefully pressing the adhesive monitoring discs to his upper arms and thighs, he fed the leads from them up toward his throat. Then he settled the olive-green neurohelmet pad over his shoulders, and threaded the monitor disc leads into their proper connections. Finally, Justin reached up and pulled the neurohelmet down over his head.

Justin shivered unconsciously as the helmet cut out all external noise and made his breathing rumble thunderously in his ears. He adjusted the helmet until the roughly triangular viewplate had centered itself in front of his face and he could feel the pressure of neuroreceptors in the proper places around his skull. He plugged wires from his 'Mech into the appropriate sockets at the helmet's throat and then spoke.

"Pattern check. Major Justin X. Allard."

Justin listened to the static crackling through his skull, then smiled as the 'Mech's computer replied, "Voiceprint pattern match obtained. Proceed with initiation sequence."

Justin's eyes narrowed. "Code check: *Zhe jian fang tai xiao*. Authorization code: Alpha Xray Tango Bravo." Now the computer was checking his codes against the vast list of authorizations and personal passwords stored within its memory. Unlike most 'Mechs, which responded only to the secret code locked into it by its pilot, training 'Mechs had to be able to accept numerous codes. Each pilot in the training cadre had his own code, which meant that anyone performing an irregular action—such as stealing a 'Mech—could be pegged by checking to see which code had last been used to activate the 'Mech.

Justin knew that it was unorthodox for him to have a personal check code in Capellan, but it ensured that none of these clowns would steal his machine. He laughed to himself. Even if they could figure out that his code meant, "This room is too small," none of them would understand the humor, nor would they be able to pronounce the words correctly. A sudden new thought sent a chill up Justin's spine as he realized that if his code ever did become known, it would only confirm the bigoted opinions about him. *Stupid, Justin*, he thought. *Better change it after this exercise.*

The computer's metallic voice knifed through his thoughts. "Authorization confirmed. Glad to have you aboard, Major."

In response to the correct codes, the control console came alive with lights and flashing buttons. The heat scales on the internal systems monitor all sat low in the cool-blue range. The data readouts on the rack of long-range missiles housed in the left side of his 'Mech's torso and the medium laser that replaced the 'Mech's right hand both reported the weapon systems operational but unarmed. Justin caressed two buttons on the targeting joystick with the fingers of his left hand, and the systems armed themselves.

Other data displays told him that both jump jets on his *Valkyrie*'s back were ready to boost him up to 150 meters at a blast. The mechanism for reloading his missiles also reported itself ready to supply twelve full flights of ten missiles apiece, though Justin knew this included the brace of missiles already loaded into the launchers.

Justin drew in one last breath of cool air, then closed his eyes and flexed his fingers. He exhaled slowly, then cleared a radio link to Leftenant Redburn's *Spider*. "Ready, Andy?"

"Yes, sir," rang out Redburn's reply.

"Good. Let's get out of here and see what these kids have learned."

2

Kittery
Capellan March, Federated Suns

27 November 3026

Justin stopped his *Valkyrie* just below the crest of a hill and turned back to watch the trainees straggling through the meadow below. The stark, snowy-white color of the 'Mechs made them a sharp contrast to the golden-brown of the dying summer grasses. A breeze swirled down into the valley's bowl and rode through the grasses in waves until it hit the wide swath of destruction made by the marching 'Mechs.

These kids are good. I suspect that after they get a battle under their belts, no one will doubt Prince Davion's wisdom in creating these training battalions—no one but the people running the military academies and the few bureaucrats who don't want their planets protected by such "green" troops. Justin shook his head. *They're really pushing themselves so that their Capellan Major will see how good they really are. Excellent!*

Justin glanced at his heat monitors. The levels still hovered in the blue range, but were nearer to the green of the next higher level. The day's warmth was not much of a danger, and none of the 'Mechs, with the possible exception of Craon's *Stinger*, should have cracked the green wall. "Andy?"

"Yes, Major?"

"See if you can have Corporal Montdidier pull his lance in a bit more. He's ranging too far north, and I suspect it's just to give Craon fits."

The warmth of Redburn's laughter almost survived transmission

12

intact. "Roger."

Justin watched as Montdidier's lance moved back toward the main line of march, then frowned as one 'Mech halted. Justin quickly scanned and identified the warrior. "Private Sonnac, why aren't you moving in? Is your 'Mech having trouble?"

"No, sir. I'm just getting odd magscan readings."

Justin reached out and punched the button on his command console that shifted his scanners from infrared to magnetic anomaly detection. A holographic display of the terrain filled the screen before him and showed each 'Mech as a glowing red pyramid or sphere. As his computer identified each machine, it tagged a glowing number beneath the symbol that told Justin at a glance the 'Mech's type, model, and designation. Other concentrations of metal—anything from an ore deposit close to the surface or a lost bicycle—showed up as a green cube until it could be identified.

As Justin turned his head, the 360-degree display continued to provide him with a tactical view that pinpointed large concentrations of metal in the area. The blue hexagon that appeared and then vanished again in his peripheral vision sent a cold chill down his spine. "Andy, check Sonnac's readings. I've got something over the hill I want to see."

"Roger."

Justin marched his *Valkyrie* up over the crest of the hill and turned to face the direction where he'd spotted the blue hexagon. Through the holographic construct, he saw that it was located deep in a wooded vale. A stream ran through the wooded area and emptied into a good-size pond. The nearby hills, covered with the red, green, and orange wildflowers, sloped down toward the pond. The whole scene, bereft of the blue scanner-ghost, looked peaceful and inviting.

And dangerous. Justin clenched his jaw. Those tranquil woods would be just the place for light 'Mechs like the *Stinger*s to seek shelter if they had to elude enemy 'Mechs. That stream would also provide cooling for overheated 'Mechs. The valley formed a superior battle arena for light 'Mechs.

Redburn's voice blasted over the radio. "Major Allard! *Cicada*s, sir! All over the place!"

At the urgency in Redburn's communication, Justin's mind went automatically into a kind of special battle mode that filtered out all emotion. "Withdraw south, Leftenant." *Just don't come this way,* he added silently, sensing something ominous behind the seeming tranquility of the vale.

"Negative, negative," burst in Robert Craon. "I've got magscan readings off the scale south, east, and north. You're clean, sir. We've got to head out west."

Justin turned his head to study the escape route that Craon suggested. His mouth went instantly dry. The blue hexagon appeared again. This time, the computer graced it with an identifier. *My God! It's a Rifleman!*

Justin snapped an order over the comm channel. "No way out here, either. Do what you can, Andy. The cadre is yours." With that, Justin turned his *Valkyrie* and jumped toward the woods. "It's a trap. All a trap. Don't run west…"

Leftenant Redburn barely heard Justin Allard's enigmatic reply to Craon, but it was too late to ask any questions. Not knowing what to do next, he nearly panicked. *Slow down, Andrew*, he told himself. *Get a grip. The Major put you in charge. He has confidence in you. Don't let him down.*

Redburn watched the ground crack open. Capellan 'Mechs— *Cicadas*—sprouted up like nightmare plants in some hideous time-lapse holodocumentary. While Craon was shouting, they had appeared on the north, south, and east sides of the valley rim. Only the west, the direction Major Allard had forbidden him, stood safely open. "Move, dammit! Move! This isn't a drill. Withdraw west, up the hillside. Sonnac, jet out of there!"

One armless *Cicada* thrust its ugly snout in front of Sonnac's position and fired its twin medium lasers. Both beams converged on the *Stinger*'s head. Armor melted and ran like wax, then the beams lanced into the cockpit. Something exploded, leaving nothing and no one behind. Sonnac's *Stinger* staggered backward, then fell lifelessly to the ground.

Redburn's magscan vision of the valley blazed with green pyramids and blue rectangles. The *Cicada*s, which weighed twice as much as any *Stinger* on the field, had no arms and sported two medium lasers and one small laser that fired in a forward arc. As data flowed across the screens on his command console, Redburn cursed angrily. Three of the *Cicada*s sported flamethrowers, and already one cadet's screams were ringing through Redburn's ears as a *Cicada* ignited the cadet's 'Mech. Outweighed and outgunned, the cadre had no other choice but to retreat.

Philip Nablus, pilot of the burning 'Mech, hit his jump jets in panic, taking off with enough speed to snuff the flames coating the left side of his machine. He came down on his feet, but stumbled and rolled into an untidy heap. A *Cicada* turned to fire at him, but the other members of Nablus's lance poured laser fire into the rear of the *Cicada*.

There's only a dozen of them, but they've got to be veteran pilots, Redburn told himself. *Still, we do outnumber them. There has to be a*

14

way.

"Pull back. Get above them," he ordered. "We'll hold the heights." Suddenly, the solution burst into his brain like a missile. "They want us to go west, so let's oblige them. Now move it, and let's see how cocky they get. We'll make them pay."

Justin's *Valkyrie* hit top speed as it reached the bottom of the hill. The blue hexagon flickered to life, and the computer placed it behind a thick stand of pines. Justin closed one eye, adjusted the target selection with one hand, and smiled. He had no computer lock, but the shot felt right. "Die, bastard," he growled as his thumb stabbed the launch button and a flight of missiles burst from the chest of his *Valkyrie*.

The launching dropped his speed from 86 kph to 72 kph, but speed did not concern Justin at that moment. The tall pines became instant torches when the first two missiles hit them, then fell away into a circle of flaming debris as three more missiles shredded them with fire and shrapnel. The remaining five missiles soared through the firestorm and slammed into the true target, lurking in its now-shattered haven.

Those five missiles burst like an exploding bandolier across the *Rifleman*'s 60-ton body. Five dents in the scarred armor showed where the missiles had hit, but Justin's initial view suggested possible damage to only one of the 'Mech's torso lasers. "Damn," he muttered.

The semi-humanoid *Rifleman*'s arms swung up, pivoting at its shoulders, and tracked Justin's *Valkyrie*. The torso swiveled at the waist, keeping the twin autocannons and heavy lasers locked onto their target. As the radar wing atop the enemy 'Mech began to swing faster, the *Rifleman* took one step out of the burning trees toward the tiny *Valkyrie*.

The *Rifleman*'s autocannons spat out a hail of slugs amid great gouts of flame. Smoldering shells rained from the shoulder ejection ports to the ground. The 'Mech tracked the speeding *Valkyrie* as best it could, sending after it a jagged trail of autocannon shells.

Too close now! Justin thought, waiting until the last possible second to kick in his jump jets, which sent him rocketing ahead of the autocannon slugs. Knowing he could not land on his feet at this speed, Justin hit the ground and rolled his 'Mech forward. Then he rose to one knee, launched another flight of LRMs, and let the launch-reaction carry him backward as twin laser lances melted the ground where he had crouched.

Only three of his hastily loosed missiles made their target, but those hit with a vengeance. One exploded into one of the *Rifleman*'s autocannon ejection ports, fusing the ejection mechanism. The other

15

missiles both slammed into the radar wing whirling like a propeller above the 'Mech's hunched shoulders. The first explosion froze the mechanism in place, and the second blast left the wing hanging by thick electrical cables.

Had enough? Justin demanded silently.

As if in reply, the *Rifleman* twisted its torso again. Its two medium torso lasers and the remaining autocannon fired on their tormentor. Up and running again, Justin eluded the assault, but knew that he could not hope to avoid disaster forever. He just had to make it worth it.

Redburn nodded as the *Stinger*s formed a line to face the oncoming enemy 'Mechs. "On my mark, as I've outlined it. Remember, they've got no jump jets, and they can't easily fire into the backward arc. Now, go!"

At his command, de Payens, Montbard, and St. Agnan jumped their lances over and behind the line of Capellan *Cicada*s. While Redburn turned his lance to face the crush of 'Mechs closing from the north, St. Omer moved his lance to repel the southern wing of oncoming Capellans. Meanwhile, Montdidier's damaged lance slid over to help. De Mesnil's lance held the center and opened up on the *Cicada*s marching at them up the hill.

Redburn smiled as he saw the Capellan warriors hesitate. *You may have thought you were fighting trainees, but these cadets are good. With one smooth operation, we've turned the ambush back on you.*

Craon landed first, having jumped his *Stinger* in a flatter arc than had the others in de Payens's lance. His 'Mech's long legs absorbed the impact of landing with the grace and strength of a cat. Craon whirled the *Stinger* about and brought his medium laser up in a fluid motion. When it fired, the ruby beam sliced virtually all the armor from a *Cicada*'s leg.

That Capellan 'Mech spun to face the threat to its rear. Craon moved wide to avoid the *Cicada*'s return fire, forcing the enemy 'Mech to pivot hard on its wounded leg. Evita Barres marched her *Stinger* forward and deliberately sighted the *Cicada*'s damaged limb. The remaining armor vaporized at the beam's touch, then the 'Mech's myomer fiber muscles parted with a snap. The *Cicada*'s leg collapsed, and the birdlike 'Mech smashed nose-first into the dirt.

The *Cicada*s on the southern wing ignored St. Agnan's lance as they jetted overhead. All the Capellan 'Mechs pressed forward, raking the defenders with bolt after bolt of laser fire. In Montdidier's lance, Reynold Vichiers's *Stinger* took heavy damage in the head and chest. Unaware that a bolt had already killed Vichiers, Bill Chartres imposed the body of his *Stinger* between his comrade and the *Cicada*s. Shafts of ruby light skewered his 'Mech even more savagely than they had Vichiers's machine. Utterly shot through, the *Stinger* collapsed in a heap.

St. Omer directed concentrated fire at the two outside *Cicada*s, while Montdidier and the other two cadets in his command hammered the two *Cicada*s closest to the center. The Capellans, in an effort to break through Montdidier's weakened lance, rushed forward and smashed their 'Mechs into the defending *Stinger*s.

St. Omer's efforts paid off handsomely. The *Cicada*s that his lance had flanked disintegrated as the heavy fire picked them apart. Once the lasers had blasted away chunks of armor, they struck deep into the ungainly 'Mechs to destroy their engines. The *Cicada*s stiffened as though seized by rigor mortis, then crashed to the ground.

Montdidier's lance took hideous damage from the charging 'Mechs, but managed to hold. Bures, whose *Stinger* had been knocked down by a *Cicada*, swept his 'Mech's legs in between those of the Capellan 'Mech. The *Cicada*'s next step shattered the *Stinger*'s limbs and tore them from the 'Mech's torso, but the effort tripped the *Cicada* and dropped it to its knees.

Thomas Berard met a *Cicada*'s charge head-on. The Capellan 'Mech hammered the smaller machine at first impact, sending shards of armor flying over the battlefield. Despite the bone-shattering impact, Berard managed to smash his *Stinger*'s left fist against the *Cicada*'s head and cracked the cockpit canopy. The Capellan pilot, disoriented by the assault, backed off just long enough for Berard to eject from his damaged 'Mech before the *Cicada* trampled his *Stinger* into spare parts.

St. Agnan's lance laid down a pattern of fire that caught the two *Cicada*s from behind and hurt them badly. Scarlet laser fire ripped through the aft armor of both 'Mechs, stabbing straight through. In the case of Berard's target, the shots burst out through the cockpit. Both *Cicada*s crumpled to the ground, where they lay smoking.

Justin's *Valkyrie* cut to the right as the heavy laser on the *Rifleman*'s left arm torched a black furrow through the meadow off to Justin's left. *It can't continue to turn!* he thought. *The torso locks up after about forty degrees. If I can get into its rear arc, the weapons can't track me!*

Justin started his *Valkyrie* running to the right, and grinned as his battle display showed him the lumbering *Rifleman*'s attempt to follow his movement. In the effort, the big 'Mech's waist locked, so that it had to make an almost comical shuffle-step to continue turning. *Perfect,* Justin told himself. *Just a bit faster, and I'll be in the clear.* He grinned

17

again and dropped his missile targeting crosshairs onto the *Rifleman*'s silhouette. He kept it there, despite the pounding, jarring strides that carried his 'Mech forward.

But wait. What is that pilot doing? Justin felt terror flash through his guts as the *Rifleman* stopped trying to track his *Valkyrie*. The larger machine stood rock-still for a moment, then twisted back in the other direction. As it did so, the Capellan 'Mech's arms swung up toward the sky and back down to lock in the rear firing arc.

"No!" Justin twisted his *Valkyrie* violently to reorient it, and tried valiantly to fire the jump jets. These frantic efforts only managed to trip up the *Valkyrie*, and he had to fight hard to regain control of the falling 'Mech.

No! Not like this! Justin stabbed the *Valkyrie*'s medium laser out at the *Rifleman*, but the gesture was useless. The *Rifleman*, swinging its weapons into line with the *Valkyrie*, scythed laser fire through the 'Mech's legs and ended Justin's futile attempt at flight.

The southern flank crushed, St. Omer, St. Agnan, and Montbard directed their lances at the Capellan center. The hellish crossfire sliced one *Cicada* to ribbons and drove the rest north. The northern wing withdrew quickly as the training battalion swept up toward it. After a savage exchange with St. Agnan's lance, the *Cicada* pilots realized that the battle was lost and chose to save their 'Mechs.

De Mesnil's gravelly voice crackled over the radio. "They're backing away, Leftenant."

Redburn looked at his magscan image and concurred with de Mesnil's assessment of the battle. "Let them run, cadets. We couldn't catch them if we wanted to." He watched the enemy 'Mechs flee and shook his head as his computer reported their running speed at better than 120 kph. *Damn, they're fast,* he thought, then shivered as his body burned the adrenalin coursing through his bloodstream.

Redburn flipped a switch on his console that instantly put his Sergeant and Corporals on a command frequency. "Report."

"De Mesnil here. All pilots alive, but Bisot and Montvalle both have leg damage. St. John lost his medium laser."

"St. Omer here, Leftenant. William Chartres is dead and his *Stinger* is gone. Minor damage otherwise. Everyone else stayed calm."

Redburn nodded and looked out toward the smoking, riddled ruin of Chartres's 'Mech. *A damn shame.* "Very well. St. Agnan?"

"Yes, sir." St. Agnan's voice came in sharp snippets of words. "I'm the only one who got tagged here, sir. Cockpit breached, and I think I have some busted ribs. Torroges lost an arm actuator, but it's been bad for awhile."

"Archie, pop your canopy so Gil Erail can get in and see what you look like." Redburn turned his attention to Montdidier's lance. "Payen, report."

It took Payen Montdidier a moment to collect himself. Even then, his voice almost broke. "Sonnac and Vichiers are dead, sir. Bures's 'Mech has no legs, and Berard's 'Mech is lost. He ejected, though, and got away fine."

Montbard and de Payens both reported their lances were virtually intact, though de Payens said that Craon wanted to know why such things never happened to anyone else running shepherd.

"Tell him it builds character," Redburn laughed, and his staff joined him. "Major Allard, how about you?"

There was no answer until De Mesnil's voice filled the silence. "I never saw him come back into the battle, Leftenant."

"De Mesnil, organize this rabble. De Payens, Montbard, form up your lances on me." Hoping the fear in his stomach would find nothing to feed it, Redburn trotted his *Spider* up over the hill. *No, God! Not the Major!* The smoke rising from the burning trees sent a tremor of dread through him. *Why does it have to look like a funeral pyre?*

Justin Allard's shattered 'Mech lay on its back. Heavy laser fire had hacked off its legs and reduced them to armored puddle. The missile autoloader clicked audibly as it attempted to feed a long-since exhausted supply of missiles into the fire-blackened ruins of the launch tubes. The right arm laser had melted clean away, and autocannon shells had ripped off the 'Mech's left arm at the shoulder.

Andrew Redburn and Robert Craon both scrambled over the 'Mech's torso, heedless of hot armor and the sparking wires of exposed mechanisms. They clambered toward the 'Mech's shattered face, then stopped short, suddenly afraid of what might be behind the jagged holes blasted through the canopy.

Redburn knew it was going to be bad. In anger and frustration, he kicked away some of the spiderwebbed glass. Carefully listening for any clue to what the darkened cockpit concealed, he lowered himself into the *Valkyrie*. When Craon hesitated, he motioned impatiently for the cadet to follow him. The cadet bleated a strangled cry as he bent down before the 'Mech's command chair.

Redburn looked up from where he pressed two fingers to Justin's bloody throat. "He's alive, Craon, and he'll stay that way if we get some evac help in here fast."

All color had drained from Craon's face, and he refused to meet Redburn's gaze. "Do you think we ought to, sir?"

Redburn's head snapped around as though he'd been punched.

19

"Are you suggesting that 'a good Capellan is a dead one?'"

Craon's jaw dropped open and horror showed in his blue eyes. "Oh God, no, sir."

Redburn's brows furrowed together with fury. "Then what the hell are you talking about? Of course, we save him."

"But, sir," Craon pleaded, pointing down at the Major. "His arm."

Redburn leaned forward and looked beyond the tangle of wires and console components that hid the left side of Justin Allard from his view. He swallowed hard and rolled back on his haunches in a crunch of broken glass and debris. "Blake's Blood," he whispered, not even realizing that he spoke. Craon was probably right. It would have been better for Allard if he'd died.

Staring down, Craon was nodding like a robot. "His arm, from the elbow down, sir. It's gone, it's just gone…"

3

Pacifica (Chara III)
Isle of Skye, Lyran Commonwealth

15 January 3027

"I don't like it, Captain." Eddie Baker's quiet voice crackled past the storm-generated static in bits and pieces. Captain Daniel Allard of the Kell Hounds mercenary unit turned his *Valkyrie*'s head far enough to watch Baker's ungainly *Jenner* waddle out of the river. "The storm's catching up with us fast. I don't fancy being out here in this walking lightning rod."

Lieutenant Austin Brand, his humanoid *Commando* following Baker's *Jenner* out of the river, laughed. "If you had a 'Mech with arms, Baker, you could swat those lighting bolts out of the air like the rest of us."

Baker, an ex-Tech who had been given the captured 'Mech as a reward for years of service, grunted in disagreement. "Just more actuators to go out."

"Can the chatter, children," Dan said, smiling to himself. *Ease up on them, Dan. Their squabbles are just battle nerves, and you know it. This scout lance works together better than almost any other lance you can name.* "Let's at least pretend to have some semblance of military order here, shall we?"

"Roger, Dan."

Daniel Allard turned his *Valkyrie*'s head around to face forward, and headed off toward the *Wasp* waiting at the crest of the hill. "How does the storm look from up there, Meg?" he asked the *Wasp* pilot.

Sergeant Margaret Lang paused a moment before answering.

"Doesn't look that bad, Captain, but the flyboys are moving their fighters inside. Must look nasty on the satellite pictures."

Dan sighed. "All right. Let's move it and get under cover. Old Stormy is living up to her name. Brand, you and I are already late for the staff meeting. This patrol is over."

"I wish the same could be said of this tour," Baker told him.

Daniel Allard laughed. *Baker's right. This is a miserable world for pulling garrison duty.* "Eddie, I'm sure if I express your disatisfaction to Colonel Kell, he'll pull some strings and get us posted elsewhere."

"No, Dan, that's all right. I could actually come to like Pacifica."

Dan's laughter filled his own neurohelmet. "You'd be the only person in the Successor States to develop that sort of affection for this world."

Chara III, a large, moonless planet in Steiner space, had proved to be one of the most contradictory places in the Inner Sphere. On one hand, the fertile soil readily accepted hybrid plants and produced fruit abundantly. The world had enough water to make it a natural paradise and to warrant garrisoning a full battalion outside the major agricultural center at Starpad. Having arrived on a placid day, the first explorer of its surface had been inspired to name the planet Pacifica.

Yet anyone who spent any time here began to wonder about the peacefulness implied in the world's name. Being a large body and lacking a moon, Pacifica rotated every fourteen TST hours. TST, or Terran Synchronized Time, related the time on any world to a traditional, twenty-four hour clock set to the rising and setting of the local sun or suns. The twenty-four hour clock divided the local day into twenty-four equal periods, with 1200 hours corresponding to local noon. A TST "hour" was, therefore, variable. Depending on a world's actual rotation, a TST hour might be much shorter than a standard, or "metric," hour. Pacifica's fast spin gave it a thirty-five minute hour as well as an unpredictable weather situation. Sudden, unexpected rain or thunderstorms were common. As many of the colonists put it, "If you don't like the weather here, just wait a minute and it'll change."

Dan worked his *Valkyrie* up the muddy hillside, following the tracks made by Lang's *Wasp*. When the Kell Hounds headquarters came into view, he smiled. *Almost home.*

Far ahead of him, Lang's *Wasp* ducked into the huge blockhouse in between the *Shilone* and *Slayer* fighters being pushed into the building. Meanwhile, the dark clouds ringing the horizon had slowly begun to drift in toward the base. To the south, beyond the blockhouse, the two barracks, and the command center, searing white lightning slashed down from distant black clouds. It took a long time for the echoes of thunder to reach the *Valkyrie*'s audio sensors, but Dan could see the storm boiling in swiftly. *Bad omen, a storm like this.* Justin always used to cite one old Capellan superstition that these storms were demons riding the clouds looking for souls to eat. Dan involuntarily crossed himself.

Turning around, he watched Baker's *Jenner* crest the hill. It looked ungainly without arms to balance it, and the nickname "Ugly Duckling" seemed more appropriate than ever. The *Jenner*, at 35 tons, was the heaviest 'Mech in Allard's scout lance, and carried the most firepower. The four launch tubes for its short-range missiles, or SRMs, ran in a line between its shoulders. Its four medium lasers fired from stubby "wings" set just above the hip joints. The way the *Jenner*'s torso jutted forward might have been a laughable sight if its powerful weaponry had not so often turned the tide of a battle. The addition of jump jets meant that the ungainly craft was actually capable of some agile moves in battle.

Compared to the *Jenner*, or most other 'Mechs, for that matter, the *Commando* following it up the hill was pure elegance. Humanoid in configuration, it carried no weapons in its open hands. Because of the camouflage patterns Brand had carefully painted on the 'Mech, the six SRM launch-tube openings in the *Commando*'s chest and the four on the 'Mech's right wrist were barely visible. A thickness on the 'Mech's left wrist betrayed the medium laser's location, but most 'Mech pilots regarded the *Commando* as nothing more than a scout, despite is weaponry. Having seen Brand pilot his 'Mech in battle, however, Dan counted the *Commando* as more than capable in combat.

Its long legs eating up the distance in an awkward jog, the *Jenner* lumbered on ahead of the other two 'Mechs. It reached the blockhouse just as the circle of storm clouds strangled the last of the sunlight and a light drizzle began to fall. Dan reached out and switched on his windscreen wipers. "You did well in the scouting run, Lieutenant. Scared the hell out of Baker when your SRM locked on to his left hip."

"Yeah, I guess I did." Brand's self-satisfaction came intact across the radio, then trailed off as he became more serious. "Lang's got to be more careful in that *Wasp*. With those SRMs, she's got more firepower than she had in her *Locust*, but both machines still rely on a medium laser for their main power. She's acting as though that monster makes her invulnerable."

Dan found himself nodding in agreement. "I'll have a talk with her. We could mention it to Colonel Kell, but I don't think the problem is at that point yet. Do you?"

Lightning-sparked static popped through the open radio connection. "No," Brand said, after a pause. "Maybe she's just got to get used

23

to the *Wasp*'s higher profile."

Glad you see that, Austin. Dan gracefully stepped his 30-ton *Valkyrie* around two bulldozers set at the edge of the makeshift spaceport. *Meg's bound to be angry with you because she thinks you cost her the* Locust.

Out beyond the bulldozers, the *Lugh*, an *Overlord* Class Drop-Ship, squatted like a gigantic Faberge egg full of lostech wonders. Behind it, as though crouching away from the rising storm's fury, a smaller DropShip, the *Leopard* Class *Manannan MacLir*, rested on the cracked ferrocrete surface. More than enough to lift the entire Kell Hounds off Pacifica, both red and black craft were buttoned up tight in anticipation of the coming storm.

Dan trailed his *Valkyrie* in after Brand's *Commando* and marched it over to the 'Mech cocoon alongside Meg Lang's *Wasp*. He disconnected his neurohelmet, popped the canopy on his *Valkyrie*, and slid down the rope ladder just in time to hear the tail-end of the tongue-lashing Meg was handing out to one of the Techs.

"I don't give a damn if you think it's impossible, Jackson. I know you can make that 'Mech more maneuverable. My *Locust* could run rings around this pile of junk!" Meg narrowed her brown eyes and brushed some strands of raven hair away from her face. "Fix it!"

Jackson, a mousy man with thick glasses, slammed his clipboard down on the ground. The papers on it exploded into a blizzard of multi-colored forms, but that didn't deflect the Tech one bit. "This isn't a *Locust*, Sergeant! I can't make it do what a *Locust* can do. Period!" Jackson looked over toward Allard, blushed, then dropped to his knees to gather up his clipboard and papers. "Sorry, Captain, for that display."

Dan Allard, towering above both Lang and Jackson, shook his head. He raked thick fingers through his light-brown hair and plucked a sodden red sweatband from his brow. "No problem, Jackson," he said calmly. As another Tech stooped to help Jackson with his papers, Dan turned to Margaret Lang and steered her away from Jackson. "A word with you."

"Yes, sir."

Out of the corner of his eye, Dan saw Brand waiting for him at the mouth of the tunnel to the command center. He waved his subordinate on ahead, then turned to Margaret Lang. "Sergeant, something's eating at you, and it has nothing to do with that *Wasp*'s performance." As he walked over to lean against the leg of a *Thunderbolt*, he waved Lang to a seat on the heavy 'Mech's foot.

"Yes, sir." Lang looked down at her boots and scratched at the sensor-pad stuck to her right thigh. "It's Lieutenant Brand, sir. I don't

24

know how to react around him."

Dan frowned. *I was afraid of this. But dammit, they work so well together.* "Meg, I know Austin feels personally responsible for the fact that your *Locust* was destroyed. I don't know if you're aware of it, but while you were in the hospital recovering from that broken leg, he pulled extra shifts and even went out with O'Cieran's jump troops to track down the bandits who planted that vibrabomb mine that killed your 'Mech."

Meg looked up into Dan's blue eyes and suppressed a laugh. "He was out with the jump infantry?"

Dan nodded solemnly. "As absurd as it may seem. On top of that, when he learned that the bandits had gotten a Kurita *Wasp* from Combine agents provocateur, he talked Cat Wilson into trotting out his *Marauder* to get that 'Mech in a dawn raid on Cat's day off."

Meg's jaw dropped open. "Cat got up before noon on a day he didn't have to?"

"Yeah." Dan squatted and pulled the helmet pad off his shoulders. "Brand's really trying to make it up to you, Meg. Don't you think its time to forgive him?"

Clearly puzzled, Meg frowned. "Forgive him? I think we're not talking about quite the same thing, sir."

Now Dan was confused, too. Sitting beside her, he leaned forward companionably, elbows on his knees. *The things they never bothered to teach me at the New Avalon Military Academy...* "Well, what *are* you talking about, then?"

Color rose to Meg's cheeks, and a smile stole across her lips. "At least part of his off-time was spent with me in the infirmary," she began. "Brand apologized over and over and promised to make it all up to me. He said he knew how much the *Locust* had meant to me, and that he really wanted to make amends."

Dan laid his left hand on her right forearm. "The *Locust* belonged in your family, right?"

Meg nodded. "Both of my mother's parents were once MechWarriors. The *Locust* belonged to my grandmother. She retired, though, to raise my mother and uncle after my grandfather died fighting against Kurita. My uncle inherited his *Warhammer*, but my mother wanted nothing more to do with 'Mechs. She married young, but my father abandoned us when I was just a few years old.'"

Dan squeezed her arm. "I'm sorry."

"Thanks." Meg swallowed past the lump in her throat and continued. "Both my mother and grandmother were bitter. Grandma trained me to use the *Locust*, and told me I could have it, provided I would never get personally mixed up with a MechWarrior."

25

She looked up into Dan's open, handsome face. "There's the problem, Captain. Austin's been so nice to me that I'm starting to fall for him—falling hard—and I think the feeling's mutual." She smiled sheepishly. "In fact, every time I look into those amber eyes of his, I know I'm right. But lurking in the back of my mind is the promise I made to my grandmother. I know I'm giving him all sorts of mixed signals, but I'm not that clear myself." Meg sighed and shrugged her shoulders. "On top of that, I know that having lovers in the same lance is not a good idea, so I don't know what to do…"

Dan shut his eyes and grimaced. *Here I am, only 28 years old, and she's making me feel like a grandfather. Eleven years with the Kell Hounds is akin to a lifetime elsewhere. By the clock, I've only got four years on both Brand and Lang, but if you consider the mileage, it's more like a century.*

Opening his eyes, Dan laughed softly. "Listen, you're getting ahead of yourself. First off, the Kell Hounds have got no rules, formal or otherwise, about relationships within the lances or battalions. We want our people to be close and to care about each other. To encourage that, but then to try to prohibit intimate relationships, would be foolhardy and impossible to police. Frankly, you, Brand, and Eddie Baker work so well together that you could start sacrificing rabbits to a full moon—if our next station has a moon—and I wouldn't really care."

Meg smiled and Dan continued. "You and Austin are two healthy, normal MechWarriors living on a world where the weather is crazy and day becomes night after seven hours. Your attraction to each other is normal, and is about the only thing on this mudball that makes any sense at all. Don't push it, or kill it prematurely. Just wait and see what happens."

"But what about my promise?" The fear and pain of betraying her mother and grandmother flickered through Meg's question.

Dan paused, then answered slowly. "I know you don't want to go back on your word, but you said it yourself—both women are bitter because of their experiences. You'll have to make up your own mind."

Meg frowned and Dan saw that she needed just a touch more convincing. "Look, Meg," he said, "my father's first marriage flamed-out for political reasons, and it ripped him up pretty badly. Even so, he tried it again. And if he hadn't, my older brother wouldn't have had anyone to pick on as we grew up."

"Your brother's a Major in the Capellan March, right?"

Her question called up Justin's image to Dan's mind, which made him smile proudly. "Justin? Yes. He's my older brother and"—Dan rose up to his full height—"I'm his *big* brother. Everyone else is back on New Avalon, just dreaming of a glorious assignment like this one."

26

Both MechWarriors laughed. Meg stood and walked a short way with Dan before she stopped to apologize to Jackson. "Thanks, Captain. I appreciate the talk."

"Sure, Sergeant. Any time." At the mention of time, Dan looked at the huge clock on the blockhouse wall. "Damn, the staff meeting! Gotta run."

4

15 January 3027

Daniel Allard sprinted off toward the Command Center, pausing once to toss his cooling vest to an astech, and a second time to accept a pair of coveralls from Master Sergeant Tech Nick Jones. He pulled on the red coveralls in the elevator ride up to the third floor, but was still pulling up the zipper before he could knock at the door labeled "Lt. Colonel Patrick M. Kell."

"Enter."

Dan opened the door and recoiled as a blast of refrigerated air struck him full on. The large room served Colonel Kell as a private office, but had ample space for the center table he'd set up for staff meetings. To Dan's left, a bank of windows looked out on the ferrocrete landing pad, offering a clear view of the lightning bolts dancing down from the dark blanket of clouds. Along the windows was a battered brown vinyl sofa left behind by the last mercenary company to pull duty—or "do time," as it had become known on station—on Pacifica. It provided seating for the only NCO at the meeting.

Ignoring his massive mahogany desk, Lieutenant Colonel Patrick Kell sat facing the door at the round meeting table. With his black hair cropped so closely, the thin scar that ran from his left temple all the way to the crown of his head stood out clearly. The scar might have been ominous if Kell's easy smile, gleaming brown eyes, and handsome features did not instantly create the urge to call this man "friend" in all who met him.

28

Kell gestured toward the unoccupied steel chair to his right. "As you can see, we began the meeting without you."

"Yes," added Kell's second-in-command, Major Salome Ward, "and I believe it's my bet. I'll see your twenty Kroner and raise you twenty." Though she had the green eyes and fiery red hair that usually accompanied a hot temper, the officers in the room knew Ward to be one of the coolest MechWarriors, in or out of battle, in the Inner Sphere.

"Yipes!" Lieutenant Mike Fitzhugh, the junior officer in Salome's Assault Lance, shot his superior an evil glance. "Forty to me? I'm out." He looked up at Dan and shook his dark curly head. "She's always finding a new way to make me earn my money."

A mischievous look twinkled through Lieutenant Austin Brand's eyes as he casually tossed the forty House Steiner Kroner onto the growing pile of blue-green bills. "I call." Lieutenant Anne Finn, the blond junior officer in Kell's Command Lance, calmly folded her hand. She smiled at Dan as he sat down beside her. "Glad you could join us."

"Said the shark to her dinner." Dan looked at the stacks of Kroner bills piled in front of Anne, and laughed. "You'd have been happier to have me contributing to your war chest there. Right, Annie?"

She merely smiled, but the long, lean black man on the couch sat up and spoke for her. "I do recall some discussion of your skill at leaving money on the table, Captain."

"I should have had you sit in for me, Cat." His remark brought a strange flash to Cat's eyes, but Dan could not identify it.

Sergeant Clarence "Cat" Wilson ran a hand back over his shaved head and laughed deeply. Of all the Kell Hounds, he was the only MechWarrior to shave to his head for better contact in the neurohelmet. "When you've played in the big leagues, you never join sandlot games."

Patrick Kell cleared his throat. "Back to business, shall we?" A worn twenty-Kroner bill fluttered from his hand into the pile of wagers. "I call."

Salome smiled hungrily. "Full house. Aces over Archons."

Brand tossed his cards into the center of the table, and Kell nodded politely to Salome. "Your deal." He turned to Allard and shook his head. "So, how is your lance doing, Dan?"

Dan cleared his throat ceremoniously. "Eddie Baker was hoping you could use your influence with your cousin, the Archon, to get us some real duty."

Kell chuckled. "Cousin-in-law, Dan. Tell Baker I'll mention it the next time Katrina Steiner comes for a beer." Kell shook his head as

29

Salome shuffled the cards. "What I really wanted to know was whether Lang is checking out on the *Wasp*."

Dan nodded, and Kell cut the cards for Salome. "She'll be fine once she works out the differences between a *Wasp* and a *Locust*. She's game enough, though. No lingering fears because of losing her *Locust*. The Lieutenant and I will keep an eye on her, and I'll keep you informed on how it's going."

Kell nodded and gathered up his cards into his strong hands. As Dan did the same, he remembered that the cards were of Lyran Commonwealth manufacture, and so he arranged them in descending order. Lacking any Aces, he put his pair of Dukes after his lone Archon. He had no 'Mechs in his hand, either, and so the numbered cards went into proper order. The four suits in the Commonwealth were Fists, Sunbursts, Dragons, and Eagles—the symbols of Houses Steiner, Davion, Kurita, and Marik. House Liao—the weakest of the Successor States—did not rate a suit.

Anne Finn gave Dan two hundred Kroner as a stake. "Not like we're playing with real money, is it?" Dan laughed and used the money to open for ten. After the others had bet or folded and he'd indicated that he wanted three cards, Dan turned to Kell.

"Is the *Intrepid*'s Captain still refusing to let Jones ship out with him after he returns here on his next run?"

Kell nodded and rearranged his cards. "We kept up a constant dialogue as his ship headed out to the jump point. He insists that we're too close to the Draconis Combine frontier for him to take a soldier on board."

Dan shook his head. "Thirty years a Tech in the Lyran Services and due to muster out a day after the *Intrepid*'s JumpShip leaves Pacifica. We can't ground the *Intrepid*, can we?"

Salome answered while Kell studied his dwinding cash reserve. "ComStar would have our tails in a sling. Somehow that lowlife merchanter weaseled a contract to haul bulk-messages to backwaters like Pacifica, and that's made him inviolate. He's afraid, though, that shipping a Steiner Tech aboard his ship would prompt the folks we know and love as the Combine to confiscate his ship—or worse."

Dan picked up his draw cards and managed to keep the arrival of a third Duke from showing on his face. "We can't just muster Jones out a day early?" Dan glanced up from his hand to see if anyone was watching him, but only Cat met his gaze with a satisfied grin.

Kell shook his head. "The Lyran Commonwealth, which has more salesmen than a cur has fleas, keeps a tight rein on its money and muster-out pay. Master Sergeant Nicholas Jones has to muster out of Pacifica on the 26th of May in order to get any of the bonus pay he's entitled to. If the computer can't check him for voice, retinal patterns, and fingerprints, his bonus goes back into the general fund."

Dan snorted. "Amen. And, in the meantime, the *Intrepid* jumps out of here and won't be back for another six months." Dan looked up at the windows and watched lightning sear through the near dark. "Six months in this place is like thirty years. There *has* to be something we can do."

Fitzhugh laughed. "Why don't you play this hand and you can buy him a JumpShip. The bet's fifty to you."

Ah, Mike, your impatience will cost you. Dan carelessly flipped the money out onto the table. "Call."

Fitzhugh flashed three tens on the table, and then Dan slapped his trio of Dukes down over Fitz's cards. He waited a half-second for Kell or Salome to make a play, then raked in the H-bills toward him.

The second knock barely sounded at the door before Cat Wilson leaped up to answer it. Opening the door a crack, he imposed his muscular body between the person in the hall and the card game. That the Colonel conducted his company staff meetings over a poker game was common knowledge among the Kell Hounds, but the outcome of the games was kept strictly confidential. The informality of the meetings could only survive if the officers knew that winning and losing did not matter. The money and bragging rights won in the weekly games remained among the deepest secrets that the Kell Hounds had.

Cat nodded and accepted a folded note from the messenger in the hallway. He shut the door and carried it over to Colonel Kell. Dan recognized the paper as the thin stock used in the communications center and noticed ComStar's logo boldly emblazoned at the head of the message. He hoped, for the barest of moments, that the message was a transfer of the Kell Hounds to an assignment far from Pacifica. The expression on the Colonel's face quickly dashed those hopes.

Kell looked up from the paper, which trembled violently in his hand. "Dan, I'm sorry."

The tone of Patrick's voice set fear churning in Dan's gut. *My God, did someone get to my father?* He snatched the message and quickly read it once, then stood abruptly. His chair crashed to the floor as Dan swept past Cat toward the windows. He smoothed out the paper that he'd unconsciously crumpled and again read the horrible words as lightning illuminated them:

WYATTSUPCOMHQ RELAY PRIORITY ALPHA REGULAR
Origin: FEDSUNSUPCOMHQ NEW AVALON
Classification: Confidential

31

To: Lt. Colonel Patrick Kell//COMKELLHOUNDS
To: Captain Daniel Allard//ATTACHKELLHOUNDS

On 27 November 3026 Major Justin Allard suffered battle-related injuries. Transferred to NAIS Medical Center 15 December 3026. Extensive trauma resulted in crude amputation of left arm. Prognosis for cybernetic rehabilitation awaiting end of induced narcotic coma. Prognosis for survival: Excellent.

Dan felt an icy claw reach into his belly and rake through his guts. He crumpled the message into a ball again and tossed it down to the floor, but none of the others made any motion to retrieve it. Dan's hands knotted into fists as his whole body quivered with rage. *No! Not Justin. Not him.*

Patrick Kell stood and silently dismissed everyone except Salome and Wilson. The three of them had known Dan since the day he'd joined the Kell Hounds as part of the core of the mercenary company. Though all the Kell Hounds would be sympathetic to the sorrows of a compatriot, the three people standing behind Daniel Allard would share his pain.

Staring out the window, Dan watched drops roll down the stormlashed pane like the tears streaming over his cheeks. *How could it be? Why doesn't that message tell me what really happened? Justin's too good a warrior to get hit in a regular skirmish. It had to be an ambush or something.*

Dan swallowed, then brushed away the tears. He turned halfway and glanced back at his friends. "Let them read it, Patrick."

Salome bent to recover the note. She pressed it smooth against her thigh, then smothered a gasp as she read. She passed the note to Wilson, but he never took it. His black eyes quickly scanned the sheet, but no emotions showed on his ebon features.

Kell stepped forward and rested his powerful hands on Dan's shoulders. "Dan, we're all sorry."

Dan squeezed his eyes shut against new tears. "He lost his arm, Patrick. He'll never pilot another 'Mech. It'll kill him."

Salome brought Dan a glass filled with three fingers of Kuritan whiskey. "You've had a shock. Drink it."

Dan hesitated, but Cat had foreseen his wish to hide any display of personal weakness. The tall black man handed Salome and Patrick similar glasses of whiskey, and even brandished one himself. "We've all had a shock." Cat reached around and dragged a chair away from the poker table. He sat in it with his chest resting against the back of the chair.

Salome went to sit on the sofa, and Dan wandered over to join her.

Patrick Kell was now leaning against the corner of his desk. "I'm going to have the crew get the *Mac* ready to take you up to the *Cucamulus*. We'll get you back to New Avalon as fast as possible."

Dan held up his left hand. "No, sir. Thank you, but no, sir." *What had gone wrong for Justin?*

Patrick waved away Dan's protest. "Listen. There's some Kell Hound business to take care of in the Federated Suns. I'll send you to represent the battalion. It's battalion business, pure and simple."

Dan looked up and forced a weak smile. "No, Colonel—Patrick—I appreciate the gesture. Really I do, but no matter how fast I travel, it will take me over three months to reach New Avalon. And even if I did get there sooner, what good would it do? That message took more than a month to reach us here, even traveling through ComStar's "A" circuit. They would have brought Justin out of his coma two weeks ago." Dan gasped and slammed his left fist down on the torn arm of the battered brown sofa.

No one spoke as he struggled to regain control of his emotions. Bitter tears streaked down his face, and he shook his head violently, flicking them off in anger. Muscles bunched at his jaws, and his face flushed scarlet. *Stop it, Dan. Get hold of yourself. Justin's probably handling it better than you are.*

"Please, forgive me," he said finally, looking around at his three friends. "I hope I've not dishonored myself in your eyes."

Cat shrugged easily. "A man loves his brother. No dishonor in that."

Salome nodded. "You were around during the Defection, when we all went through our own private hells. You were there for us. Now it's our turn."

The Defection. They all thought of it that way, and they all carried the scars. After a strange battle on Mallory's World with that Kurita commander—one Yorinaga Kurita—Colonel Morgan Kell had quit the unit and entered a monastery on Zaniah III. Two-thirds of the Kell Hound Regiment had left at the same time. All that had happened eleven years ago. Patrick still wondered why Morgan had not trusted him with a full regiment, and Salome still wondered why Morgan had left her. And Dan never did understand why, as soon as he joined the Kell Hounds, they had fallen apart.

Patrick Kell nodded slowly in echo of Salome's words. "We've all been through so much together, Dan," he said, keeping his vow never to speak of the Defection. He faltered, then recovered himself. "I know what it is to have an older brother, and to lose him. But we all worked together and built up this unit into the best mercenary battalion around." Patrick nodded at Cat and Salome. "We share your pain."

Dan smiled weakly. "I appreciate this. I just hope Justin made it through…you know…all in one piece mentally." He drank a slug from his glass and relished the burning in his throat. "I remember how, when we were growing up, other kids used to beat up on Justin because he was half-Capellan. I used to want to help him fight, but win or lose, he always kept me back. 'My fight, Danny,' he'd say. When I'd tell him that he was my brother and that it was *our* fight, he'd laugh and tell me I could have whatever he couldn't handle."

Patrick smiled warmly and sipped his whiskey. "I've heard good things about your brother Justin. Always hoped he'd want to join the Hounds."

Dan nodded. "Me, too. I can remember when he announced his intention to enroll in Sakhara Military Academy. He told my father he wanted to be away from New Avalon to keep from taking advantage of the Allard name, and my father took that rather well. Justin told me he wanted to become a MechWarrior because, in a BattleMech, everyone becomes equal. From that moment, I decided to become a MechWarrior, too, because I wanted to be Justin's equal."

Salome reached out and kneaded the muscles at the back of Dan's neck with her strong, slender fingers. "I bet there's another message rattling around in some ComStar center that would tell you that Justin is doing fine. The New Avalon Institute of Science has made so many breakthroughs lately. At least your brother's getting the best possible care."

"Dan, are you certain you don't want to head out? I'm not saying we can function without you, but the *Cucamulus* is yours if you want her." Patrick pointed out the window at the *Manannan MacLir*. "I'll have the *Mac*'s crew stand by, just in case."

Dan shook his head, drained his glass, and stood. "No, but thank you. Thank all you." He smiled calmly. "I'm sure Justin will be fine. As the aerojocks like to say, 'Any wreck you walk away from is a good one.'"

Dan's head came up and he smiled even more broadly. "I've got work to do here, and Justin would think poorly of me if I didn't accomplish it. After all, someone's got to figure out a way to get Master Sergeant Jones off Old Stormy when his time comes."

Patrick Kell smiled. "Understood, Captain. Just remember, the door's always open."

Daniel Allard nodded, but Kell's words barely registered with so many thoughts speeding through his own mind. *I'll find out who did this to you, Justin, and I swear, his blood will be on the hands of an Allard.*

5

Solaris VII (The Game World)
Rahneshire, Lyran Commonwealth

15 January 3027

The black and blood-red groundcar sliced through the gray
drizzle, cutting around piles of debris scattered over the ferrocrete
street. As the car's headlights burned away the dark shadows hiding
alleys and doorways from view, pedestrians scrambled back out of the
light. Recognizing the car, they knew, as certain as the clouds never left
Solaris VII, that to ambush that vehicle was to die.

The ground car crossed the burned out "no-man's-land" between
Cathay and Silesia—the Capellan and Lyran quarters, respectively, of
Solaris City. The tongsmen of Cathay ignored the vehicle as it left their
area of influence, but the "unofficial" wardens of Silesia snapped
respectful salutes at the darkened windscreen as the car sped past on a
whispering cushion of air. The vehicle turned left at the first unblocked
street and stopped finally before the narrow doorway of a nondescript
building.

Air hissed as the gull-wing door on the driver's side of the car
swung upward. No interior light came on, for the driver refused to be
silhouetted for a sniper's convenience. Stepping quickly into the rain-
slicked street, he snapped the door down shut. With long-legged
strides, the driver headed toward the smoked glass door.

Once inside, the man swept off the slouch-brimmed black hat
from his shaved head, and handed it and his spattered rain cloak to the
checkroom attendant. He quickly followed that with a 10 C-bill tip, and
smiled at her reaction. "Oh, thank you, Mr. Noton," the girl gushed in

35

astonishment. He could tell by the look in her eyes that she could hardly believe that he'd given her a ComStar Bill. Most of her tips had to be in House Bills or, worse yet, Solaris scrip, the underground currency that paid for most of the illegal doings on this world.

"It's real, child." His deep voice had an edge that did not quite match the warmth of his smile, but the girl never noticed. Noton turned from her, straightened his double-breasted blue satin shirt, and fastened the last two buttons at his left shoulder. Feeling how tightly his shirt stretched across his barrel chest, he knew that if he grew any stouter, he'd have to abandon the paramilitary dress that all MechWarriors favored. Noton thought better of it then, and smiled to himself. *As long as I am a MechWarrior, I will continue to dress as one.*

Gray Noton straightened up to his full height and strode boldly down the dim hallway and up the half-flight of stairs against the left wall. A slender, nervous looking doorman glanced up as Noton filled the doorway, then smiled. "Welcome back to Thor's Shieldhall, Mr. Noton. There is someone waiting for you up in Valhalla, but Mr. Shang hoped you would have a moment for him. He's down here in Midgard, back watching the matches."

So, he's waiting for me, is he? That he knows I've returned is obvious, but did he know of my other meeting? And, if so, how? Noton smiled easily. "Thank you, Roger." He deposited a 20 C-bill on Roger's desk. "Mr. Shang does not know that I am meeting someone else here?"

Roger laid a long-fingered hand over the C-bill, which vanished as though absorbed straight into the man himself. "I certainly did not tell him, sir, but he is resourceful, as you well know." Roger stopped for a moment and absently tapped nicotine-stained teeth with a finger while he was thinking. He narrowed his eyes. "Mr. Shang just came in and announced he'd be watching the fights in our holoroom. I offered him a private viewing room in Valhalla, but he declined."

Noton nodded slowly. "Very well, Roger. Thank you." *You must be more careful, Gray. If Shang can guess that you'd show up at Thor's Shieldhall on your first night back on the Game World, you've become predictable—fatally predictable.*

Turning from the doorman, Noton took one step into the darkened room and studied the crowd. Garish phosphoron designs of diverse colors and intensities decorated the U-shaped bar. He watched intently, but recognized none of the faces revealed by dazzling but tantalizingly short bursts of light. Beyond the tables and off to the right were more brilliant lights rotating above the dance floor. The harsh white illumination they splashed over the bar resembled searchlights racing along prison walls. An occasional beam would fragment into rainbows as it lanced against some patron's oversized gem, but mostly the lights served only to heighten the corpselike pallor of those destined to remain in Midgard.

No one to fear in the land of the dead, but it's the ones you don't see that get you. Noton shook himself slightly. *Ease off, Gray. You've not lost your edge. He eluded you, but you got him in due course.*

Gray blinked against a momentarily blinding spotlight, then looked around him. Thor's Shieldhall—a place so chic and popular that it needed no exterior signs—divided its clientele into two distinct classes: the masses and the privileged. If anyone of the former had enough luck or initiative to find out where Thor's was located, he was welcome to spend time and money in Midgard on overpriced drinks, loud music, and the garish ambiance. Ordinary customers actually paid for the chance to spot members of the privileged pass through Midgard on their way to Valhalla.

Valhalla, Hall of Slain Warriors. Gray Noton suppressed a laugh, knowing that he was probably one of the few who understood and appreciated the real meaning behind that name. Whether it was the masses longing for admittance or the MechWarriors and slumming nobles of the Successor States, most people thought of Valhalla as a haven, a heaven, for the human stars of Solaris. There, one could see and perhaps speak with legendary MechWarriors—the gladiators of the Game World—such as Snorri Sturluson, Inigo de Onez y Loyola, Antal Dorati, or even the current champion, Philip Capet.

Visiting and resident nobles and their guests swelled Valhalla's population and often outnumbered the MechWarriors. Many nobles owned a string of BattleMechs, and they selected MechWarriors the way their Terran ancestors might have selected jockeys to race thoroughbreds millennia ago. Those "stabled" 'Mechs dominated, perforce, the heavyweight leagues on Solaris, while owner-operators wallowed around in the lighter classes. If an independent dared challenge a noble's 'Mech pilot, the independent became a long-odds shot—not for winning, but for surviving.

Noton cut through the crowd and headed deeper into Midgard, toward the open end of the bar. Ignoring invitations to join people he did not know or wanted to forget, he continued toward a far doorway leading into a wide and deep room. The backlight from the massive holographic display dominating the center of the bowl-shaped auditorium made it easy for Noton to find Tsen Shang. Descending the steps to the third terrace, he quickly passed by one crowded booth after another, until he reached the one where the Capellan awaited him.

"Greetings, Tsen," Gray said, sliding onto the seat opposite. He knew better than to offer Shang his hand. Instead, he bowed his head and the Capellan graciously returned the gesture.

Shang signalled to catch the eye of a server. The gesture silhouetted his hand against the glowing blue hologram of a battling *Valkyrie* in the center of the room. Though Gray had many times studied Shang's hands in meetings like this, he never overcame a feeling of slight disgust at the sight of them. The affectation seemed unnatural and gave Shang a delicate and foppish appearance. Gray knew, however, that anyone who accepted that impression could be in as much trouble as someone who believed a *Valkyrie* posed no threat to a *Rifleman*.

Shang, in Capellan fashion, had grown out the fingernails on the last three fingers of each hand to a length of ten centimeters. Decorated with gem chips and goldleaf, the distinctive nails marked Shang as a Capellan of culture and wealth. This coincided with the image he cultivated on Solaris and, in addition to his ownership of two heavy 'Mechs, was enough to grant him entry to Valhalla whenever he visited the Shieldhall.

Noton shuddered slightly because he knew Shang so well, perhaps better than did anyone else on Solaris. Tsen Shang answered to masters in the Maskirovka, the Capellan secret police. He ran a string of spies on Solaris and often worked with free agents, like Noton himself, to gather information for his superiors on Sian, the Capellan capital world. In keeping with Shang's true identity, the nails were much more than a concession to fashion.

The female server appeared and squatted to keep from blocking the two men's view of the hologram battle. Despite the din raised by the room's other spectators, Shang's half-whisper was still commandingly clear. "Another plum wine for me, and a PPC for my companion."

Noton shook his head. "Beer. Timbiqui dark, if you have it."

Shang smiled. "Timbiqui dark, then." He slid a small bowl toward the woman. Scraps of a blue-green skin and fruit pits the size of navy beans rattled around in it. "And another bowl of *kincha* fruit, please." Shang waited for her to scoop up the bowl and retreat before he spoke.

"Welcome, Gray. Congratulations on your mission."

Noton frowned. "Congratulations? That mission blew up in our faces. Your superiors sent me out to bag a training cadre, but all I did was destroy a *Valkyrie*. That MechWarrior was good." *Too damned good,* Gray thought.

"Indeed." Shang fell silent as the server returned with their drinks. She placed the bowl of fruit in the center, but Shang quickly slid it toward himself. He lifted a *kincha*, and with great skill born of much practice, sliced through its thick flesh with the carbon-fiber reinforced,

38

razor-sharp nail of his little finger. "That *Valkyrie*'s pilot was none other than Major Justin Allard."

Noton smiled ruefully. "So that's the Allard that Capet speaks of so often. No wonder he fears him. Capet's not bad, but Allard is better."

Shang peeled back the *kincha* flesh and carved off a sliver of the fruit's sweet meat. "*Was* better. Though your attack did not kill him, it ended a brilliant career. According to our agents on Kittery, you blew off his left forearm. Allard's still alive, but he'll never lead troops again. After what he did on Spica, we praise his removal from Hanse Davion's service."

Noton grimaced. *Had I known that, I would have killed him. Never would I so maim another MechWarrior that he could not fight again.* Noton looked up and saw Shang lost in the pleasure of tasting the *kincha. Ah, Shang,* he thought, *has the Maskirovka made you forget your days as a MechWarrior? You have become so careless, and your addiction to* kincha *marks you as one of Liao's Lost Legion. You disgraced yourselves when you lost Shuen Wan to Marik. Do you forget what it is to be a MechWarrior because you wish to forget losing the* kincha's *homeworld, or is it that you believe MechWarriors are below your exalted height as a spymaster?*

Shang opened his eyes. "I have arranged for your payment, as usual." Shang fished a silvery slip of paper from the pocket of his green silk jacket, and passed it across the table to Noton. Gray waited until Shang's attention returned to the *kincha* before reaching out for the paper. In the dying holo-light of the scarlet *Wasp* collapsing above him, he squinted and studied the ticket.

"Steiner Stadium, fifth fight?" Noton frowned. "The bet is too small to make any money on Philip Capet."

Shang nodded and his dark eyes flashed. "It has been arranged."

Noton pulled back and slowly shook his head. "You've fixed a fight with Capet in it? Impossible. He won't lose on command. We both know that—especially not against Capellans."

Blue light flashed from diamond chips as Shang waved away Noton's concerns. "He's in his *Rifleman* and he'll be fighting the Teng brothers. They'll both be in *Vindicators.* Your bet is that he'll leave Fuh Teng alive."

Noton nodded. "Sze Teng will die?"

Concentrating more on the *kincha* than his answer, Shang nodded diffidently. "He has lost his nerve. He disgraces ancestors who, two hundred years ago, made the *Vindicator* a 'Mech to be feared. He knows it is time to die."

I will never understand your Capellan ways, Gray thought. *They are…unnatural.* "But won't that affect how he fights?"

Shang flicked the *kincha* pit into the bowl. "He has been told that he will die in the rematch after he and his brother defeat Philip Capet."

Noton took a long drink of beer to forestall any comment. The brothers Teng were Maskirovka, too. They would follow Shang into Solaris's sun if he so commanded them. Noton lowered his glass. "Is there something that you want me to do?"

Shang thought for a moment, then nodded. "The MechWarrior who organized the defense on Kittery while you fought Major Allard is Leftenant Andrew Redburn. Keep your eyes and ears open and let me know anything you're able to learn about him."

Noton smiled and rose to leave. He made no move to drain his glass of beer, as other MechWarriors or denizens of Solaris might have. Shang's eyes flicked toward the beer and Noton suppressed a smile. *Capellans—so bound up in traditions that confuse me, but still so easy to read. Because I leave that expensive, imported beverage, you take it as a sign that I am prosperous. Likewise, you will abandon your prized* kincha *fruit to prove to me your own affluence. You will respect me for what I do, while I find your action laughable.*

"Again, Gray, I offer you the praise of House Liao for your mission. I look forward to sharing similar successes with you in the future."

Noton smiled in the dimness of Midgard. "And I with you, Tsen."

Leaving Shang to his *kincha* fruit, Noton climbed the terrace steps and cut back along a narrow catwalk to a door linking Midgard with Valhalla on the far side of the garishly lit bar. Opposite the bar was a section of tables and booths kept intentionally dark. A bank of coolers set into the ceiling was so efficient at sucking up the smoke of everything from opium to Turin leaf that Noton caught only a hint of the acrid drugsmoke while passing among the tables. He never looked down, never tried to identify anyone in the cherry glow of a pipe, but marched straight ahead toward and through the shadowed doorway in the wall.

Noton brushed aside a thick black curtain and walked swiftly up a ramp that doubled back on itself and brought him to a lobby roughly above where he had spoken with Roger earlier. Set into the floor was a pressure plate where Noton stopped to allow the identiscanner's ruby red beam to play over him. Behind a clear, impact-resistant glass panel to his left, a security guard smiled. "Welcome, Mr. Noton."

Gray nodded in a brief salute. Facing him across the short lobby was a dark glass wall that prevented anyone from seeing into Valhalla, but that allowed those already inside to monitor approaching newcomers. From time to time, the denizens of Valhalla amused themselves by watching the guards conduct undesirables back down to Midgard, but most paid little attention to new arrivals.

Noton smiled, thinking that only one person there would be

41

anxious about his arrival. As the wall's central panel slid noiselessly into the ceiling, Gray Noton entered Valhalla.

In accord with its name, Valhalla had been constructed as a Norse warrior's vision of paradise. Long and wide, the whole room was constructed from rare, imported woods cut into rough, unfinished planks. Animal skins hung from the walls, and garishly painted shields decorated pillars and posts. A holographic bonfire raged in the center of the room. Along with holographic torches stuck into wall brackets, the fire provided virtually all of the light for Valhalla.

Running the length of the room, from the door to a raised dais at the far end, were crudely built tables and benches. MechWarriors filled the tables, seating themselves in a rough hierarchy of skill and reputation. The best MechWarriors sat nearest the dais. The new warriors, or those on their way down, sat nearest the door. Male and female servers hurriedly passed up and down among them, carrying wooden mugs frothy with Tsinghai ale, or depositing plates of steaming meat and fresh bread before the customers.

Along either side of Valhalla, gray woolen curtains cut off dark alcoves from view. Alongside most of these hung a shield decorated with the arms of the MechWarrior or noble who owned that alcove. The nobles' booths were clustered nearer the door than were the alcoves of the MechWarriors. Even so, everyone on Solaris VII knew where the real power lay. Though it might be a great honor to sit with Snorri Sturluson in his alcove near the dais, it was usually more profitable to visit back further with a Duchess or Count from any one of the Successor States.

Noton waved a friendly greeting to the first few MechWarriors he knew, though he did not linger to chat. He usually enjoyed the company of other 'Mech pilots, even those doomed to live and die in the tempest world of the Games on Solaris. Tonight, however, there were other, more important matters on his mind.

Lo, though I walk through the valley of death, I shall not fear — *I shall not linger*...Noton knew that any MechWarrior found in Valhalla was superior to 80 percent of the MechWarriors on the planet, and could best 90 percent of the MechWarriors in the Inner Sphere. He also knew that the Game World of Solaris was a deadend for Mech-Warriors because, unlike 'Mech pilots in service to the Lords of the battling Successor Houses, no one here could retire to a title and liege-gifted riches. As the name Valhalla suggested, these MechWarriors were already as good as dead.

Or they'll get smart and get out, as I have, Noton thought, admiring the shield that decorated his alcove. The device, a wispy, almost comical, ghost centered in a red crosshairs, reminded everyone

42

of Noton's past glories. *Legend-killer, they named me and my Rifleman, and I spilled more alcove-owners from their havens than has anyone before me or since I "retired." Now, as an information broker, I consort with royalty and spill leaders from their thrones.* Though some MechWarriors believed that Gray had betrayed their profession by making such a switch, most did not care. No one cared less than Gray Noton himself.

Noton parted the curtains secluding his alcove. "Good evening, Baron von Summer," he said to the dark-haired, corpulent noble from the Lyran Commonwealth who sat waiting for him. With the Baron tonight was a female companion, a strikingly beautiful blond with ice-blue eyes. She smiled and extended her hand toward Noton. "I am Contessa Kym Sorenson, late of the Federated Suns." A diamond and ruby ring sparkled up at Noton. "I am pleased to meet you, Gray Noton."

He kissed her hand, noticing its velvety softness and the perfection of her manicure—right down to a nail polish color that exactly matched her eyes. "The pleasure is all mine, Contessa."

The Contessa stood up gracefully. Her blue satin blouse, which mimicked the double-breasted styling of Noton's tunic, had not been fastened all the way at the left shoulder. Gathered at the waist with a linked silver belt, it defined her lithe figure most flatteringly. She also wore silky black trousers and riding boots. Though the boots were not yet a fashion rage on Solaris as on other worlds, they looked enough like battle gear to give Noton pause. *Is she a MechWarrior...*

Despite the Contessa's grace of movement and choice of clothing, Noton answered his own question after a moment's reflection. *She's no MechWarrior. Not with those hands.* He frowned slightly as she moved toward the curtain. "You are leaving us?" he asked.

Enrico Lestrade, the Baron von Summer, added a mute protest and offered the Contessa his hand.

With her free hand, she flicked back her shoulder-length hair and smiled. "I will perhaps return another time, Mr. Noton." She reached out and squeezed Lestrade's right hand. "I assume that you and Enrico have some business to discuss, which I would not wish to interrupt. Until we meet again."

Noton held the curtain open for her. "I shall look forward to that time." He let the curtain fall behind her, and then turned on Enrico Lestrade. "You insist on a private meeting, but then bring a woman with you? No wonder your uncle prefers to keep you here on Solaris instead of on Summer! I'm surprised he didn't get you posted as a diplomat to Luthien." Noton paused, then added cruelly, "No, I expect he couldn't risk your starting a war with House Kurita, could he?"

43

The Baron stammered, then gained control over the flow of gibberish that had begun to spill from his mouth. "She knows nothing. You have become far too suspicious for your own good, Noton. The Contessa is newly arrived here. I met her at a party last night—a party thrown by the head of the Solaris Battle Commission—and she asked me about Valhalla. Could I pass up the chance to escort her here? No. Quite simply and absolutely, no." Seated in the corner, Lestrade glowered at Noton like a child refusing to eat his ashqua.

Noton frowned, too, and sat down in the large wooden chair at the head of the narrow table. *Either you're an incredible fool posted here to keep you from doing too much damage, or you're hiding your own schemes behind this foolish facade. I will take steps to find out which it is.*

Wooden planks formed the alcove into a three-sided box. Touching a button hidden beneath the table's edge, Noton activated the low hiss of a white-noise generator to assure him that no one would overhear any subsequent conversation. "How do you know she is harmless?"

Lestrade snorted derisively. "My dear Noton, after many a year of dealing with the bored daughters of rich industrialist fathers, I can spot one from a myriameter off. As it so happens, though, I have learned that she was booted out of the Federated Suns because she refused to join her father's business." The Baron smiled at Noton. "Her family made the engine in your ground car, in fact. You still do drive the Typhoon?"

Noton nodded. "Sorenson Mechanicals." He touched another button, and the wooden panel opposite him slid up to reveal a holovision viewscreen. "Steiner Stadium, fifth fight tonight." In response to his voice, the computer scanned through Valhalla's available library. Finally, after a blizzard of partial images stormed across the screen, there appeared the frozen image of a *Rifleman* facing off against twin *Vindicators*.

Before the taped battle began to unfold, Noton added a command. "Display only the results."

Lestrade frowned. "A most uninteresting fight."

Noton grunted. *More the fool, I begin to think...* White lettering superimposed itself over the BattleMech images. Noton smiled. Fuh Teng had survived and would be able to fight in another month. He had lost his brother, however, and the battle, to Philip Capet. Beneath the official results, the computer added a footnote describing this as Capet's thirteenth straight victory in the Open Class, and the first time he'd failed to kill a Capellan opponent.

Lestrade sniffed. "He should have killed the other one. I lost because he did not."

Noton regarded Lestrade harshly. The chubby Baron's red shirt, black vest, and red pants made him look more like an actor from some heroic comedy than a nobleman. Suddenly exasperated with the man, Gray demanded, "What was so urgent that you asked for this meeting?"

"Some people," the Baron began—while Noton instantly substituted the names of Duke Frederick Steiner and Duke Aldo Lestrade—"believe that there might be ways of diverting a JumpShip from a particular course."

Noton frowned. *Definitely the fool.* "If you're talking about stealing a JumpShip, stop right there." The ultimate example of lostech, JumpShips were vessels capable of instantaneous, 30 light-year leaps from star to star. And they were jealously guarded by anyone lucky enough to own one. "No one I know would dare steal a JumpShip. Especially since the Federated Suns began its anti-hijacking measures last year."

Lestrade wrinkled his nose. "Well, not actually a JumpShip. It's a DropShip they want. A DropShip with some special people aboard."

"Military DropShip?"

Lestrade shook his head. "No, just a DropShip."

Noton pondered the thought. Often enough, a passenger line or cargo hauler kept JumpShips at certain central jump points. DropShips—craft capable of traveling from space to a planet's surface—arrived insystem via one JumpShip and were then transferred to another outbound ship. Because a JumpShip generally required a week to recharge its Kearny-Fuchida jump drive, the relay system helped speed up the shuttle between stars.

Noton nodded. "That's more possible. What ship? Where?"

Lestrade smiled weakly. "I don't have that information yet. I know that the ship will be in the vicinity of Terra, so your contact would have to be near there to strike. We anticipate a two- or three-month leadtime on this."

"Good." Noton knew that despite the week-long waits between jumps and the seemingly leisurely pace of jump travel, any operation to hijack a DropShip full of passengers would require split-second timing. "It will be expensive."

Lestrade nodded and produced a little notebook from his vest pocket. "These people will pay an advance of up to sixty-thousand C-bills to cover operational costs…"

"Eighty-five thousand," Noton said.

Lestrade looked up as though Noton had stung him. "I'm only authorized to give you sixty-thousand."

"Get new authorization." Noton leaned forward. He knew that if these "people" were desperate enough to want to hijack a DropShip, they'd be desperate enough to pay well for it. "I assume you want these certain passengers held for a certain amount of time. Preparing a place to hold a DropShip's worth of people will be costly. While you're talking to your people, tell them my cut of the operation will be fifty-thousand, up front, and my people will want a balance of three hundred thousand C-bills upon completion of the mission."

All the blood drained from Lestrade's face. He looked at Noton, then glanced at his notebook, and back up at the mercenary. "That's way over budget…"

Noton smiled like a fox. "No, it isn't. They can supplement the payments by collecting ransoms from the families of the passengers. My people will have to take serious risks in this operation, and they won't even consider it unless the price is right."

The Baron swallowed hard. "I will pass the message along."

Noton nodded. The only person bound toward Terra that could possibly interest the Steiner/Lestrade faction of the Lyran Commonwealth would have to be a courier from Archon Katrina Steiner to Prince Hanse Davion of the Federated Suns. Kidnapping that courier would delay the growing alliance between House Davion and House Steiner. While that alliance was gaining Katrina Steiner more power with each passing day, it stood squarely in the path of her cousin, Frederick Steiner, who had his own designs on the Lyran throne. Noton assured himself that Frederick Steiner and his ally, Duke Aldo Lestrade—Enrico's uncle—would pay well to sabotage that Steiner-Davion alliance.

Noton stood and guided the visibly perspiring Baron to the curtain. "Contact me when you have some real figures to discuss, Baron. Until then."

Noton half-turned back to his alcove, but a bold voice shouted his name. "Noton, did you watch my fight?"

Noton shook his head slowly. "No, Capet. If I wanted to see the sort of battling you do, I'd have only to toss a C-bill in the street and watch the crippled orphans of Cathay scramble for it."

Philip Capet, seated on the dais at the room's far end, slammed his flagon against the table. It struck hard, shattering against the oak wood surface and spattering golden ale over his companions. "How dare you!"

"How dare I what, Capet? How dare I point out that the Emperor has no clothes?" Noton turned to face the front of the room and rested balled fists on his narrow hips. *Capet, you fool, have you begun to believe you're as invincible as the fight commentators claim?*

Noton's voice dropped to a razor-edged growl. "Your *Rifleman* grossly outclassed those two *Vindicator*s. Your fight should have ended quickly. In Steiner Stadium, with all that open ground, you should have killed both pilots in a minute or less. Five minutes. Ha! You toyed with them. You did not treat them like MechWarriors."

Capet shook his head. His curly salt and pepper hair was cropped closely to his scalp, but his bushy black moustache gave his visage a menacing, angry look. Added to that were a hooked nose broken once too often and a jagged scar plucking the corner of Capet's right eye into a perpetual squint that matched his habitual sneer. He now graced Noton with one of those looks.

Capet forced a harsh laugh. "You washed-up fighters are all the same. I've been in the wars, Noton. I've seen combat the likes of which you'll never know." Capet spat on the floor. "I didn't toy with those Capellans. I gave them a few more minutes of life than they deserved."

Capet stabbed a finger at Noton. "If I'm such a street-brawler, why don't you come out and defeat me, eh, Noton? Or has retirement softened you?" Capet faced his audience. "Noton's been gone these last few weeks getting a tummy-tuck and a facelift." Turning back to Noton, he added, "You should have gotten some backbone while you were away."

Noton laughed aloud. "That's the difference between us, Capet. You don't know when to shut up. You also don't know how vulnerable you really are. I don't care about your hatred for Capellans or your God-awful ego, but stay clear of me. If you don't, I swear that the *Legend-killer* will be your death."

7

New Avalon
Crucis March, Federated Suns

27 December 3026

Consciousness seeped into Justin Allard's brain drop by drop. As the doctor slowly dialed 10ccs of dexamaline into the IV monitor, the drug slowly ate away the narcotic coma induced by other drugs. The doctor looked over at the EEG monitor, smiled as brain activity increased steadily, and quickened the pace of the dexamaline infusion.

Disjointed and fragmented, words and feelings flashed across Justin's consciousness like firefish striking at the surface of a murky pond. Shrapnel bits of pain and memories of fire stung him, and he latched onto the pain long enough to give his mind some focus. He located that pain—a tiny, almost lost shard of it—in his right forearm. From that pinpoint of awareness, he began to recall that he had an arm and a body, which led him to the knowledge that he was still alive.

Random scenes from memory suddenly bombarded him. First came the intense fear for his command that he had felt upon discovering that *Rifleman*. Then the battle began to play itself out again, but in such shifting colors and slow movements that his recollection twisted into a surreal nightmare. Missiles exploded into flowers that sprouted teeth and bit into 'Mechs made of balloons.

The doctor watched brain activity increase rapidly and so brought down the dexamaline level again. A nurse pressed a cool cloth to Justin's forehead and drew his sheets down to the waist to cool him off.

Justin's dream battle evaporated in a cold rush of reason. *Impossible to happen. It cannot exist. I do not wish to dream it.* Those three thoughts, short but connected, descended into the black pit where Justin found himself, and he clung to them like the lowest rungs of some ladder. Slowly, laboriously, he reached up and grasped another thought. *I have pain. I am alive.*

The acrid scent of his own perspiration almost blocked the room's harsh antiseptic odor, but Justin caught it. Memories of hospital visits tore at him, but he refused to succumb to them. *I am in a hospital. I must have been injured.* With that thought came another impression that confirmed it. Justin finally felt the bandages circling his head and covering his eyes.

Panic shot through him with a jolt. *No, not blind. Dear God, anything but that!* He tried to lift his right hand to touch his face, but the doctor restrained him gently to keep the IV needles from tearing free. Justin, feeling resistance, immediately abandoned the effort to use his right arm and commanded his left hand to act instead.

It took almost superhuman strength, but his left arm responded. Bending at the elbow, it jerked upright, then flopped over and struck Justin heavily in the chest. In that instant, terror and confusion ripped away at Justin's sanity.

What is it? What's wrong with my arm? He could feel his forearm pressing against his chest, and there was a dull ache where his fingers had poked hard into his ribs, yet he still felt his left hand and wrist extended straight down from his upper arm!

A sharp, authoritative voice drilled through Justin's blind panic. "Stop, Allard! Wait! Stand easy, Major." The command, voiced like an order from a superior officer, hit Justin with the force of a physical blow. It shattered the chaos of anxiety that was swallowing him, and he grabbed at it like a drowning man at a life preserver.

Justin's parched lips opened with difficulty. He tried to speak, but only a harsh croaking came from his throat. Smashing down another jolt of fear, he again tried to speak. "Water."

Instantly, the bed began to rise, elevating his head and torso. Whatever had fallen on his chest no longer pressed against him. Justin heard the gurgle of water pouring from a pitcher into a cup, and his burning thirst swept away all other considerations.

"Slowly, Major." A straw rested against his lower lip and Justin greedily sucked in the cool water. In a habit born of two years' garrison duty on Spica, he held the water in his mouth for a second or two before swallowing. He drank more with the same deliberate care, then shook his head.

With the straw withdrawn, Justin turned his head in the direction from which he'd heard the commands. "Am I blind?"

The commanding voice softened a bit. "No. There are bandages

49

over your eyes because you've been in a narcotic coma. The drugs dilate your pupils, and so we bandaged your eyes to prevent any accidental damage to your vision."

Justin nodded slowly. "You will remove them? Now?"

"If you wish," the voice replied, after a moment's hesitation. "Nurse, dim the lights and draw the window shades." The doctor paused, then spoke even more softly. "There are some things you may want to understand first."

Justin shook his head. *What could be more important than my vision?* "I want to see first, doctor. Any problem I can see, I can defeat."

Justin felt the line of cold steel slide down beside his right ear as the doctor carefully scissored through the bandage. With two quick snips, the wrappings tumbled down over Justin's nose, but two cotton pads still covered his eyes. He felt pressure briefly against his eyes, then the nurse pulled away the pads.

"Open your eyes slowly, Major. Everything will be dark, but that's because we've darkened the room. Go ahead. Open."

Justin took a deep breath and opened his eyes. They snapped almost immediately shut as even the low light seared into them. Once more, he forced his eyes open and blinked them rapidly, finally becoming accustomed to the darkness. *I can see!* His smile almost cracked his dry lips, and brought a hearty chuckle from the doctor.

Justin turned his head to the right and focused. The doctor, a tall, sandy-haired man, returned his smile. Justin squinted and finally succeeded in reading the name on the doctor's white coat: James Thompson, M.D. "Dr. Thompson. Thank you. I am Major Justin Allard."

Thompson laughed. "Yes, Major. I know that." He turned toward the plump nurse standing at the foot of Justin's bed. She wore no nurse's cap to restrain her curly riot of blond hair, but had gathered it at the nape of her neck with a ribbon. "This is Nurse Alice Forrester."

Justin nodded at her, and she returned the gesture. *I can see! Thank God, I can see.* "So, doctor, what is it you think I should understand?"

The doctor hesitated, but Justin saw his gaze flick toward the far side of the bed. Justin turned his head slowly and looked down.

There, nestled like a viper in the sharp folds of the starched white sheets, Justin saw the blackened steel thing that had engulfed his left forearm.

New Avalon
Crucis March, Federated Suns

8 January 3027

A helmeted and visored guard swung open the heavy bronze door to Hanse Davion's private planning chamber. Quintus Allard saluted the bodyguard with a curt nod of his white-maned head, then swept into the room. His slightly oversize green jacket and loose pants hid a strong, lean body that belied the years Quintus showed in the color of his hair or the wrinkles around his blue eyes.

Prince Hanse Davion, sole and undisputed ruler of the Federated Suns, looked up from the massive antique desk and frowned. *Something must be very wrong*, he thought. *Never, in the five years that Quintus has been acting Minister of Intelligence Investigations and Operation has he looked so disturbed*. The man's anxiety and anger was palpable. "What is it, Quintus? Has something happened to Justin?"

Allard shook his head and moved toward the wall console that controlled the office holoviewer. "Justin's doing well. The doctor released him only a week after he came out of coma, and he spent the New Year's holiday with my wife, his sister Riva, and me. He pushes himself, and Doctor Thompson is pleased with the gross mobility Justin is showing with the, ah, the..." The voice of Hanse Davion's master of counter-espionage trailed off as he looked at his own left hand and twisted it up and down.

The Prince was relieved, but still concerned over what was troubling Quintus. "If Justin is fine, what *is* the matter?"

51

Quintus held up a green and gold holodisk, with a look of distaste. "This arrived in the company of more lawyers and 'security' men from the Capellan March than ought to be allowed on any DropShip. Michael Hasek-Davion seems to think I can't handle the Counter-Intelligence Division in addition to the IIO Ministry, and so is trying to help me."

What the hell is that scheming idiot up to now? Hanse wondered. He leafed through a pile of papers, and plucked a shipping schedule from the middle of the stack. He held up the sheet for Quintus to see. "How did they get here so fast? I haven't been expecting any ships from New Syrtis. Nothing due in for two weeks."

Quintus nodded and shoved the holodisk into the viewer. "Your beloved brother-in-law learned of Leftenant Redburn's departure from Kittery for the Awards Ceremony. Because you approved the expense of having Redburn travel on the Command Circuit, Duke Michael decided to send a few representatives of his own along. The Command Circuit worked its normal wonders, of course. The DropShip passed from JumpShip to JumpShip and made the voyage from Kittery to New Avalon in twenty-four hours instead of two months. Some of Michael's own men had been on Kittery conducting an investigation, and so they just boarded the ship with Redburn and got permission from Michael to proceed. This holodisk was recorded from a ComStar transmission, and they brought it with them."

Hanse's blue eyes turned to slits as barely controlled anger flashed across his face. "Wait, Quint," he said. "Before you start playing that tripe, let me get Ardan in here." The Prince punched a button on his desk. "Find Ardan Sortek and ask him to join me in my office, please."

Hanse Davion, often known as the Fox because of his cunning, suppressed his fury and forced a smile. "You have taken care of Michael's representatives?"

The pall lifted from Quintus's face as he smiled broadly. "Decontamination for the next thirty-six hours. Seems the batch number on their Kentares flu vaccine indicates that they got a bad dose, so we're running a full set of shots and blood tests on them."

The Prince of the Federated Suns laughed. "Always best to be cautious." *Well done, Quintus. Very well done.*

The chamber's massive door again opened to allow in Hanse Davion's friend and advisor, Ardan Sortek, who was carrying an armful of folders. Younger than either of the other two men, Sortek had the fit form and handsome face that any Davion recruiter might have wished to reproduce on recruiting posters all over the realm. Ardan smiled warmly at the other two men, his brown eyes twinkling, then his own expression changed to one of concern as he saw the worry on his friend's face. "What has Michael done now?" he asked.

Hanse Davion returned Ardan's smile, though somewhat wanly. *As always, my friend, you see the truth at the heart of everything.*

Quintus, too, was glad to see Ardan. Though Sortek was a military man who hated the compromises and shadowy dealings that politics often forced upon himself and Hanse Davion, he had amazing political instincts. Indeed, he had managed to uncover and defeat a plot hatched by Maximilian Liao, leader of the Capellan Confederation, to substitute a double for Hanse Davion. Had it not been for Sortek's resourcefulness and intelligence, Max Liao might have succeeded where all his legions had failed miserably. Through his fake Hanse Davion, he might have taken over the rulership of the Federated Suns, the most powerful realm in the Inner Sphere.

Hanse waved Sortek to a chair. "We're not certain yet, but this holodisk is a message from Michael. It should be explosive."

As if sparked by Hanse's final word, Sortek extended the files toward Allard. "Some of your men said they'd found the originals for these files while they were decontaminating the luggage that came in with Michael's 'representatives.' They also added the top file, which is a complete rundown on each of the men Michael has sent."

Allard took the files and set them down on a corner table. He dimmed the lights, then punched the viewer's start-up button. After an initial burst of static, a golden lion on a field of bright green filled the screen. As Michael Hasek-Davion's personal crest was fading from the screen, Sortek noted drily, "Is it just me, or is that lion looking more and more Capellan every time we see it."

Hanse exaggerated a frown. "You can't believe that Michael might be talking to Liao, could you?"

"Ha!" Sortek laughed.

Michael Hasek-Davion's face materializing on the screen cut off all further comment. Only seven years Hanse Davion's senior, the Duke of New Syrtis wore his long black hair in a braid that curled around and up over his shoulder like a snake. His restless green eyes, just slightly too close together, kept shifting away from the camera, failing utterly to convey sincerity. His voice, though deep and well-suited to speech-making, carried no conviction.

"Greetings, brother. Your sister Andrea is well and sends her love. She is anxious for your welfare and hopes you are as fit as ever." Unknowingly referring to the brief period when Liao's double ruled in Hanse's stead, Michael continued, "Your bout with the Kentares flu last year worried her greatly."

Hanse smiled in the shadows. "Michael could never lie that well.

53

He'll never know how close Liao came to winning the Federated Suns." With a nod, he saluted Quintus for his efforts in killing the news of the Liao plot.

Michael Hasek-Davion moved back from the camera, and the focus adjusted to take in the whole of the Duke's austere office. The tiled floors and white plaster walls were patterned after dwellings from the North American deserts on Terra, but the neo-cubist artwork and campaign maps tacked to the walls destroyed any of the peacefulness envisioned by the architect who had created the office. Hasek-Davion perched himself on the corner of his desk.

"It is not easy for us to speak with you about the following matter, Prince Davion, because it calls into question your motives toward the Capellan March. Yes, we fully acknowledge your anger with us because we refuse to commit our troops to your war with Kurita in the north, but House Liao eyes us with hungry intent. How well could I serve you as a Marchlord if I allowed you to strengthen one front, only to lose another?"

Michael shrugged, then his face darkened with thinly disguised outrage. "How is it that you have not yet begun prosecution against the worst traitor the Federated Suns has ever seen? How is it that you have turned the resources of your vaunted New Avalon Institute of Science to help restore a vile quisling to his health? How can you justify anything but death for Justin Allard?"

The vehemence in Michael's voice cut off any opportunity for the room's trio of occupants to comment. "Justin Xiang Allard, the son of your own counter-intelligence chief, has betrayed the Capellan March on more than one occasion. You knew of, but chose to overlook, his dismissal of Sergeant Philip Capet. You yourself had pinned the Gold Sunburst upon Capet's chest for his selfless valor on Uravan. How Allard's dismissal of such a hero could escape your notice is beyond me—unless that report somehow never reached you."

Though Hanse knew Quintus Allard was not so insecure as to need reassurance, he turned to him with a look that said, *I know he lies.* The grim smile on Allard's ashen face showed that the man took the Prince's meaning.

"We are certain, Prince Davion, that you have seen reports on the ambush that cost Justin Allard his arm. Many people might have put his injury down to bad luck. My investigators, however, have uncovered information suggesting that the treasonous half-caste merely ran afoul of his incompetent confederates and was attacked before he could identify himself."

Michael reached behind him and pulled up a thick folder. "Unsupported conjecture? No, it is not. It is fact. We have countless reports of

Major Allard spending much of his spare time among the indigs of Kittery. We know of contacts he's made with the local Tongs, and how he has gained control of them. While reports to you might have indicated a pacification of Kittery's largely Capellan population, my agents report that Allard had them biding their time until the moment when they could overthrow our authority."

As Michael replaced the file on his desk, the camera slowly drifted in toward a close-up. "We realize this may seem like a trivial matter to you, but it is of the utmost importance here in the Capellan March. Our people already believe that your attention is consumed entirely with the Kurita front and the slender threads of an alliance with the Lyran Commonwealth. They feel you do not care about them and that you are willing to strip us of troops, 'Mechs, and resources merely to keep the Combine from your neck."

Michael stared out from the screen. "If Justin Allard is not tried for treason—and we assure you that he is a spy of the highest order—what are my people to think? You know well how difficult it is to maintain an effective empire when civil unrest saps your strength from within. I would hate to think that the kind of problems that plague the Free Worlds League might also befall *you*. My people are at your command in pursuing the just resolution of this matter."

The screen faded to black, leaving the three men silent in the darkness. Then, as static flashed like a blizzard across the screen, Quintus Allard rose stiffly from his seat and dialed the lights up brighter.

How dare you threaten me with a civil war! Hanse thought angrily. *I have not forgotten, Michael, that Anton Marik's forces in the Free Worlds League civil war were backed by Maximilian Liao. Have you tipped your hand to me, brother mine, or are you just too stupid to see that Liao would use you as shabbily as he did Anton Marik? Recall, Michael, that Anton Marik is dead...*

Hanse looked over at his MIIO Minister and felt a pang in his heart. "Gentlemen, let us review our options. Michael gives us little choice other than to sacrifice Justin Allard to keep the Capellan March a part of the Federated Suns. Are things that bad out there?"

Quintus shook his head and concentrated to clear away the shock he had felt at Michael's message. "His allusion to the civil war in the Free Worlds League is an idle threat. Michael knows that many of the people in the Capellan March see him as no more than your half-sister's consort. I doubt that he could get enough popular support to pull off a revolt."

Ardan Sortek leaned forward in his chair and loosened the collar of his dark blue uniform jacket. "I think Quintus is right, but Michael could influence his people to resist our sending troops from the Capellan March to other fronts. We're nowhere near spread as thin on the Capellan border as House Liao is, but Liao can still cause trouble. The assault on Stein's Folly turned out badly for them eighteen months ago, but a strike that deep behind our border scared some people badly. Michael is right when he suggests that further attacks would devastate morale and definitely slow down the production of vital goods. That spells unrest rather plainly."

Hanse rose but said nothing until he had gone to sit behind his desk. "Quintus, have we had any confirmation of Michael's dealings with Max Liao?"

The white-haired man shook his head. "There is still only suspicion, except for official meetings that are matters of protocol—new ambassadors presenting their documents or Council of the Arts meetings and the like. We've also got the 'officially reported' texts of discussions, but no private meetings have been recorded, and so my cryptographers have no way to determine if Michael uses some elaborate code in the meetings. Anasta over at the NAIS has done some interesting work with rapid, high-frequency transmission of data, which is later slowed down and decoded. Without a recording, though, we can't begin to look for that sort of thing."

Hanse frowned. "No reported absences...no time when he could have been off meeting with Liao?"

Quintus shook his head again. "It's possible that Max has created a double for Michael, but it's unlikely. Barring that possibility, there's no way he could have gotten out of sight long enough for a meeting with Max Liao." Allard hesitated, then added, "Check that. Michael could have jumped out, met with Liao for four or five hours, and then jumped back in during a tour of some border worlds he took back three months ago. Still, it's highly unlikely."

Sortek stood and looked from Allard to Prince Davion. "I don't know about the two of you, but I don't need any proof of Michael's duplicity. I can *feel* it in my guts."

"As can I." Hanse's quiet agreement accompanied Allard's solemn nod. "Quint, you know I must ask this. What are the chances that your son is a spy?"

Sortek immediately fixed Hanse with a harsh stare, but the Prince ignored it. "Is it possible that we've all missed some sign? It's true that he worked hard for acceptance in some circles because of being half-Capellan."

Quintus rubbed his temple thoughtfully as he stared at the floor for a moment. Then he straightened up and stared at Hanse.

"As an intelligence officer, I would have to say that sending a

56

half-Capellan officer to head up a garrison/training force on a world we've only controlled for twenty years is a risky proposition. On one hand, his natural command of the tongue and his appreciation for the culture provide a bridge to normalizing relations with the native population."

Quintus grimaced, but went on purposefully. "On the other hand, it could be very easy for enemy agents to coopt such an officer if he were to feel betrayed or persecuted by his own troops or superiors." Quintus shrugged helplessly. "I don't know about Justin. All I can do is review the evidence Michael's men have gathered and see what I can come up with."

Hanse smiled and nodded. "I know you'll do your best, Quintus." The Prince of the Federated Suns stood up, fingers poised against the polished surface of his desk. "It seems, gentlemen, that we agree. I believe that Michael Hasek-Davion wants to take my place, and I believe he'd league himself with the devil—or Max Liao—to do so. Both of you know how much I'd like to pay back Max Liao for the little trick he played on me when he put a double here on my throne....If I could, I'd like to pay him back a hundredfold." He paused then, and the dramatic effect was not lost on his two visitors. "Yes, my friends, I think we can use Michael to get at Max himself."

Ardan Sortek and Quintus Allard smiled at their leader. "Let us begin," Hanse continued, "to feed Michael the kind of troop figures, locations, and projected movements that will show him we're not abandoning the Capellan March. You, Quintus, will meanwhile thoroughly track the Liao countermoves as we shuffle our troops. I want to know exactly who I can trust in the Capellan March."

9

10 January 3027

"Hello, doctor. How are you?" Justin slowly completed one series of tai chi chuan circular moves, then stopped. He plucked a white towel from a bench in the hospital's Solarium and mopped his sweaty brow. "Do you need me for some more tests?"

Dr. Thompson shook his head. "Not exactly." As the doctor sat down on the bench, Justin dropped to sit facing him on the carpeted floor. "I watched your exercises for awhile. What do you think of the arm?"

Justin frowned darkly and looked down at the metallic prosthesis. *I hate it, utterly and completely. It's lifeless, and because of its lifelessness, I'll never again pilot a 'Mech.* The wrist remained cocked at the slight angle he'd set for his last series of motions. The fingers, locked like claws, curled back toward his palm stiffly. Justin rotated his arm so that his palm faced up, then back down again. *It mocks me, pretending to be a suitable replacement for the limb I've lost. But, no, this is not what the doctor really wants to know. He cares only for how it functions, not my feelings and thoughts about having a metal arm.*

"The elbow works very well, and these exercises have helped to give me a feel for where the limb is now. I'd guess that comes from the weight and pressure on the lower part of my arm." Justin narrowed his eyes and tried to make a fist with his left hand. "When I move the fingers or wrist, I get some slight feeling, but nothing I can control." Justin shrugged. "I'd rather have my real arm back. Perhaps that

58

feeling will fade when I gain control of the wrist and hand."

Dr. Thompson leaned forward, elbows resting on his knees. "Justin, you may never gain control of the wrist or fingers of that hand. It's true that we have prostheses that are fully articulated, but those cases were different from yours. Those people did not suffer the kind of extensive damage as you did to your forearm."

Justin listened and understood, but he could not allow himself to acknowledge any truth in the doctor's statement. He nodded, however, feeling sweat trickle from the hairline around his ears. "You said before that the others still had muscle tissue in their forearms, which you were able to attach to artificial ligaments and tendons to give them hand and wrist control."

Thompson nodded slowly. "Right." He took Justin's prosthesis by the wrist and gently bent it back toward Justin's shoulder. Pointing at the elbow, he continued his lecture. "The only thing we had to work with on you, however, were portions of your radius and ulna, and the ganglia in your elbow. It's actually the muscles of your upper arm that control your elbow and lateral arm motion. All you have to drive your fingers and wrist are impulses from the nerves in your elbow."

Terror crawled maggotlike through Justin's stomach. He wiped his face with the towel again. "So, what you're telling me is that I cannot ever control this hand."

The doctor shook his head. "No. With years of hard work, such as your tai chi chuan, you'll gain control of the motors and truncated myomer fibers threaded through your forearm. With persistence, you should eventually be able to perform gross motor functions with that hand." The doctor flexed his own fingers. "You'll never play the piano, but you will be able to pluck and eat a grape."

Anger flashed through Justin's dark eyes and he stood abruptly. *I don't want grapes! I want a 'Mech!* His right hand contracted into a fist, and he shut his eyes in the fight to control his emotions. When he opened them again, he scowled at Thompson. "Why don't you just go ahead and tell me what you've avoided saying before? Why don't you just tell me I'll never pilot a 'Mech again?" He stared down at his inert hand. "Why don't you just tell me I'm a useless cripple?"

The doctor pursed his lips and slowly shook his head. "I won't tell you that because I don't believe it's true."

Fury flashed through Justin's eyes. "Don't tell me about training programs and therapy, Doc, because I don't want any part of it. Without a 'Mech, I'm nothing. Imagine having to spend the rest of your life only being able to watch medicine instead of practicing it…not taking care of patients…just watching. Imagine all your friends and relatives trying to console your loss, pointing out all the silver linings in these dark clouds. By God, I'll find a way to get a 'Mech back under me."

Doctor Thompson smiled and nodded his head. "I told them over in Biomechanicals that you were the right choice for that arm."

What? Justin stared up at the doctor. "I don't understand."

"Does the expression 'lab rat' mean anything to you?" Thompson reached into the pocket of his white coat and pulled out a device. It was a black plastic rectangle, about fifteen centimeters long and a centimeter wide, capped by a clear lucite section. The clear plastic cap fit flush onto the rectangle, but the upper face had been chiseled back diagonally to present a flat face toward whomever held the device. Justin turned it over and noticed an opening for a computer jack on the bottom side. "Do you know what this is?" the doctor asked.

Justin took the device and turned it over. "I think I've seen something like it before. It's a diagnostic tool used for checking MinerMech remote controls."

Dr. Thompson smiled. "Very good. As you know, most Miner-Mechs are run by remote control instead of by human pilots. A radio link is plugged into the command console below the left-hand joystick, and all commands to the joystick are delivered over tightbeam broadcast." Thompson pointed at the unit Justin held. "They use that thing to make sure remote units are relaying the correct information to the joystick control. That one's been modified to check for input into a BattleMech. We chose to model it on a *Warhammer* because of the various weapon systems that machine employs."

Justin nodded, then looked up, puzzled. "Why tell me this?"

The doctor reached out and took hold of Justin's artificial arm. He pulled the middle and ring finger back until they lay flat against the back of Justin's synthetic hand. The MechWarrior stared as though the doctor were a madman, then he heard a click at his metal wrist. He looked down and saw a small slit in the metal around his wrist.

The doctor released his arm. "Slide that panel back."

Justin did so, and by the time he'd slid it back a half-centimeter, a tightly coiled ribbon cable sprang out like a striking snake. At the end of the gray cable was a light blue jack. He shifted the testing rod to his left hand, closed the steel fingers around it, and snapped the cable jack into the opening on the test rod's bottom.

Instantly, a riot of color swirled across the lucite viewer atop the rod. "Easy, Justin, relax. You don't want to burn it out," Dr. Thompson said calmly, sensing Justin's intense excitement. "Close your eyes and think about opening your left hand. Don't frown. You can still feel the nerve connections…I know because I hitched the artificial neurore-ceptors to them."

Justin exhaled slowly. *Easy now, Justin. Be calm. Just feel your fist opening.* Almost immediately, Dr. Thompson congratulated him, but Justin waited until he could harness the rising well of enthusiasm in his chest before he dared open his eyes. Slowly, almost like a child peeking through his fingers at a terrifying holovideo, Justin looked at the cube. All the lights, except for a burning red dot in the center of the display, had died.

Dr. Thompson smiled. "O.K. Let's take this slowly. The boys over in Theoreticals would be dancing just to see you do that much." Thompson pointed at the dot centered on the display, and drew a line from it up toward the top of the viewing area. "You'll notice, as you think about having your hand manipulate a 'Mech's joystick that you get a red arrow on the viewing face indicating in which direction you're shoving the joystick."

The doctor gave a nod, and Justin slowly commanded his phantom arm to move the joystick forward. The dot flickered a couple of times as Justin false-started. He swallowed hard and concentrated. The red dot stretched and lazily unfolded itself into an arrow pointing at the top center of the display. Justin willed his hand to pull back, and the arrow reversed itself. He smiled broadly and looked up. "It's slow, but it's working."

Thompson laughed aloud. "Slow? I've got colleagues over at the NAIS who said you'd never be able to get it to move at all."

Justin, infected by Thompson's enthusiasm, laughed as well. "Should have had money on it, Doc."

"True enough."

Justin took a deep breath. *My heart's pounding like an autocannon full open and firing hot.* Then he looked up at Thompson, feeling like a child afraid to be told it was all a dream. "I can target things. How do I shoot them?"

"That's a warrior for you. I put you back together, and all you want to do is take other folks apart." Dr. Thompson licked his lips. "All right. A *Warhammer* control has three thumb buttons, as well you know. The center operates the particle projection cannon. Successfully pressing it will give you a blue light on the display. Left thumb is a medium laser and creates a green light. Right thumb is the button to launch SRMs and will give you a yellow light."

Justin nodded and tried imagining each position. *Carefully now. Let's punch the center. Nope, dammit! Again...* His efforts met with meager success, but he did occasionally trigger one of the three large weapons. "What else? It's been awhile since I sat in a *Warhammer*, but I seem to recall two trigger buttons on the joystick as well."

Thompson shook his head. "Take it easy, Major. Men have spent

61

careers building that toy you're playing with. Try one step at a time…"

Justin frowned. "Doc, this is my life we're talking about here. Just let me know all the tricks this thing will perform, and then I'll practice."

The urgency in Justin's plea hit home. "Yes. I understand," Thompson said, patting Justin on the shoulder. "Now, the index finger triggers an orange light on your display, and that stands for a small laser. The last thing, which gives a violet light, is the machine gun. That's triggered through your middle finger."

Thompson watched as Justin closed his eyes and concentrated for a moment. Each of the weapon system lights burst to life in sequence, and the doctor smiled. "Blake's Blood! I can't wait to get you on a monitor and have you do all this. Prince Davion's going to be handing out fellowships left and right for this."

Dr. Thompson shook his head as the lights danced through the lucite block. "Good Lord, Justin, give the device a rest. Remember, too, that this system only works for the left-side weapons. Your right hand will still have to operate the other weapons."

Justin opened his eyes and laughed. "I think I can trust it to do that, Doctor. I don't know how to begin to thank you." Justin extended his good hand to the doctor and pumped his arm warmly. "This gives me hope that someday I will really pilot a 'Mech again." He raised the test rod high like a trophy.

Before Dr. Thompson could reply, the Solarium doors burst open, and both men froze. A pair of CID guards dressed in black and tan riot gear, with stun-sticks in hand and full visors that hid their faces, held the doors open and stood at attention. A small, almost cadaverously thin man with a wisp of hair curling over his high forehead marched into the room. Keeping his hands clasped behind his back, the man stared at Justin Allard with eyes full of hate. "Major Justin Xiang Allard?"

Justin recoiled at the man's tone. He pronounced his middle name—his Capellan mother's family name—as though the word were something bitter, even obscene, on his tongue. *If this was all a dream, it just became a nightmare.* "You know me, Count Vitios. What made you decide to crawl from under your rock to venture this far from the safety of the Capellan March?"

Justin felt a tremor go through Dr. Thompson's arm. The doctor freed his hand from Justin's grip and extended it toward the Count. "I am Dr. Thompson." When the small man ignored the gesture, Thompson pulled himself to his full height and snarled, "This man is my patient, and I would like you to leave us. *Now*."

Vitios snapped a look at the doctor, then pointed at Thompson, while addressing his escort. "Restrain him or remove him." A CID guard leveled his stun-stick in Thompson's direction, but Justin spoke and prevented either man from acting foolishly.

"What is it you want, Count Vitios?" Justin looked up at the guard nearest Dr. Thompson. "Leave him alone and go get my father."

The Count's evil little chuckle dripped its icy melody up and down Justin's spine. "Even he will not be able to help you, Justin Allard."

Justin snarled and balled his right hand into a fist. "What are you talking about, you malignant dwarf?"

The Count smiled for the first time in Justin's memory. "In the names of Prince Hanse Davion and Duke Michael Hasek-Davion, it is my duty and distinct pleasure to place you under arrest for treason."

10

Tharkad
District of Donegal, Lyran Commonwealth

10 October 3026

Simon Johnson, Chancellor of the Lyran Intelligence Corps, closed the file and stared at it silently for a second. His fingers unconsciously traced the legend, "Ultra Secret," and finally came to rest against the bulging capsule worked into the folder's construction. He slid the folder over to the edge of the table, crushed the capsule, and let the slender document fall into the round disposal bin.

In seconds, the chemicals that mixed together when he broke the capsule exploded into a blue-green flame that consumed the folder. The blaze painted his plain face and white hair with ghoulish tints. Johnson watched the flames until he could no longer feel the heat of the flash fire, then looked up at the room's other occupant.

Katrina Elizabeth Steiner, Duchess of Tharkad and Archon of the Lyran Commonwealth, regarded Johnson with eyes so gray they were like slivers of steel. Though she had lived more than a half-century already, Katrina was as lithe, tall, and blonde as ever. Her strong features were still handsome, though one could easily see she had been a great beauty in her youth. "Your thoughts, Simon?"

Johnson glanced at the small device he'd placed on the table. The colored LCD display still registered no traces of active or passive monitoring devices in the area, but he kept his voice low and soft nonetheless. "If the signature and personal holograph of Quintus Allard were not woven into the fabric of the paper itself, I would not believe the plan." Johnson focused his black eyes on the charred

64

remains of the folder. "That House Liao actually produced a double for Prince Davion and actually put him in Davion's place is chilling. This explains, in part, our troubles during the Galtor Campaign and the lapse in your relations with the Federated Suns."

The Archon rested her elbows on the arms of her chair and steepled her fingers. "Could it happen here, Simon?" The Archon watched him closely, but could not pierce his thoughts. *You always play it so close to the chest, Simon. Thank God, you're with me, not against me.*

The LIC's Chancellor chewed his lower lip. "It is possible, of course, but it would be very difficult. To make such a substitution would require the duplicity of so many people that it would probably disrupt all normal activity." Johnson closed his eyes, pursed his lips, leaving the Archon to wonder whether the white-haired man had actually fallen asleep. Then his eyes opened, and Katrina caught a brief flash of a hellish fire playing through them. "Perhaps, if you were to suffer a serious injury that required hospitalization, another person could be substituted for you in a hospital. Your convalescence would allow a gradual conditioning of the substitute, and would let people forget what you were like." He slowly nodded his head. "Yes, it *could* happen here."

Johnson's eyes slitted, and the Archon smiled wryly. *I know you, Simon. The first thing you'll do when you leave here is review hospital procedures and staff records.* "I shall attempt to be very careful in the future, until you are able to assure me that such a thing could not happen."

Johnson's gentle nod confirmed his understanding of her jest, but he felt no need to trade quips with her today. Instead, he fixed the Archon with a steady gaze. "That is not what you wanted to ask me, is it, Archon?"

Katrina shook her head gently. "Could we do what Liao did? Could we transform someone into a double?"

Again, as always, Simon Johnson did not speak until the answer had fully formed in his mind. "Yes, we could do what Max Liao did to prepare his double of Hanse Davion. The intensive training we give to the orphans inducted into Lohengrin would be sufficient to brainwash fanatic loyalty into a double. It works for our anti-terrorists, so why wouldn't it work for a deep cover agent? It's certainly possible to create a profile on a subject, and then train someone to fit that profile. Finding a subject of the appropriate age and physical characteristics is perhaps the easiest part of the plan."

The Archon nodded, then broke eye contact as she played with the ring on her right hand. "I sense hesitation in your answer."

Johnson smiled. "From what little Quintus confided in his report, I believe Liao's plan would have collapsed because of a gross flaw. Liao's scientists blanked the double's mind, then force-fed him with Hanse Davion's memories. The double had all the memories, knew all the facts, but, he did not, of course, have Hanse Davion's mind. If he had, Davion never would have been able to win a contest to prove that he was the genuine Prince because the other individual would have been just as *real*."

The Archon frowned. "You're saying the double would have broken down? Mentally, I mean, not physically."

"Yes. Each person has his own way of storing information." Johnson held out both his hands, palms up. "For example, if I say the word "crusader" to both you and our court historian, Thelos Auburn, each of you will respond with a different impression. Because, Archon, you are a MechWarrior, you will think first of a 'Crusader' as a BattleMech model. Auburn will probably recall the various political groupings known as 'Crusader' movements throughout past millennia. Though each of you would be familiar with the other's image of 'Crusader,' your cognitive networks would have stored those facts away differently."

The Archon smiled. "In short, you're saying that the Liao imposter had stored Davion's memories according to his own cognitive structure." Katrina Steiner narrowed her eyes. "Given cultural differences, the double could have been caught thinking in a Capellan manner."

A curt nod confirmed her conclusion, and Johnson expanded upon it. "Also, because the network was still there, I suspect that the imposter's memories were merely suppressed. I think they must have withdrawn, almost the way the core personality does in some cases of multiple personality. Whenever it emerged, the person would have gone mad, or would have been very angry with Liao for enslaving his mind. Hanse Davion already hates the Capellans well enough. The idea of Hanse Davion with a grudge against House Liao is not one I would like to contemplate, especially if I were seated on Sian."

Truer words were never spoken. The Archon laughed. "So, would we have difficulty creating a substitute for someone?"

Johnson shook his head. "Not at all. We could not, and would not, enslave a mind as Liao did. An actor, for example, could slip into a role well enough to handle 99 percent of the matters a leader must handle. With the proper delegation of authority, the realm might not even notice the hand of a temporary leader at the helm."

Johnson smiled and reached for another folder. "I took the liberty, Archon, of bringing this with me." He opened it and looked up at her.

66

"Whom did you have in mind for the creation of a double? Loki agents can pick up any of the people in the files today."

"As ever, you have anticipated me." Katrina whispered the name of her candidate. Johnson licked his thumb, paged through blue and yellow sheets of paper, then stopped. He smiled. "Oh, yes, we have some excellent candidates…"

Jeana Clay coasted the racing bicycle down the final hill as she pulled her water bottle free of the bike's frame and squirted some of the warm liquid into her mouth. Savoring the water, she sprayed the rest over her face and down her arms. A quick glance at her watch brought a smile. *Knocked thirty seconds off that last leg*, she thought, well-pleased with herself. Her smile continued to light up her pretty face as she hunkered down and pedaled the bike up the last little rise and into the driveway of the house where she had lived alone since her mother's death.

Old Mr. Tompkins looked up from trimming his shrubs and waved at her. "Getting faster, Jeana. You'll surely win this year's Tharkad Triathlon!"

"Thanks, Mr. Tompkins, for your confidence." She stopped the cycle and swung off. She slid it into the anti-theft rack that she'd welded together herself years ago, then straightened up to her full height and walked back to where the older man stood. "I just hope my unit doesn't have exercises that weekend."

Tompkins smiled and looked almost cherubic. "They won't, child, and I have a feeling it would take more than that to keep *you* from that race."

Jeana peeled the fingerless gloves from her hands and nodded. "Yeah, my CO is pretty good about letting me race. I think he feels that my wins reflect well on the 24th Lyran Guards, being as we're such an untried unit."

Tompkins winked. "I knew Leutnant-Colonel Orpheus Thomas when he was a lad, before he wandered off to Donegal to recruit all of you MechWarriors for his unit. He's a proud man, and I can tell that he appreciates what you do for the unit."

The tall, slender MechWarrior smiled. She grabbed her riding jersey by the shoulders and gently tugged at it while making a face. "I'm going change out of these sweaty things and catch a shower." Jeana began to walk away, but turned back long enough to add, "I'll let you know if I'm going to be able to race."

At her own door, Jeana slipped a mag-key from the waistband of her riding shorts and inserted it into the lock. The door clicked and she ducked inside. The cooler, which she had not set particularly low, had made the house positively arctic. When she doublechecked the thermostat, however, the dial still sat where she'd left it. Below the thermostat, the lights on house alarm system all glowed reassuringly green.

Jeana passed through the kitchen and jogged up the stairs, barely glancing at the closed door of the master bedroom before entering the sanctuary of her own room. *It's silly, Jeana. There's no reason why you shouldn't move into that room.* She sat on the bed to untie her shoes. *Keeping the room as a shrine to your mother won't bring her back.*

Jeana shook her head and forced herself to abandon that line of thought. She'd covered it before, many times, and all the "what ifs" and "I should haves" could not reverse what had happened to her mother. Yet, Jeana could not shake the feeling that if she *had* been home that night, no intruder would ever have killed her mother.

Jeana pulled off her blouse, wadded it up into a ball, and tossed it into a basket. Socks, shorts, and underclothes quickly arched after it. Then she stood, stretched, and went into the cleaner to start the shower running. As steam filled the small, white-tiled room, Jeana flicked on the radio to listen to something other than her own sad thoughts.

As Jeana stepped into the shower, she was unaware of the door of the cleaner opening behind her. With her eyes closed and water rushing over her face, it was only the cool draft of the shower curtain being pulled aside that alerted her to danger. She turned from the watery spray and stared in horror at the hooded intruder.

Loki! The thought burst into Jeana's mind like an inferno rocket as she caught sight of the emblem on his collar. She balled her left fist and swung at the intruder without thinking, but her feet slipped and she started to fall. *What is someone from State Terrorism doing here after so long? How did they find me?*

The Loki operative's first dart missed Jeana's falling body, and her aborted punch forced him to step back. She broke her fall by tearing a faucet handle from the shower and gathering her long legs beneath her. She uncoiled and hit the agent with a tackle that smashed him back into the handbasin. He grunted, then spun away out of her grasp.

Jeana grabbed a towel and threw it at him. It unfolded like a JumpShip's solar collector and prevented the agent's second dart from hitting her. He continued to back away out into the hall, and Jeana dove at his legs. Her wet feet slipped at the last, draining her attack of much of its power, but the fury and anger born of guilt over her mother's death more than compensated for it.

Her shoulder hit the intruder in the shins, and she gathered his ankles in a savage hug. Unbalanced, the agent flailed helplessly with one hand, but failed to grab the stair railing. He crashed down the stairs, careening from side to side, and then lay very still.

Jeana gathered herself up on hands and knees, then felt a sting against her right buttock. Numbness spread like a blush, and her nerveless limbs refused to support her anymore. She fell to her left and stared up at the man silhouetted in the master bedroom's doorway. "Yes," she heard him say, "an excellent candidate." In her befuddled state, Jeana could make no sense of those words at all.

The air-ambulance driver smiled reassuringly at Mr. Tompkins as two white-suited medics gently lifted the stretcher into the back of the craft. "Don't worry, Mr. Tompkins. You did the right thing in calling us when you heard her crash down the stairs. She's very lucky to have a concerned neighbor like you."

The older man shook his head as Jeana vanished into the air-ambulance. "She's so young...only twenty-five. First, her mother dies, then this." He frowned. "A heart attack, you say?"

The driver nodded. "Stress-induced, but really secondary to some damage done when she caught Yeguas fever while training with the 24th last year. It'll normally leave folks alone, but one in a million develop a heart defect." The driver shrugged. "It's in the doctors' hands now."

The driver turned to leave, but Mr. Tompkins grabbed his wrist. "You'll let me know where they've taken her? I'll visit."

The driver laid his hand over that of the older man and patted it warmly. "I'll keep you informed. Remember, if you hadn't called, she might not even have the chance she's got now. The Commonwealth needs more citizens like you."

11

Tharkad
District of Donegal, Lyran Commonwealth

11 January 3027

Jeana's eyes snapped open and the brilliant white of the room's walls and ceiling sizzled pain into her eyeballs. She shook her head once, then unconsciously rubbed the sore spot. *Feel muzzy from whatever they hit me with.*

Jeana raised her hands to shade her eyes. *Good, I'm not restrained.* Her eyes narrowed. *The duty of a prisoner is to escape. Name. Rank. Serial Number.*

She sat on the room's only stick of furniture—a rickety wooden chair—and studied her surroundings. The whole ceiling glowed with a light that burned away all shadows except those hiding beneath her chair. It also bleached her black jumpsuit a pallid gray. It was no surprise that there were neither insignia or labels on the suit or slippers she had been given. Jeana had nary a clue to where her Loki abductors had taken her.

She heard a click from across the room, and then the outline of a door traced itself in gray lines against the white wall. Jeana stood and quickly walked over to it. Pushing it open, she slipped through and stopped dead in her tracks.

Standing there in the center of the room, with arms folded across her chest, was none other than Archon Katrina Steiner. "Do you know who I am?" she asked Jeana.

Jeana hesitated as she stared into the Archon's gray eyes. "Sergeant Jeana Clay, LCAF, 090-453-2234-12." She stood at attention and drew her head up high. Though as tall as the Archon, Jeana felt dwarfed. *Is this a trick? Am I hallucinating?*

The Archon smiled. "Very good, Sergeant. At ease. I am Archon Katrina Steiner, and this meeting is neither a dream nor a nightmare." She waved Jeana toward a chair at a small table and also seated herself. The remaining pair of seats were vacant.

Jeana hesitated, then crossed the room and sat down. She'd seen the Archon countless times on holovision or in person at 'Mech unit reviews. She'd met her when the Archon had awarded medals for the triathlon two years before, and all that told Jeana that this was no illusion. *It is Katrina Steiner. But what does it all mean?*

The Archon smiled to put Jeana more at ease. "I'd like you to know that I understand the sense of loss that you must feel for your mother." Katrina reached out to place a hand on Jeana's wrist. Her gray eyes clouded over slightly, then she forced a weak smile. "Though it has been seventeen years, I still feel keenly the loss of my husband. You have my sympathy."

Jeana bowed her head. "Thank you, Archon." She bit back tears of guilt and loneliness.

Katrina's eyes narrowed. "You also have my promise that the LIC will find your mother's killer and will deal with him or her."

"Again, thank you, Archon." Jeana looked up. "You will forgive me, Archon, but may I ask why I am here?"

The Archon nodded, her yellow hair framing her face softly. "I cannot answer for the melodramatic means used to conduct you here—though I have been assured that they were essential—but I can address your main question. You are here so that I may ask you to undertake a mission of extreme danger. It will also be one demanding selfless concentration. It will be a totally consuming operation and could very possibly end with your death."

Thank God, it's not for the other reason. Jeana sat up to her full height. "Anything, Archon. I will do anything you ask."

Katrina smiled. "I had expected no less a prompt answer from a member of the 24th Guards. Though you remain untested in battle, your loyalty is unquestioned. Yet, I would not have you agree so readily to a mission I have only begun to describe."

The Archon took up a folder from the table and opened it. "This mission will mean that you will never again be able to participate in the triathlons you love so well."

Jeana shook her head. "No matter. "

The Archon continued to read. "It means you will never again see your friends in the 24th."

Jeana shrugged. "We will be together in service to you, Archon."

71

The Archon's voice tightened. "This mission will mean you'll probably never again pilot a 'Mech."

Jeana hesitated, then slowly shook her head again. "Please, Archon, before you read any more, understand one thing. Everything I am, and everything I have, comes from House Steiner. There are some things your files cannot tell you about me, because they are things I would confide to no one." Jeana's eyes flicked down to her hands, then back up into the Archon's gray stare.

Forgive me, mother, but I must do it. "This is not the first time we've met, Archon."

Katrina Steiner nodded thoughtfully. "I recall awarding you a silver medal two years ago."

Jeana shook her head. "No, that was not our first meeting, either." The Archon narrowed her gray eyes and their electric fire made Jeana's words catch in her throat. She looked down and shyly continued to speak, as though confessing some horrible crime. "We first met twenty-two years ago, when I was only three...on Poulsbo." Jeana's head came up. "You sang to me so I'd not cry while Loki agents questioned my father downstairs in our house..."

The Archon stiffened and the muscles at the corners of her mouth bunched. "Your file says nothing..."

Jeana shook her head. "That was your husband's doing. Before he died, he made sure to cover our tracks so that no one could get at us. My mother kept your secret from everyone but me. I don't think she would even have told me, Archon, except that she had no other answers to a daughter's questions about her father. You knew him by his code-name—Grison."

The Archon rocked back in her chair, then recovered herself and smiled bravely. "I owe your father my life. When my DropShip landed on Poulsbo, I guessed that my uncle Alessandro saw me as a threat to his own power as Archon. But in the arrogance of my youth, I never dreamed he would dare to move against me. For me, the trip was merely a routine inspection of a military base. The Bangor base, after all, is a strategic site in the Commonwealth."

The Archon took Jeana's hands in hers. "What did your mother tell you about your father?"

In the glow of the memories that had warmed her childhood, Jeana smiled. "She told me that I got my height and my green eyes from him. She said that she had loved him fiercely and that he knew he would be meeting his death that night. He told her it would be dangerous, but that he also believed you'd be a better Archon than Alessandro ever could. He said you'd be an Archon worth dying for." Tears gathered in Jeana's eyes and streamed down her cheeks.

Katrina reached up and brushed away the girl's tears. "Your father was brave man, Jeana. Alessandro's men made their move to kidnap me while I was dining with the Duke of Donegal, Arthur Luvon—my future husband—and his cousin, Morgan Kell. Morgan was fresh from the Nagelring Military Academy and had been assigned to the Duke's personal guards. I'd known Arthur for years, but we'd just been friends, and so meeting him and Morgan on Poulsbo was a pleasant surprise.

"Alessandro's agents attacked us, but we beat them back. We fled into the night, and lost ourselves in the streets of Bangor. We had no idea what might be a safe haven until a man found *us* in a dark bar one evening. He walked up and said simply, 'I'm from Heimdall. Loki wants you. Therefore, they won't get you. Call me Grison. Let's go.'"

Katrina squeezed Jeana's hands. "Your father was the sort of man who could inspire confidence and trust in so simple and direct a greeting. I'd heard horrible stories about Heimdall, the underground organization opposed to the Lyran Intelligence Corps and to Loki, in particular. I believed those stories until your father spoke to us. In that instant, I knew that Heimdall posed no threat to me. With the Loki after us, I even understood the need for Heimdall. The three of us went with your father, and that must have been the night you and I first met."

Jeana nodded and swallowed past the thick lump in her throat. "My mother said he organized a raid that got you off Poulsbo."

The Archon nodded solemnly. "Your father and his comrades in the Bangor cells of Heimdall provided us with clothing and disguises. They raided the military side of the Bangor spaceport so that we could slip into the civilian sector and steal a small shuttle. We succeeded and managed to escape. I later learned that the craft was stolen from a Heimdall sympathizer who covered our escape."

Jeana nodded. "Loki ops shot my father after he blew the radar tower."

The Archon's lower lip trembled. "I know. Arthur had a radio link with your father. He blew the tower so that we could escape. The last thing your father said to us was, 'You're free. Return the favor to the Commonwealth.'"

The Archon stood and turned away. "I tried to find out your father's identity, to reward him and the others, but I could never crack Heimdall's security. I don't even think ComStar knows what Heimdall is." Her lips pressed into a thin, grim line, Katrina turned back to Jeana. "I was able to tighten the reins on the LIC, and the Loki no longer runs rampant." The Archon nodded at the folder. "Had I known, I never would have allowed Loki agents to be the ones to bring you here."

The Archon clasped her hands behind her back. "In view of your

73

family's sacrifices, though, I cannot allow you this duty. To release you is the least I can do to honor the memory of your father."

Jeana shot to her feet. "No, Archon! You cannot deny me the chance to serve you. You have rewarded me and the people of Heimdall many times over." Jeana balked, but knew that Katrina deserved to know all of it.

She bowed her head and completed her confession. "Your husband was a member of Heimdall. He had been a member for years, and though neither he nor my father recognized one another, the Duke of Donegal trusted my father. Later, in the five years left to him, your husband saw to it that the families and cell-members of Poulsbo were well-cared for."

Jeana pointed to the folder from which the Archon had been reading. "Your husband engineered the restructuring of my history files, and he secretly endowed many of us with monies or other bequests. I went to Slangmore on a scholarship that he arranged, and I'm sure he assisted the children of the others who helped you, too. As I said before, everything I have and everything I am is because of you."

The Archon started to speak, but Jeana would not be interrupted. "My father died because he believed in what you would do for the Commonwealth as Archon. You said you'd spare me this difficult duty out of honor for my father's memory. But to accept the mission would allow me the greatest tribute I could pay to that memory. The reason I became a MechWarrior was to continue what he believed in. Though it meant losing her daughter, my mother never flinched from the same mission."

Jeana opened her hands. "Now I have nothing and no one but you and the Commonwealth. What could you ask of me that I would not willingly agree to carry out?"

The Archon's head came up and she impaled Jeana with a harsh stare. "What I ask of you is a total sublimation of yourself. Jeana Clay will, in fact, cease to exist. You will undergo a minor amount of reconstructive surgery. You will spend the next six months in an intensive learning environment where everything you are will be broken down and discarded. You will learn to do everything differently, and you will receive neither medals nor applause for your efforts. In fact, the mark of your success will be total anonymity."

The Archon pointed to the folder that contained most of the details of Jeana Clay's existence. "If you accept this mission, you will be forgotten forever."

In reply, Jeana simply pulled herself to attention.

The Archon nodded slowly. "Johnson was correct. You are an excellent candidate." She stood up and drew Jeana to her feet as well.

Looking the girl directly in the eyes, Katrina Steiner said, "Jeana Clay, will you accept the role of my daughter's double for now and all time?"

Albert Tompkins watched the members of the 24th Lyran Guards walk away from the gravesite and into the mist. The old man brushed tears off his cheeks, then placed a white rose on the loosely packed earth. "Rest well, Jeana Clay. Though your life was cut short, you made all Heimdall proud."

12

20 January 3027

Count Anton Vitios narrowed his brown eyes and nodded to the military tribunal. He turned so that the holovid camera in the courtroom's corner would catch him at his best. "The prosecution calls Leftenant Andrew Redburn to the stand."

Redburn wiped his moist palms against his trousers as he stood up, then shuffled through the crowded aisle where he'd been seated, whispering apologies as he went. Once clear of the packed gallery, Redburn straightened his dress uniform jacket, took a deep breath, and walked toward the bailiff, who held a low wooden gate open for him.

Though Redburn was holding himself ramrod-straight outwardly, his guts had turned to icy slush. He took his place at the mahogany witness stand while a court clerk held out a leather-bound copy of *The Unfinished Book*. "In the name of the freedom-loving people of the Federated Suns, this court calls you to a pledge of truth," the clerk intoned. Redburn raised his right hand and placed his left firmly on the book's brown cover. "In the name of duty, faith, and honor, I pledge this sacred oath," Redburn declared, feeling the solemnity of the time-honored phrases. He licked his lips. "So help me God."

Vitios stood at the prosecution bench and conferred with the aide who had interviewed Redburn. Seated at an identical oaken table across the aisle were Major Justin Allard and his lawyer. Redburn shivered. *Justin stares straight ahead*, he thought. *It's almost as though he's not even in the room.* The sight of the black leather glove

76

on Justin's left hand gave Redburn a start, but fascinated him so much that he missed Vitios's first question.

"I asked you to state your full name and rank." The irritation in the prosecutor's voice had characterized his whole performance in the courtroom, and Redburn suddenly dreaded what he had hoped would be his chance to help his friend.

"I am Leftenant Andrew Bruce Redburn." Redburn allowed himself to linger over the "r's" in his name. Though he'd struggled mightily to suppress his accent during his cadet days at the Warriors Hall on New Syrtis, he summoned it now in the defiant spirit of his Scottish ancestors, whose motto was *"Die fighting!"* Redburn gripped the railing of the witness stand and met the prosecutor's black stare.

Vitios pointed to a folder. "I have studied your deposition, Leftenant, and it has been entered into the official record." The man's face suddenly reminded Redburn of a hungry raptor stooping toward its helpless prey. "How did Major Allard come to be with your unit on that training exercise?"

"I requested his participation."

Vitios nodded. "Did you not request his participation several times before he agreed to attend the exercise?"

Redburn swallowed. "Yes, sir."

"How many times?"

Redburn narrowed his eyes and decided to go on the offensive. "Four times, in writing. Perhaps the Count does not understand that the Major was busy."

Vitios smiled coldly. "Oh, I understand how busy your Major was, Leftenant. After all, that is what this trial is about, isn't it?" Vitios turned his attention to the deposition and flicked it open. "In fact, you did not have confirmation from Major Allard that he would join you until the day before the exercise, when you had a private meeting with him. Is that not correct?"

Redburn nodded uneasily. "Yes, sir."

Vitios dramatically cupped his right elbow in his left hand and tapped his pointy chin with his right index finger. "In your deposition, you characterized the meeting as urgent. What did you speak about?"

Redburn bit his lower lip. "I expressed to the Major my concern over some unrest in the training battalion. I told him that his participation in the exercise would help morale and might regain him some of the respect due a MechWarrior of his reputation."

Vitios made a hissing sound as though the Leftenant had said something that pained him. "This 'unrest' in the battalion. What was that about?"

Redburn shrugged and tried to downplay the gravity of the

question. "Recruits seldom like their CO, especially when he's hard on them."

Vitios stepped forward, then spun to face the gallery. "Come now, Leftenant. You know the real reason for the dissatisfaction in the battalion, don't you? Were there not demonstrations of support for Sergeant Philip Capet? Weren't the troops furious because Major Allard, without provocation, had dismissed a Gold Sunburst winner?"

"That may have been part of it, Count Vitios."

Redburn's hopes that he'd parried the Count's dangerous thrust died on the Count's riposte. "And part of that unrest was due to Major Allard's trafficking with the indigs, wasn't it? How could these recruits trust a man who regularly traveled among, met with, and preferred the company of the enemy to what should have been his own people?"

"Objection!" Justin's attorney shot to his feet and stabbed the air with one finger. His left hand struggled to shove his glasses back into place before they could fall from his face entirely, but his intense stare did not change. "The prosecution is leading the witness and has stated his question in a totally prejudicial manner."

The ranking tribunal officer, Major General Sheridan Courtney, turned toward Count Vitios. "Sustained. Be more careful, your Lordship."

The Count nodded. "Leftenant, did Major Allard visit with indigs on any sort of regular basis?"

"I suppose he did."

"Indeed, Leftenant, he did. Have you forgotten the Community Relations Committee meetings each week? Have you forgotten how he liked to take his first meal in the restaurants of Shaoshan upon returning from field exercises? Have you forgotten his hiring indigs to work as personal servants in his home?"

Redburn looked down at the polished wood-tile floor. "No, sir."

Vitios's voice lost none of its edge. "Why were you stationed on Kittery, Leftenant?"

Redburn's head snapped back up and his anger rocketed through his answer. "To protect the world and the frontier."

"From whom, Leftenant?"

Redburn spat out his answer. "From the Capellan forces of Maximilian Liao."

"The very people the Major spent so much time with. Correct, Leftenant?" Before Redburn could answer, Vitios pressed a new question upon him. "Do you know Shang Dao?"

What the hell is he getting at now? Redburn nodded. "I was introduced to him."

"By Major Allard?"

"Yes."

Vitios nodded. "Isn't Shang Dao the leader of the Yizhi tong in Shaoshan?"

Redburn frowned. "I believe he is."

Vitios canted his head slightly. "I thought the CID had identified the Yizhi tong as a Capellan organization, and that contact between Federated Suns personnel and the tong was forbidden. In fact, you dismissed a cadet on a charge of trafficking with restricted personnel, didn't you?"

Redburn hesitated. "I...it was not like that."

Courtney glared down at Redburn from the bench. "Answer the question, Leftenant."

"Yes, sir." Redburn held up his head. "The cadet was dismissed for his addiction to opium. We felt the problem would lapse once he left Kittery, and we did not want the charge of opium substance abuse to haunt him for the rest of his life."

Vitios almost smiled. "Commendable, Leftenant, but the fact remains that Major Allard regularly met with Shang Dao in violation of the CID directives, didn't he?"

Redburn hung his head. "Yes, sir."

Vitios turned back to the prosecution desk and picked up a file. "I have here, and have entered into the record, a transcript of your 'Mech's battle-recorder. In reviewing your transcript, and the transcripts from the other 'Mechs in the battalion, I must congratulate you on your quick thinking and calm under fire. You saved your command from a savage ambush."

Redburn nodded. He shot a glance toward the defense table, and died inside. Leftenant Lofton, Justin's lawyer, was urgently whispering something into his client's ear, but the Major gave no sign of hearing him. He just stared straight ahead, as though trying to burn a hole through the courtroom's gray marble walls by force of will.

When Vitios smiled, he might have been a python spotting a fat pig. "We know the Capellan 'Mechs were waiting for you. Why was that?"

"We are required to file forms with the civilian government in Shaoshan detailing where we plan to travel."

Vitios nodded. "Shang Dao is a member of the civilian government, isn't he?"

Redburn shrugged. "That information is not very secret, your Lordship. When we stopped at noon that day, food peddlers from Shaoshan came out and sold us lunch."

Vitios frowned, but Redburn cut off any comment. "Sir, we MechWarriors bake inside our machines. None of us want to eat

79

anything that's been cooked in the same oven if we can avoid it. Remember, sir, that government contracts go to the lowest bidder, which says a lot about the quality of rations, especially out on the frontier."

Courtney gaveled the courtroom's laughing spectators back to order, and Redburn took heart when even Justin's distant and harsh expression had lightened a bit.

Vitios swallowed Redburn's good feeling in one gulp. "What did Major Allard say to you when Private William Sonnac, whose *Stinger* was positioned above the *Cicada*s that would kill him, reported strange magscan readings?"

Redburn frowned. "He asked me to check Sonnac's readings. That's standard procedure."

"But that's not all he said to you, is it, Leftenant?"

"Sir?"

Vitios flipped through the transcript. "Let me refresh your memory, Leftenant. Major Allard said to you, 'Andy, check Sonnac's readings. I've got something over the hill I want to see.'" Vitios turned and stared at Justin. "Doesn't that strike you as a little odd, Leftenant? Here you are, trapped in a bowl-shaped valley and your commanding officer leaves a junior officer in charge of green troops in a hostile area while he goes over a hill to check something whose existence no one else can verify?"

Vitios gave Redburn no chance to reply before he waded in like a boxer to hammer home his points. "You acknowledged his command, then shouted, 'Major Allard! *Cicada*s, sir! All over the place!' His reply to you is, 'Withdraw south, Leftenant.'" Vitios turned a page and began to drift over toward the defense table. "A private, Robert Craon, burst in there. 'Negative, negative,' he says. 'I've got magscan readings off the scale south, east, and north. You're clean, sir. We've got to head out west.'" Vitios looked up and half-turned to face Redburn. "Is that how you remember it, Leftenant?"

Redburn nodded. "Yes."

Vitios's eyes glowed fiercely, and Redburn felt as though he were suddenly plunging through deep, dark space. "A senior officer, the graduate of a superior military academy, and a Diamond Sunburst winner for his actions on Spica, has just learned that his command is surrounded. What would we expect from this sort of man? Wouldn't such a commander return to rally his troops? He's only half a klick over a hill. Didn't you expect him to return, Leftenant?"

Redburn swallowed hard and drew in a deep breath. "Yes, sir."

"Of course you would, Leftenant." Vitios opened his arms to include all the officers in the gallery and the three men on the tribunal.

"Anyone with military experience knows a commanding officer does not abandon his men. But what is Justin Xiang Allard's reply to this urgent appeal by his troops? 'No way out here, either. Do what you can, Andy. The cadre is yours.' He abandons his command, then adds, 'It's a trap. All a trap. Don't run west…'" Vitios shook his head. "He abandons them and dashes their hopes for any sort of escape."

Vitios smiled conspiratorially at Redburn, and dropped his voice to a malicious whisper. "You did feel betrayed, didn't you?"

Redburn hesitated, then nodded his head with resignation. "Yes."

"And so you were." Vitios looked to Courtney. "I am finished with this witness."

The Major General looked at his watch. "Given the hour, this court will adjourn."

Lofton shot to his feet. "Objection, Your Honor! It's only three-thirty! We cannot adjourn before I have a chance to cross-examine the witness."

"Leftenant Lofton, need I remind you that Prince Davion is holding a reception for Leftenant Redburn tonight. I will not have this man too badgered and exhausted to fully participate in this great honor."

Lofton removed his glasses and narrowed his dark eyes. "No, but you'll retire and a whole evening will pass before I can purge your mind of the prejudicial testimony that Count Vitios has wrung from this valuable witness."

Redburn looked up at Courtney. "I can go on, sir."

Courtney's gavel slammed into the bench. "Enough. Court is adjourned until nine-thirty tomorrow morning. As for you, Leftenant Lofton, one more statement like that and you'll spend the night in a cell with your client because I'll hold you in contempt."

13

22 January 3027

"No, Major, I won't put you on the stand!" Leftenant David Lofton glared at his client. "Your story of what happened in the field that day is utterly unsubstantiated."

Justin stared into the mirror as his right hand labored to button his dress jacket shut. "Leftenant, you must allow me to testify on my own behalf. I read the text of General Courtney's speech at Andy Redburn's reception two nights ago. He already believes I'm guilty."

Lofton snarled in frustration. "What could you say? What could you add that would justify your giving Vitios a direct shot at you?"

Justin spun about. "Courtney is a commander of men. He's made battle decisions before. I served under him. I can convince him of my innocence. I can touch that chord deep inside every soldier who's ever had to make a decision that sent men out to die."

Lofton shook his head violently. "Are you mad? Recall, Major, that it was your unorthodox action on Spica that saved Courtney's command. If you and Colonel William Dobson hadn't flanked Liao's Blackwind Lancers, Courtney would have died without having to face the shame of being trapped by those Capellan units." Lofton cursed under his breath. "I wish Dobson hadn't died on Galtor. We could have used his testimony to your bravery."

Justin nodded slowly. "And I could have used his friendship."

Lofton shook his head. "Redburn was...*is*...your friend, and Vitios made mincemeat of him. He'll do the same with you, Major, and

82

that's the reason I won't put you on the stand."

Justin tugged at the black glove on his left hand. "Absolutely?"

Lofton shrugged and picked up his briefcase from the table. "I think I made some headway with Redburn's cross-examination yesterday. He got a chance to use his wit, and it worked in our favor to delay until after Prince Davion awarded him the Silver Sunburst. I don't want to give Vitios a shot at you, Justin, because he'll hurt you badly."

Justin pursed his lips and nodded slowly. "This is your battlefield, David. Just remember I'm ready if you need reinforcements."

Leftenant David Lofton forced a smile and led his client out into the maelstrom. *I hope, for your sake, Major, that this trial doesn't get to the point where I need your help.*

"Objection, Your Honor!"

Courtney shrugged and looked toward Lofton. "Yes, Leftenant?"

Lofton adjusted his glasses. "If it please the court, the prosecution cannot use the holovid tapes of investigators on Kittery as testimony. To do so would violate my client's right to face his accusers. Because I cannot cross-examine those witnesses, their testimony cannot be allowed."

Vitios placed the tapes back on the desk. "Your Honor, though I would never think of denying Leftenant Lofton the chance to crush my witnesses—as he has so ably done thus far—I would hasten to point out that tapes have been allowed in court before." The titters that sprang up at Vitios's sarcastic reference to Lofton's inability to break witnesses died as the prosecutor's aide typed furiously on a keyboard.

Vitios turned to face the large viewscreen to the right of the witness stand. "As you can see, in the case of *Muije versus Nebula Foods*, the court allowed the plaintiff to present holovid tapes because of the prohibitive cost in time and money of bringing witnesses to the site of the trial."

Lofton's laugh startled the court. "Your honor, this is ridiculous. *Muije versus Nebula Foods* is a civil case over two hundred years old, and this is a military trial! The plaintiff, in this case, is a member of the Armed Forces of the Federated Suns." Lofton turned to face his adversary. "It strikes me that if Duke Hasek-Davion can afford to send his own hatchetman to persecute my client, he can damn well afford to send witnesses."

Courtney's gavel thundercracked silence throughout the courtroom. "That will be enough Leftenant! You, yourself, have reminded the Court that this is a military trial. Now the Court will remind you of the same and demands that you conduct yourself in a military manner!"

Lofton bowed his head. "Yes, sir."

Courtney drew his bushy gray eyebrows together in a way that filled Lofton with cold dread. "While your objection might have some merit in another case, or even at another point in this proceeding, it has no bearing here. The witnesses on these tapes are experts in their fields, and it would be well beyond your ability to impeach their testimony. The tapes contain information needed to adjudicate this case. Proceed, Count Vitios."

"No!" Lofton stalked forward. "Am I to believe, based on what you have just said, Your Honor, that you have already reviewed the tapes?"

Courtney nodded his silver-maned head. "I have, Leftenant Lofton, and I see no reason to let your objection stand. Overruled."

The courtroom lights came back up as the image of the last Hasek-Davion expert faded from the viewscreen. Vitios, poised perfectly in the center of the courtroom, opened his hands to include the whole audience. "In short, Your Honor, the witnesses have confirmed that Major Allard's *Valkyrie* was damaged by autocannon and laser fire, as he has maintained. They found enough chemical residue and spent projectiles from an autocannon to suggest, as Major Allard reported, that he tried to evade the 'Mech shooting at him. But, because of their inability to recover data from Major Allard's damaged battle-recorder, they have no way of verifying his claim to have fought off a *Rifleman*. In fact, given the evidence in the field, they have concluded that he faced an *UrbanMech*—the lightest 'Mech known to carry an autocannon."

"Objection! The prosecution is making a statement, not asking a question. This is neither the time nor the place." Wearily, Lofton stood and leaned over the defense table, supporting himself on his two hands. No one in the courtroom could fail to read the exhaustion in his slumping frame or the nervous tic tugging at the corner of one eye.

"Sustained." Courtney looked over at the Corporal acting as court stenographer. "Strike those comments. Count Vitios, please call your next witness."

The Count graced Lofton with a sly nod of the head, then smiled cruelly. "The prosecution calls Quintus Allard to the stand."

Justin's father marched stiffly down the aisle from the gallery, anger flashing like lighting from his blue eyes. He allowed himself to be sworn in as though it were the most onerous task he'd ever been asked to perform. He glared at the prosecutor.

Vitios smiled almost graciously. "State your name for the record, please, and your position."

Quintus's nostrils flared. "Enough games, Vitios. I'm here. I'm

84

your Judas, so just get it over with."

Vitios nodded curtly, then looked to Courtney. "Your Honor, you can see that this will be a hostile witness." With the judge's nodded acknowledgement, Vitios started in. "You are the head of the Davion Counter-Intelligence Division, are you not?"

"Among other things, yes." Quintus spat out the words out as though they were poison.

Vitios smiled without compassion or sympathy. "In your capacity as Acting Minister of Intelligence Information and Operations, did you attend the interrogation of a captured Capellan MechWarrior by the name of Lo Ching-wei?"

"Yes."

"In this interrogation, did you identify him as a member of the Yizhi tong of Shaoshan? And did you identify him as one of the people who claimed some knowledge of the ambush in which your son was injured?"

Quintus tightened his grip on the witness box railing to white-knuckled intensity. "Yes, to both counts."

"What did he identify as the type of 'Mech that destroyed your son's *Valkyrie*?"

Pain creased Quintus Allard's face as the answer came reluctantly from his lips. "An *UrbanMech*."

Justin quickly whispered something to his lawyer, and Lofton stood. "Objection, your Honor. This is hearsay evidence."

Vitios wheeled and stabbed a finger at Lofton. "Are you doubting Quintus Allard's sworn word? Obviously, this man is fighting me as hard as he can, and yet you object?"

Lofton removed his glasses and leaned toward Vitios. "Need I remind you, my Lord, that it is not the veracity or credibility of a witness that makes his testimony admissible or not."

Courtney's gavel slammed into the bench and broke the tension much like the bell ending a round of a prize fight. "Leftenant Lofton, return to your place. Overruled!"

"Overruled!" Lofton grabbed for a stack of law disks and would have thrown them at the judge except that Justin restrained his arm. Lofton snapped around and stared at his client as though he'd stabbed him in the back. Justin merely shook his head resignedly. Lofton sank mutely back into his seat.

Vitios turned again on Quintus Allard. "Lo Ching-wei also surrendered the identity of an agent within the Federated Suns forces in Shaoshan, did he not? What was the designation the tong gave to this agent?"

Muscles bunched at Quintus's jaws. "They called him Ivory."

Vitios closed his eyes and clasped his hands before him like a man in prayer. "And what is that designation in Capellan, Minister Allard?"

"Xiangya."

Vitios smiled. "Louder, please. I did not hear it."

"Xiangya!" Quintus raked his fingernails over the oak railing. "There. I've said it. Is that enough?"

Vitios's dark eyes snapped open. "No, that is not enough. In the interrogation, Lo identified the agent, didn't he? He identified him as your son, Justin Xiang Allard, didn't he?"

Quintus bit back angry tears. "Yes, he identified him as my son."

"But you were not satisfied with this identification. You directed a full-scale investigation that included a sweep of the Kittery base computer for security codes. What was your son Justin's activation code for his 'Mech?"

Quintus stared up at the ceiling. "Zhe jian fang tai xiao."

Vitios closed on him. "In English, Minister."

Quintus lowered his head and stared bitterly at Vitios. "This room is too small."

Vitios smiled. "This room is too small. This phrase has another meaning among the Yizhi tong, doesn't it?"

"Yes. It signifies that the speaker fears that someone is listening in on the conversation, and the phrase is a warning to be careful."

Vitios turned to point at Justin Allard. "And this phrase—of all the possible codes he could have used— in either Capellan or English, is the one he chose. Ironic, isn't it, that he chooses an enemy expression for caution as the password to his 'Mech."

"Do you expect me to respond to that?"

Vitios shook his head. "No, I suppose not. I withdraw the question. I am finished with this witness."

Leftenant Lofton leaped to his feet. "I have only one question for this witness." As he started to phrase it, Quintus slowly shook his head. Justin clutched at his lawyer's sleeve, but Lofton marched straight into the trap, heedless of the warning signs. "Mr. Allard, do you believe your son is a traitor?"

Quintus looked down at his shoes. "I don't know. I just don't know."

14

30 January 3027

"David, you *must* put me on the stand!" Though speaking in a low tone, Justin's voice seethed with anger and filled the prisoners' holding room. "I need my chance to speak."

Lofton shook his head. "It will do no good."

Justin smiled coldly, but his brown eyes had become dark slivers of fury. "Oh, it *will* do some good, David."

Lofton's nostrils flared. "Since when have you become a lawyer? Do you think I'm oblivious to what's going on out there? They might as well have strapped you to a K-F drive and jumped you straight into the grave. I look at you and see an officer who cared for his men and who tried to normalize relations with a conquered people. I see a man proud of his mixed heritage, and I see a man who's been decorated for bravery…"

Justin thrust his right hand at the Lieutenant. "You see that, perhaps, but you stand alone. To them, out there, I'm the rogue. They gave me everything: a name, a place to live, a career, and their trust. The problem is that they're so used to hiding the skeletons in their own closets that they imagine everyone else is, too. My case gives them a chance to direct their fears and hatred at a living target. Well, I'm ready to shoot back, David, and you have to give me the chance."

"Justin, Vitios will crucify you. You saw how he forced your father to say things he didn't want to say. You heard how he twisted the interpretation of your normal behavior to look like the sinister machinations of a master spy. What can you do on the stand that will help you?"

Justin shook his head. "Nothing."

"Exactly…"

"Nothing but point up what an absolute travesty this whole trial has been from the start."

Lofton thrust his face at Justin. "No! If you go rogue in that courtroom, if you sink down into the pits with Vitios, they'll kill you. Treason is still a capital offense, Justin, and if you anger enough people out there, you'll be dead."

Justin looked up and met Lofton's concerned stare with a blank one. "David, put me on the stand, or I'll find a lawyer who will."

David Lofton slowly straightened up, then rebuttoned his dress jacket. "Very well, Major, you'll have your wish." Lofton stared down at his client. "One thing, though. When I told you what sort of officer I had for a client, you said I was alone in my opinion. Don't you believe in yourself?"

Justin shook his head slowly. "The only thing I believe right now is that I made a mistake in leaving my mother's people to live with my father."

Lofton turned from his client and returned to the defense desk. "Thank you, Major Allard, for your cooperation." Without looking up, he added, "I am finished with this witness, Your Honor."

Courtney nodded. "Your witness, Count Vitios."

Vitios stalked Justin Allard like a tiger that has tasted human flesh. He stopped his pacing directly before the witness box and met Justin's hot glare with one of arctic frigidity. "What comes to mind, Major Allard, when someone calls you 'yellow?'"

"Objection!" Lofton vaulted out of his seat and stepped toward his client. "The prosecutor is insulting my client with irrelevant questions."

Vitios shook his head. "I will show relevancy, Your Honor."

Courtney waved Lofton back to his bench, then turned to Justin. "Answer the question, Major."

Justin let the hint of a smile flicker over his lips. "Generally, I would assume that someone who called me 'yellow' was accusing me of being a coward, but when a small-minded bigot like you uses the term, I assume it is a racial slur."

Vitios stepped back. "Quick to take offense, aren't you, Major?" Justin opened his mouth to reply, but Vitios started another question first.

Lofton smiled and split the confusion with a loud voice, "Objection. My client has not had a chance to answer your question."

Vitios, slightly off balance, growled. "I withdraw the question."

"No," Justin interjected. "I'd like to answer it. I understand, Count Vitios, why you hate the Capellan Confederation. I know your family died in a Liao raid on Verlo. I know the attack came after insurgents had poisoned the local garrison forces and I know you've been looking under beds and in closets for Capellan spies ever since. I've heard your hatred of me in everything you've said since we first met after the battle of Valencia on Spica. Your blind prejudice disgusts me."

"Does it, now, Major Justin Xiang Allard?" Vitios returned to the prosecution table, picked up a file, and began to flip through it as he spoke. "You associate with known Liao agents. You speak their tongue and are accepted in their homes. You use a catch phrase from a tong as your 'Mech's personal security code. You abandon your men to a Liao ambush during an exercise you never wanted to participate in to start with! Forgive me my blind loathing, Major, but something here stinks, and the facts say that it's *you*!"

Vitios slammed the folder back down on the desk. "Major Allard, you nearly cost the Federated Suns over forty-eight million C-bills in equipment, the lives of thirty MechWarriors, and the world of Kittery. You sold out the people who accepted you as one of their own and who gave you everything you have! You betrayed everything that humans hold sacred anywhere in the Inner Sphere, and you betrayed your honor as a MechWarrior!"

The prosecutor raked fingers back through his thin brown hair, and wiped flecks of spittle from the corners of his mouth. "You take the stand and have your attorney feed you questions so that you can trot out your unsubstantiated fabrication of a battle with a 'Mech three times the size of your *Valkyrie*. Then you ask us to believe that story. But I know the real truth, you lying son of a Capellan slut, and so does everyone else in this courtroom!"

"Enough!" Spoken in a voice born to command, that single word silenced the uproar that had seized the spectators. The attention of everyone in the courtroom turned toward the bronze double-doors at the rear of the room, and the spectators were riveted by what they saw. Flanked by Ardan Sortek, Quintus Allard, and CID guards, Prince Hanse Davion strode smartly into the room. "I have heard enough!"

Hanse pushed open the low wooden gates and admitted himself to the center of the courtroom. He looked at Count Vitios, who seemed to recoil from the cold impact of the Prince's gaze. The Prince then looked up at Major General Courtney. "I would address the court."

The judge nodded nervously. Hanse turned slowly, then pointed

89

at Count Vitios. "You are, without a doubt, the most shameless creature it has ever been my sad duty to acknowledge as a subject. Your very manner is offensive to me and any clear-thinking person alive today. You do not wear your bigotry like a uniform; it has utterly consumed you and poisoned everything you do. I accepted you as prosecutor as a favor to Duke Michael Hasek-Davion, but I do not owe him enough to put up with you any longer. You will leave New Avalon tonight!"

Hanse turned so that he could address both the Tribunal and the gallery of spectators. "As I have watched this trial, it appears to be an indictment of a whole nation, not an adjudication of the guilt or innocence of one MechWarrior. This trial, and the manner in which it has been conducted, is an example of power and hatred run rampant. Leftenant Lofton's valiant attempts to win justice for his client have been crushed by the vilest of legal trickery. I call this whole procedure a mockery of everything the Davions honor and hold dear."

Hanse smiled, as he turned toward the Tribunal. "Certainly, you must recognize that there is no solid proof of Justin Allard's guilt. The facts—those few that the Count has actually managed to present—are all circumstantial. Yes, Allard's Capellan middle name may be close to that of the tong designation for an agent, but would he or his spymasters have been stupid enough to choose such a codename? Have enough respect for House Liao to dismiss that idea immediately."

Hanse shrugged. "Perhaps Major Allard did display poor judgement in moving off to investigate the *UrbanMech* hidden further ahead. And yet, if he believed his men were faced with a possible ambush, this might have been the most prudent course of action. Strip him of his command, as you must, but is a simple act of negligence to cost him his life?"

"No command!" The Prince's words had hit Justin like a meteorite and visibly crushed him. He leaned forward heavily, hands pressed against the dark wooden railing of the witness box, staring at Hanse Davion's back. At Justin's outburst, the Prince spun around to face him. Justin gestured with his right hand at the crowd. "Do not spare me the full depth of hatred that these people—your people—feel for me. They look at me and see no further than the shape of my eyes or the color of my skin. All my life I have fought against the legacy of having a Capellan mother. I became more loyal to House Davion than anyone else I knew because I hoped—prayed—that what I held in my heart would make me like everyone else in my flesh. But that did not happen."

Anger flashed through Hanse's blue eyes, and his face registered pain at the bitter rage in Justin's voice. "Beware, Major. I offer you your life!"

"Ha! Life? For what? So that I can continue to protect these ungrateful slugs who fatten themselves in the Federated Suns core while their countless countrymen work and sweat and die to keep them safe? Do I want to live to protect animals like Vitios there…so that they can continue their witchhunts?"

Davion's ice blue eyes flared. "Don't push me, Major. I'm being generous with you. Do not presume, however, that I owe you even as much as the life I offer you."

For a half-second, Justin's eyes closed, then they jerked open. The pain of a lifetime showed in them and seemed to flood through the room. Justin smashed his black-gloved hand into the witness box railing, shattering it.

"What you offer me is as much a life as this is a hand! You flatter yourself to imagine I might be grateful." Justin stared at Hanse Davion, fury making his eyes shine with a malevolent light. "What is it, then, Prince Davion? Do you want to keep me as you do Ardan Sortek? Is not one captive MechWarrior enough?" Justin spat on the floor. "The life you offer me is as shallow as House Davion's conception of justice!" His anger spent, Justin cradled his lifeless arm against his chest and trembled.

Immobile as a statue, Hanse Davion stood within the silence that settled heavily over the room. Finally, he nodded slightly, the motion growing as he gathered his thoughts. "Very well, Justin Allard. I will give you what you most desire."

The Prince turned on his heel and stared up at Courtney. "Sentence him as you will. It makes no difference. I will strip him of his rank and commute any sentence to a lifetime in exile." The Prince turned again, this time picking out Quintus Allard among the crowd. "You, Quintus Allard, no longer have a son named Justin. He no longer exists, and no one will ever speak his name to me again."

Finally, Hanse Davion set his malachite gaze on Justin Allard himself. "I give you back your Capellan name, traitor. Justin Xiang, there is no place for you in the Federated Suns. You will be taken to any world willing to accept you, as long as it is beyond the borders of the Federated Suns." Hanse's head dropped for a moment, then came back up. "And if you wish to learn the true depth of justice in the Federated Suns, return here and we will drown you in it!"

Ardan Sortek and Andrew Redburn stood in the control tower, watching while the DropShip *Sigmund Rosenblum* accepted its final passenger. As Justin Xiang passed up the ramp and into the ship's dark interior, Redburn turned from the window. "I'm sure, Colonel Sortek, that Justin—I mean Major Allard—did not mean what he said in

91

court."

Ardan Sortek smiled knowingly and rested a hand on Redburn's shoulder. "No need for you to apologize, Leftenant. There was a time when I, too, believed that I was wasting away here on New Avalon. I went back into the field, but after a harrowing adventure or two, I realized that a man at peace with himself can be useful anywhere." He looked out as the DropShip's engines ignited and the egg-shaped ship slowly shuddered skyward. "Your friend has a lot of pain in him, and he'll not be satisfied until he can deal with that. I take no offense at anything he said while so sorely troubled."

Redburn nodded. "It's a waste of a damn good MechWarrior."

Sortek shrugged. "On Solaris VII, he'll be with plenty of his own kind." Sortek's next words caused Redburn to smile. "And while he's trying to sate that anger, I imagine he'll be hell on wheels there on the Game World."

"But I know he's innocent, Colonel Sortek, and when I return to Kittery, I'll get the evidence to prove it. His *Val* was empty of LRMs after the battle. No *UrbanMech* could have survived that barrage. It had to have been a *Rifleman*."

The smile drained from Sortek's face. "I suppose they've not told you about your new assignment, have they?"

Redburn froze. "I was told that I'd ship back to Kittery and resume command of the training battalion."

Sortek shifted his weight from one foot to the other, and shook his head. "Eventually you'll get there, Leftenant. But first, you and I will be shipping out to the Lyran Commonwealth. I've got inspections and official functions to attend. Now that you're a hero, we'll give a lot of influential people a chance to have their holographs taken with you."

Redburn frowned with puzzlement. "Isn't there someone else, say, from Redfield or from Galtor, who could go?"

Sortek shrugged and led the other man to the elevator. "Nothing more stale than yesterday's heroes. Besides, some people want to know how this training battalion idea is working out. Lots of resistance in House Steiner to MechWarriors trained in anything other than the Academies. Your men, and their performance against the Liao ambush, are hot right now."

Redburn nodded, but barely heard the words. *Good luck, Justin. I know that deep in your heart you're one of us. Somehow, I'll find a way to prove it.*

15

1 January 3027

Jiro Ishiyama bowed deeply out of respect for the wrinkled old monk who had led him through the twisting tunnels of the Zen monastery. Above them, on Echo V's barren, wind-scarred tundra, icy cyclones shrieked as they scourged the planet. Ishiyama fought the shiver provoked by the planet's chill, and respected the old monk even more because of his indifference to the cold.

Indeed, Ishiyama was swathed in the warm folds of a heavy coat, while the monk wore a simple black robe. Though the air was cold enough to show both men's breath, the monk wore only sandals, and had neither gloves to protect his hands nor a hood to protect his shaved pate. In the monk's eyes, however, Ishiyama saw no superiority or disdain for this visitor from far Luthien. Instead, Ishiyama read pity for the man who does not know himself well enough to exist as one with the cold.

The monk looked beyond Jiro Ishiyama and wordlessly directed the two initiates bearing the visitor's lacquered trunks to pass around them. The initiates, bowing only their heads because of the burdens on their backs, passed through the garden to the small hut reserved for the *cha-no-yu*, the tea ceremony. The two initiates vanished into the hut for a moment, then returned to bow deeply to the monk and his visitor before disappearing into the dark tunnels of the monastery complex.

The monk inclined his head and half-smiled. "*Sumimasen*, Ishiyama Jiro-sama," he began slowly. "Excuse me if I speak slowly because we use words sparingly here."

Ishiyama bowed. "I am honored by the words you grant me." He looked out over the rock and bonsai garden that filled the underground cavern. The pale white gravel had been raked in long, undulating waves that truly made one feel that he were viewing a frozen ocean. Larger rocks, from the gray of granite to the glassy black-purple of obsidian, thrust up through the stone surf like defiant islands. Nestled in the naturally carven niches, bonsai trees pushed up as though part of the rock, while carefully nurtured mosses clung to the rock, adding the proper verdant touches.

The tea house stood in the center of the garden, and though of obvious human construction, it seemed to be an organic part of the garden. Styled after a pagoda, complete with wood lattice, rice-paper screen walls, and a red-tiled roof, the well-worn granite used to construct the tea house made it look as though the structure were even older than the garden itself. From beneath the tip of the tea house's peaked roof, gray smoke drifted almost imperceptibly.

Ishiyama breathed in and smiled at the familiar, pleasing aroma of burning cedar. Again, he bowed to the monk. "All is perfect. Your faithfulness honors the Dragon." The monk, obviously pleased, bowed his head. Both men knew that, as perfect as the garden might seem, Ishiyama would alter it in some subtle way to make it yet more perfect, and to bind it into the *cha-no-yu* that he had travelled more than two hundred light years to perform.

"*Do itashimash'te*, Ishiyama Jiro-sama," the monk replied softly. "It is we who are honored that the Dragon sends you to grace us with your skill. Be assured that your preparations will not be disturbed. In four hours, I will send Kurita Yorinaga-ji to you."

"*Domo arigato*." Ishiyama bowed deeply and did not straighten up until the monk had silently departed the chamber. Ishiyama studied the garden. As his eyes followed the path of flat stones leading from the entrance to the tea house, he allowed himself to become absorbed in the beauty the monks had created. The garden, by its artistry and resonance, touched him deeply and peeled away layers of emotion and inner conflicts. The scene restored him to the centered feeling of peace that his trip across seven jump points had stripped away.

Ishiyama forced his mind to the cavern and the garden and his mission. He removed his thick, quilted mittens, stuffed them into his coat pockets, pulled off his boots, and then crossed to where a bamboo rake lay hidden in a shadowed niche. Brandishing it with the care and reverence a warrior might give to his 'Mech, Ishiyama slowly stepped out onto the stone path. Three stones out, he used the rake to gently tease four small pieces of gravel onto that third stone. He did nothing

94

to change or repair how the gravel had fallen, and it might have been only that the last person to rake the gravel had been careless.

Ishiyama allowed himself a brief smile. *Deliberately careless.* Ishiyama knew that Kurita Yorinaga-ji would immediately spot the small white pebbles on the broad gray steppingstone. He knew, too, that Yorinaga-ji would take them as the first sign that the perfect universe, the universe that had trapped him, was changing.

Ishiyama looked up and concentrated. *If the tea house is Luthien, then...* He turned to the left and squinted. Reaching out with the butt of the rake, he gently pressed it into the gravel. *Mallory's World, the site of Yorinaga-ji's disgrace, would be here.*

Ishiyama reversed the rake and used the broad, toothed end to subtly alter the flowing wavelines around the mark he'd made for Mallory's World. Slowly, and with a patience bordering upon the superhuman, he reworked the gravel until one could see, if one knew how to look, minute ripples spreading from that point. Advancing ahead three more path-stones, Ishiyama completed the eleventh concentric ripple-ring—one for each year since Yorinaga-ji had disgraced himself. It was now just over an hour since he had first laid eyes on the garden.

Ishiyama backtracked to the garden's edge, and removed his coat and hat. The chill air sliced through the midnight-blue silken kimono he wore, and Ishiyama unconsciously retied the silver obi a bit tighter. Though difficult to see in the soothing half-light, a dragon figure coiled around the kimono, woven into the garment with slightly darker blue thread.

Ishiyama again studied the tea house and compared it to Luthien's location on the star chart he'd memorized. Further to the left than the mark he'd made for Mallory's World, and just a bit closer to the tea house, he touched one edge of the rake into the sea of pebbles to mark the location of Chara. With benign and skillful care, he flipped the rake over and used its flat edge to smooth away any trace of his original mark on the stones. Only the briefly broken lines of the stone-sea currents suggested that any movement had occurred.

Ishiyama allowed himself another smile. *Most would miss it.* He shook his head. *But not Yorinaga-ji.*

Finally, Ishiyama walked the path to the tea house, but he did not enter it. Instead, he carefully walked around the tea house's narrow ledge out onto the ocean of gravel behind it. He sighted a perfect spot to represent the planet Echo, and boldly touched the rake butt into the gravel to mark it. Backtracking, he raked the stones back into their previous pattern. By the time he had returned to the tea house, only the invisible depression representing Echo gave any clue to his passage.

95

Though Ishiyama knew Yorinaga-ji would never look out behind the tea house to see his work, he also knew it had to be done. *It makes the garden mine, and makes the* cha-no-yu *complete. Yorinaga-ji would expect no less of me, and because of that, he has no need to confirm the presence of the mark.*

Ishiyama worked his way back down the stone path, carefully avoiding the four pebbles, and returned the rake to its niche. Gathering up his coat and boots, he carried them to the tea house, where he knelt at the doorway, bowed once, and slid open the door.

He should have expected it, but the tea house's simplicity and beauty took his breath away. The waiting area, built slightly below the interior chamber where the *cha-no-yu* would actually take place, had been constructed of hand-fitted woodwork. The pieces of wood had been chosen for their color and grain, and polished to a softly glowing sheen. Though one could make out the seams between the different pieces of wood, the natural patterns in each piece flowed together and provided the illusion that the whole floor and lower walls had been laid in with one huge piece of wood.

The paper used to make the walls seemed, at first glance, to be unadorned. No landscapes or calligraphed snippets of wisdom spoiled the panels' translucent beauty. As Ishiyama slowly slid the door panel shut behind him, he saw that the paper did bear a decoration. It had been worked, with great subtlety and delicacy, as a watermark into the paper itself. Thus did Ishiyama see images of trees and tigers, of waves and fish, of hawks and hares and, of course, of the Dragon.

Silently, out of respect for the setting and because no noise was required, Ishiyama crossed through the waiting area and slid open the door to the raised room where he would perform the *cha-no-yu*. The two black lacquered cases lay just to the right of the tall brass urn rising up through a square opening in the floor. Ishiyama did not need to see the thin gray ribbons of smoke twisting through the hot air to know that a fire burned within the urn. He could feel the waves of heat washing off the urn itself, and the scent of burning cedar filled the room.

In the center of the room, Ishiyama saw a low, rectangular table. It had been oriented perfectly with the shape of the room, and Ishiyama now changed that. Instead of leaving the table's narrow end to coincide with the narrow parts of the room, he gently slid it around on the polished oaken floor so that it sat almost perpendicular to its earlier position. Still, he did not fully straighten it, but left it canted at a slight angle and pushed off-center. *Perfect symmetry traps the mind within the bounds of reality.*

Ishiyama knelt down to open the first case. Inside, swathed in thick folds of foam padding, lay the Coordinator's own tea service set.

Taking a deep breath to calm himself, Ishiyama fought the panic and weight of responsibility that threatened to crush him from both inside and out. *The Coordinator has entrusted me with these items so that I might perform a delicate mission. I will not fail him.*

The first things he withdrew from the case were three *tatami*, the mats on which the participants would kneel during the ceremony. The first, a brilliant red, Ishiyama placed at the wide side of the table that lay deepest in the room. He withdrew a small ruler from inside his kimono and made sure that the red mat lay exactly twenty centimeters from the edge of the table.

On the other side of the table, Ishiyama unfurled the second *tatami*. This one was a rosy-pink, and he made sure it lay thirty-five centimeters from the table's edge. Finally, at the narrow end of the table closest to the brass charcoal urn, Ishiyama unrolled his own plain mat for the ceremony and placed it forty-five centimeters from the table's black edge. His end of the table, because of the diagonal alignment, placed him below either of the other mats.

Ishiyama did not hurry as he unpacked the other necessary items, nor did he glance at his watch. He had an innate sense of time and its passage, as did anyone trained as a tea master. He knew his preparations would extend beyond the time the monk had estimated for sending Kurita Yorinaga-ji to him, but he also knew Yorinaga-ji would not enter the tea house's central chamber until invited.

Ishiyama unwrapped the bamboo ladle that had been in the Kurita family for the last four hundred years. It was rumored that Coordinator Urizen Kurita II had stopped his aircar when he had seen a remarkable stand of bamboo on Luthien, thinking it would make a fine tea ceremony ladle. Just after he had descended from the car to cut off a piece of the bamboo, Urizen's car was blown up by a bomb secretly planted by a rival. The Coordinator was, fortunately, already well away from it. Tradition had it that because something utterly Japanese had saved the Coordinator's life, Urizen instituted the reforms that raised medieval Japanese culture to become the heart and soul of the Draconis Combine.

Ishiyama smiled as he reverently set the ladle down on the floor. *Urizen remained Coordinator until he resigned at the age of 101, and retired here to Echo. He formed this monastery and served as its head, under the title of Colonial Governor—nothing less would do for him—until his death. How appropriate to use this ladle here, today.*

Ishiyama carefully unwrapped the cerulean blue tea bowl and set it on the table. Beside it, he placed the bamboo spoon and whisk. Reaching into the first case again, Ishiyama produced the black-lacquered, wooden tea chest, which he set down reverently near his end

97

of the table. It was a gorgeous piece, with a red and gold dragon circling both body and lid. Ishiyama knew that it was the same chest used at the meal where the Coordinator, Takashi Kurita, had first seen his future wife, the beautiful young Jasmine. The chest's placement, while utilitarian, would allow Ishiyama's intended guest an opportunity to study it.

Finally, Ishiyama lifted the Coordinator's own water urn from the chest. The simple bowl was not at all as grand as the other objects in the room, yet its slightly crude manufacture invited all manner of speculation about its origin. Ishiyama reveled in one of the more popular tales claiming that the Coordinator had formed it from the armor of his first 'Mech kill, or that it was all he had left of his first 'Mech. Just touching it sent a thrill through him. He allowed himself a flight of fantasy in which a young Takashi Kurita sat hammering the pot into shape so that he could heat water and have tea while war thundered around him.

Ishiyama shivered when it dawned on him that Yorinaga-ji might actually have been present when the Coordinator first shaped the pot. Until the time of his disgrace, Yorinaga-ji had been a battalion commander in the Coordinator's own 2nd Sword of Light. *Some even credit him with Prince Ian Davion's death!* Ishiyama shook his head. *How could one so brave have so dishonored himself?*

Ishiyama picked up the ladle in his right hand and held the pot in his left. He moved toward the urn-pit where the ceramic jar full of water had remained hidden from view. Setting the tea urn between his knees, and canted with one edge on the floor, Ishiyama uncovered the jar and sank the ladle into the water. He let the ladle drink briefly, then drew out one full measure of water. Carefully turning the urn so that the water could wash the insides, he dripped liquid into the urn. Though no sediment or dirt showed in the water that had pooled in the urn, Ishiyama poured it out into the pit and then filled the tea urn with three more ladles of water.

Ishiyama recovered the water jar and set the ladle back down on his own plain *tatami*. Then, as though lifting an offering to unseen gods, he placed the tea urn onto the brass fire urn. Pleased with his preparations so far, Ishiyama knelt back on his heels and again drank in the peace of the tea house.

After a moment's respite, he crossed back to the lacquered cases. Gently folding his coat and boots, he fitted them carefully into the now-empty first case. After closing it, Ishiyama slid the case just enough out of the way so that it would still be visible. His guest would see it and surely wonder at what secrets it contained.

16

Jiro Ishiyama, tea master for the *cha-no-yu*, opened the second case and pulled a small gong and hammer from it. After carrying it to his place at the table, he set it where his body would shield it from the guest's view. Returning to the case, Ishiyama removed the kimono he wore and pulled on the black one that lay like a congealed shadow at the bottom of the case. Then he also drew from the case a black hood with a mesh front to hide his face yet allow him to see what he needed to do.

After folding his kimono and laying it in the case, Ishiyama pushed the case back alongside its companion. He left it open so that the white interior—*not unlike an alligator's mouth*—yawned open to invite trust and the contemplation of a journey.

Ishiyama crossed to his position and pulled on the black hood. Using a fir twig that he had carried within his kimono, he reached up to place it into the fire urn. The twig immediately burst into flame, filling the room with the scent the Coordinator so admired. Ishiyama breathed it in deeply it and settled back to enter a more contemplative frame of mind.

The peace he sought eluded him, dancing like a butterfly just out of reach. Instead, his mind bubbled with images from the many stories he had heard about Yorinaga-ji over the years. A distant cousin of the Coordinator, Yorinaga had been a fierce MechWarrior and one of the few men to match Takashi in *kendo*, the art of the sword. Three years

99

after being credited with Prince Ian Davion's death on Mallory's World in 3013, Yorinaga had been given the honor of leading the 2nd Sword of Light in an attempt to take that same world. Ishiyama recalled, too, the news reports of Yorinaga in action that he had seen as a child. He even remembered the pride that had swelled in his young heart, for he had idolized Yorinaga. The bitter taste of bile rose to this throat as he once again relived his hero's downfall.

The story, as Ishiyama had heard it many times, was one of honor, and it should have ended with Yorinaga slaying his enemy in grand style. The 2nd Sword of Light had surrounded the Kell Hounds's 1st 'Mech Battalion on Mallory's World and was advancing to destroy them when Colonel Morgan Kell marched his *Archer* out to the head of his force. In Japanese fashion, he suddenly began to announce his lineage and all the bold things his line had done.

Yorinaga, out of respect and honor for his foe, marched his own *Warhammer* to the forefront of the gathered Kurita troops and broadcast his own lineage and their accomplishments. All the MechWarriors watching the confrontation knew that the battle would be decided between their commanders. Ishiyama had often heard the jest that the tension was so thick that the Lyran traders might have to come in to export it.

Kell's *Archer*, armed with long-range missiles and four medium lasers, conceded much to Yorinaga's 'Mech. The *Warhammer's* main armaments were its two medium lasers and twin particle projection cannons, known commonly as PPCs. In a close battle, the *Warhammer's* short range missiles and two small lasers made it even deadlier. Everyone knew that the *Archer* would die, and they hoped its pilot would die with honor.

By all accounts, the battle pitted two master MechWarriors against each other. Kell did not retreat to a range where his LRMs would give him an advantage. Instead, he used his incredible agility to make his 'Mech a nearly impossible target, while using his fore and aft lasers to score random hits on his foe.

Yorinaga, as always, fought a self-possessed battle. He tried to concentrate his fire, as was his custom, on one part of his foe's 'Mech, but Kell's twisting and dodging made that difficult. Yorinaga used his medium and small lasers to keep Kell at bay while his PPCs cooled, and he staggered their use so that Kell could not advance while the *Warhammer* ran hot.

Some observers had described the fight in terms of a martial arts match, while others had regarded it more as an odd dance-of-death. Ishiyama had tracked down all the accounts of the battle, which had so melded in his mind that he felt a perfect understanding of each move

100

and its complicated nuances. It disturbed him deeply to understand the battle so well, yet not be able to understand how his idol could have met such disgrace.

Finally, Kell's medium lasers seemed to have knocked out the *Warhammer*'s right PPC, he sailed in at Yorinaga. To meet him, Yorinaga's right PPC came up and loosed a bolt of argent electricity. The energy slashed into the *Archer*'s right shoulder, searing completely through it. Within a heartbeat, Yorinaga's shot dropped the *Archer*'s melted right arm to the ground, and the maimed 'Mech stumbled to its knees. Kell was finished.

Yorinaga's *Warhammer*, barely thirty meters distant, leveled both PPCs at the stricken Kell Hound. Silver-blue energy erupted from both weapons, but the bolts missed their intended target and instead melted sand into glass beyond Kell. Morgan Kell, in desperation, triggered two flights of LRMs, which sent forty missiles flying from his 'Mech's torso against Yorinaga's *Warhammer*.

Though the flight was too short to arm the warheads, the missiles slammed into the *Warhammer* and battered it savagely. Some propellant tanks exploded and washed the Kurita 'Mech in sheets of golden-red fire. Other missiles smashed and dented armor plates, or crushed heat sinks and shattered joints. Yorinaga's *Warhammer*, though it remained standing throughout the onslaught, might have been a toy abused by a hateful child.

Yorinaga trained all his operable weapons systems on the *Archer* as it rose to its feet, but could not score a hit. It seemed as though Yorinaga's *Warhammer* refused to acknowledge the target's existence. Ishiyama had even heard the stories of MechWarriors present at the battle who said that Kell's dead 'Mech vanished like a ghost from their instrument readings. While lasers flashed and PPC lightning burned the air into ozone around his machine, Morgan Kell did only one thing. His 'Mech, though not built for it, bowed as best it could toward Yorinaga.

Ishiyama remembered the shock in the voices of MechWarriors who had witnessed the barbarian mimicking their traditions. They waited for Yorinaga to destroy him, then to give them the command to destroy the rest of the Kell Hounds. Instead, when Yorinaga's voice filled their ears, they heard a simple haiku:

Yellow bird I see
The gray dragon hides wisely
Honor is duty

Some believed that the enemy's missiles had injured Yorinaga and that this was his death haiku, but it was soon followed by his order that the regiment withdraw. One *Chu-i*, a Lieutenant recently attached to the unit, protested that the *Tai-sa* must be injured and out of his mind. At that, Yorinaga turned both PPCs on the *Chu-i* and melted his *Panther* in a hellish whirlwind of lightning. All understood, then and there, that Yorinaga had some reason for his actions, and so they obeyed him absolutely.

Up to that point, Ishiyama could accept all that Yorinaga had done, for he had acted honorably. He did not surrender. As his men withdrew, all that Lord Kurita would have lost was a *Panther* and the chance to take the world. But, so the whispered stories went, Yorinaga cracked his 'Mech's canopy and tossed out both of his swords to where Morgan Kell could retrieve them.

After the battle on Mallory's World, Yorinaga had traveled to Luthien to report in secret to the Coordinator. It was said that he asked for leave to commit *seppuku*, but that the Coordinator denied him the honor. Instead, Yorinaga was exiled to the monastery on Echo V, and had been there ever since. Aside from this visit by Ishiyama, the only contact with the outside world had by Kurita Yorinaga-ji—the *ji* appended to his name to signify entry into the monastery—was his annual request that the Coordinator permit him to commit *seppuku*.

Ishiyama reached over and picked up the small hammer. He struck the gong softly, but with enough power for the sound to penetrate the paper walls. Again he struck it, again and again until five distinct tones rang out, each one filling the dying echo of its predecessor. After the fifth sound, Ishiyama replaced the hammer, lowered his head and waited.

Slowly, as befitting its great antiquity, the door slid back. Even through the hood of his visitor, Ishiyama could recognize the face. The glittering dark eyes and the long, thin nose lent Yorinaga-ji a noble aspect many men would have killed to possess. Yet Ishiyama could see from the deep creases around Yorinaga-ji's eyes that exile had not been kind to this man.

Yorinaga-ji, moving with the fluid grace natural to a superior MechWarrior, squatted inside the tea chamber and slid the door shut. He turned slowly, but Ishiyama knew, despite the respectful inclination of the man's head, that Yorinaga-ji studied the room the way a field commander might survey a battlefield. Though Ishiyama had expected some hesitation when his visitor saw the red mat on the other side of the table, Yorinaga-ji gave no sign that he noticed.

The MechWarrior-monk crossed to his position at the table and knelt on the rose pink *tatami*. He never looked in Ishiyama's direction. Instead, he bowed deeply toward the Coordinator's empty position, and held the bent-over position for longer than most men could have tolerated. Then, slowly, he straightened up.

Ishiyama, distracted by the crest worn over Yorinaga-ji's breasts, and on the sleeves and back of his kimono, hesitated and almost spoiled the whole *cha-no-yu*. The crest, showing a fierce yellow bird reflected in the eye of a dragon, had been born in the first line of Yorinaga-ji's haiku, and formed an image of his disgrace. All Draconians knew that the Yellow Bird was the Dragon's only enemy, and Yorinaga-ji had retreated from his chance to kill the Yellow Bird when he saw it.

Ishiyama salvaged the ceremony by bowing deeply to the Coordinator's position and holding the bow for even longer than Yorinaga-ji had. He then bowed to Yorinaga-ji and held that bow for nearly as long as his bow to the Coordinator.

"The Coordinator says, *Komban wa*, Kurita Yorinaga-ji." Ishiyama's voice, barely more than a whisper through his mask, came almost as an echo of words from the absent Coordinator's throat.

Yorinaga-ji bowed, but made no reply.

Ishiyama lifted the blue tea bowl up onto the lacquered table. Using Urizen's ladle, he dipped steaming water from the tea urn and brought it down slowly enough for the steam to form a thick white curtain between the urn and the table. In three fluid motions, he filled the bowl with water, releasing a cloud of steam with each move.

As the steam dissipated, Ishiyama again whispered. "The Coordinator says he wishes to apologize for not replying to your annual request to commit *seppuku*. He admits that his own weakness has kept him from contemplating this life without you. He says that he has never replied because he could only deny your requests, and that denial would bring you pain."

Again, silently, Yorinaga-ji inclined his head toward the invisible Coordinator. He paid no conscious attention to the man acting as the Coordinator's surrogate because, as long as the other man wore the black costume, he did not exist. Yet, the tea master's skill was such that, as he added crushed tea leaves to the water and mixed them with so dexterous and easy a motion of the whisk, Yorinaga-ji relaxed unconsciously for the barest of moments.

Ishiyama, his senses almost supernaturally alert during the *cha-no-yu*, sensed Yorinaga-ji's momentary relaxation, and his heart leapt up. Ishiyama immediately gained control of himself and set the whisk down on the table. He cupped the bowl of tea in his hands, utterly ignoring the heat, and placed it before the Coordinator's position.

"The Coordinator says he has found a way to grant the release you desire, while also allowing you to fulfill your duty to him and preserving him from grief for your death." Ishiyama reached out for the tea bowl, rotated it 180 degrees with slow precision, and lifted it across the table. Without a sound, and without a ripple breaking across the top

103

of the tea, he placed the bowl before Yorinaga-ji.

"The Coordinator says that he will form an elite unit around you. They will become the *Genyosha*—the Black Ocean—and you will be their leader. You will train them and pass on the knowledge and skill for which you are so well-known. You will be able to select fifty men, one for each year of your age, from all the forces in the Combine. Then, aside from an ISF liaison officer, you will have no superior but the Coordinator."

Ishiyama lowered his head. "You will be *Iemoto* of the Genyosha for, once you have given them all that you are, they will train fifty men, and those fifty will train fifty until all our forces have your heart and mind."

Ishiyama waited, but Yorinaga-ji did not move. Ishiyama knew that he had presented Yorinaga-ji with his deepest desire. Ishiyama suppressed the desire to smile nervously, but he did marvel at how well the Coordinator knew this man who had been in exile for eleven years.

Ishiyama's voice again filled the room with sounds less substantial than the steam curling up from the tea before Yorinaga-ji. "The Coordinator asked me to mention, as a small item of interest, that plans have already begun for the utter destruction of the Kell Hounds."

Yorinaga-ji inclined his head ever so briefly. Some emotion that Ishiyama could not identify strobed across Yorinaga's face, but was swallowed in the self-control fortified by his exile. Without looking down, Yorinaga-ji unerringly cupped the tea bowl in his hands and raised it to his lips.

BOOK
2

17

Solaris VII (The Game World)
Rahneshire, Lyran Commonwealth

20 February 3027

"*Zao*, Fuh Teng."

Justin Xiang's greeting startled the MechWarrior. Fuh Teng half-turned to see who had crept up on him so quietly, and his movement caused a piece of equipment to shift. Teng's Tech, half-hidden inside the *Vindicator*'s PPC assembly, cursed loudly. Fuh Teng narrowed his eyes. He did not like the looks of the man who had spoken, but could not identify him.

Fuh Teng bowed his head slightly and returned Justin's greeting. "Hello. Is there something I can do for you? You should not be in here, you know."

Justin nodded and thrust his hands even deeper into the pockets of his leather jacket. "So they tried to tell me at the gates. I am Justin Xiang, and I want to fight for you."

Teng frowned. "I need no pilots. I cannot afford them." He looked up at the *Vindicator* looming above them in the darkened warehouse. "I exhausted my resources piecing this 'Mech together from what remnants I could salvage of my last 'Mech and the 'Mech my brother died in."

Justin nodded. The Tech, Tung Yuan, appeared from inside the PPC, and the glare of his arc-welder bleached the color from Teng's face while sinking his eyes into deep shadows. The Tech snapped an order in Capellan. Before Teng, hampered by the brace stiffening his right knee, could move to comply, Justin responded. Easing his duffle-

107

bag from his right shoulder, he crossed to the crate that the Tech had indicated and plucked a silver cylinder half a meter long and half that wide from the plastic foam inside the box.

He held it up toward the Tech, saying, "This is an R-4721 PPC Inhibitor." Justin frowned at Teng. "If you put this in the PPC, you'll get all the flash with none of the punch."

Teng snatched the cylinder from Justin and handed it up to the Tech. "Yes, Xiang, that is true. But it is also true that I do not want the punch."

Justin shook his head. "But if you win the match in Steiner Stadium tonight, you'll have enough money to refurbish your *Vindicator* from top to bottom, and to hire a half-dozen pilots to work for you. With a few well-placed bets, you could even win enough to buy another 'Mech and start a stable."

Teng behaved as though he'd heard none of Justin's words. "Xiang, Xiang..." he mused, then suddenly smiled tensely. "Oh yes, you're the MechWarrior that Hanse Davion banished to our little world. Well, you may have been special where you came from, Justin Xiang, but without a 'Mech, you're nothing here." Teng shrugged, then smiled again weakly. "Understand. I do not mean to be harsh, but there are certain rules here on the Game World."

Justin narrowed his eyes. "You mean you've been ordered to lose the fight."

Teng smiled and the lines around his eyes betrayed his age. "I know survival is the key, and I feel more vulnerable out in Cathay than I do in any of the stadiums. The local oddsmakers have connections within the tongs, and are willing to use them to protect their profits." Fuh Teng shrugged philosophically. "I will be given another chance to win a large purse when it suits the purposes of the planet's masters."

Justin nodded solemnly. "So, in this case, your advice to a warrior without a 'Mech is that he should bet on your opponent?"

Teng nodded. "Your age belies your wisdom."

Justin smiled and bowed. Teng, knowing that the interview had ended, turned back to supervising the repair of his 'Mech. He never saw Justin's gloved left fist arc out and crash into his head. With a quiet gasp, Teng sank into a heap on the floor, and the tool he'd been holding clattered beside him on the ferrocrete.

When Tung Yuan poked his head back out of the PPC, his eyes popped open wide at the sight of his fallen employer. Justin merely smiled up at him. "Switch that inhibitor out of the PPC and blank the recognition system so I can link up with the machine."

Grinning broadly, the Tech nodded assent. Justin winked at him and added, "Then we'll tie up Teng here, and find someone willing to

108

take a very specific bet on this fight at nice, long odds."

Tung Yuan ducked back into the *Vindicator*'s PPC housing. Though he never saw the grim smile take hold of Justin's face, he heard him mutter, *Now, Hanse Davion, I begin to take my revenge. You will long remember this day.*

"My dear Gray Noton, how pleased I am to see you've made it!" Enrico Lestrade, clad in a navy blue dress uniform with more medals and gold braid decorating it than were available in most of the Successor States, moved through the crowd gathered in his private box at Steiner Stadium. He enthusiastically grasped Noton's extended right hand in both of of his own, pumping it furiously. "You honor us with your visit."

As other of Lestrade's guests turned to stare at Noton, he forced himself to smile, inwardly trying to decide whether to shatter Lestrade's clammy, fleshy hand. Instead, he grabbed Lestrade's right elbow tightly and gently squeezed. "So kind of you to invite me here to watch Teng battle Wolfson. It should be a good match."

Lestrade winced at the pressure on his elbow and quickly freed Noton's hand. Lowering his voice, he said, "We should speak. Come to my office."

Noton nodded and followed Lestrade back to a small room. As the door closed behind him, shutting out all the party's noise from the soundproof cubicle, Noton touched a button on his watch and waited for a red light to glow on the face. When nothing happened, Noton smiled to himself. *He's not recording this meeting, and that makes him a fool.* "You have the ticket, Baron?"

Enrico Lestrade nodded. He flexed his right hand several times to try to get some feeling back into it, and frowned at Noton during the process. "I'm sorry, Noton, but that is how I greet all my guests."

Noton's eyes slitted. "I trust you do not have covert deals with all of them." *Doublecross me, Baron, and you will regret it.*

Enrico shook his head and began patting his pockets in search of the betting ticket. "No," he said, "most are visitors from the Commonwealth, and a few from the Federated Suns. Wolfson, being one of the Capellan Mafia—as Capet has so quaintly labeled his pack of warriors—is a great draw. I've even invited him up here after the match."

"You did *what*?" Noton's voice exploded in anger. *If you've done anything to suggest that this fight is fixed, I will have you flayed alive.*

Lestrade recoiled from Noton's tone, as though from a heavy blow. "Come now, don't take me for a fool. I did not invite *him* up. I invited the winner." Smiling conspiratorially, he found the silvery slip of paper and extended it toward Noton. "Just because we know who will win doesn't mean we need to broadcast it."

Noton took the ticket and let a slow smile transform the mask of fury his face had become. His fee, 50,000 credits, had been used to place a bet at two-to-one odds that Wolfson would win. With the fight fixed, Noton got double his fee from the bookmakers on the planet, and no one could trace the transfer of wealth. "Very well. Let us rejoin the party."

Enrico beamed. "You'll be pleased to know, Noton, that the Contessa is here this evening." Enrico opened the door and escorted Noton among the guests, making a few preliminary introductions. Then he slipped away into the chattering crowd. Noton excused himself from a conversation about the neo-abstraction of the Deia traditionalist school, and navigated a path toward the bar.

The bartender smiled up at him. "Sir?"

Noton glanced at the various types of beer half-buried in a tray of ice, but changed his mind. *Business is over. I can afford to drink, especially if Lestrade is paying.* Noton smiled. "A PPC, Steiner, straight up."

The bartender smiled knowingly and set a brandy snifter on the counter. Into it, he poured four shots of grain alcohol, and because Noton had specified "Steiner," he cut it with two shots of peppermint schnapps. He reached for a sprig of mint, too, but Noton warned him off with a shake of his head. The bartender smiled and handed him the drink. "Be careful. That stuff can etch glass."

Noton laughed and cradled the snifter in one hand. He swirled the clear mixture around and watched as it picked up and distorted the sights and colors around him. With a pleased smile, he raised the glass to his lips and swallowed a mouthful of the liquid before it could fully numb his tongue.

"Not a sipping drink, is it, Mr. Noton?" Contessa Kym Sorenson commented as Noton screwed his eyes shut against the drink's jolt.

Noton relaxed his face, then opened his eyes. "You are a most welcome vision, Contessa." She wore high-heeled black boots gathered at the ankles, black trousers, and a sleeveless, strapless satiny green shirt that matched the silk scarf knotted around her pale throat. Noton smiled, took her outstretched hand, and raised it to his lips. "Please, call me Gray."

The Contessa nodded and smiled. "Gray, it is." She turned and leaned against the bar, glancing wearily from the milling crowd to Gray. Pointing at his drink, she said, "Does that make these gatherings any less stuffy?"

Noton shrugged his wide shoulders. The light rippled off the black velvet of his tunic, whose wide "V" of gray velvet running from one shoulder to his waist and back up to the other shoulder made the MechWarrior seem more slender. "Lestrade runs with a rarified crowd. I remember many of these people from the days when the Battle Commission honored me with parties because of my victories out in the Arenas. They've always been stuffy, and, yes,"—he looked down at his drink—"I've found PPCs a great help."

The Contessa turned to the bartender. "I'll have a PPC, too."

The bartender smiled as Noton, standing behind the Contessa, signaled the man to dilute the drink by half. "How would you like that, my lady?"

The Contessa frowned and turned to Noton. "Gray?"

Noton smiled. "The drink has several variations, each one known by one of the Great House names. I drink the Steiner variant, which cuts the white lightning with peppermint schnapps. The Liao version cuts it with plum wine, and the Kuritan dilutes it with *sake*—or aviation fuel, whichever is handier." Noton paused for a moment, trying to recall the other variants. "Davion cuts it with bourbon, or tequila, if you're in the Capellan March."

The Contessa wrinkled her nose. "And Marik?"

The bartender brandished a bottle of ouzo and the Contessa smiled. "I'll have mine Marik." The bartender quickly complied and handed her a snifter identical to the one that Noton was holding.

Noton led the Contessa away from the bar to the first row of chairs looking out over the Arena. "You'd best sit down before you drink that. The first one is something of an experience." Noton waited for her to sit, then dropped into a plush red seat beside her, and began to swirl his drink.

The Contessa aped his motion. "Why do they call it a PPC?"

Noton laughed. "The particle projection cannon is one of the most powerful weapons a 'Mech can carry. It packs a nasty punch, just like this drink." Noton nodded toward her glass. "The trick is to get it down before."

"Before what?"

Noton quickly drank and swallowed. "Try it and see," he whispered hoarsely.

The Contessa reared her head and tossed off the PPC. She swallowed, then coughed and wiped the tears that sprang to her eyes. She waved a hand in front of her mouth for a couple of seconds, then swallowed again. "I see." She coughed again lightly. "My mouth is numb."

Noton smiled. "In about thirty minutes, that numbness will hit your brain. You ought not to notice the stuffiness of the party."

The Contessa smiled and turned to look out the massive window.

111

Below, in a sandy, open arena reminiscent of the coliseums of ancient Rome, a trio of medium 'Mechs battled twice their number of more agile, lighter 'Mechs. Nearly invisible and impossibly delicate, a criss-crossed cage of wires surrounded the arena, separating the killing area from the glassed-in spectator galleries and, above them, the luxury boxes.

The Contessa pointed to the wire mesh. "What is that?"

Noton, sitting back as the drink spread its warmth through his body, knit his brows in concentration. "That is a detonator grid. Any missiles flying from the arena will hit it before they hit the spectator windows. The windows are covered with the same sort of high-impact plastic used in 'Mech canopies, but no one wants to take any chances."

"What about lasers or PPC shots?"

"The grid will siphon off PPC energy. The windows themselves are reflective." Gray laughed and leaned forward. "I remember once using the window to bounce off a shot at a foe's weakened aft armor." He nodded toward the arena. "There can actually be a 'home field advantage' for a warrior who fights regularly in one arena."

Kym furrowed her blond eyebrows. "Neither of the two men we're here to watch is from the Commonwealth, and so neither would have that advantage?"

Noton pursed his lips and watched as one of the battling Mech-Warriors ejected right before his 'Mech exploded. "Billy Wolfson, the guy who will pilot the *Hermes II*, has fought in this arena more times than has Fuh Teng, though Teng has more fights overall."

"Won't a *Vindicator* take the *Hermes* apart? The *Hermes* surrenders five tons and some weaponry." Another explosion down on the killing floor flashed yellow and orange light against Kym's face and hair. "I should think Teng will walk all over this Wolfson."

Noton smiled carefully. "That's what the bookmakers believe. They have Teng a two-to-one favorite over Wolfson."

Kym smiled impishly. "But…"

"But?"

Kym laid her hand on Noton's thick forearm. "You obviously have your own opinion, Gray. Who do you think will win?"

Noton chuckled softly to himself. "Touché. This is Teng's first fight in several weeks. His knee is now braced, and he's fighting without his brother at his side. I think that Wolfson, who is a good fighter on his way up, will win the contest."

Down on the battlefield, two of the medium 'Mechs finished off the last light 'Mech, and the maintenance crew appeared to clear away the debris. They worked quickly and efficiently to tow any 'Mechs unable to leave the arena on their own.

112

Behind Noton and the Contessa, Lestrade's other guests also noticed that the fight had ended. With a whispered rustle of silks and satins, the guests quickly took seats overlooking the field. A few cursed their luck concerning bets on the last battle, and several loudly predicted the outcome of the fight they'd all come to watch. Whenever any overheard pronouncement seemed particularly absurd, Kym turned to Noton and both of them shared a silent laugh.

"Ladies and gentlemen of all nations and races," boomed an announcer's voice. "This is the ninth fight on this evening's card. In the Medium Class, from the stable of Lord Brighton, we have a *Hermes II*. Its pilot, for this evening, is Billy Wolfson."

The cheering in Baron von Summer's box echoed, in a small part, the thunderous ovation from below.

18

Solaris VII (The Game World)
Rahneshire, Lyran Commonwealth

20 February 3027

Justin Xiang reached out with his right hand to adjust the volume on his external microphone. The crowd's applause for Billy Wolfson and his *Hermes II* did not surprise Justin, but the vibrant insistency of it did. *They dearly want him to win.* The loud ovation rasped across his brain like sandpaper and threatened to release the anxiety he'd earlier managed to lock away with a round of tai chi chuan exercises.

I've never fought before an audience, Justin thought, then involuntary laughter filled his neurohelmet. *That's the least of your worries,* he reminded himself. *You've never fought without your left arm before, either.*

He glanced over at the synthetic limb. The ribbon cable, freed from the compartment at his wrist, had neatly clicked into place on the arm rest, and Justin had closed the fingers of his metal hand around the joystick. He did not want the limb falling and jerking the cable free in the middle of combat. Checking and doublechecking, he verified his ability to control the *Vindicator*'s left arm. The 'Mech's hand and the small laser both functioned normally, as reported by the test lights flashing on his command console. He also verified that the missile control was operational for the LRMs. Though they launched from the *Vindicator*'s torso, their controls were also on the left joystick.

Justin's "good" hand controlled the 'Mech's major weapons. The PPC occupying the whole of the *Vindicator*'s right forearm, and the medium laser built into the 'Mech's head were both controlled by the

114

right hand. The joystick control led the targeting system, and the buttons fired the weapons exactly the way Justin remembered it in the simulator on Sakhara.

Justin watched Wolfson's *Hermes II* march into the arena. Slightly to the right and just above the 'Mech's waist, Justin saw the wide maw of an autocannon. Remembering how the *Rifleman's* auto-cannon had shredded his *Valkyrie* in the duel on Kittery, he felt a sudden cold chill.

In an effort to regain control of himself, Justin focused upon the humanoid 'Mech he had to destroy. He knew that it carried a medium laser in its right forearm. Though a formidable weapon, it did not worry him. *That flamer, on the other hand...*

The weapon formed the 'Mech's truncated left arm. Six canisters of fuel, each about the size of a small aircar, ringed a slender cylinder. It opened into a nozzle that most resembled the muzzle of an ancient blunderbuss and measured almost a full meter across. Despite attempts to keep it painted, the nozzle showed only the carbon buildup easily associated with a flamethrower.

Justin nodded his head as the blue and gray *Hermes* stopped and raised its right hand to salute the crowd. That flamethrower could bake him inside the *Vindicator* and force him to eject. Though fire really could not damage his 'Mech, it could prematurely end the fight and rob him of victory. *I cannot allow myself to lose.*

The announcer's voice burst in on Justin's thoughts. "And from Teng Stables, we have a *Vindicator!*"

Justin slowly and deliberately walked the humanoid *Vindicator* onto the field. *It had been* Vindicators *that had once turned House Davion back at Tikonov. How fitting for me to use one now to embarrass the Federated Suns.* Justin raised the 'Mech's left arm to wave at the crowd huddled invisibly behind the mirrored arena walls. Though he heard none of the applause given to Wolfson, he forced the irritation away. *Victors deserve praise, not combatants.*

The announcer's voice, tinged with excitement, again filled the arena and Justin's neurohelmet. "We've just received word that Baron von Summer has issued an invitation for the victor to come to his private box after the battle," Justin heard him say.

Wolfson's *Hermes* turned toward Lestrade's box and saluted, and Justin's 'Mech followed suit, though its pilot performed the action without thought. *He knows. He must know the fight has been rigged.* Justin chuckled to himself. *Billy Wolfson is in for a rude shock.*

"Let the game begin!"

The *Hermes* immediately triggered a burst of autocannon fire that raked across the *Vindicator*, blasting small craters into the torso armor.

115

Justin jerked his 'Mech to the right and dropped to one knee as the *Hermes*'s laser sliced through the air and splintered against the windows around the arena.

Justin popped open the LRM compartment in the *Vindicator*'s chest and launched a flight of five missiles at the *Hermes*. Wolfson quickly moved his 'Mech to the left, keeping the PPC out of line, evading all but one of the missiles. The one that hit peeled back some armor on the *Hermes*'s left leg, while the other missiles exploded against the protective screen.

Concentrate, Justin! You can't afford any sloppy shots! He darted a quick glance at the prosthesis to assure himself that the cable had not broken free. *Wolfson thinks the fight is fixed. Use it against him.*

Wolfson's return shots from both the autocannon and the medium laser slammed into the *Vindicator*'s chest. Autocannon rounds smashed into Justin's armor, tearing divots from it. The laser, firing on the same targeted spot, cauterized the autocannon wounds and melted them into ugly scars. The *Hermes* followed up its shots and closed the gap between the two 'Mechs.

Justin continued to circle his *Vindicator* to the right, then stopped and pivoted on his left foot to swing around and lunge at the *Hermes* with his PPC. His right index finger tightened up on the trigger, and his middle finger jerked the trigger for his medium laser. The heat monitors in the cockpit blazed up from green into the red zone, but Justin ignored the computer's keening complaint about excess heat. The *Hermes*, moving in, strolled directly into his fire zone.

The laser stitched a stuttering line across the *Hermes*' eyes, and the 'Mech jerked as Wolfson reacted to the blinding scarlet light. The beam itself did little more than melt an outer layer of the pilot's canopy, but the shot distracted Wolfson from the need to turn and face the *Vindicator*'s attack.

An azure whip of pure energy lashed out at the *Hermes*. The PPC's beam stabbed at the *Hermes*'s left arm and ripped armor from the flamer with the ease of a cyclone tearing shingles from a roof. The beam caressed the *Hermes* for less than three terrible seconds, but that was enough to strip all but the barest of armor from the smaller 'Mech's fearsome weapon. Suddenly, the flamethrower became a bomb strapped to the side of the *Hermes*, and Wolfson's quick turn showed that he realized the outcome of the fight was not fixed, after all.

As Justin's *Vindicator* moved toward the *Hermes*, Wolfson brought his 'Mech's right arm up and triggered a blast of laser fire to hold him back. The ruby energy beam bubbled ablative armor on the *Vindicator*'s torso, but failed to penetrate further into the 'Mech's working parts. When it did nothing to slow the *Vindicator*'s advance,

Wolfson began to sprint his 'Mech off across the arena.

Justin hit his jump jets and launched a flight of LRMs, aiming the missiles deliberately wide and to the right of the *Hermes*. They exploded in a line of flaming geysers that brought the *Hermes* up short while the *Vindicator* soared above it and almost grazed the arena's mesh roof. Justin grounded the *Vindicator* to the left of the *Hermes*. *Nowhere to run, nowhere to hide, Wolfson.*

Sweat poured down Justin's face and tasted salty on his lips. Ahead of him, the *Hermes* turned. Its medium laser fired a red bolt of energy, while its autocannon boomed out a staccato accompaniment to the rain of metal it spat out. The autocannon slugs plucked away at the armor on the *Vindicator*'s left leg and dotted it with jagged gashes. The laser drilled into the armor on the *Vindicator*'s center torso and burned away the last of it. Enough of the laser fire had penetrated the armor to burn into the heart of the *Vindicator*.

Justin cursed as a red light ignited on his control board. The last of the laser's energy had damaged his 'Mech's gyrostabilizer and would force him to concentrate more on each little motion or get spilled to the ground. He slapped the heat override control and sneered. *This ends now.*

Missiles arced from the *Vindicator* and smashed into the *Hermes*'s right side. The missiles exploded into brilliant orange fireballs, and the *Hermes* staggered as armor plates ripped free. Before the *Hermes* could recover, the blue whiplash of Justin's PPC scourged the newly opened wound. What little armor the missiles had spared, the particle beam evaporated into a metal steam. Melted slag coursed down the *Hermes*'s front, but the beam had failed to bore into the 'Mech's internal structures.

The *Vindicator*'s laser flashed to life and stabbed into the other 'Mech's left arm. It vaporized the remaining armor and shredded the flamethrower's mechanisms. The beam sliced up into the *Hermes*'s armpit and baked the shoulder actuator. The left arm, locked in a slightly forward position, smoldered and began to leak flamer fuel.

Justin cleared a tightbeam channel to his opponent, "Wolfson, your flamer's leaking. Bail out now."

Justin could almost feel the fear coming through the radio link, but Wolfson's words belied it, "Can't. Got a 100,000 credit bond against surrender. You ain't getting that from me."

Justin shook his head and droplets of sweat ran down his neurohelmet's viewplate. "Dammit, you idiot! I don't want it. Get out!"

"Go to hell, you Capellan bastard!" The *Hermes* raised its right arm. The laser and the autocannon both came to life as Wolfson attempted the impossible feat of exchanging shots with a 'Mech that outgunned him. The laser cut flecks of armor from the *Vindicator*'s PPC, and the autocannon shredded the armor on the 'Mech's right leg, but neither shot did enough damage to take the *Vindicator* down.

Justin's flight of missiles sent three explosive charges into the *Hermes*'s right leg, blasting twisted sheets of armor from the thigh. The laser burned into the same limb, excising even greater hunks of armor from the thigh. Neither attack damaged the limb, but that hardly mattered as the PPC flared to life.

The PPC's azure beam drilled through the melted armor on the *Hermes*'s right breast. As the artificial lightning bolt ate into the 'Mech, blue fire burst from the muzzle of the *Hermes*'s autocannon, and a dull explosion belched a black column of smoke from the hole in the 'Mech's chest. Sparks flashed within the oily haze and the *Hermes* seemed to fold in upon itself.

Suddenly, Wolfson jerked his 'Mech upright and charged. As the *Hermes* lurched forward, it accelerated to 97 kph, living up to its name. Wolfson held the 'Mech's right arm wide, and came in for a tackle. His laser flared to life at the last second, but the beam cut wide of its intended mark.

Justin's *Vindicator* ducked under the *Hermes*'s outstretched arm and buried its left fist into the other 'Mech's flank. The giant analog of Justin's own metal hand crushed internal circuitry and came away with wires and the autocannon's ammo chain trailing on it. His medium laser, hastily aimed, sawed yet more armor from the *Hermes*'s right thigh.

Wolfson spun his *Hermes* on its right foot and tried to kick back at the *Vindicator* with its left leg. He failed because Justin's punch to the *Hermes*'s middle had crushed part of the gyro housing. The *Hermes* merely spun to the ground. It landed hard on its left shoulder and ruptured the flamer fuel tanks. Even as the wounded 'Mech settled onto its back, the viscous liquid washed over its torso.

The small laser on the *Vindicator*'s left arm struck like a neon-scarlet viper. The coruscating energy stream ignited the flamer fuel, sending a huge white-yellow tongue of flame licking up at the arena's roof. The fire snapped and crackled in Justin's ears, but did nothing to mask the screams and applause of the spectators.

The *Hermes*'s faceplate blew upward. Wolfson hit his eject button and his command chair exploded out of his 'Mech's head, spinning up into the conflagration. Almost instantly, the chair's gyros kicked in the escape rockets and jetted the chair out of the danger zone. Singed and smoking, Wolfson's chair landed at the *Vindicator*'s feet.

The *Vindicator* squatted over the ejected pilot. Wolfson

scrambled to free himself of the command chair. but the *Vindicator* dropped its hand over the chair and encased it in a cage of fingers. Within his cockpit, Justin reached out his right hand to dial his directional mike in at Wolfson.

"The next time you call me bastard, little man, you'd better win, because otherwise I'll kill you for it."

19

Gray Noton stared out at the killing field and watched his fortune dissipate with the smoke from the *Hermes* as the maintenance crew extinguished the fire. He cursed inwardly at the loss. *I should have known that anything Lestrade arranged would fail and that the little weasel will never reimburse me. I'd love to try, but I can't extort more money from Lestrade without ruining my own reputation.* He also realized that Teng's victory had cost him more than just the fifty thousand credits wagered on the battle. It would cost him five thousand credits to have Teng killed, and probably another ten thousand to make sure that the investigation of Teng's death did not lead back to him. *Damn! I hate the costs of doing business.*

Kym reached out and squeezed Noton's left forearm. "That fight was incredible!" She paused and studied his face. "Gray, you didn't have money on it, did you?"

Noton started, then forced a smile. He shrugged. "A bit, but nothing really." He narrowed his eyes. "Teng has apparently learned to fight while recovering from his injuries."

"Foul!" someone cried behind Noton. The spymaster turned and watched as people pointed at a small holovidscreen set into a wall beside the door. The camera had focused upon the fight's victor as he climbed down from the *Vindicator*'s cockpit. "That's not Fuh Teng!"

What in hell? Noton got up and shouldered his way through the crowd. A couple of people made to protest, but changed their minds at

120

the look of angry concentration on Noton's face. He reached the front ranks and stared hard at the man who had just won the battle.

The MechWarrior's dark hair, almond-shaped eyes, and yellowish skin marked him as Capellan, but Noton had never seen him before. As the camera concentrated on the victor's face, Noton did recognize the wolfish look of hunger. He knew that he had once worn that same expression. *This one is a killer.*

"Not fair!" shouted a noble from the Federated Suns, brandishing bet stubs as though they were legal documents. "We wagered that Billy Wolfson would defeat Fuh Teng! We were cheated!"

"Shut up!" Noton snapped at him. "Just shut up. If you look at your tickets, you'll see that you bet on a *Hermes II* defeating a *Vindicator*." Noton stabbed a finger back at the arena viewport. "That was not a challenge match. Neither pilot specified the warrior he was to face. You may not like it, but anyone who owns stables of 'Mechs knows that a last-minute change of pilots is not illegal. The machines battle, and any fool old enough to bet should have known that a *Vindicator* would eat a *Hermes* alive!"

Noton posted one arm on either side of the holovision screen. The camera had panned back as the MechWarrior pulled on a jumpsuit. Noton's heart caught in his throat as he caught a glimpse of a blue-steel forearm slipping into a sleeve. Even before he had time to voice his suspicion, the name "Justin Xiang" appeared on the screen as the announcer stumbled his way through an impromptu history of the fight's victor.

Justin, freshly showered and clad in a black leather jacket over a blue jumpsuit, entered the elevator and pushed the button to close the door. "Baron von Summer's box," he said. "I am expected."

The elevator, responding to his voice command, jerked upward, then glided smoothly to the left. Halfway around the arena, it slowed and stopped.

The door opened and Justin found himself staring out at a semicircle of hostile people. "Go away, traitor," spat one white-haired gentleman. "You are not wanted here!"

Justin frowned but made no reply as Enrico Lestrade broke through the crowd to offer Justin his hand. "Pay no attention to them, Justin Xiang. They are angry because you cost them money." Behind the Baron, Gray Noton and Contessa Kym Sorenson had drifted in through the angry guests.

"He betrayed Hanse Davion, Baron!" The noblewoman who spoke wore a tartan that Justin identified instantly. *She was from Firgrove.* Andrew Redburn was a native of that same Capellan March

121

coreworld and had hung a blanket of the same pattern on the wall of his Kittery quarters.

The noblewoman shook a fist in Justin's face. "This man sold out the Federated Suns to House Liao just the way he cheated here tonight."

Justin opened his mouth to reply, but Contessa Kym Sorenson thrust out a finger at the woman. "Always complaining, aren't you, Doris MacDougal? One might think Firgrove's major product was gripes. But then it'd have to beat out excuses, wouldn't it?" Kym straightened up and took in all the Federated Suns nobility with one harsh stare. "You all bet your nationality, but just because Hanse Davion's troops regularly defeat Liao's soldiers doesn't mean the same has to happen here. Perhaps gripes and excuses fall behind one other product of Firgrove—errors of judgement!"

The Davion nobles drew back from the Contessa's assault, but Enrico Lestrade did not let them escape. "This man won, and he is my guest. You'd not want me to go back on my word, would you? As I recall, all of you thought that an invitation to the victor was a good idea, especially when you thought it would be Billy Wolfson! Whoever doesn't like it here may leave right now."

Lestrade's challenge broke the ranks of the angry nobles, who drifted off in pairs or trios to stare coldly at Justin. Their remarks, which included words like "traitor" and "bastard", were voiced just loudly enough to reach Justin. Kym Sorenson glared back at the Capellan March nobles and slipped her arm through Justin's as she steered him toward the bar and well away from the deprecating whispers.

Away from the angry nobles, Justin jerked his left arm from the Contessa's grasp. "I do not need your protection, my lady!"

Kym flashed an arctic blue stare at Justin. "I am not protecting you, Mr. Xiang," she said coldly, looking past him toward the other Federated Suns contingent. "I despise boors and poor losers," she said. "You are merely a convenient vehicle for getting under their skin."

Am I? Justin snorted. "Typical behavior for a Federat."

Kym's eyes narrowed to slits. "My, we have a sharp tongue, and we've picked up the local slang quickly, haven't we?" She stabbed a finger into the center of his chest. "I'm not going to be saddled with your anger at everything to do with House Davion. I'm here because my daddy finds it embarrassing that I share the view that most Capellan Marchers are parasites on the body of the Federated Suns. I haven't been afraid to say that out loud, either, which is not very good for business. Hanse Davion kicked you out of the Federation. It was my father who booted me. Cut back on your jump jets."

Justin boldly appraised Kym Sorenson, then slowly nodded. *She*

122

sees me as a way to strike back at her father and the Federated Suns. I find her very attractive, and very different. "Very well. You're right. As they say, 'Enemy of my enemy is my friend'. I am Justin Xiang, and I did appreciate your help back there."

The hint of a smile broke through Kym's angry expression. "And I am Contessa Kym Sorenson. Pleased to have been of service." Kym extended her right hand and Justin enfolded it in a warm grasp.

Justin noticed that she held onto his hand just a bit longer than necessary, giving it a little squeeze before she released it and turned toward the large man with a shaved head standing beside her. "Justin Xiang, this is Gray Noton."

Justin extended his hand to Noton and met the firm grip with an equal amount of power. Neither man tried to crush the other's hand, but their grips conveyed a great deal about each man's considerable strength of personality. "Gray Noton...I remember hearing about some of your fights on the flight insystem. You must have been very good...Many people referred to up-and-coming fighters as 'new Gray Notons'."

Noton smiled quizzically. "I have not lost all my ability, but I bow to one of your skill. You turned the *Hermes* with that flight of missiles. Not many fighters here on Solaris would waste munitions that way."

Justin smiled. "Ascribe it to the bad habits I picked up during Operation Galahad, those military exercises that Prince Davion put his troops through last year. He is generous with missiles, and as a battalion commander, I had to find new and interesting ways to use them."

Noton smiled warily. "I believe that Solaris is not at all prepared for you, Justin Xiang."

Justin laughed and offered Kym his left arm. "Shall we?" Justin pointed toward the bar. "I'm definitely in the mood for drink."

Kym Sorenson reached out and stabbed the glowing blue button on her Hurricane's dashboard. The passenger-side gullwing door descended on a whisper and shut out the cold, moist air. She closed her eyes and leaned back in the driver's seat. The gentle vibration of the aircar relaxed her.

Her index finger punched a number into the car's phone. She heard the chittering hum of a dial tone, then the piercing wail of a computer carrier before the phone muted the sharp sound. She punched in several more numbers, then picked up the receiver and spoke only one word, "Contact."

Putting the phone down, Kym watched raindrops splash across the Hurricane's windscreen. A shadow flashed in front of the vehicle, and she opened the passenger door in response to Justin's light knock.

The Capellan MechWarrior slid into the thickly padded leather seat and tossed his bag into the small storage area behind Kym's seat. He started to open his mouth, but Kym pressed the fingers of her right hand to his lips.

"I don't know why I'm doing this, either, Justin. Suffice it to say that I'm very attracted to you." She glanced back over her shoulder at the garish red and yellow phosphoron facade of the Morpheus Hotel. "I will not have you stay in that place. Need you more of an explanation?"

Justin kissed her fingers and shook his head.

20

Nicholas Jones cleared his throat nervously. "I don't think this is going to work, sir."

Lieutenant Colonel Patrick Kell shifted his gaze from the dignitaries alighting from the Lyran DropShip and looked at the sergeant. "Mr. Jones, don't tell me you're anxious about how Joss will react?" *Get any paler and I'll send for a medic.*

Jones stammered. "W-well, sir, I am close to retirement, and I am still part of the Lyran Commonwealth Armed Forces, even though I've been assigned to your command. I don't want any problems, if you know what I mean."

Patrick's chuckle did little to hearten the enlisted man. "Don't worry, Nick. I doubt she'll even notice your uniform. Now back in line. They're here."

Patrick Kell stepped forward with a smile and extended a hand to Hauptmann-General Sarah Joss. "Welcome to Pacifica, Hauptmann-General. As always, the Kell Hounds are honored by your visit."

The Lyran officer, her long blond hair glittering with highlights from the dying sun, frowned. She looked beyond Kell at the collection of Techs and astechs in the Kell Hound unit dress uniforms. "I hope you have an explanation, Lieutenant Colonel, because I do not find this amusing at all."

Kell winked at her and cleared his throat to cover the sound of Jones's stricken gasp, then turned to the man following behind her.

125

"Colonel Sortek, how very good to see you again. Shall I introduce you to my staff?"

Pacifica's growing breeze drove dust along the ferrocrete of the spaceport and tousled Sortek's brown hair. He squinted and looked closely at the men and women standing with Kell. "They've changed since I last saw them, haven't they, Patrick?" Sortek offered Kell his hand and the two MechWarriors shook hands heartily.

Sortek immediately turned and brought Leftenant Redburn forward. "Patrick Kell, meet Leftenant Andrew Redburn."

Kell smiled warmly. "Welcome to Pacifica, Leftenant."

Redburn nodded and shook Kell's extended hand. "Thank you, Colonel."

Kell laughed. "Call me Patrick." He turned back to Hauptmann-General Joss. "Please don't look at me that way, General. I'm not doing this to embarrass you before these distinguished guests, despite the fact that the Kell Hounds hate duty here." Joss opened her mouth to protest, but Kell cut her off with a friendly laugh. "No. We've something more diabolical planned."

Kell turned to Nick Jones. "Captain Allard, please conduct the troops inside before a storm starts blowing." He nodded to the woman wearing Major Ward's uniform. "Mare, would you be so kind as to ask Major O'Cieran's jump troopers to roust the last radio outlet to see if it's reported the bait is down?"

She nodded and spoke into the radio microphone clipped near her left shoulder. Kell turned to his guests. "Smile, my friends, because the Kurita insurgents want to make sure you have a pleasant visit. We've jammed their audio pickups, but there'll be someone watching with binoculars to confirm your identities."

Joss frowned. "What did you mean by calling us bait?"

Kell laughed. "Kurita has had elements of the 2nd Sword of Light orbiting Chara IV for the past two weeks."

The expression on Joss's face darkened like the stormy Pacifica sky. "We scanned nothing from the nadir jump point."

Kell led his guests across the ferrocrete toward the 'Mech bays. "And you wouldn't, General, because they took care against that. The problem is that they did not take Captain Janos Vandermeer into account."

Sortek laughed. "Is that old pirate still in charge of the *Cucamulus*? I thought he'd be dead by now."

Kell shook his head. "He's too mean to die." At the blank stares of both Joss and Redburn, he quickly explained. "Vandermeer, over the years, has collected an enormous amount of information about alternate jump points. Most JumpShip captains use the zenith or nadir

126

points of the system sun's gravity well to jump in and out of a system because that's where it's easiest to recharge the Kearny-Fuchida drives. But a safe jump point merely needs to be sufficiently distant from any object of mass in a system. Many of the early Star League captains used to bring in their ships much closer to a system's planets to save the DropShips time traveling to and from from the planet."

Joss's grin lit her pretty face. "Vandermeer has the *Cucamulus* in a position where he spotted the Kurita vessels?"

Kell nodded. "That's a confirmed kill, General. The second your JumpShip appeared in system, Janos reported Kurita preparations." Kell looked at his watch. "Their DropShips are scheduled to land in three hours." He looked up at Sortek. "So, Colonel, did they ship you out on this tour just to look, or did your Prince give you a toy to play with?"

"What?"

Kell stepped into the 'Mech bay, and the three visitors stopped just inside the doorway. Kell waved his hand at the empty hangar. "The Kell Hounds own half the Kurita spies on Pacifica. We know the ETA, landing sites, and troop strengths for two of the three DropShips. As you can see, my hounds are out waiting for our visitors." Kell hid the situation's grim seriousness behind a smile. "Would you like to join us?"

Sortek laughed, but turned to Hauptmann-General Joss. "What do you think, General?"

Before she could answer, Kell cut in with one last comment. "Trust me, Sarah, this'll beat anything else Pacifica has to offer in the way of nightlife."

The *Kiken*'s pilot brought the *Overlord* Class DropShip to a soft landing beyond the night-cloaked hills where the main body of the Kell Hounds waited hidden. Storm clouds boiled up and quickly filled the hole burned through them by the DropShip's ion engines. Thin threads of argent lightning crackled through the clouds as the energy released into the atmosphere built and flowed through the storm system.

The egg-shaped DropShip settled down on the moist ground in an artificial fog. Its weapons turrets revolved like bug-eyes on stalks as the gunners sought out any hostile targets. Air hissed from within the pressurized ship as the crew blew the hatches. Ramps descended from the 'Mech bays, allowing the 'Mechs to troop slowly from their steel cocoons. As the Kurita spies had reported, the Kell Hounds had no fighter cover up. As nearly as the Kuritans could tell, the Hounds did not know that their ships had landed.

Daniel Allard glanced over at his ops board for the fiftieth time to reassure himself that the "land-line" indicator remained lit. While it burned its cool blue, Allard's communications came and went without fear of interception on a slender optic fiber stretched out behind his *Valkyrie*. On the other end, Colonel Kell waited in his *Thunderbolt*.

"We have confirmation, Patrick. This is part of the 2nd Sword of Light. I've got a company of *Panther*s, a mixed medium lance of SHD-2K *Shadow Hawk*s with PPCs, and *Griffin*s—two of each."

Kell's voice crackled back into Dan's ears. "What else do they have, Dan? They should be unloading the heavy stuff now."

Dan studied his scanner displays again and swallowed hard. He toggled between the two reports the battle computer offered him on the scanner screen. "Here's the bad news, Patrick. I've got a *Dragon*, perhaps one of the new *Grand Dragon* designs."

Dan ordered up magnification on his main monitor and keyed the reference number—0-931787-84-Xp-74d—into his battle computer. The cursor blinked down at the bottom of the screen, then the computer redrew the complete scanner diagram and added the stored information from that file. "I've got a match. It *is* a *Grand Dragon*, so it's sporting a PPC in the right arm and a third medium laser in the right torso." Dan looked up at a light flashing on the scanner display. "This is odd..."

"What, Dan?" Patrick Kell's voice remained even, despite the commanding urgency in his words.

"The *Panther*s are forming up into a spearhead, with the medium lance on the west flank and the *Grand Dragon* in the middle. They're coming right at you, but the *Dragon*'s not moving. It seems to be waiting for something."

Kell's light laugh traveled to Dan ungarbled and brought with it the assurance of victory. "Perfect. The lighter 'Mechs are drifting out to establish a perimeter without the *Dragon*'s firepower. Remember the plan, Dan. The Kuritans consider "five" to be a lucky number and things in fives to be an omen. Let's take five 'Mechs out in the initial ambush, and it'll spook them. Coordinates transmitting...Now. Good luck."

"And to you, Patrick. Severing land line and returning to command of my lance." Dan punched the blue land-line button and it died. He radioed a tightbeam broadcast back to Brand, and his Lieutenant replayed it for Meg Lang and Eddie Baker. It provided them with targets for their initial attacks, and secondary targets after that. Dan quickly reviewed the assignments and shook his head. It would not be pretty.

The eastern wing of the *Panther* formation came up over the hills surrounding the landing site. One *Panther*, which Dan's computer labeled "Able"—the last one in the wedge—stood atop the hillock, only a hundred meters from where Dan's *Valkyrie* lay beneath a scanner baffle. The *Panther*'s head swung slowly from side to side as though the MechWarrior inside imagined himself the lord of all he surveyed.

Dan trained his medium laser's targeting crosshairs on "Able," but brought his LRM sight to rest and lock-on to the next *Panther*— "Bravo"—in line. He kept both target icons following the appropriate 'Mechs almost automatically as he focused his attention on the spearhead's lead *Panther*. It had stopped short and brought up the PPC on its right arm.

A light flared in Dan's cockpit, signaling the attack. "Fire!" Dan stabbed his thumb down on the left-hand joystick and launched a flight of LRMs at the further of the two *Panthers*. Six missiles struck their target. Five smashed into the left side of the 'Mech's chest and succeeded in chipping away armor in a glowing metal rain. The sixth missile exploded against the other side of "Bravo's" chest, but failed to check the involuntary rotation the other missiles had imparted to the *Panther*.

Dan's medium laser lanced into "Able" and seared an ugly scar into the armor of its right arm. SRMs, launched by Brand's *Commando* and Lang's *Wasp* peppered the "Able" from head to toe. Medium laser fire pierced the smoke and flames left behind by the missile, and shredded the armor on the 'Mech's right leg. Dan saw myomer-fiber muscles corded around titanium 'Mech bones. *Able's doomed. That leg won't take much more damage.*

He brushed the fingers of his right hand across the toggle switch, and his scanner immediately reported "Bravo's" condition. Laser fire from Baker's *Jenner* had added to the damage his LRMs had done. All the armor from the *Panther*'s left torso had been blown or lazed away to expose the 'Mech's circuitry and other vital parts to the murderous fire from the ambush. Hanging in tatters, the armor on the right leg and right torso showed further damage from the *Jenner*'s battery of medium lasers.

Dan looked up and saw Cat Wilson's black and red *Marauder* step from ambush. The hunched-over 'Mech thrust its right claw at the wedge's lead *Panther*. The *Marauder*'s right PPC spat a jagged bolt of man-made lighting. The blue fire licked greedily at the *Panther*'s chest and instantly vaporized all the armor it touched. The *Marauder*'s twin medium lasers slashed surgically at the *Panther*'s left arm and stripped it of armor as though it were so much bark off a tree. *The Marauder*'s autocannon blasted the *Panther* and gouged massive craters in the armor over the 'Mech's right thigh.

Bethany Connor's *Crusader*, moving up through the jungle behind Wilson's *Marauder*, similarly targeted the lead *Panther*. Panels flicked open on the *Crusader*'s forearms. Two flights of LRMs burned into the night sky. The missiles spiraled down into the *Panther*, and one complete flight crushed the 'Mech's chest like a hammer-blow. Fragments of armor, frozen in mid-flight by the strobing explosions, filled the air like a flight of frightened birds. The rest of the *Crusader*'s missiles tore at the *Panther*'s right leg, denting and blasting away armor.

Fire from Ward's Assault Lance ripped mercilessly into the *Panther* designated "Echo." Diane McWilliams's *Rifleman* and Mary Lasker's *Trebuchet* combined their fire to strip armor off their target. The *Trebuchet*'s twin LRMs flights bracketed the *Panther* and blasted every shred of armor from either arm. Four of the LRMs smashed into the *Panther*'s head and ripped away part of its armor, giving the 'Mech a torn lip and a scorched face. The *Rifleman*'s autocannon fire easily peeled off the *Panther*'s chest armor, while its pair of medium lasers melted all but the last of the enemy 'Mech's right leg.

Colonel Kell and Lieutenant Finn combined their attack to hideous effect on the *Panther* that Dan's readout nicknamed "Foxtrot." Kell trained his *Thunderbolt*'s large laser on the 'Mech's right torso, and the ruby beam boiled the armor away like honey on a stove. Finn's *Orion* added its medium laser to the wound and burned through to the interior. Sparks flashed as circuits melted on the enemy 'Mech. The thick black smoke curling from the wound suggested that the laser had burned away a number of heat sinks. Without them, no 'Mech could operate for long, especially a PPC-armed *Panther*.

Major Salome Ward in her *Wolverine*, and her lancemate, Lieutenant Fitzhugh in his *Catapult*, concentrated their fire on one of the modified *Shadow Hawk*s. The *Catapult*'s two launching racks, located where its bird-like 'Mech should have had wings, flipped open to corkscrew thirty LRMs through the Pacifica darkness. They struck in waves, and exploded thunderously. With so much fire concentrated on the *Shadow Hawk*'s left arm, it appeared utterly consumed. As the fire melted into the night, the *Hawk*'s left limb lay completely vulnerable. Mangled beyond use, the hand and forearm hung frozen in place.

The *Wolverine*'s SRM flight exploded in an even line across the *Shadow Hawk*'s torso. Though the *Wolverine*'s autocannon and medium laser blasted and burned huge slabs of armor from the *Shadow Hawk*'s left side, they had failed to breech the armor. The medium lasers of Fitzhugh's *Catapult* sliced through the *Shadow Hawk*'s right leg armor, laying bare the myomer muscle. This left the 'Mech scanner-tagged "Golf" with the appearance of having only one of its trouser legs on.

130

Leftenant Redburn's *Hunchback* stepped into the open and chased a *Griffin* out from amid the flames and smoke. The massive, boxy autocannon perched on the *Hunchback*'s right shoulder vomited fire and metal, a hellish stream that tore through the *Griffin*'s chest like a crosscut saw. Armor fragmented and spun away in jagged shards of waste-metal. Simultaneously, the *Hunchback*'s medium lasers chopped armor from the *Griffin*'s left flank and arm.

The ferocity of Redburn's assault staggered the *Griffin*. The potency of Hauptmann-General Sarah Joss's attack finished it. Joss's *Warhammer* seemed to regard the stricken *Griffin* pitilessly, as the 'Mech raised its PPCs.

One blue bolt flashed from the *Warhammer* and probed the *Griffin*'s half-melted left arm with a savage touch. Armor exploded and rocketed across the battlefield as blue lightning further mauled the damaged arm. Joss's attack left the 'Mech's limb twisted and fused to the shoulder in a fire-blackened lump.

The second tongue of electrical fire launched itself into the *Griffin*'s heart, stabbing into the *Griffin*'s chest and melting all that it touched. Fire roared through the 'Mech's torso and jetted out through every heat sink and maintenance crawlway in the 'Mech's body. The *Griffin* shuddered and twitched as the blue lighting tightened every myomer muscle in its body. The 'Mech fell back heavily, the center of its chest a cherry hellpit, and lay staring up at the sky.

Confidence flared to life in Dan's heart. *We've hammered them hard and badly damaged six 'Mechs—better than we'd planned. They've got to pull back.* Then Dan looked up as another 'Mech marched from the DropShip's titanium womb. The ground trembled beneath its massive feet. His scanners instantly studied it and provided a data readout. Humanoid in configuration, the 'Mech's hunched shoulders hid its small head. Huge winglike counterbalances for the arms projected up past the shoulders. The left arm ended in a crude club, while the scanners reported that the right arm and the twin chest-muzzles contained PPCs.

Oh, my God! Dan's mouth went dry as the *Awesome* filled his monitors. He shuddered as his confidence wavered like a candle in a tornado. Suddenly, he remembered what they always said at the New Avalon academy, joking to hide the terror in the thought. *"It's not over until the Assault 'Mechs have finished playing.*

21

The Kurita *Awesome* lumbered forward like a starving man toward a feast. The pilot raised the 'Mech's mace-like left fist as a threat while surveying the battlefield. He trumpeted a widebeam challenge to anyone foolish enough to fight him, and began to recite his impressive list of battles and victories. It was apparent from the casual way the *Awesome* moved and feinted toward possible foes that the pilot did not expect anyone to be so foolish as to pick up the gauntlet.

Ardan Sortek's *Victor* waded through burning *Panther*s and stepped over the fallen *Griffin*. Resplendent in the blue and gold of the Davion Home Guards, it looked utterly out of place among the 'Mechs camouflaged for jungle warfare. The battlefield flames skittered in glittering highlights off the humanoid 'Mech's gold trim, but failed to pierce the dark canopy over the cockpit. As smoke from the *Griffin* twisted up and around it like offertory incense, the *Victor* waited.

The *Awesome* turned, and the pilot shifted the mace in a salute to his enemy. The mace fell and the PPC mounted on the right arm came up in the same motion. The battle slowed as the two massive Assault 'Mechs opened the gates of hell to attack one another.

Three ropes of icy blue plasma groped over the *Victor*. Wherever they touched, armor melted like wax under a blowtorch. The PPC beams encircled the *Victor*'s legs in an energy snare and tightened. Armor bled down the legs of Sortek's 'Mech in steaming rivulets, nearly stripping the right limb naked. Yet the horrible energy failed to crush the *Victor* as it would have any of the other 'Mechs on the field.

Sortek's counterattack blazed forward in a cyclone of sizzling metal and ruby spears of light. The projectiles streaming from the autocannon in the *Victor*'s right arm flayed armor from the *Awesome*'s right leg. The medium lasers on the *Victor*'s left arm stabbed out in tandem, slicing long slivers of armor from the left side of the *Awesome*'s chest. The *Victor*'s SRMs, launched from four tubes over the Assault 'Mech's left breast, blasted sheets of armor from the *Awesome*'s mace-arm.

Again the *Awesome*'s PPCs flared to life, their blue energy vipers striking at random. One gnawed armor from the torso of Sortek's *Victor*. The other two nipped armor from the 'Mech's arms, but Ardan Sortek's machine gave no sign of noticing. Instead, it returned the fire, giving better than it got.

The *Victor*'s autocannon burst scourged the remaining armor from the *Awesome*'s left arm, but failed to destroy the now-exposed myomer muscles. Meanwhile, Ardan's lasers vaporized armor on the *Awesome*'s left leg and right arm, and his four SRMs ripped an angry scar across the enemy 'Mech's head. The *Awesome* flinched, as though the pilot were shaken by the explosions.

As Dan watched the war between the two titanic 'Mechs, he realized that the rest of the battle had stopped in an informal truce around the two Assault 'Mechs. All of them knew that those two pilots would decide the outcome of their petty struggle. This battle would make history, and the two MechWarriors fighting it were destined for immortality. Just to be present was an honor any MechWarrior would cherish.

The *Awesome* again belched out three spears of artificial lightning. One drilled to the center of the *Victor*, and managed to punch a small hole through Sortek's armor without breeching it entirely. The energy singed the gyrostabilizer deep in the 'Mech's chest, however. The *Victor* shuddered and staggered, but Sortek's cool hand on the controls righted the enormous machine before it could topple. The other two shots, which melted angry weals on the *Victor*'s left arm and torso, did nothing but burn armor and paint from their target.

Sortek's angry counterpunch slammed into the *Awesome*'s left shoulder, stripping the myomer muscles from the limb, then snapped the titanium bone like a dry stick. The heavy limb spun off through the smoky darkness and blasted a hapless *Panther* to the ground.

The *Victor*'s lasers stabbed out from its left wrist to slash armor from the *Awesome*'s torso. Metal steam rose from the lasers' ragged incisions, and molten metal dripped from the wounds. At the same time, the SRMs spiraling out from the *Victor*'s chest exploded great

133

craters in the armor of the *Awesome*'s left thigh.

Sortek, fighting against the damaged gyro, boldly jetted his *Victor* to the right. The tactical shift caught the *Awesome*'s pilot by surprise because few warriors ever expected an Assault 'Mech to be jump-capable. The Kurita pilot's attempt to pursue came too slowly. He hurriedly triggered the *Awesome*'s PPCs, but only one of them hit. It lashed out at the *Victor*'s right flank and boiled away armor, but that did not stop Ardan Sortek.

Sortek's *Victor* circled and closed like a tiger smelling blood. Two laser lances skewered the *Awesome*'s left flank, eroding armor and washing it away in a flash of ruby light. SRMs drilled through the hole where the *Awesome*'s left arm had once hung and landed inside the 'Mech's thick chest. The missile hits splashed coolant from shattered heat sinks thoughout the 'Mech.

Sortek stabbed his autocannon forward and nearly touched it to the *Awesome*'s wounded flank. The weapon's unholy metallic hail crushed straight through the enemy's remaining armor and opened a gaping wound in the chest of the *Awesome*. The projectiles filled the 'Mech with jagged, ricocheting shrapnel. Pieces of circuitry rained out of the wound amid myomer fibers and pulverized structural components. Worse, as the autocannon shells ate into the *Awesome* like cancer, they consumed the fusion engine's shielding.

The *Awesome*'s head burst open. The pilot vaulted out in his command chair seconds before a geyser of silver-gold fire ripped up through the cockpit. Freed of all constraints, the captive sun that had powered the 'Mech now turned on its charge. Superheated plasma boiled up and out from the *Awesome*'s belly. It grew and grew into a roiling cloud of golden energy, then exploded free of the big 'Mech's shell.

The scattered bits of armor and weaponry peppered the forces gathered around the *Awesome*. The 'Mech's right arm spun off in the light of the artificial sun and snapped a *Shadow Hawk* off at the knees. Whirling armor fragments and the explosion's force toppled some of the lighter Kurita 'Mechs, while Dan fought to control his *Valkyrie* against the armor shards peppering it.

The *Awesome*'s spectacular death broke the truce on the battlefield, but it also shattered the Kuritans' spirit. As resistance evaporated, the Draconian assault withered. Delirious over the battle's outcome, but not foolish enough to pursue the enemy back inside the protective umbrella of the DropShip's weapons, the Kell Hounds allowed the Kuritans to withdraw.

* * *

Patrick Kell wiped beer foam from his upper lip and nodded at Dan Allard. "Your lance came out all right?"

Dan settled back against the couch in Kell's office. Next to him sat Salome Ward. Beyond her, Cat Wilson had perched on the couch's arm. Kell was behind his desk while Redburn, Sortek, and General Joss had seated themselves at the poker table. Positioned beside the door stood Major Seamus Fitzpatrick and Major Richard O'Cieran.

Dan nodded in response to Kell's question. "We beat those two *Panther*s pretty bad. I'm the only one who took any damage, though. A couple of SRMs to the chest as the *Panther*s retreated. We'd moved inside their PPCs' effective range, which gave the *Panther* pilots a couple of targets that they just couldn't hit." He shrugged easily, and everyone understood that the damage was insignificant.

Kell turned back to Major Fitzpatrick. "Seamus, what did your flyboys find?"

Fitzpatrick, a red-haired pilot slender almost to the point of cadaverousness, smiled like a fox in a henhouse. "We had one company of *Panther*s, who must have been very green because they waved when we made our first pass." Fitzpatrick noticed the frown on General Joss's face and quickly explained. "We're flying aerofighters that we captured from the Kuritans a long time ago. With advance word on this attack, we decorated the underside of our craft with appropriate decals." Fitzpatrick's smile and easy posture admitted that the ploy might not be fair, but his company was attacking dirt-pigs, and everyone knew that MechWarriors would fall for anything.

General Joss narrowed her eyes. "I hope the tactic worked."

Fitzpatrick nodded enthusiastically. "Bagged an even dozen and came away without a scratch." The Major turned to Kell. "Rob Kirk got his sixth 'Mech in this operation. We'll need to set a date for his award."

Kell nodded and scribbled a note to himself. "So, Richard, did your men encounter any trouble?"

Major O'Cieran pushed a hand back through steel-gray hair. This short and barrel-chested man looked more like a Master-Sergeant than a Major, but his talent for tactics and organization far exceeded anything an NCO might grasp. "No difficulties. As you directed, we rounded people up for questioning, but confiscated no broadcasting equipment."

General Joss frowned. "Isn't that irregular, Colonel Kell?"

Kell looked at his boots for a moment before answering. "That it is, General, but right now, we know who the spies are, and we are able to monitor their communications. They gave us the information about two of the three landing sites, and that's how we were able to plan our

135

ambush. If we take the spies and their equipment, Kurita will just put more in and we'll have to find them all over again."

"What happened with the third landing site?" Ardan Sortek interjected.

Kell reached down and took a yellow sheet of paper from his desk. "The DropShip came down in Branson's Swamp. That's a bog about a hundred klicks north of here. It looks like the ship got mired and finally fought its way free."

O'Cieran spoke up. "A group of my recon boys scouted the area. Looks like a *Union* Class ship. We found no tracks to indicate that anything got offloaded. Furthermore, our ground ops people reported that the ship's performance and acceleration profile said it came and left with the same mass."

Kell frowned. "How long was it down?"

O'Cieran's nod showed that he shared his commander's concern. "Two hours."

Redburn leaned his chair back. "Excuse me, sir, but we've got peat bogs on my homeworld of Firgrove. If the Kuritans used pumps to load water into their DropShip, wouldn't it have the same mass, regardless of what they dropped off?"

Kell chuckled in a low voice. "On target, Leftenant, as you were earlier this evening." He looked over at Fitzpatrick. "Did the *Panthers* jet out of the DropShip?"

The Major nodded. "Hung there like balloons."

Kell bit his lower lip, then drained the last of the stout from his mug. "We'll tighten things up around here. We have to assume that a full company of *Panthers*—at the very least—is operational and waiting on Pacifica. I'll have the computer section calculate the Drop-Ship mass versus any configuration of jump jet-equipped 'Mechs to see what's the most horrible thing we can come up with."

The staff nodded their understanding, and Kell smiled. "Pending that report, this meeting is formally dismissed." Kell nodded to Ardan Sortek. "I now convene the first annual Ardan-Sortek-saved-our-asses party!"

Ardan Sortek and Andrew Redburn found Daniel Allard down in the 'Mech bay watching the Techs swarm over the *Victor*. Arc torches bonded new armor plates to those partially melted by the *Awesome*'s assault. One astech crawled into the *Victor*'s chest through the hole that a PPC had drilled into it. His long, low whistle echoed through the whole 'Mech, and set the three MechWarriors to laughing.

Ardan Sortek extended his hand to Dan. "It was good seeing you again, Dan. I look forward to our next meeting."

136

Dan chuckled. "Just see if you can talk Prince Davion into giving us a better contract than the one we've got with Katrina Steiner, O.K.? I don't mind working for Kell's kin, but she never gives us exciting duty."

Sortek raised an eyebrow and studied his 'Mech again. "Are you sure you mean that?"

Dan laughed. "Touché." He jerked a thumb at the *Victor*. "Jackson, our best Tech, tells me they're going to rebuild a gyro housing from some pieces of the *Awesome*. We'll fix this baby up and repaint it for you. You'll get it back as good as new." Dan shot a covert glance at some of the astechs. "But don't be surprised if your company insignia changes to the Kell Hounds."

Sortek nodded, then caught sight of Colonel Kell and General Joss out of the corner of his eye. "I'd best catch up with them. I'll give your best to Quintus and your mother when next I see them."

Dan nodded. "Just don't tell them that I got hit in battle."

Sortek nodded and walked away. Leftenant Redburn looked after him, then hesistated. "Sir?"

Daniel Allard smiled. "Please call me Dan. You know we're informal here. What is it, Andrew?"

"Andy—that's what your brother called me." Redburn saw pain lance through Dan's eyes and swallowed hard. "I'm sorry, sir. I know Colonel Sortek gave you a holodisc from your father, and I know he spoke to you about the trial." Redburn stopped and waited.

Daniel Allard nodded, and the Capellan March Leftenant continued. "I don't know what they told you, Captain, but I was there…at the battle and at the trial. I know your brother didn't abandon us. I know he wasn't a spy. I don't care what the court found."

Dan reached out and rested his hands on Redburn's shoulders. "Andy, I appreciate what you've told me." He swallowed past the lump choking him. "You knew Justin, as I did. He's my brother, and I'll never believe he's a traitor until he proves it to me."

Redburn smiled. "That's the way I feel, Dan." Redburn stepped back and saluted.

Daniel Allard returned the salute smartly. *Please God, Justin, don't betray our faith in you.*

22

20 March 3027

Fuh Teng gave Justin Xiang the thumbs-up sign from his perch on the scaffolding. Seconds later, Tung Yuan appeared from inside the tall 'Mech's right arm, removed his welding goggles, and snapped the armored panel into place. Reading the smile on Teng's face, and seeing it reflected on Justin's down below, he laughed aloud.

"We will show Capet's protege no mercy, Justin Xiang."

When the Tech suddenly frowned as though seeing something he did not like, Justin whirled sharply, prepared to rebuke any visitors. His anger evaporated just as quickly as it had come. Contessa Kym Sorenson, clad in a blue leather jumpsuit cinched at the waist by a silver belt, smiled at him. She slipped into Justin's outstretched arms and kissed him.

"I want you to come home in one piece, lover," she whispered.

Justin hugged her and breathed deeply the musky perfume she wore. "I can think of no place I would rather be, my love," he murmured. Through the blond veil of her hair, he could see Gray Noton studying the 'Mech towering over all of them. Justin let his right arm slip around Kym's waist, then turned to face Noton. "What do you think, Gray?"

Noton squinted and raked his gaze up and down the 'Mech. "A *Centurion* is not held in very high esteem here on Solaris. I hope you got it cheap."

Justin snorted. "Cheap enough." He smiled at Kym. "It's only a

138

loan, you realize."

She raised an eyebrow. "I hope you don't think I just *give* money to the men I live with. I do expect some repayment…"

Noton pointed at the *Centurion*'s right arm. "I see you've added some armor to the right arm, but it looks like you stripped it from the left. You've got to realize that the LRMs the *Centurion* packs in its left breast are not going to be much use here in the Factory."

Justin nodded. The Marik arena had been built on the site of an abandoned factory where 'Mechs had once served to move parts. The structure was built to 'Mech scale, just as any normal building would be built to human scale. Marik interests from the Montenegran area of Solaris City had bought the factory and sowed it with thousands of remote cameras. With the audience ensconced safely in another building, warring 'Mechs could wander through the derelict structure to ambush one another in a dangerous multilevel game of hide-and-seek.

Noton looked Justin in the eyes. "I've heard that the fight's been fixed."

Justin nodded solemnly. "It seems that I cost a number of people big money a month ago when I took Fuh Teng's place and won. Certain interests have made it known to me that I'm to lose to Peter Armstrong this evening. I take it that Armstrong is Capet's best fighter in the Medium Class?"

Noton shrugged. "Probably, though Wolfson will be better as he gets more experience. You refused the fix?"

Justin brandished his steel hand, saying, "Never, *absolutely never*, will I kowtow to anyone who swears allegiance to Hanse Davion or the Federated Suns!" Kym shivered slightly, and Justin hugged her a bit tighter.

Noton smiled. "So, you will never accept a fix?"

Justin's eyes all but closed as he shook his head. "Never bet against me, Gray. No matter what your sources tell you, I will always win."

Kym turned Justin's face toward her with her one hand. She kissed him long and deeply, encircling his neck with her arms and pressing her body against his. "Win for me, Justin."

"My pleasure."

Kym pulled away from Justin and slipped her arm through the crook in Noton's arm. "After you win, Gray and I have a surprise for you."

Justin smiled, "Yes?"

Noton laughed. "Win and I'll introduce you to Valhalla…"

139

*   *   *

Justin signaled his readiness to the arena controller. The huge elevator doors opened like jaws and Justin felt the camera focusing in on his *Centurion*. The announcer's voice burrowed into his brain.

"And here, ladies and gentlemen, is the challenger. Justin Xiang in his *Centurion*, the *Yen-lo-wang*. It's named after the Chinese god of the dead, the King of the Nine Hells. That's quite appropriate, too, because Xiang has been hell on the three foes he's faced in his month here on Solaris Seven. This is his first fight outside the *Vindicator* owned by his partner, Fuh Teng. Peter Armstrong and his *Griffin*, the *Ares*, will have their work cut out for them. Welcome to 'Night at the Fights' for March 20, brought to you by…"

Justin punched a button and shut off the sound. Sweat began to trickle down his temples as he waited. Once the green light had flashed to life on his control console, he could wander out into the Factory's shadowed interior. He smiled because he knew the "live" fight would actually begin ten minutes before the broadcast over the local pay-for-play holovision systems in Solaris City. The lag-time would be used to build up spare tape, allowing the producers to cut boring footage or add in advertisements without losing any of the action.

The green light ignited. Justin lumbered his humanoid *Centurion* forward and did exactly what he knew his foe was doing. As he punched several buttons on his command console, a schematic of a *Griffin* drew itself in shades of red and gold. *Know your enemy as yourself.*

Justin studied the display and reviewed his foe's strengths and weaknesses. Armstrong's *Griffin* sported LRMs fired from a launch pod on the 'Mech's right shoulder. *That PPC in its right hand could mean trouble.* The *Griffin*, Justin read, also carried more armor than the *Centurion*. That accounted, in part, for its five-ton weight advantage over the *Centurion*. Highly regarded as a distance-hitter on the battlefield, the *Griffin* was a formidable foe.

Justin switched his 'Mech's main scanner mode from magnetic anomaly detection to infrared because of all the scrap metal strewn throughout the Factory. In heat-detection mode, the scanner displayed all cool blues and greens, except for the area he'd just marched his *Centurion* through. There, the latent traces of heat glowed red and yellow, but they dissipated fast.

How will Armstrong evaluate the Centurion? Justin narrowed his eyes and stepped over a barricade of twisted girders and fire-blackened ferrocrete. *He'll recall that the Luxor autocannon in the right arm often jams. He won't try to sneak up on me because one of my two medium lasers covers my rear arc. He knows we both pack LRMs, so he'll*

140

probably expect a long-range duel. Justin smiled to himself. *In fact, we'll probably spar at range, and he'll hope my Luxor autocannon jams...*

Justin picked the *Centurion*'s path through metal debris like a child working his way through a rusty junkyard. Through the cable hanging from his left wrist, he guided the 'Mech's huge left hand. Closing its fingers on small chunks of ferrocrete, he moved them out of the way. Unmindful of the arena cameras, he cleared himself a little space and hunkered down in his *Centurion*.

Justin watched for the director's green light on his dash. He remembered his pregame production briefing. If both combatants had settled in to ambush one other, which would make for a boring fight, the producer would flicker the light three times. That meant both MechWarriors had to get moving or else the production company would withhold the combatant's portion of royalties for the fight. Justin waited, but the light never ignited.

I did not think Armstrong would dare attempt an ambush. Aren't I the treacherous Capellan traitor who has defeated Wolfson and killed two other Federated Suns expatriots? Already the media mentions how Philip Capet and I have met before, and they suggest that none of the Federats here on Solaris will be able to stop me except for Capet himself. Justin shook his head, then shut his eyes against the burning sting of sweat. *Fools. Utter fools.*

He licked his lips and tasted the salty sweat, marveling at how the Tharkan Broadcast Company controlled the fights and their presentation. As a TBC representative had told him, three or four TBC JumpShips were getting the broadcast beamed out to them a minute or two before the public saw it. They would jump out to begin the distribution of the game tapes throughout most of the Inner Sphere. TBC had production studios built right into its DropShips so that they could add editing and extra commentary before the tapes were beamed down to a world's local broadcasting company.

Within a month, the TBC man had said, the fight will have played on every Steiner world and half the worlds of Davion, Marik, and Liao. Justin laughed to himself as he recalled the man assuring him that they'd crack the Kurita market soon. *Sure*, he thought, *and Takashi Kurita sleeps with a teddy bear!*

Justin looked up and adjusted his scanner, which showed faint blue rectangles sinking down through the ferrocrete above him. *The sound and vibration baffles built between floors hide the sound of him, but they don't trap the heat.* Justin looked over to his right, back where the ramp from the upper level fed out onto his floor. He saw nothing but a momentary flicker of yellow.

I can imagine the announcer. Martial music in the background rises slowly to heighten tension. 'Will our champion, Peter Armstrong—Philip Capet's hand-picked fighter in the Medium Class—fall prey to the Capellan ambush?'

Justin reached out with his right hand and firmly grasped the targeting joystick jutting up from the command chair's arm. The red button on top triggered his autocannon, and the trigger under his index finger would fire the forward medium laser. Justin swallowed hard and found his mouth suddenly dry.

The gold crosshairs on his viewscreen hovered at the right edge of his forward view. Though the sensors and neurohelmet provided him with full, 360-degree vision, almost undetectable lines broke the circle into parts corresponding to his firing arcs. If he tried to target something outside a weapon's arc, the crosshairs would lose all intensity.

Do I wait until he has walked past me and then hit him from behind? Do I attack straight on and give him a chance? That would be the honorable thing. Justin narrowed his eyes. *The man belongs to Hanse Davion. He deserves no honor.*

Slowly, and with a stealth ridiculous for such a large machine, the *Griffin* inched into sight. Humanoid, with two fully manipulable hands, it looked much like a jump trooper dressed in bulky space armor. Its pistol-like PPC rested casually in its right hand. The LRM launch canister riding on its right shoulder moved up and down in fits and starts as Armstrong sighted it on probable targets ahead.

Justin laughed. This was the first time he'd ever seen a 'Mech swagger! He reached out and flicked his external speakers on.

"It's over before it begins, Armstrong!" Justin brought the *Centurion* to its feet, and extended the autocannon's muzzle at the *Griffin*.

The *Griffin* opened its arms wide. "Take your best shot, yellow dog." For the cameras, Armstrong made the *Griffin* shake its head, as though in pity. "I'll let you die fast, Xiang."

Justin's thumb stabbed down on the fire button. The Pontiac Autocannon/20 for which he'd sacrificed his LRMs and installed in place of the Luxor, spat out a cloud of projectiles. Like metal locusts, they stripped the *Griffin*'s forward armor. Metal and ceramic chaff rained down around the *Griffin*'s legs as the *Centurion*'s medium laser skewered it. A wave of amber heat washed out of the middle of Armstrong's machine as the laser melted some of the engine's shielding. The 'Mech shuddered, too, which Justin hoped was an indication that the gyro had also been damaged.

Badly shaken, Armstrong triggered all his weapons. Fire shot from the missile canister as each LRM took flight. Six of them hit and tore armor from the *Centurion's* right side. The errant rockets detonated behind the *Centurion,* scattering scrap metal and shattering ferrocrete blocks in fiery explosions.

Armstrong then snapped his PPC into line with the *Centurion's* chest. The charging coils glowed for a second, giving Justin enough time to switch the scanners from heat to visual before the lightning could burn out the sensors. The artificial lightning bolt stabbed out toward the *Centurion,* but crackled off above it with Armstrong's hasty shot. It struck a rusty I-beam and reduced it to a puddle of slag.

Justin redirected the autocannon and caressed the firing button with his thumb. The *Centurion* shook violently as the autocannon vomited another metal blizzard at the *Griffin.* The swarm of projectiles ate into the *Griffin's* right arm, peeling armor from it like rind from a naranji. Myomer fiber strands in the 'Mech's hand snapped apart, and the PPC's charging coil exploded in a burst of argent fire. The weapon fell smoldering to the ground.

Justin's laser stabbed deep into the *Griffin's* heart. Fire boiled through the 'Mech's chest, spitting out pieces of melted and broken circuit boards. The 'Mech wavered and stumbled back, but Armstrong fought to gain control. Reaching back with its left hand, the *Griffin* steadied itself as fire geysered from its torso.

Justin waited for the canopy to split and for Armstrong to eject. *The 'Mech is lost! Your engine's shielding is gone! Get out!* He watched the *Griffin's* LRM canister swivel toward the *Centurion,* then cant back as the 'Mech went out of control. Instead of flying at Justin, a full flight of LRMs launched into the ceiling.

The *Griffin's* black faceplate exploded outward. Flames spouted from it as though the *Griffin* were a fire-breathing monster. Again the LRM canister blasted away blindly at the ceiling. Debris and ferrocrete crashed down in huge chunks onto the *Griffin.* Unsteadied, Armstrong's *Griffin* dropped straight down, as though its legs had been suddenly cut from under it. It now leaned back pitifully against the Factory's ferrocrete wall.

Justin shook his head slowly. If not for the fires burning in its chest and head, the huge 'Mech might have resembled a man sleeping peacefully against the wall. Justin balled his *Centurion's* left hand into a fist. *Perhaps someday I, too, will know such peace.*

23

Solaris VII (The Game World)
Rahneshire, Lyran Commonwealth

20 March 3027

Noton tossed Justin a towel as he came out of the cleaner. "Risky business substituting the Pontiac 100 for the Luxor," he said, seating himself on the narrow wooden bench beside Justin's locker. "Doubles your firepower, but severely cuts your range. Especially because you sacrificed your LRMs for it. *Yen-lo-wang* is a fine infighter, and the surprise worked well in the Factory, but anyone else will kill you with LRMs and PPC fire."

Justin finished drying off and wrapped the towel around his waist. He pressed it to himself with his inert left hand while he tucked it in with his right. "Calculated risk, Gray. That's something you understand, isn't it?"

Noton leaned back against the wall. "I don't know that I follow you…"

Justin smiled and swung open his locker door. He reached in and pulled a plastic comb from the top shelf, then pressed it into his left hand and painstakingly sculpted the fingers to hold the comb securely. Watching himself in the fly-blown mirror, he used it to slick down his hair.

"Gray, I've only been here a month, but I know your type."

Noton raised an eyebrow. "My type?"

Justin nodded. "You know that fighting in the Arenas is a dead end. You've not fought in a while—or so the record of public fights shows—but you've got a Typhoon and powerful friends. You're

144

shrewd." Justin looked over at the information broker. "I'd like to think I'm shrewd, too."

A third voice broke in on the conversation. "It wasn't too shrewd, Xiang, to ignore our advice to you about the fight."

Justin turned and lowered his hand. Three men—two large men flanking a smaller, slightly older man—stood just inside the door. The smaller man chomped on a cigar and pointed a thick finger at Justin. "You cost me money tonight."

Justin shook his head. "*You* cost you money tonight. I told you I'd not throw the fight. You should have listened."

"No, Xiang, *you* should have listened." The little man snapped his fingers. Balling their fists, his twin goons stepped forward. "Rock, Jeff, tear his arm off and break his legs with it."

Justin dropped into a crouch and swept in toward the two thugs. Leaping up, he snapped a kick to Rock's face. With his jaw shattered and his nose leaking blood, Rock toppled backward. Collapsing like a rag doll, he smacked his head hard on the ferrocrete floor.

When Jeff swung a fist at Justin, the MechWarrior grabbed the thug's wrist with his right hand and lifted it up and over his own head. Without relinquishing his grip, Justin pivoted beneath the hoodlum's arm and brought the wrist twisting back with him. Justin locked the arm, then snapped his own left forearm down on Jeff's elbow. The joint cracked audibly as it broke, but the thug's scream of pain swallowed the sound.

Justin released the goon and vaulted over the other incapacitated hood. He grabbed the small man by the throat and drove him back to the wall. Twisting his own hip so that the man could not kick or knee him, he waited until his foe's labored breath was the only sound either of them could hear.

Justin stared mercilessly into the smaller man's eyes. "Listen to me now, because I will not tell you again. If you ever try to fix one of my fights, I will ruin you financially, then I'll kill you in degrees." Justin raised his left hand and wished, for a moment, that the comb had dropped away during the fight. "I've picked up soldiers in a 'Mech's hand, and I know how delicate those devices can be. I also know how rough they can get. I assure you that you don't want to have personal knowledge of their roughness, *ni you dong*?"

The bookie shook his head fervently. "I understand, *wo dong*."

Justin smiled coldly and relaxed his grip. "*Hao. Zou kai yijing!*" He released the man and jerked a thumb at the two goons. "And take them with you. I never want to see you again. If I do, I'll kill you."

Noton refrained from laughing as Jeff and the bookie dragged the unconscious thug from the room. He sputtered a chuckle when the door finally shut behind them, then shook his head. "I thought you said you were shrewd. Now, how was that shrewd?"

Justin pulled on a blue and black silken coat, which hung to just below the waistband of his black trousers. He carefully adjusted the cuff of the left sleeve over the glove covering his metal hand, then tied the blue sash around his waist and let the long ends dangle down at his left hip. Pulling on his boots, he looked over at Noton.

"That will make the Federats here on Solaris more angry. It guarantees me more fights and larger purses. You and I both know the fights here are not combats as much as they are theatrical spectacles. If I'm to fight battles with high purses, I have to be someone that the spectators can either love or hate. Doing things to make the Federats' blood boil is money in the bank."

Noton stood. "Is that why you've taken up with Kym?"

Justin smiled and nodded acknowledgement of Noton's perception. "You mean, has the idea of a Capellan lying with a Davion woman —and the anger it must arouse in men like Capet—ever occurred to me? I'd be lying if I said no." Justin looked up. "You realize, of course, that she sought me out for the same reason, don't you?"

Noton nodded. "I saw that from the first."

"I'm sure you did." Justin swung his rusty locker shut and spun the combination. "We both started out using each other to get back at the people in the Federated Suns." Justin smiled sheepishly. "But, as exiles, we share a bond that seems to knit us together tightly. Back in the Federated Suns, I'd never have gotten to know her, but now I believe I may actually be in love with her."

"I envy you," Noton said with a smile. Then he opened the locker room door for Justin. "Kym's bringing my Typhoon around. Next stop, Valhalla!"

The darkened glass door opened onto a silent Valhalla as Noton, Justin, and Kym approached. MechWarriors were seated up and down the length of the tables running through the center of the long hall. Each had his head bent forward, as though in prayer. Up on the dais, sandwiched between Billy Wolfson and Philip Capet, a chair sat hidden beneath a shroud of black satin.

"What is this?" Noton shouted laughingly. "Is this Valhalla, or is it a funeral home?"

Capet's head snapped up as if on a spring. He glared at Noton, then flushed as his gaze fell upon Justin. "You have gone too far, Noton, bringing that quisling scum in here!" Capet thrust an accusing finger at Justin Xiang. "There!" he shouted. "There is the Capellan traitor who killed Peter Armstrong. Look on him and see the face of a

146

coward!"

"Coward!" Justin's denial exploded from him. He released Kym's hand and stalked forward. "Coward? No one in this room can call me that, least of all you, Capet." Justin laughed and looked around as the curtains over many alcoves fell back. "I see you have not shared the secrets of your past with those here."

Capet narrowed his eyes. "We have all seen the kind of liar and coward you are, Xiang. Vids of your trial played long and well here on Solaris. We heard how you abandoned your men to a Capellan ambush. Even your father admitted you were a spy. Why should anyone here believe anything you say?"

Justin nodded slowly. "Actions speak louder than words, Philip. When will you come after me?"

Capet hesitated, but no one noticed because Billy Wolfson shot to his feet. "He'll not get the chance, slant. You defeated me because you took Fuh Teng's place…"

"You mean, I put up a fight!" Justin spat out the words at Wolfson, who colored visibly. Both shared the knowledge of the fix, and Wolfson burned with the shame of having been so careless.

Wolfson slammed a fist into the table. "I will kill you, Xiang! Rig up your 'Mech any way you can. It makes no difference to me. I'll destroy you, no matter what!"

Justin nodded eagerly. "Done. Just don't be as stupid as Armstrong."

Wolfson glowered at Justin. "What?"

"Don't believe what Capet tells you is the mark of a man." Justin reached back and slipped his arm around Kym's waist as she came forward. Off to his left, Noton pulled aside the curtain of his alcove, and waved the MechWarrior and his lady into the private booth.

Kym slid onto the bench and moved toward the center of the table. Gray took his place at the head of the table while Justin seated himself beside Kym. Noton touched a button and the wooden panel concealing the holovision screen slid up into the wall.

Noton waved at the screen. "Would you like to see a replay of your fight?"

Justin shook his head. "I've never enjoyed reviewing my performance. That goes double for those training tapes they loved to make at the Sakhara Academy."

Noton nodded understandingly. "I agree, though I maintain a complete library of battles here. If you ever want to review the fights of an upcoming foe, please feel free to use this booth."

That could be very useful. Justin nodded to his host. "Thank you, Gray."

The three of them looked up as the curtain slid back slowly. A servant smiled sheepishly, saying, "Just a second, folks, and I'll be gone." He turned away, then swung a silver wine caddy into the booth. Condensed moisture ran down the shining exterior, and ice brimmed up over the top. Protruding from the ice pack was the neck of a wine bottle.

The servant produced three glasses and set them on the table. He also handed Noton a small envelope. Noton slid a thumbnail beneath the flap and withdrew the card. He turned it over, then handed it to Justin. "It's in Capellan, which I can't read."

Justin accepted it wordlessly. When he had read it, he looked up with a smile. "It says, 'The honor of the House of Xiang rises like the sun. My compliments. Signed, Tsen Shang.'" Justin glanced over at Noton. "A friend of yours?"

Noton nodded. "One of my shrewder friends, Justin. I'll have to introduce you." He looked over at the server and nodded for him to pour.

The young man smiled. "I hope you realize this is from Palos. Not only is it the best Capella has to offer, it's the best in the Successor States. Mr. Shang had to ship this stuff in himself because we can't get it here." He stripped the lead foil from the cork and freed it of the wire cage. Carefully, he worked the cork loose, then covered the bottle with a cloth as he freed the cork with a muffled pop. The server poured for all three, then retreated silently.

Gray raised his glass. "To your skill and intelligence, Justin. May you live long here on Solaris, and get all that you desire."

Justin, abstaining from drinking to a toast in his honor, waited for his friends to lower their glasses. "To my two friends," he said, in turn raising his own glass. "May they help me to stay alive here on Solaris, and to get all that I desire." Justin drank, very much enjoying the piquant sweetness of the wine.

He looked up at Noton. "This Tsen Shang must be well connected. I recall someone on Spica offering three bottles of this vintage to ransom his damaged *Valkyrie*."

Noton smiled and set his empty glass down. "He's well connected, indeed. He even owns two heavy 'Mechs, though he lacks a pilot."

"Then we two should meet, don't you think?" Justin drained his glass. "After all, I'll be needing a heavy 'Mech if I'm to kill Philip Capet."

24

Solaris VII (The Game World)
Rahneshire, Lyran Commonwealth

20 March 3027

Darkness cloaked Kym Sorenson as she slipped out from under the thick coverlet. Rearranging the bedcovers, she bent down and drew the quilt up around Justin's shoulders, then knelt to kiss him lightly on the forehead. "Sleep well, lover. I'll be back soon." A quick glance at the empty glass on his bedside table told her he'd not notice her absence.

Despite her confidence in the depth of Justin's drugged sleep, Kym gathered up her clothing and carried it outside their room to dress. Over the garments she'd worn to the fight and to Valhalla, she pulled on a heavy coat and then tucked her golden hair up into a wide-brimmed hat.

Kym flipped up the collar of her coat against the wet, rainy wind as she left the villa and crossed to the Hurricane. At a touch, the door swung up and Kym slipped into the driver's seat. The door descended and locked tight as she tapped the ignition code out onto the dashboard's number pad. The engine hummed to life, and the Hurricane rose up on a cushion of air.

The lights of Solaris City sparkled like raindrops on a spiderweb of streets as Kym guided the Hurricane down from the hills of the Davion sector, known locally as the Black Hills. She steered the vehicle onto Bunyan Road, then brought it to a halt before a moderately well-kept apartment tower.

She hurried from her aircar to the glassed-in vestibule, where she pressed one particular button twice, waited for a three-count, and then pressed it four more times. While waiting for the tenant to open the door, she looked around anxiously but saw no one else in the outer darkness. With a rasp like that of an angry beast, a buzzer sounded, but stopped abruptly as Kym yanked open the door. She darted inside the building, but went no further until she was sure the door had clicked shut behind her.

Instead of going to the lobby elevator, Kym turned to the fire door on her right. She opened it and stepped cautiously into a long, dimly lit corridor. Passing quickly through it, she reached the apartment building's rear exit. From there, she slipped out into the dark alley behind the building.

Kym hurried on through the night until she reached an avenue named Twain Street. Stepping out from the alley onto the street, she resumed a relaxed pace. Strolling past a restaurant, she paused as if making an impulsive decision, glanced at the holovid menu display, then went in.

Once inside, Kym removed her hat and shook out her hair, which cascaded over her shoulders as she moved toward a rear booth. When a smiling server handed her a menu, Kym leaned back to study it in leisurely fashion.

A deep male voice whispered from the speaker hidden in the cushions just behind her head. "Report."

Kym yawned. "Contact with Shang. Noton is interested in Xiang, and Xiang is susceptible to Nasodithol. He did not notice it in a drink, and was highly suggestible under its influence."

Kym stopped speaking as the server returned to her table. "Coffee, please. Nothing else."

When the server was again out of earshot, the voice hissed in Kym's ear like a snake. "Satisfactory. Continue to encourage Xiang's entry into Noton's service. He will be most useful there. Be aware that Fuh Teng is Maskirovka. Take care." The flat, emotionless voice paused. "The Minister would hate for you to find it expedient to kill his son."

Gray Noton sank back into the shadows across Bunyan Street when he saw Kym reenter her Hurricane. Pressing his hand over his right ear, he listened carefully to the agent reporting to him over a radio. Noton smiled and watched the aircar rise and disappear down the street.

Come all the way down here for a cup of coffee, Kym? I don't think so. Especially not after you cajoled half a kilo of that special Atocongo

150

blend from Enrico Lestrade a week ago! There's nothing at that restaurant that you'd want, at least not to eat or drink. Remembering Lestrade's assurances that Contessa Sorenson was nothing more than a bored rich girl, Noton laughed. *You fooled him, Kym, but that's no great feat. You didn't fool me. And that will cost you more than you want to know.*

25

The DropShip's retrorockets blasted snow from the landing pad. The howling wind whirled in at the spherical *Union* Class craft, but the billowing clouds of snow broke the wind's fury. The *Cougar* landed heavily on its four steel feet. The second the Captain cut the ship's engines, the raging blizzard smothered the DropShip in a blanket of snow.

Moving at a snail's pace, a square patch of snow detached itself from the landing pad and rose skyward. As wind blasted the snow from its roof, the gantry grew upward. It stopped opposite the *Cougar*'s smallest hatchway and secured a canopy to the craft's hull.

Ardan Sortek stood back as an Ensign cracked the *Cougar*'s hatch. She smiled and waved Sortek forward into the room at the top of the gantry. Ardan moved quickly and shivered as the frigid winter wind of Tharkad nipped at him despite the canopy. Leftenant Redburn followed closely behind.

Why is Tharkad always so cold when I visit? Ardan crossed to the elevator in the rear of the gantry. He pushed the black button on the wall, then turned to Redburn, who was tugging nervously at his dark green dress jacket. Ardan laughed, thinking that Andrew looked as nervous as a MechWarrior dropping naked into a combat zone. "Easy, Leftenant. You look fine."

Redburn's face flushed scarlet and his eyes nearly bugged out. "Easy? This is the Archon we're going to meet." He followed Ardan into the elevator as its doors yawned open for them.

Ardan nodded and pressed a button to shut the door. "And the Archon-Designate, and the whole of the Lyran Commonwealth court."

Redburn wilted before his eyes. "Oh thanks, Colonel, that makes me feel much better." The elevator, independent of any command, sank faster than Redburn's self-confidence.

Ardan laughed again, then straightened himself up and arranged his own dress tunic as the elevator slowed. He wore a blue uniform with gold trim because, unlike Redburn, he was not attached to a combat unit in the Capellan March. Despite the color differences, their uniforms looked similar and distinctive. The sunburst design, which started at the left shoulder and shot four rays extending out and down to the middle of the jacket, created a brilliant, asymmetrical double-breast. Tight-fitting trousers tucked snugly into cavalry boots. Completing the uniform were rowelless spurs, remnants of ages-old cavalry traditions and the mark of a MechWarrior in the Federated Suns.

Ardan reached out and adjusted the Silver Sunburst on Redburn's chest. With a certain satisfaction, he noted that the medal matched the uniform's silver trim. Redburn looked down nervously, but smiled as Ardan winked. They both turned to face the heavy elevator doors as they opened.

Ardan Sortek grinned at the sight that greeted them. Standing in the small receiving room, Katrina Steiner and her daughter, Melissa Arthur Steiner, returned his smile warmly. Stepping from the elevator, he took the Archon's extended hand. "I am honored, Archon."

"And I am very glad to see you, Ardan Sortek." Katrina turned to her right. "You remember my daughter?"

Ardan laughed heartily and swept Melissa into a bear hug. "The best nurse an ailing MechWarrior ever had." He hugged her tightly, then held her out at arm's length. "Let me look at you."

Melissa Arthur Steiner shared her mother's height and steely gray eyes, but her blond hair was a shade darker, a legacy from her dead father. More lithesome than her mother, she nevertheless showed strength in her regal bearing and in the sharp fire of her eyes. In keeping with Lyran custom, Melissa's light-blue eye shadow extended in a feathery pattern from the corners of her eyes and curled down onto her high cheekbones.

"You have become lovelier than ever in the two years since we last met, Melissa!" Ardan hugged her again, stepped back, but still held her right hand in his left. *Ah, she will make Hanse Davion very happy.*

Melissa smiled brilliantly. "I miss the time we spent together while you recuperated here, Ardan, but I'm glad you have not again needed my ministrations." She gave his hand a squeeze, then reluc-

153

tantly released it.

"You're not alone in either thought," Ardan admitted quietly. He turned toward Redburn, inviting him forward with a wave of the hand. "I should like to present my traveling companion and friend, Leftenant Andrew Redburn. Archon Katrina Steiner, Duchess of Tharkad, and her daughter, Melissa Arthur Steiner, Archon-Designate and Landgrave von Bremen."

Redburn snapped to attention and saluted. Katrina Steiner returned the salute and glanced reprovingly as Melissa raised a hand to her mouth to smother a giggle. The Archon stepped forward and offered Redburn her hand. "I am pleased to meet you, Leftenant. News of your brave deeds has preceded your arrival in Tharkad."

Redburn nodded. "The honor is mine, Archon."

Melissa took Redburn's hand in both of hers. "Forgive me, Leftenant. I'm afraid I cannot understand how a man so courageous on the battlefield can be so baffled in a social situation."

Ardan started to answer, but Redburn decided to speak for himself. "I think, Archon-Designate, the difference is that, on a battlefield, if I don't know what else to do, I can always shoot." Redburn smiled sheepishly. "That could get very messy in social situations." The four of them laughed at Andrew's witticism, which help to relieve his anxiety.

"I'm afraid, Leftenant, that you and the Colonel will be thrown to the social wolves tonight at the reception," the Archon said, leading the quartet out through a small door and into a large, underground maintenance facility beneath the spaceport. She pulled back the wrist of her quilted parka to glance at her chronometer. "Because the weather delayed your landing, things have already begun."

The Archon guided them toward a hovercraft and stood back as the door slid upward and melting snow dripped from it to the ground. Melissa preceded the others into the craft's dark interior. She seated herself with her back to the hovercraft's pilot and Leftenant Redburn sat down in the jump seat beside her. Ardan Sortek took the seat opposite Melissa and the Archon sat facing Redburn.

The Archon pressed a hidden pair of buttons. The hovercraft's door slid shut and the clear partition between the driver's compartment and the back slid open. At a nod from the Archon, Melissa stood up and said something in a low voice to the hovercraft pilot. The driver rose, too, and moved to the seat Melissa had vacated while Melissa made her way to the driver's seat.

When the whole exchange was complete, Katrina Steiner smiled. "Leftenant Redburn...Ardan," she said as the hovercraft pilot removed a woolen cap to let free a rain of golden hair around her shoulders, "I would like you to meet my daughter, Melissa."

Ardan Sortek, standing in the Archon's offices, turned to Simon Johnson and shook his head. "Even seeing them stand side by side, I cannot tell them apart. You have done a superior job." Ardan had suppressed a shiver, however, as he thought, *This reminds me too much of what Max Liao almost accomplished with his duplicate of Hanse.*

Johnson smiled. "I did nothing." He pointed to the Melissa on the right. "Jeana has worked long and furiously to become the Archon-Designate's double. Because she has voluntarily adopted the role, we believe she will be superior in her job." Johnson glanced over to where Redburn stood talking to the Archon and raised an eyebrow.

Ardan shook his head only slightly, as if to say, *Redburn knows nothing of the double, or of his true purpose here.*

Johnson took his cue from Ardan's curt shake of the head. "Thank you, Jeana. You may withdraw."

Jeana nodded and retreated from the room through one of the private and secure corridors built into the palace for the royal family's protection in even wilder times. Melissa crossed to a bookshelf and pressed a switch. The whole bookcase swung out to reveal a hidden bathroom and vanity. She glanced in the mirror. "I always feel an urge to make sure I'm still me after Jeana and I spend time together." She smiled and turned back toward the room. "Sometimes she seems more me than I do."

Ardan caught the tremor in Melissa's voice. He nodded to Johnson, then walked over to the girl. "What do you mean, Melissa?"

The Archon-Designate shrugged her bare shoulders, then tugged at the top of her gray gown. "Jeana is eight years my senior. She's a MechWarrior and she's so much more mature than I am. It's scary the amount of discipline she has and how commanding is her presence."

Ardan reached out and placed his hands on Melissa's shoulders. "You seem to forget how commanding is your own presence, Melissa, and how you've grown into your duty. I can see it." *Remember, Ardan, though she is a woman in form, she is only seventeen years old. Melissa may have matured since last you saw her, but she has a way to go before she's ready for the responsibilities that await her.*

Melissa frowned and bit her lower lip. "When I look at her, I see the person I could be. Perhaps I should just let her rule in my place when the time comes."

Ardan rocked back on his heels. "What's this? Why is she more worthy to rule than you?"

Melissa looked down at her feet. "She's a MechWarrior, just as my mother was—and as all the Archons have been."

155

Ardan gave Melissa's shoulders a squeeze. "As I recall, you did not study to become a MechWarrior."

"I was too skinny. They trained me for infantry." The dejection in her voice slowed her words to a dirge.

Ardan reached out with his right hand and tilted the girl's head up so that he could look her in the eye. "I seem to recall that you did well in that training. Didn't you once tell me to tell Hanse that he'd be getting a wife who could command the household infantry while he ordered his 'Mechs about?"

Melissa shook her head. "Those were games, Ardan. Jeana has had the will and discipline to become a MechWarrior and a champion triathlete. And she gave it all up to help protect me. That's the sort of sacrifice I could never make, and I don't think I'm worthy of someone else making such a one."

Ardan noticed Leftenant Redburn hovering by his shoulder. "Yes, Leftenant?"

Redburn swallowed hard and looked down at his feet. "Begging your pardon, sir, and your Highness, but I overheard that last remark." He looked up, embarrassed, and his brown eyes searched their faces for understanding. "I'd not intended to, you understand, but the Archon wants a word with you, Colonel. What I wanted to say, though, is that I think I understand some of what the Archon-Designate is saying."

Ardan narrowed his eyes, but found only pained innocence on Redburn's face. *Just saying what you have, Leftenant, has taken more courage than anything you've done on a battlefield. I respect you for it.* Ardan dropped his hand from Melissa's shoulder. "Please, Leftenant, share your thoughts." Ardan smiled at Melissa. "I'll be right back."

Melissa composed herself, then looked up at Andrew. "Yes, Leftenant Redburn?" Feeling on the defensive, her voice and manner grew icy, but her obvious vulnerability kept the tone from wounding him.

Redburn hesitated, then bobbed his head and spoke. "I know what you're afraid of, because I've been there. I've looked into the faces of raw recruits in a training battalion. I know that some of them, no matter how well I work with them, will die in their first battle. I know they'll go to their graves wondering why I wasn't there to save them. I know that just by trying to give them the skills they need to pilot a 'Mech, I'm probably teaching them just enough to kill them." Redburn looked down at his balled fists. "It's a hell of a responsibility."

Melissa nodded unconsciously. "How do you handle it? How can you accept it?"

Redburn shrugged and looked into Melissa's gray eyes. "I do the

156

best I can because I know others would do worse. I hope my men's faith in me will make them believe in what I tell them. I pray that the training will give them something—anything—that will save them in a tight spot."

Redburn smiled wistfully. "The trick of it is, your Highness, that people just want someone to tell them everything is fine, or they want someone to blame when things go wrong. They want someone else to shoulder the responsibility so that they can get on with whatever else they need to do. I accept the responsibility for my men, just as you accept the responsibility for your people."

"Yes, but how do I know I can stand up under the pressure?"

Melissa's plea bored through Redburn like a PPC blast. He forced a smile to his lips, but his voice remained grim. "I don't know the answer to that question. I don't think anyone ever does until the time comes and they either stand or fall." Redburn's head came up and he winked at Melissa. "I do believe, however, that the only folks who even think about the question are the ones who have what it takes."

26

Tharkad
District of Donegal, Lyran Commonwealth

10 April 3027

Katrina Steiner, standing on the raised dais at the northern end of the Grand Ballroom, waited until the servants had circulated long enough to serve all the guests a glass of the rare wine. Then she lifted her glass toward the vaulted ceiling and smiled as the clear liquid reflected the image of her cousin Frederick—who stood pouting below the edge of the dais—and stood him on his head. "It is my great pleasure to welcome all of you here this evening."

She looked over at Ardan Sortek and Leftenant Redburn, who stood flanking Melissa on one side of the dais. Ardan's eyes betrayed his discomfort at being singled out during the reception. "I would like to offer a toast to our esteemed visitors from the Federated Suns," Katrina continued. "Colonel Ardan Sortek and Leftenant Andrew Redburn, the Lyran Commonwealth salutes your courage."

Most of the assembled members of the court lifted their glasses like so many marionettes controlled by the Archon's hand. Ardan noticed that Frederick Steiner and Duke Aldo Lestrade were a bit sluggish in their own response to the toast. *Perhaps their pained expressions mean that the Archon has ended their scheming by slipping them hemlock instead of this excellent champagne*, he thought wryly. *If so, I'll find a way to ship a bottle of whatever they're drinking to Duke Michael Hasek-Davion...*

Ardan stepped away from the wall and lifted his glass. "If you will permit me, Archon, I was instructed to offer the following toast in the name of Prince Hanse Davion. 'I salute the beauty, valor, and intelligence of the Steiner women. Long may their steady hands steer the Lyran Commonwealth's ship of state.'"

Ardan nodded to the Archon, who accepted the compliment graciously, then smiled at Frederick. The raw hatred in Frederick's eyes echoed a similar blaze in Duke Lestrade's, but both men bowed to social necessity and joined the toast.

Melissa smiled and offered her hand to the slender, dark-haired man approaching her. The man kissed her hand gently. "A pleasure of the highest order, as always, your Highness."

Melissa's face froze into a plastic mask of royal dignity. "How gracious, Baron Sefnes." She turned toward Leftenant Redburn. "The Baron is Duke Michael Hasek-Davion's representative here on Tharkad. Surely, as you both are from the Capellan March, you must know each other."

Redburn shook his head, and the Baron answered for both of them. "The Capellan March is a large holding, Highness."

Melissa reddened slightly. "Of course. How silly of me."

The Baron nodded at Redburn. "That is not to say that I have not heard of Leftenant Redburn. The Duke himself has commented on how much he appreciates what the 1st Kittery Training Battalion has done."

Redburn snorted. "He has an odd way of showing it."

The Baron, shocked by Redburn's vehemence, frowned. "Whatever do you mean?"

"I mean that the Duke sent Count Vitios and a pack of 'investigators' to Kittery to ruin the best MechWarrior in the March."

The Baron sneered. "You cannot be referring to that Capellan, Xiang, are you?"

Redburn nodded curtly. "That trial was a joke. Major Justin Allard is no more a traitor to the Federated Suns than am I or are you."

Baron Sefnes hissed and drew back. "Be careful what you say, Leftenant. Your arrogance will lead to no good. Haven't you seen the fights on Solaris?"

Redburn shook his head. "Colonel Sortek and I have been on an inspection tour."

"Suffice it to say, Leftenant, that Justin Xiang is doing his best to kill every Federated Suns MechWarrior on the Game World." The Baron's words sent a chill down Redburn's spine.

"Impossible!"

The Baron's frown sharpened his features and made him look like a rodent. "As I said, Leftenant, be careful of what you say." He smiled hungrily. "You'd not want any of us loyalists to think you a sympathizer, would you?"

Ardan Sortek looked over and saw Baron Sefnes approaching Melissa. *That sycophant! I trust him about as far as I can throw my Victor.* He glanced back toward Frederick Steiner and saw the anger still smoldering in his eyes. Chuckling inwardly, Ardan made his way toward the Duke of Duran.

Extending his hand, Ardan said, "Your Grace, I don't believe we've met before. I am Ardan Sortek."

The Duke grimaced and extended his own hand toward Ardan with the reluctance of a man asked to greet a leper. He shared the family trait of piercing gray eyes, but the scar running from the corner of his right eye up toward his hairline diluted the effect of his arctic stare. He inclined his graying head slightly, then offered Ardan a thin-lipped smile. "Your reputation precedes you, Colonel."

Matching the Duke's powerful grip, Ardan shook the other man's hand. "As does yours, Duke Frederick."

Steiner freed his right hand and probed the scar by his eye. "I see your career has left you without scars, at least not visible ones, Colonel. I fear that I have not been so fortunate."

A frown flashed across Ardan's face. *Petty, isn't it, to remind me of the 'delusion' I suffered when recovering here on Tharkad. I'm sure you've kept the story of my psychological difficulties circulating, haven't you? If you only knew the truth—that it was all a part of Maximilian Liao's plan to destroy the Federated Suns.*

Ardan smiled and riposted, "Of course, your Grace, my career has not been nearly as long as yours." Ardan watched with feigned innocence as his thinly veiled comment on the Duke's age hit home like an SRM. "Please call me Ardan."

Frederick Steiner winced as Ardan waited for him to reciprocate the offer of familiarity. Duke Lestrade, reading Steiner's transparent anguish, forestalled any action by limping forward and thrusting his pudgy hand at Ardan. "I am Aldo Lestrade." He nodded toward Steiner. "Like my friend, the Duke, I, too, have suffered the physical toll of a valiant career serving in a front-line unit."

Ardan nodded. Aldo Lestrade clutched his champagne glass in a steel and plastic left hand. Ardan knew that the prosthesis extended to the Duke's shoulder, and he also knew that the Duke's limp came from a hip-joint replacement. *That Kurita raid may have taken part of your body, but it did nothing to dull your mind,* Ardan thought ruefully. *By referring to Steiner as "the Duke," you prevent me from expecting any familiarity from him. Neatly done.*

Ardan smiled courteously. "I know your homeworld of Summer has been raided by Kurita, but I was unaware that you were a MechWarrior, Duke Lestrade."

160

The short, stocky man smiled and spread his hands. "Life on Summer is itself service in a front-line unit. My father died in a Kurita raid. I nearly did as well. It seems that my family dared not allow me to undergo the training for fear I'd be shipped away from my world to die defending someone else's holding."

"Yes," Ardan said, cocking his head slightly. "I do recall reading in Thelos Auburn's *Origins of the Three Great Families* that yours suffered miserably. Indeed, I would suggest that it was almost providential that you, the youngest of your family, outlived older siblings and managed to take power."

Frederick Steiner quivered with rage. "What might you mean by that, Colonel Sortek?"

Ardan smiled innocently at Katrina's cousin. *Do you ask if I am accusing the Duke of murdering his father during a Kurita raid, just as he got rid of the others standing between him and the throne?* "Why, I merely meant to compliment the Duke on his ability to survive. I have read texts of his speeches, and if the Commonwealth leaves Skye as wide open as he describes, I marvel at his ability to live in such a dangerous area."

Lestrade reached out and laid his artificial hand on Steiner's arm. "Calm yourself, my Duke, I took no offense." Turning back to Ardan, he added, "But I believe the Colonel thinks my thesis incorrect…"

Ardan held up his glass, and a passing servant refilled it. He waited until Steiner and Lestrade had been similarly refreshed, then replied to the Duke's statement. "Perhaps, without the benefit of a military education, you underestimate the strength defending you. Not three weeks ago, I watched the Kell Hounds repulse a raid by elements of the 2nd Sword of Light. A better mercenary battalion you'd be hard pressed to find."

Lestrade shook his head slowly. "True enough, but what is one battalion in a holding as vast as the Isle of Skye? Besides, that raid is the exception that proves the rule. You soldiers think of worlds as squares on a chessboard, and your 'Mech units as the pieces on that board. To you warriors, especially when not engaged in a line unit, the squares on the board are empty."

Lestrade nodded toward Duke Steiner. "Those commanding line units, on the other hand, realize that each world has a life of its own. Though a raid may not result in the loss of a planet, it always generates hardship for the inhabitants. That perspective is easily lost when you only view the situation on a strategic level."

Ardan laughed. He relished the anger in Steiner's eyes, and the shock filling Lestrade's face. "I am amazed at how like my Prince you sound, Duke Lestrade. This lack of feeling for a world's natives is

161

exactly why he suggested—and the Archon accepted—my visit. I will see the places where men have fought, and I will meet the natives. Through further exchanges and stronger ties between our two nations, we will address the very issue you raise."

Though reluctant to leave Steiner and Lestrade as they writhed over his favorable comparison of their views and those of Hanse Davion, Ardan excused himself. He returned to the dais and laid a hand on Redburn's shoulder. His arrival prompted Baron Sefnes to withdraw quickly, and Redburn was finally able to unknot his fists.

Melissa smiled. "Ardan, you're a cross to a vampire."

"Salt to a slug, more like," Redburn grumbled. "So help me, Colonel, if you'd not arrived, I'd have punched his eject button! Blake's Blood, he's as bad as Vitios!"

Ardan shook his head and snorted. "No one is that bad, Andrew."

Redburn nodded sheepishly. "I guess not."

Melissa reached out and brought a fourth person into their circle. "This is Misha Auburn," she said. "Thelos Auburn's daughter and my best friend. Misha, this is Ardan Sortek and Leftenant Andrew Redburn." Melissa hooked her left arm through Ardan's right. "You men are far too handsome to be locked away here in political discussions. Let's go to the ballroom and dance."

A quick glance from Ardan told Redburn that there was no appeal of the sentence, and so he offered Misha his right arm. He smiled as she deftly slipped her hand into the crook of his elbow. "I pray, Miss Auburn, that you are either an able instructor or that your feet will move swiftly from beneath mine."

The dark-haired young woman laughed throatily, and a mischievous glint illuminated her brown eyes. She brought her right hand to rest on Andrew's right forearm as they walked down the wide corridor behind Ardan and Melissa. "And I pray, Leftenant, that you have the MechWarrior's legendary agility so that you may avoid stepping on my feet. I fear this gown was not created with an eye toward swift movement."

Andrew chuckled lightly. Misha's black-sequined gown covered her slender body from floor to throat and from neck to wrists like a snake-skin. Slits up the sides extended only as far as her knees, but he could not see that the dress hampered her movement any. "Forgive me, Miss Auburn, but you move as if born in that gown. And please, call me Andrew."

She gave his arm a slight squeeze. "And I am Misha, Andrew." She turned and smiled at him. "Let me suggest that if we survive each other's skill at the dance, we should enjoy the winter sports here in Tharkad tomorrow. That is, if you have nothing else planned."

162

Andrew nodded his head and guided Misha into the darkened ballroom. Splashed against the domed ceiling, stars twinkled in the exact pattern they would have taken had the roof been glass and the blizzard a memory. The orchestra filled the room with sensuous music, but the song had enough intensity for both the younger and the older listeners. Its tempo even infected Andrew, who seemed able to follow Misha's instructions with ease.

Out of the corner of his eye, Andrew saw Ardan and Melissa dancing, too. He could not hear what they were saying, but the smiles on their faces and the laughter in their bodies revealed the lightness of the conversation. He nodded to Misha, then gestured with a tilt of the head at their two friends. "It's good to see the Colonel enjoying himself."

Misha smiled. "Melissa nursed him back to health after his trauma on Stein's Folly. They became very close. She has been looking forward eagerly to this visit."

As the music slowed and faded around them, Misha and Andrew retreated to the edge of the dance floor. "You dance very well, Andrew," she said.

"Ah yes," he told her. "We may attribute that to the superior skill and grace of my teacher." Misha took the glass of champagne that Andrew offered her from the bar and touched it to his glass.

"To great combinations," she said.

27

11 April 3027

"Good afternoon, Misha…Andrew." Ardan strode into the living room of Redburn's suite, stopping to warm his hands before the fire blazing like a nova in the fireplace. "I trust your skiing went well?"

Redburn nodded and set his brandy snifter down on the low table before him. "Yes, sir."

Ardan smiled at Misha. "I trust, Misha, that you worked the Leftenant hard and that he did nothing to dishonor the Federated Suns?"

Gracefully uncoiling herself from the sofa, Misha shook her head. "He learns quickly, Colonel, and did very well." She reached down and squeezed Redburn's hand. "If you leave him here on Tharkad, I'm sure he'd pick up enough within two weeks to teach those Federated Suns Mountain Troops whatever they need to know."

Ardan nodded slowly. "Indeed." He looked at Redburn. "I'm afraid that duty now calls, Leftenant." Misha made to get up, but Ardan waved her back. "No, Misha. Please stay. I'll only steal him for a little while. He'll return within the hour."

Redburn seconded Ardan's invitation with a hopeful smile, and Misha nodded. He stood up slowly and stiffly, then looked at Ardan. "Should I change first?" Wearing a thick pullover, blue corduroy knickers, and thick wool stockings, he looked far too casual beside Ardan's neatly pressed blue uniform.

"No, Andrew, that will not be necessary." Ardan turned and

164

walked from the room. Redburn caught up with him in the corridor, but neither man spoke. Their silence continued unbroken until they'd entered a small, nearly featureless room and Simon Johnson closed the door behind them.

Johnson stood while the two Federated Suns officers sat in the gray iron chairs. He narrowed his black eyes and addressed himself to Ardan. "How much does he know?"

Redburn felt a sinister thrill as Ardan answered, "He has not been briefed."

"Very well." Johnson dragged a chair around before him, but seated himself on it with his chest against its back. "I will keep this simple, Leftenant. I could have let you read a file, but you would probably find all the details boring. As you are aware, Leftenant, the more you know, the more you might reveal."

The Chancellor of the Lyran Intelligence Corps exhaled, then watched Redburn for a moment before beginning to speak. "Five years ago, in 3022, Hanse Davion and Archon Katrina Steiner signed an agreement on Terra. Your visit is but one of the exchanges made possible by that treaty. For example, I believe that two Lyran Commonwealth students entered the Warriors Hall in your final year there."

Redburn nodded. "I knew of them, but they served in other cadet companies."

Johnson nodded curtly. "No matter, except that you are aware of the treaty and some of its effects. What you do not know is that the treaty has some secret provisions. What I will reveal to you now is known only to a handful of people, for reasons that will become painfully obvious." Johnson winced. "I believe that even that is too many, but there is nothing I can do about it."

Redburn saw Ardan nod in silent agreement with the Chancellor. He swallowed hard. "If you do not feel that I should know this…" *What is it? What could be so important?*

Johnson waved away Redburn's protest. "No one would believe you if you told the story. I fear, however, that those with ambition will use their knowledge to secure power during this delicate time. You see, Andrew Redburn, Prince Hanse Davion and Archon-Designate Melissa Arthur Steiner are to be married on Terra, on the 20th of August, next year, in 3028."

Redburn took the news like an autocannon salvo to the head. His mouth dropped open and a legion of questions clamored at his mind. Instead of vocalizing that babble, he shook his head and kept his mouth firmly shut.

Johnson waited a moment, seeing Redburn's need to compose himself. "Melissa has met her future husband once, on Terra, when the treaty was signed. She was a child then, and the betrothal seemed more a game to her than reality. Since that time, her contact with the Prince has been restricted to messages exchanged through Colonel Sortek." Johnson nodded at Ardan, and the hint of a smile tightened the corners of his mouth. "Though the Colonel has told Melissa much about the Prince, and the messages have pleased her, it is not the same as a flesh-and-blood meeting."

Redburn nodded. "Like fighting in a simulator."

Johnson paused and smiled more fully. "An apt analogy. While I debate the wisdom of this enterprise, both the Archon and her daughter insist that Melissa must travel to the Federated Suns to meet Prince Davion. I have managed to convince them that I should handle the travel arrangements. You have already met one part of our preparations. Jeana Clay will double as Melissa, traveling with Colonel Sortek on some further inspections. Including you two, less than a dozen people will ever know that the real Melissa has actually left the Commonwealth."

Redburn nodded. "I assume, then, from the way the conversation is going, that I am to return to the Federated Suns in the company of someone who just happens to be Melissa Steiner?" Redburn narrowed his eyes. "Wouldn't transshipping her amid a mercenary unit, say Richard's Panzer Brigade, be safer?"

Ardan shook his head. "You, Andrew, being a hero and something of a media figure, will attract the attention of everyone watching. During the long voyage on a commercial liner, your contact with Melissa-in-disguise will not be noticed. That is because you, in essence, will have a large target painted on your chest. Melissa will pass unnoticed on the same ship."

Redburn nodded and Johnson smiled. "Very good, Leftenant. I feel better now. As soon as Melissa selects her traveling name and we have assembled an identity around it, you will be briefed further."

Ardan and Redburn rose to leave, but Johnson added one more remark before they could escape the room. "Oh, and Leftenant—be careful. Though Misha Auburn is Melissa's best friend, she does not know any of this. In fact, she has spent much time in Jeana's company without guessing at the exchange. Still, she has trained well to take over for her father as court historian when he retires. The Auburns have an instinctive nose for conspiracy. Watch yourself."

Melissa looked up from the computer screen and over at Jeana. "I think I have it."

"Have what?" echoed her own voice from Jeana's throat.

"I have the name I'll travel under. I will become Joana Barker."

166

Jeana frowned. Melissa wondered for a moment if she really looked like that when angry or puzzled. "That sounds familiar, Melissa, but I can't place it."

Melissa smiled triumphantly. "I've cobbled it together from one of the books I read. Do you remember 'Sweeney Todd'?"

Melissa's twin shivered. "That ghastly tale about the demon barber of Fleet Street?"

Melissa nodded. "Sweeney Todd's real name was Benjamin Barker, and his daughter's name was Joana. No one ever called her Joana Barker, but that was her true name. That's what I'll use."

Jeana yawned. "If you want to select a name from this ancient literature you seem to devour, why not pick something more romantic? Why not become Irene Adler?"

Melissa wrinkled her nose with distaste. "A Lestrade might select a name from Sherlock Holmes, but not me. No. Joana Barker married a tall, handsome man, and lived happily ever after, I'm sure. That's the sort of omen I want watching over me as I travel to meet…"—Melissa blushed at the thought—"…my bethrothed…my Hanse Davion, my future husband."

28

Nashira
Dieron Military District, Draconis Combine

15 April 3027

Hands folded serenely behind his back, Yorinaga Kurita watched though the large window as the first of the *Genyosha* engaged in calisthenics. Broken down into groups of five, including the *Chu-i* leading each, the twenty-five men performed in perfect unison. Utterly faithful synchronization made each man a finger on one hand, and the training would make all five into a fist.

"*Sumimasen,* Kurita Yorinaga-sama." *Sho-sa* Tarukito Niiro stood respectfully back and away from his master. The Major, one of the first staff officers Yorinaga had honored with acceptance into the *Genyosha,* bowed deeply. He straightened up again when Yorinaga graced him with a nod. "Forgive me, *Tai-sa,*" Tarukito begged, honoring Yorinaga with the Japanese form of his title, "but the *Taishi* requests your presence." *Taishi* meant "Ambassador," and was the name the staff officers had given to the local liaison officer for the Draconis Combine's Internal Security Forces.

Yorinaga bowed his head. Though no sign, no flicker of emotion, passed over Yorinaga's face, Tarukito Niiro knew that he comprehended all that had been said and all that had been left unspoken. *Yorinaga understands, from the way I worded my message, that the* Taishi *actually demanded the* Tai-sa's *presence. He must know that I would sooner commit* seppuku *than deliver such a harsh message.* Tarukito allowed himself to hope that Yorinaga would realize that the ISF man, Shinzei Abe, was forcing his officers to act as a buffer,

168

thereby reminding them that he, the *Taishi*, controlled their fates.

Yorinaga nodded slightly as Tarukito moved from his path. Yorinaga passed his right hand through the gray hair that had grown out in his months away from the monastery. Tarukito Niiro, already stationed on Nashira when the call for volunteers had gone out, had applied immediately for a staff position. He gladly took a reduction in grade from *Chu-sa* to *Sho-sa* to serve in the *Genyosha* with Yorinaga.

Yorinaga strode through the corridors with strong, sure strides. Only the gray hair and the crest staring at Tarukito from Yorinaga's back reminded him of the MechWarrior's age and long history. *Only his silence reminds me that he was disgraced.* Tarukito paused at the door to Yorinaga's office to remove his boots, as Yorinaga had done. Then they both entered to face Shinzei Abe.

"*Konnichi-wa,* Kurita Yorinaga-san," Shinzei intoned respectfully. He executed his bow with the correct sincerity, but its depth and swiftness mocked the gesture. The ISF liaison officer straightened up before Yorinaga had a chance to return the bow. His anger and contempt showed plainly on his broad moon-face.

Yorinaga ignored Abe and knelt behind his low desk. When he looked up, Tarukito noted Yorinaga's frown at seeing that Shinzei Abe had not removed his boots before entering the room. Yorinaga's shock increased as he saw the source of Shinzei's insult. He stiffened, then bowed.

The prisoner—for a man in such rough shape and bonds could be nothing less—knelt opposite the *Tai-sa*. The welts on his body must have caused him pain, but he bowed deeply. Though he nearly fell over as he tried to straighten up, the man ground his teeth and controlled his body with an iron will. Bringing his bruised and battered body erect, the prisoner said smoothly, "*Konnichi wa,* Kurita Yorinaga-sama."

Shinzei Abe lashed out with his left hand and smashed the man in the face. The blow snapped the prisoner's head back, but even Tarukito saw that the man had moved with the blow, aborting its full effect. Tarukito half-rose from his knees, but Shinzei Abe dropped a hand to the neural whip at his belt. Tarukito glanced at Yorinaga, but the *Tai-sa* signaled him back to his place by the door.

Yorinaga looked at Shinzei Abe and mutely invited him to kneel. Tarukito watched the simple motion of Yorinaga's right hand. It floated like a leaf falling from a tree, but it brought Shinzei to his knees like an avalanche. Yorinaga nodded slightly, then narrowed his eyes and wordlessly demanded an explanation from the ISF officer.

Shinzei smiled coldly. "You have doubtless recognized this traitor, Yorinaga-san. Narimasa Asano, as you will recall, served with you eleven years ago in the 2nd Sword of Light Regiment. He traveled

169

here to join the *Genyosha* without orders or permission. He traveled here even though the invitation to join the *Genyosha* was specifically *not* extended to officers who had served with you in the past."

Yorinaga nodded slowly, but the intensity never left his expression. He stared at Shinzei Abe, and after a moment, the ISF officer felt compelled to offer further explanation.

"Because he abandoned his command and proceeded, illegally, to travel 230 light years to this place, I assumed, naturally, that he is an agent of House Davion or House Steiner."

Yorinaga cocked his head ever so slightly to show puzzlement. "No," Shinzei Abe answered the unvoiced question. "He has not revealed the identity of his masters under torture. I bring him to you because only the garrison commander can grant me the permission needed to execute him."

Tarukito watched distaste flash across Shinzei Abe's face. Tarukito himself had transmitted the order that placed a limit on the ISF liaison's powers. He remembered, with relish, relaying the Coordinator's answer to Abe: "Yorinaga is the master of the *Genyosha*. Life and death are his to give or take. His men are to be as devoted to him as he is to me. You are not to interfere with him. Security is your only concern."

Yorinaga flicked his gaze from Shinzei Abe to Narimasa. Life seemed to flow from Yorinaga's eyes into Narimasa's body. With a slight inclination of his head, Yorinaga invited Narimasa to explain himself.

Narimasa again bowed deeply to the *Tai-sa*. "It is as Shinzei Abe has told you, Yorinaga-sama. No invitation to apply to your command was given to me, but I learned of the *Genyosha* from other sources. As soon as I heard that you had come forth, I knew that I must serve with you again. Since the time I served in your command, no other superior officer has inspired such deep respect. I knew, though I risked death, that I must, at least, try."

Narimasa licked his swollen, cracked lips. "I traveled aboard DropShips by disguising myself as a common laborer. No one watched me or cared where I went as long as I helped get work done on time and well. In some places, I traveled among the *Yakuza* and shipped aboard their pirate craft. Finally, after a journey of more than two hundred light years, I arrived here. I reported to your staff two days ago, and since that time, Shinzei Abe has been my host."

Yorinaga glanced at Tarukito. The *Sho-sa* in turn regarded the *Taishi*. "Why did you not inform Yorinaga-sama of Narimasa Asano's arrival? Why did he not appear in the daily arrival lists?"

Shinzei Abe lifted his head and stared down his narrow nose at

170

Tarukito. "I decided that his accomplices might inadvertently reveal themselves if he seemed to be overdue. That he is guilty of many crimes against the Dragon is not in question. Preventing the discovery of the *Genyosha* is. Even you, Major, will recall that the Coordinator made security my responsibility."

Tarukito Niiro straightened up and graced Shinzei Abe with a look of pure poison. "You recall but one line from a message you should have memorized in its entirety. The Coordinator reminded you that all the *Genyosha* officers and men are to be as devoted to Yorinaga-sama as the *Tai-sa* is himself devoted to the Coordinator."

Tarukito glanced at Yorinaga. He accepted Yorinaga's nod as permission to continue, then waded in against Shinzei again. "Narimasa Asano is obviously such a man. Forget that he threw a career away to travel here. Forget that he was willing to forfeit his life to travel here. Examine only the action of traveling here. Months on worlds working at tasks far beneath him in order to reach this world. Not only is this man devoted to Yorinaga-sama, but he is resourceful and does not surrender. What better recruit could we ask for?"

Shinzei Abe snorted derisively. "You could ask for a recruit who follows orders."

Tarukito narrowed his eyes. "Precisely why you are only a liaison officer, Shinzei Abe, and nothing more." He turned to Yorinaga. "Permission to show Narimasa Asano to proper quarters, sir?"

Yorinaga bowed his head. Lifting it again, he reached out his hand for a small lacquered box on his desk. From it, he withdrew a brush and small jar of black ink. After drawing a sheet of paper from one corner of his desk, Yorinaga dipped his brush into the ink. With bold strokes, he defined several characters. Setting the brush down, he reached into the box again and pressed his personal seal to the bottom of the paper.

Tarukito took it from Yorinaga's outstretched hand, and regarded it dispassionately. When he noticed Shinzei Abe's interest, he smiled. "As you have ordered, *Tai-sa,* I will conduct *Chu-sa* Narimasa Asano to the suite next to yours."

"*Domo arigato,* Niiro Tarukito-san." Narimasa Asano bowed from the waist. "You have been most kind to me, *Sho-sa.*"

"*Ie,* it was nothing." Tarukito returned the bow. "I am more than happy to help a fellow officer, especially if it displeases the *Taishi.* The uniform fits you well, *Chu-sa.*"

"*Hai!* Your quartermaster did exceedingly well in fitting me." Narimasa glanced at his reflection in the mirror on the wall of his living room. The room, which was L-shaped, bent around the cleaner and kitchenette from the front door to the bedroom. The straw *tatami* and

171

two brush painting landscapes alone decorated the apartment.

Narimasa sighed. "It has been a long time since I wore the green *ni*." He rubbed his hand over the symbol for "two" on his shoulder. "For this alone, I would have braved many of the perils I faced coming here."

"Forgive me for asking, *Chu-sa*, but you were a *Chu-sa* in the 2nd Sword of Light, were you not?" Tarukito, being well-bred, did not look Narimasa in the face as he asked the question, the better to avoid their mutual embarrassment.

Narimasa Asano nodded his head slowly. "The Dragon's memory is long and unshakable. After the disgrace on Mallory's World, the Coordinator broke up the Command Lance and sent us to different places. I believe that they thought what we had witnessed in the battle between Yorinaga and Morgan Kell had shattered our spirits."

"*Sumimasen*, Narimasa-san, but I do not follow what you are saying. What could have been so horrible?"

The elder MechWarrior shook his head. "At times, I recall it as a nightmare. I watched Kell's *Archer*—plainly, visible through my *Marauder*'s canopy—vanish from my tactical displays. I shifted through all the scanner modes, but it would not register. Though I could see the *Archer* with my eyes, my weapons refused to acknowledge it."

Tarukito shivered. *This is every MechWarrior's nightmare. The foe that cannot be destroyed.*

Narimasa nodded as though he'd read Tarukito's thoughts. "After we were scattered throughout the Combine, I became a *Chu-i* and once again commanded a single lance, as I had done in the early days out of Sun Zhang."

He suffered a reduction from Lieutenant Colonel to Lieutenant! Tarukito shook his head. "Forgive me the inquiry."

Narimasa smiled easily. "*Ie*. I have endured much, Tarukito-kun, but I never abandoned my duty during that time. I must admit, however, that I might one day have committed *seppuku* if this chance had not revived my hopes of honor."

Tarukito frowned. "Why would you do that, *Chu-sa*?"

Narimasa's eyes narrowed to slits. "I was almost assigned to Duke Ricol's service."

Tarukito blanched, then caught himself. "Surely you would have been able to deal with the Gray Death Legion, Narimasa-san."

The elder MechWarrior nodded slowly. "Perhaps, but not as the leader of a *Panther* lance. That is all they would have let me do. Fortunately, I learned of this assignment and began my journey." Narimasa's head came up and he looked hard at Tarukito. "Be wary, Tarukito-kun, for the Gray Death Legion is not that far behind Wolf's Dragoons or the Kell Hounds in deadliness."

"But *Chu-sa*, Wolf's Dragoons now work for the Dragon, and the Kell Hounds will soon be destroyed." Narimasa Asano stiffened suddenly, but it was not because of Tarukito's words. Feeling a shadowy presence behind him, Tarukito whirled to see what it was. Then, like the *Chu-sa*, he bowed to Yorinaga.

Yorinaga returned their bows as best his kendo armor would allow. He carried the helmet under his left arm and his wooden, swordlike *shinai* in his left hand. He quickly glanced at Narimasa and the uniform, then allowed himself a small smile and nodded his head. Tarukito saw that the two men shared something more—a look, nothing else—before they bowed to one another.

Narimasa turned to Tarukito. "Please remember, *Sho-sa*, that the Kell Hounds escaped death once before, years ago, and even the first half of the operation set into place on Pacifica went less well than planned."

Yorinaga withdrew a folded sheet of paper from his chest armor and extended it to Tarukito. Opening it carefully, the *Sho-sa* read it with an expression that seemed to mix horror and relief. "This is horrible, *Tai-sa!* For Shinzei Abe to die in a kendo accident. To have his windpipe crushed by a strike." Tarukito shivered. "Shouldn't I transmit this message immediately?"

Yorinaga shook his head slightly, then turned as Shinzei Abe, similarly attired in *kendo* armor, came up to where they stood. The ISF liaison officer stopped before Yorinaga, and glared at the two junior officers. "Well, Yorinaga-san, shall we? I have meetings this afternoon and," he added, staring at Narimasa, "investigations to complete."

29

Damn! That Victor *runs cool.* Seated in the cockpit of his *Valkyrie*, Daniel Allard adjusted his infrared scanner to a finer gradation of heat. The display immediately redrew the *Victor* in shades of red and blue. Also within the scan zone, the other 'Mechs in his lance brought the flickering of color to the edges of his scanner.

Over the land connection, Dan called to Salome Ward. "He's coming our way, Major. We expect contact in fifteen seconds."

"Luck, Dan. Don't let the fox bite the hounds." Her calm reply brought a smile to Dan's face. Looking at his heat scanner again, he brought the crosshairs for his LRMs into line with the *Victor*'s heat shadow. *Three, two, one.* "Flight away!"

Computer-projected trajectories scored red paths for his missiles across his combat monitor, but the *Victor* suddenly hit its jump jets. The sudden burst of heat released by the ion jets overloaded Dan's screen and bathed his cockpit in white fire. Alarms screamed in his ears as his sensors reported heavy scanning and a preliminary lock onto his *Valkyrie*.

"Punch it, now, Scout Lance! I'm marked!" Dan wheeled his *Valkyrie* blindly amid the jungle and smashed into a tall tree. He rebounded, then punched his jump jets and flew straight up through the tree's branches. *I hope I can see to come down.*

"Move it, Baker!" Austin Brand's voice knifed into his ears. "Damn! *Victor* came down on top of him and used the AC on his head.

174

Baker's gone!"

"Flight away!" Meg Lang spoke more calmly and Dan visualized her systematically coaxing data up on her monitors as she sent two SRMs at the *Victor*. "No hits for the LRMs, but Brand's SRM salvo hit seven out of ten in center torso. Damn! I only hit a leg."

Dan squinted and his control panel swam into view. He saw the opening in the jungle where the *Victor* had come down on top of Baker's *Jenner*. Turning the *Valkyrie*, he jetted toward the opening on another ion cloud. *Come in behind and POW!* His finger caressed the fire button and another flight of LRMs coursed toward the *Victor*.

Suddenly the *Victor* rose up through the canopy and hung suspended on a jet of ion flame. As the autocannon that was the enemy 'Mech's right forearm came up, alarms again wailed in Dan's ears. Stabbing a button, he abruptly cut his jump jets. The *Valkyrie* started to fall as the *Victor*'s autocannon rose into line, but the surprise move did not save him.

Lights exploded across his control panel. The computers told him that the autocannon's stream of slugs had peeled his *Valkyrie*'s chest armor like an orange, and had juiced the center of his 'Mech to boot. Warning lights flashed to tell him that the fusion engine's shielding had been chipped away. The internal heat monitor readouts spiked into the critical red band. In a slow voice that mocked the urgency, his computer suggested, "Evacuation would be prudent."

The *Valkyrie* was dropping like a rock. The trees in Pacifica's jungle might have broken the 'Mech's fall, but the *Valkyrie*'s landing snapped off branches and crushed whole trunks. As his 'Mech came down finally, Dan smashed back against the rear wall of the cockpit so hard that it stunned him. Helpless as a turtle on its back, Dan lay sprawled and his 'Mech faithfully imitated his nerveless body.

Through the *Valkyrie*'s faceplate and the branches strewn over it, he watched the *Victor* descend. The Assault 'Mech straddled its smaller cousin, its head tipped down so that the pilot could watch his victim. The *Victor*'s autocannon swung into line with the *Valkyrie*'s head, but Dan could do nothing as alarms screamed around him.

Suddenly, the computer screens reported a monstrous cloud of LRMs arcing in at the *Victor*. *Sixty of them! That's the* Catapult *and the* Trebuchet! The computer also reported heavy laser fire blasting into the *Victor*. The missile impacts blotted out the enemy 'Mech's outline on the scanner screen in a fiery tornado. When the 'Mech's outline appeared again, it was dotted with impact sites like spots on a chiroptopard's pelt.

The *Victor* hung its head. "O.K., troops, the computer shows the *Victor* 50 percent stripped of armor and the head utterly gone. Nice hit with the large lasers, Diane."

"Roger, Colonel Kell. Thanks." Sergeant McWilliams, the *Rifleman* pilot from Ward's Assault Lance, sounded pleased with her performance. "You shouldn't have gone after Captain Allard. That was the only predictable move you made."

Dan laughed. "Roger that. Damn it, Patrick, you never told us you were checked out on a *Victor*."

The *Victor* reached down and helped Dan get his *Valkyrie* back on its feet. "Nagelring likes its graduates to survive. My cadet company rebuilt a *Victor* captured from Kurita. Handle really well, don't they?"

Salome's answer struck home with both lances. "Well enough to crush a Scout Lance, to be sure. But not enough to take on a company by itself. Let's remember that, people. The bigger the 'Mech, the more people gunning for it."

Lieutenant Colonel Kell's voice followed Salome's comment quickly. "Truer words, Kell Hounds, couldn't come from ComStar. Let's get back to the base. Salome…Dan…executive staff meeting when we get back."

Patrick Kell leaned against the edge of his desk, arms folded. Salome Ward and Dan Allard sat on the worn sofa by the window. Seamus Fitzpatrick joined Richard O'Cieran at the poker table. Cat Wilson, the only non-officer, lounged near the door.

Kell looked up from a folder. "The computer projections give the best percentage chance that the Kurita force on Pacifica is a company of *Panther*s. That also complies most with the mass equations relating to the water-for-'Mechs substitution that Leftenant Redburn suggested on his visit. Comments?"

O'Cieran nodded. "I've had my men on exercises in the swamp area, but nothing extensive. We've seen signs of someone living out there, but Branson's Swamp has been a haven for *Yakuza* and other outlaws since long before Kurita lost this world. We've narrowed possible encampments to some of the larger islands, but we can't check them out unless we go in forcefully. I've not done that because we agreed last time that we don't want to let them know that *we* know of their existence."

Patrick Kell nodded curtly. "That's a plan I intend to stick with. Just continue your sweeps in the daily exercise schedule you have. Dan?"

"I don't believe the *Panther* company was meant to be part of the invasion."

Kell's thick brows knitted in concentration. "Explain."

176

Dan nodded. "O.K. We knew of the other two landing spots through our spy network, right? We didn't know of this one, and I think Kurita wanted to slip the *Panthers* in on us secretly. If their attack with the main force couldn't drive us off, they'd have this other company in place. They didn't even let their people on Pacifica know what is going on."

O'Cieran frowned. "What about the other *Panther* company? The one the aerojocks took out?"

Dan hesitated, then continued. "I think Kurita meant for them to be a diversionary force. If we'd gotten reports of a *Panther* or two wandering around out there, we'd have sent my lance or your troops to meet them. A dozen *Panthers* would certainly have overwhelmed such a small force."

Salome shifted her position on the sofa and looked at Dan. "Why the huge main force?"

Dan shrugged and Cat Wilson levered himself away from the wall. Although Wilson had refused a commission many times during his tenure with the Kell Hounds, the officers considered Cat very much a member of the executive staff. He half-smiled and squinted his dark eyes as though attempting to penetrate the mystery surrounding Kurita's actions.

"The Dragon never forgets. Takashi Kurita still burns from our last encounter on Mallory's World. Whenever Kurita decides to come after us, they'll come hard and try to crush us bad."

Patrick Kell smiled broadly. "As always, Cat, you make a whole lot of sense. Added to what Cat's just said, I'd say that Kurita will either evacuate those *Panthers*, or reinforce them. Until then, they'll probably stage a few raids on some of the agro-complexes."

Dan stood. "I think I should point out, Patrick, that *Panthers* are known for their ability to fight in cities. This spaceport is about the closest thing Pacifica has to a city of any importance in this area. If reinforcements arrive in system, I'd bet they'll make their move here."

Kell looked around the room and saw mute nods of agreement. "Good point." He looked over at O'Cieran. "Rick, have your troopers with SRM launchers replace the missiles with infernos."

At the mention of those napalm rockets, every MechWarrior in the room felt a slight shiver of horror. Infernos exploded in close proximity to a 'Mech, covering it with jellied fuel that ignited on contact with oxygen. The fuel clung to a 'Mech, leaving it awash in fire. Inferno rockets caused a 'Mech's heat to soar and could roast a Mech-Warrior inside his craft in seconds. It was the one infantry weapon that all MechWarriors feared, and 'Mechs seldom carried them as ammo for their own SRM launchers because of the inferno's volatility.

Jump Infantry Major O'Cieran took the order without batting an eye. "I'll also put an order through the computer system notifying all the Techs and astechs that it's again time for them to qualify with small arms, just in case the Kurita spy network is still tapped into our system. I can't imagine the *Panthers* coming in without some infantry support, and the mass of a company of troopers would be lost as a rounding error in your computer projections. We might as well have the hired help with us as against us."

Kell nodded solemnly, as he looked around at his staff. "Tell all your people to carry sidearms. Let's tighten things up, but let's not make it look too conspicuous." He looked up and was about to dismiss the meeting when he suddenly remembered something else. "Oh, Dan, whatever happened with the Nick Jones situation? Have you figured out how we're going to get him offworld on the *Intrepid*? I asked General Joss, but she said she couldn't speed up the paperwork because we're in the Isle of Skye. That means Lestrade will be watching everything with a quark-projection microscope."

Dan smiled and shot a glance at Wilson, who acknowledged him with a bare flicker of the eyes. "Cat and I came up with a plan that ought to work." He jerked a thumb at the window behind him, which showed the rapidly settling night. "Because Pacifica has this fourteen-hour rotation, and we run on TST, it's anyone's guess as to what time or day it is. We thought we'd just, ah, push the official clock ahead a day. May 25 becomes May 26 to everyone on the planet, and Jones musters out with his papers all dated properly."

O'Cieran's eyes narrowed. "Wait a minute. You and Cat have watch duty the night of the twenty-fifth." He laughed as the two of them feigned innocence. "Don't give me any of that. Besides, I'm conducting some night operations on the twenty-fifth, and now the day won't exist."

Cat's low bass rumbled like thunder. "Seems to me, Major, that your troopies, who have their alarms tied in with the base computer, will be sleeping secure in the knowledge that they'll be awake well before you come for them. Won't they be surprised…"

Everyone laughed, though O'Cieran's chuckle came a bit lower and more sinister than the rest. "Perhaps this plan has merit, Cat," he admitted. "Of course, you and Dan will cover the watch for me, right?"

Cat looked at Dan, who shrugged back. "We had that in mind all along, Major, because we knew how important the field exercise was to you."

Kell laughed aloud. "Gracious of you, Cat, to have thought so far ahead."

Cat glanced at Dan. "His idea, really."

Dan glared back at Cat. "Couldn't have done it without you."

"Very well. In forty days, we lose one day, and Master Sergeant Jones gets shipped off this wet rock." Kell looked out the window at the thunderstorm sailing in from Branson's Swamp. "A fair exchange, I think."

Sho-sa Akiie Kamekura hunched over his comtech's shoulder and stared at the flickering amber computer screen. In the corner of the screen, the date and time ticked down with military precision. Across the screen scrolled the hundreds of messages flowing through the Kell Hound base computer. The comtech's fingers flowed across the keyboard and typed a routine inquiry.

Kamekura straightened up, but avoided bumping his head against the low ceiling of the the man-made cavern. *I abhor being trapped here like a mole in this bunker.* He stared into the dark, where he could just barely make out the sparks made by Techs working on the *Panther*s back in the 'Mech bays. *Stuck in this musty cellar amid the swamps, I am being wasted.*

The comtech spoke without turning to face his commander. "Here it is, *Sho-sa*. The *Leopard* Class DropShip *Karasu*, the one they call the *Manannan MacLir*, is due back in two days, and the *Victor* is scheduled to be transshipped up to the JumpShip *Tsunami*."

Kamekura nodded silently and withdrew quietly. Thoughts and plans ran riot in his head, then slowly congealed into a masterstroke of brilliance. *I need a victory to prove how worthy I am of a real command. Without the* Victor, *my* Panthers *can deal with those enemy 'Mechs. Especially if the jump troops can infiltrate the base and demolish the Kell Hound barracks.*

He breathed in to call his aid, *Chu-i* Bokuden Oguchi, but the man materialized out of the gloom as though summoned by thought alone. Kamekura controlled an involuntary shiver. "Oguchi-kun, the strike force is scheduled to arrive here on 25 May, correct?"

"*Hai,* Kamekura-sama." The man hesitated, then added, "Planetfall is expected 27 May. We strike three different agcenters that morning to draw the Kell Hounds away, and then the strike force lands on them like a hammer."

A sly grin tightened Kamekura's thin lips. "Imagine instead, Oguchi-kun, our launching a surprise attack on the Kell Hound barracks during the early darkness on 26 May. We destroy their barracks facilities with explosives and have our infantry slay any MechWarriors who survive to try to make it to their 'Mechs."

Oguchi nodded enthusiastically. "Luthien would surely reward such forward thinking. Bold strokes make the Dragon happy. The

179

capture of everything the Kell Hounds have taken from us would please the Coordinator even more than the mere destruction of the mercenary scum."

Kamekura smiled openly. "Oguchi-kun, from your lips to the Dragon's ears."

30

20 April 3027

Justin stared at the screen in Gray Noton's Valhalla alcove. Sweat pasted black locks to his brow and trickled down to wet his lips with its saltiness. Though he desperately wanted to look away, he could not force himself to do so. "Rewind and show it again." His voice, barely raised above a fearful whisper, sounded like the sibilant murmuring of a madman.

The screen images blurred, then focused themselves into a *Rifleman* blazing away madly at an *Ostroc*. *Yes, the headless* Ostroc *circles as I did in my* Valkyrie. The *Rifleman* slowly spun and tried to bring his autocannons into line with the running 'Mech as it paced around Steiner Stadium. Autocannon slugs churned the dirt behind the *Ostroc* as the pilot loosed flight after flight of SRMs at the *Rifleman*.

Justin stiffened as a phantom rose from his memory, raking sharp talons across his consciousness. "Slow motion!" He snarled the command, half to make the computer obey and half to force himself to sit through it again. The *Rifleman* snapped its recoiless arms up and around, just as had the *Rifleman* on Kittery! The 'Mech pivoted back at the waist and scythed its deadly fire through the *Ostroc*'s legs.

Sepulchral fingers walked their way up Justin's spine. He looked down at his left hand...or where it should have been. He licked his lips and swallowed past the desert dryness in his throat. Trembling like a child, he stared at the screen and the logo painted on the *Rifleman*'s broad breast. The name echoed unceasingly through his brain.

Legend-killer.

Gray Noton looked up as Justin sank into the Typhoon's seat beside him. *He looks as though he's been through hell!* "Hey," Gray said. "Are you all right?"

Justin nodded woodenly, then something sparked in his eyes and he let himself smile. "Sure, no problem. I'm just a bit anxious about this fight."

Gray mirrored Justin's smile and punched the vehicle's ignition code into the dash console. "Did the tapes tell you anything about Wolfson?"

Justin shrugged casually. "Enough. He doesn't mind running his 'Mech a bit hot. Actually, I reviewed fights featuring *Riflemen.* You were pretty good, Gray."

Easy. Noton forced himself to smile despite the pain ripping through his stomach. He concentrated on navigating his way from Silesia before he answered. "I did my share. I always liked fighting in a *Rifleman.*" He looked toward Justin, but the MechWarrior was staring straight ahead.

Justin finally nodded slowly and turned back toward Noton. "I don't know if you're aware of it, but I lost my forearm in a fight with one."

Gray stiffened. "No, I wasn't aware of that. All I remember them talking about at the trial was an *UrbanMech.*" He steered around to the barricades and sent the Typhoon into Cathay.

Justin laughed harshly. "Vitios probably thought up that little piece of fiction all by himself. It was a *Rifleman,* all right, and one piloted by a very good warrior. Someone told Wolfson I'd have reason to fear a *Rifleman,* so that's what he chose for the fight. Bad choice."

Noton frowned, telling himself to be careful. "Why's that? You're fighting in the Cathay arena. In that jungle, the firepower that the *Rifleman* packs will be helpful. That machine's a monster, with its ACs over large lasers in the arms and medium lasers on the torso." Noton smiled. "I know because I sent enough 'Mechs to the scrap heap…"

Justin's eyes narrowed. "True enough, Gray, but jungle will make target acquisition difficult. The pilot that took my left arm was good. Even as good as you if you're still up to your game vids. But Wolfson's a kid with a hate on for me. He'll make a mistake."

Noton turned and looked hard at Justin. "Just remember this, my friend. *Yen-lo-wang* is really only packing one weapon. I don't count the lasers or that modification to the *Centurion's* left hand. If your autocannon goes out, you're in trouble. And Wolfson's not going to let

182

you punch out."

Noton slid the Typhoon down the ramp beneath the Liao Arena and Park. He released the passenger door, which rose up to let Justin out. Justin turned before alighting, and rested his left hand on Noton's shoulder. "I appreciate the warning, Gray. And while you and Kym are up there in Tsen Shang's box enjoying the battle, don't go betting against me."

Justin settled the neurohelmet over his head. One by one, he plucked the 'Mech's quartet of connector wires from his dead left hand and snapped them into the helmet's sockets. As the neural receptors pressed against his skull, the sound of his breathing filled the helmet's confining closeness. He shut his eyes and forced himself to forget the fear he'd felt while watching the fights in Noton's alcove.

This isn't Kittery, Justin, and Billy Wolfson is not Gray Noton. The second that thought formed itself in his mind, he suddenly realized that he'd discovered the identity of the MechWarrior who had maimed him. *No,* he told himself. *Don't think about it now. There'll be time later, much later. Dwell on it now, and Billy Wolfson will kill you, no matter how clumsy he is. Use your anger, but against Wolfson first.*

"Pattern check. Justin Xiang." Anger seeped into his voice, though the computer neither noticed nor cared. His nostrils flared as he remembered Wolfson calling him a "slant" and a "bastard." *You're going to die for those remarks, Billy Wolfson, and I'll spit on your grave.*

Static burst in his ears like thunder from a distant storm. "Voice-print pattern match obtained. Proceed with initiation sequence."

Justin smiled. "My heart belongs to the woman with hair of gold." Kym's image flashed through his mind and banished the last, bitter traces of his fear. *I've not lost everything.* "Authorization code: *Ba si jiu ling.*"

"Confirmation of authorization. *Yen-lo-wang* awaits to eat the dead." The computer's voice, flat and emotionless, died as all the 'Mech's systems flickered to life.

Justin reached over, took firm hold of the middle and ring fingers on his metal hand, and wrenched them back flat against the back of his hand. That popped open the little cavity in his wrist and let the computer cable dangle free. Justin snapped it into the port on the left arm of his command chair, then folded the metal hand around the joystick.

He raised his 'Mech's left arm and smiled at the titanium-sheathed blades attached to the last three fingers on the 'Mech's hand. He'd had them added to *Yen-lo-wang* in honor of Tsen Shang. The jutting, triangular shards of metal looked fearsome and could slice into another 'Mech's armor, but Justin tended to agree with Noton's assessment of the weapons. *If I get in close enough to have to use these blades, it will be a very desperate fight, indeed.*

The fingers on Justin's right hand flicked over the control panel. As he hit one button, the cultivated tones of the arena announcer's voice filled his helmet. Though the man had probably studied hard to disguise his accent, Justin recognized the rough edge of the announcer's speech as a sign that the man was from the Lyran Commonwealth. *Probably a big-time TBC man brought in for the broadcast.*

"Yes, indeed, folks, we've got a spectacular contest for you tonight. You're all aware of the sensational rise of Justin Xiang. Just two months ago, he arrived here on Solaris as an unknown. In his first battle, he pitted his *Vindicator* against a *Hermes*, winnning that fight easily. Soon enough, he switched to a *Centurion*, and used that much-maligned 'Mech to stalk Peter Armstrong in his *Griffin*, the *Ares*. *Yen-lo-wang*, Xiang's specially modified *Centurion*, surprised Arm-strong—and he died surprised."

"That night, so we hear, hot words flew between Xiang and Billy Wolfson. Wolfson vowed that he'd kill Xiang. Xiang, meanwhile, defeated certain fighters over the next two weeks, which brought him within challenge distance of Billy Wolfson."

Justin doublechecked his equipment as the broadcast's color man explained the pyramidal arrangement of fights and challenges among the MechWarriors on Solaris. Justin had, by virtue of his six victories, moved up from the unranked fighters to the sixth of eight ranks. That placed him one rank below Wolfson. Even if Wolfson had not threatened to kill him, Justin's new rank would have made the Fed vulnerable to a challenge.

"So, you're saying that Xiang, if he wins this match, might be in striking range of Philip Capet?" asked the announcer.

"Yes, Karl, but that will not be easy. He surrenders much in the way of weaponry to the *Rifleman*. Though Wolfson has never fought in a *Rifleman* before, that 'Mech mounts enough weapons to be dangerous even in the hands of an amateur."

As the green light flashed on Justin's control panel, he looked up through the cockpit canopy to see the massive bronze doors opening before him. The arboretum's muted light writhed over the Chinese ideograms and symbols cast into the doors. It also revealed the damage done by stray missiles. Such wanton destruction of rare and ancient artifacts brought a new throb of anger to Justin's pulse. Once more, he caught and subdued the emotion.

As in the Factory, the Cathay arena had been built with holovision in mind. Scattered throughout the massive forest were holovision cameras that would record every instant of the coming battle. Hidden in the brush or disguised by vines and Spanish moss, the cameras relayed everything to a legion of editors, who fed their pictures to the master editor. He, in turn, sculpted an exciting program and sent it out for broadcast.

Justin stepped the *Centurion* forward and shivered involuntarily. *So like the rainforests on Spica!* He adjusted his scanner controls so that the magscanners would operate, but would only overlay images of anything 'Mech-sized. He did not want holovision cameras appearing all over his screens.

From what he'd seen of Wolfson's earlier fights, his foe would probably be coming at him from almost directly across the arena. Justin quickly studied the narrow path leading into the thick rainforest and believed that he recognized Wolfson's position from one battle vid. *South here, and I'll hit that broken canyon area.*

He turned the *Centurion* south and hurried through the low brush. He squeezed his 'Mech between some tight tree stands, then loped out onto the low ground. The groundskeepers had provided a sandy riverbed to break up the area between large islands of greenery. *A perfect place to play hide and seek,* Justin thought, with a knowing smile.

Suddenly, his sensors exploded and burned the *Rifleman's* yellow silhouette onto his forward screen. The 'Mech sprang from behind a hillock and leveled its arms at Justin. The large laser on the *Rifleman's* right arm bathed the *Centurion's* right arm with its scarlet fire. Armor boiled and melted on *Yen-lo-wang's* limb, but held even as the *Rifleman's* autocannon ripped chunks of armor away from the same arm.

Justin, ignoring the medium laser that flashed at him and missed, brought up his autocannon. He dropped his jaw and opened a radio line to Wolfson. "It's all over, Billy. At this range, you're history." Justin tightened his finger on the autocannon's trigger.

Nothing happened.

31

20 April 3027

"Gray!" Kym's silvered fingernails sank into Noton's arm. "What's happening?"

Noton's drink splashed to the ground, forgotten. He leaned forward, ignorant of the pain in his arm, to better see the image on the viewing screen. "The autocannon! It's jammed!"

"Oh, God!" Kym's breathless whisper was trampled beneath the stampede of comments from the other spectators in Shang's private box. "He's got nothing else!"

Noton wrinkled his forehead as he strained to see. "No, he has those titanium nails," he murmured. Like some half-remembered invocation, he repeated the words, "The nails and his brain."

Jammed, dammit! Justin spun his *Centurion* back behind a hill as the *Rifleman's* left arm appeared. He saw the flash of the large laser reflected from a thousand shiny leaves. The staccato bark of autocannon fire hammered through the jungle, but neither weapon touched his *Centurion.*

Blake's Blood! Justin watched as his helpful computer outlined the *Rifleman's* capabilities. Their speeds matched exactly, but the *Rifleman's* weaponry grossly outclassed the *Centurion. Even if my damned autocannon worked!*

Justin sent his *Centurion* sprinting north. He worked around the tight spaces, then swung back into line with them in case Wolfson

186

decided to follow on a direct line. Behind him, Wolfson sent bolt after bolt of coherent light burning through the forest. None of it touched the *Centurion*, but Justin had the distinctly unsettling feeling that Wolfson merely wanted to bracket him.

He's playing with me. Idiot…he should finish me.

Justin glanced at his own heat levels and saw that his 'Mech was handling the buildup admirably. His status monitor showed the blinking outline of an autocannon shell in the Pontiac 100's breech. He lifted the 'Mech's right arm and rotated it. *Damn! Armor melted over the gas exhaust port!*

The bole of a tree exploded on Justin's left as the *Rifleman's* left autocannon launched its cargo of metal. Justin's phantom left hand dropped the rear laser's crosshair on target and loosed a bolt of ruby fire at his tormentor. It sliced armor from the *Rifleman's* torso, which made Wolfson bring his 'Mech up short.

I'm still dangerous, Wolfson. Justin smiled and slipped his *Centurion* deeper into the rainforest. *Don't worry. I'll be back.*

A smile crept over Noton's lips as he watched the *Centurion* vanish amid the thick forest. "Yes, Justin, yes. Get away." Noton sat back as side-by-side comparisons of the status of the two 'Mechs bled onto the screen.

"There! The Capellan is in trouble." A white-haired man whose thick middle and scarlet nose betrayed his area of true expertise, gestured toward the screen with a frothy mug of Timbiqui. "Never should have modified that monster. Armor's almost gone on the only weapon he's got. *Rifleman's* gonna kill him."

Kym shot Noton a worried glance. Noton patted her hands, then turned and stood. "Is that your guess, or your opinion?"

The drunkard straightened up. "Son, in my day, I blew *Centurions* apart with glee out there in real battles." He looked at the others in the room. "Fought with the 10th Lyran Regulars, I did, and sent Marik *Centurions* home in pieces."

Noton nodded, then leaned forward. His voice dropped to a bass whisper, but no one had difficulty hearing him. "Then you'd not be afraid to accept a bet for one thousand C-bills, would you?"

The man swallowed hard, but could not resist the challenge. "Done."

Noton smiled and surveyed the audience. "Anyone else?"

Justin examined the autocannon's exhaust port again. Though the weapon used caseless ammo, it still needed to vent the explosive gases produced when the propellant exploded in the breech. Without the

187

open port, the gun's built-in safeguards would not allow the weapon to fire. If it did, the gun would burst and could possibly explode all the ammo in the *Centurion*.

Hopeless. It'll take Tung a week to open that tube up again. He'll probably have to replace it. Justin glanced at his monitors to see if the *Rifleman* had continued pursuit, but his foe had stayed put. *I don't want to do this, but I'll be damned if I'm going to carry live ammo for a weapon I can't use.*

Justin punched a button. A port normally used for loading ammo slid open in the *Centurion*'s back. Justin flipped a switch, then punched the button again. In a long stream, the autocannon's shells, all two-hundred rounds, shot out over the green landscape. Once the ammo had been utterly evacuated, the port snapped shut.

Justin glanced at his monitor. *Why hasn't the* Rifleman *moved? I couldn't have damaged anything inside.* Justin punched up the computer projection of damage done by his laser blast. *Ninety percent chance of internal damage…Even so, at best, his engine is kicking out a little extra heat.*

Wait! Justin flicked his scanners over from magnetics to infrared. The jungle faded away into a background of blacks, blues, and dark greens. The *Rifleman*, where Justin could see it between blue stripes of tree trunks, glowed orange and red.

Justin almost laughed aloud. *Yes, how stupid of me not to have seen it sooner…Wolfson almost fried himself running after me while firing wildly like that.* Justin flexed the *Centurion*'s left hand and looked at the gleaming blades on the last three fingers. Smiling to himself, Justin turned his 'Mech to face in the direction of the *Rifleman*.

Ready or not, here I come, Billy Wolfson. One of us has lived too long.

The *Centurion*'s loping run carried it around toward the east. Justin allowed the *Rifleman* tantalizing glimpses of his 'Mech as he brought it in closer. *If I can just keep the useless right arm covering my flank, he can shoot all he wants.* Sweat stung Justin's eyes. *Gotta be close.*

The *Rifleman* turned. The silhouette pulsed yellow-white on the lower part of its arms. Twin laser bolts ignited tunnels through the green canopy, but neither struck the *Centurion*.

Justin watched on his monitors as the *Rifleman* continued to track his 'Mech. Wolfson kept the larger machine turning slowly to match the *Centurion*'s orbit. As breaks in the woods allowed, Justin made the orbit decay. Like an errant planetoid, the *Centurion* slowly spiraled in toward the hottest thing in the artificial arena-solar-system.

Again and again, Wolfson lashed out at the *Centurion* with his large lasers. The beams continued to miss the swiftly moving *Centurion*, but succeeded in burning an open kill zone 300 meters around the 'Mech. When heat made using the larger lasers impractical, Wolfson blasted away at the *Centurion* with his autocannons, though their voracious appetite for ammo soon tempered their use.

Justin tightened the circle again, and Wolfson reacted as though Justin were a moth to flame, never imagining that his *Rifleman* might be a neck to Justin's noose. Justin's view of the *Rifleman* flared and vanished, but he saw what he had been waiting for. *Now!*

The white-haired warrior thrust a fist in the air. "Yes, the *Centurion* dies now!"

Noton stared unbelieving at the screen. Justin's *Centurion* appeared on the fringe of the kill zone. He circled fast, while the *Rifleman*, turning at the waist, tracked centimeters behind him. "No, God, no!" Noton slammed his right fist into his leg and felt Kym's hands tighten on his left arm. "Not again, Justin! Not what I did to you."

The *Rifleman*'s arms tipped up and came around behind as the torso twisted back. The old man laughed in triumph, and the first tears sprang to Kym's eyes. Noton tasted bile at the back of the throat. ""Better *I* had killed you, Justin."

Justin saw the *Rifleman*'s arms swing toward the sky. He planted the *Centurion*'s left foot and cut sharply to the right. He raced straight in at the *Rifleman*'s back, making himself an easy target. The *Rifleman*'s arms snapped down easily and Wolfson brought all four weapons to bear on the suicidal *Centurion*.

One heavy laser washed the remaining armor from the right arm of Justin's 'Mech, locking the *Centurion*'s shoulder in a tangle of fused myomer muscles. The second laser vaporized armor on the *Centurion*'s left thigh. The right autocannon's hail tore armor from the *Centurion*'s left breast, while its twin ripped jagged scars across the 'Mech's right thigh.

Undaunted by the damage the *Rifleman* had inflicted, the *Centurion* stiffened its left hand into a spearhead. Safely inside the firing range of the *Rifleman*'s long arms, Justin hesitated just long enough for Wolfson to realize his error. Tightening the grip of his phantom hand, Justin stabbed the 'Mech's left hand into the *Rifleman*.

The titanium blades slashed like a meat cleaver through the *Rifleman*'s inferior rear armor. Coolant shot out in glowing yellow-green geysers as the nails slashed heat sinks apart. Effortlessly, they punctured the *Rifleman*'s engine shielding. The heat of the resulting explosion washed silver fire over Justin's screens, but he merely flicked off the infrared without a thought. He closed *Yen-lo-Wang*'s left fist around the *Rifleman*'s gyrostabilizer—snapping the titanium nails off—and ripped the crushed mechanism free of the dying 'Mech's body.

Wolfson's 'Mech tottered and fell, even as Justin threw his *Centurion* backward. Like a vengeful djinn freed at last from its bottle-prison, the plasma powering the *Rifleman* blossomed into a gold-white ball of roiling energy. It lifted the *Rifleman* up as though the 60-ton 'Mech were a toy. It sucked the soul from the jerking, twitching machine, then dripped what remained into a fiery puddle at the feet of Justin's *Centurion*.

The announcer turned and stepped away from Justin Xiang. The holovision camera and its harsh light tracked the "personality" and let shadows cloak Justin. The commentator smiled and stared into the camera, despite its dazzling glare. "There you have it, fight fans. Justin Xiang's exclusive post-fight statement, and what a scathing condemnation of Federated Suns fighters it was! Only on TBC, the Home of Champions!"

Justin scowled and fought his way through the crowd of media people. He nodded at the twin mountains of muscle the Liao arena had posted as guards by his dressing room. One of them opened the door while the other kept the crowd at bay.

Safely inside, Justin leaned against the door and relished the steel's chill. Sweat still dripped from his black hair and ran in streams down his temples and neck. He smiled, then levered himself away from the doorway. "Ever come that close, Gray?"

The bald MechWarrior shook his head. He tossed Justin a thick white towel, and waited for him to wipe off his face before answering. "No. You came closer than any MechWarrior I know."

Justin snorted and raised his artificial fist. "But not closer than I've been before." He patted his neck with the towel. "That tactic, the one Wolfson used, was the same one that *Rifleman* used against me on Kittery. Wolfson didn't realize that the tactic is flashy and looks great on vid, but it has a flaw."

Noton narrowed his eyes. "Weak back armor on a *Rifleman*."

Justin smiled. "Yeah. I'd not thought about it, really, until I stopped running. My brother Dan—he's with the Kell Hounds—described a move an aerojock named Seamus Fitzpatrick pulled in his *Slayer*. He did an Immelmann and blasted the back of a *Rifleman* while it was still shooting at the rest of his flight."

Noton smiled. "Fancy flying."

"Fancy, indeed." Justin shrugged. "Anyway, Billy must have

learned about the tactic that got me and tried to repeat it. But you know what they say…"

"Yes?"

"Fool me once, shame on you. Fool me twice, shame on me." Justin pulled off his cooling vest and tossed it in a hamper. "Where's Kym?"

Gray smiled. "She said she'd catch up with us later. I'll be your transport until we find her. I think she has a surprise for you."

"Great!" said Justin as he turned on the shower and a steaming curtain passed between them. "I love surprises."

32

20 April 3027

"Report."

Kym stretched and sipped her coffee. "This goes directly to the Minister. Tonight I heard Gray Noton say that he was the one who wounded Justin. Justin Xiang is innocent."

Static popped in the speaker, then the male voice spoke with its customary emotionlessness. "Explain."

Kym smiled at the server and waved away the coffee refill the girl offered. "In his most recent fight, Xiang found himself in a situation that matched his report of his wounding on Kittery. The *Rifleman* used the same tactic—tracking right, inverting the guns, and tracking left— that got Xiang previously. As all that was going on, Noton said, 'Not again, Justin. Not what I did to you. Better *I* had killed you…'"

The discarnate voice slowed. "Implication: Noton was the *Rifleman* pilot who wounded Xiang on Kittery. Noton was offplanet at that time. Conclusion: Your deduction is probably correct."

Kym licked her lips. "Do I tell Xiang?"

Another static-punctuated pause answered her. "No. Not on my authorization. Information will be forwarded fastest by ComStar. Proceed normally."

Kym nodded. She lingered thoughtfully over her coffee even though the meeting had ended. *I am his mistress. Though he tries to hide it from me because I am from the Federated Suns, I can see how bitter he is.* She shivered, remembering what he had told her. *He's giving back as good as he got in his trial, but it will consume him.*

She finished her coffee and glanced at the hidden speaker. *I hope I can tell him soon. It may be the only chance to save Justin Allard from Justin Xiang.*

Kym buttoned her overcoat and raised the collar. The usual evening mist had actually become a drizzle. Retracing her steps toward the alley, she stayed beneath as many awnings as possible to keep the oily moisture from her clothes. Thinking of little more than that, she entered the alley.

Shadows swirled around her as a hand seized at her from the darkness. Kym was too fast for it, however. She grabbed the thumb, locked the wrist, then gave it an added twist that splintered it with a wet crack. Then she spun her attacker off into the shadows. As she began to step forward to finish him off, something heavy slammed into the back of her neck and the world exploded.

Stunned, Kym pitched forward and splashed helplessly into a scummy puddle on the alley floor. The tepid water clung to her face and hair like vomitus. Rough hands grabbed her by the armpits and dragged her deeper into the alley. Where it widened to form a small ferrocrete court behind the apartment building, the men tossed her at the steps like a sack of wet laundry.

A booted toe slid roughly beneath her right shoulder to flip her over onto her back. "You see, Justin. I told you she had a surprise for you." Noton's words had an ominous undertone. "Sneaky as a *Javelin*, this one."

Kym looked at Justin, but the alley's feeble light backlit him so that only his silhouette was visible. Yet, she almost felt Justin's fury. Rage gathered in his dark outline like lightning within a thunderhead. He hugged his left arm to his chest. *My God,* Kym thought. *He's the one who hit me from behind. That hand!*

There was agony in Justin's halting words. "Where were you just now? What were you doing?" His voice begged for any shred of a believable story, but the anger that shuddered across his shoulders threatened to mock anything she might offer.

Kym looked down at her feet. "I was...I just wanted...I was just having coffee!"

Noton's laughter stung like a neural whip. "We'll have to peel you like an onion to get the truth, won't we? That little bistro is a place where Davion agents get orders. Don't bother to deny it. Tsen Shang has already confirmed it for me."

Justin's silhouette grew taller and his hands dropped to his side. "What were you doing there?" His voice no longer begged for excuses. It demanded compliance. "*Answer me.*"

193

Kym darted a glance at Noton. "Don't believe him, Justin. I love you and Noton is the one who…Unngghh."

Justin's left-handed slap fractured Kym's jaw with a loud crack. "Whore!" he shrieked. "You worm your way into my confidence, into my heart, just so you can steal my very life from me!" Justin's metal fist rose again, but he stayed the blow. "You manipulated me—not for yourself and what you wanted—but for *them!*" He stabbed a finger back toward the bistro and, beyond it, to the Black Hills.

The first burst of pain had shocked Kym into utter clarity of mind, but its echoes nibbled at her sanity and devoured her confidence. The fears held at bay during months of balancing on the razor's edge of an undercover assignment finally overwhelmed her. The stiff defiance in her body melted. She curled her legs up toward her chest and hugged them with a low moan.

As she lay there, Kym heard the click of a pistol being armed. The she felt the cold metal pressed to her temple. She waited helplessly, knowing that there was no deliverance from the despair and terror that engulfed her.

"No!" Justin's voice reached out and touched her. Though she recognized it, she understood that it would never again soften with any trace of his former warmth and affection. "No, you will not kill her. Take this whore to the Davion representative on this world. I have a message for him—and for her other masters."

She sensed Justin's presence. She could smell him, and for a moment, the scent brought back vivid images of their lovemaking. As his hand, his human hand, settled on her shoulder, she screwed her eyes shut even tighter. His touch would never again have the intimacy or gentleness of a lover's. *As it would have just an hour ago.*

"Hear me, Judas, and carry my message to your whoremasters, Prince Hanse Davion and Quintus Allard." Justin paused as he gathered his thoughts. "You have driven me from you, yet you seek to maintain your hold upon me. I am not yours. I have never been yours. I will never be yours. Spare me your lies and plots and false information. You refused to call me friend, now know me to be your worst enemy."

33

Tharkad
District of Donegal, Lyran Commonwealth

24 April 3027

The clerk at Meier-Star Travel answered the holophone with a smile frozen on her face. "Meier-Star Travel. From A Place to Zwipadze, we'll get you there. And how may I help you?"

Melissa, her hair hidden by a brown wig and her gray eyes by dark contacts, smiled. "I wish to book passage to New Avalon."

The clerk nodded. "Direct, cruise, or local?"

Melissa paused as though considering the alternatives. "Direct would get me there in three weeks, correct?"

The clerk's fingers skittered across the terminal's keys. In response to her inquiry, data rolled through the text window beneath Melissa's picture. "Yes, three weeks. Is speed urgent, or is this more of a pleasure trip?"

"A vacation, I think, but I do have to get to New Avalon by July or August." Melissa shrugged and smiled innocently. "I've never really traveled between stars before."

The clerk nodded. "Many of our customers are out for the first time. Direct will get you there in three weeks, but the cost is prohibitive."

The girl glanced as Joana Barker's credit history rolled past on the screen. "You pay more for less time in transit. It would cost over 100,000 Kroner."

Melissa's eyes flew wide open. "Can't afford that! Not on my teacher's pay."

195

"Well, a local trip will never get you there by summer." The clerk typed some more, then smiled. "I can book you passage on the Monopole *Silver Eagle*. It's a *Monarch* Class DropShip that's been refitted for extra luxurious travel. It will get you to New Avalon within your timeframe and also give you a chance to see places like Skye, Terra, Fomalhaut, and Mallory's World."

Melissa frowned. "All those stops, and we still get there in time?"

The clerk smiled reassuringly. "Monopole owns the DropShip, but jumps from star to star aboard independently owned JumpShips. This gives Monopole access to a far larger fleet of JumpShips than one firm could ever hope to put together. Because the JumpShips are waiting insystem when you arrive, you pass through the recharge points quickly. That's how you'll have time to explore the interesting worlds."

Melissa nodded. "It sounds perfect."

The clerk frowned. "The *Silver Eagle* leaves in two days. Is that a problem?"

Melissa shook her head. "Not really. What is the cost?"

"Moderate. Luxury passage is 20,000 Kroner, but we can get you a private room for 8,500 Kroner."

"Splendid!" Melissa clapped her hands.

The clerk nodded as data on Joana Barker again flickered across the screen. "Your tickets will be waiting at the spaceport. The *Silver Eagle* leaves on April 26." The clerk hit the "Enter" button on her terminal and locked in Joana Barker's passage among the stars. "Enjoy your trip," the clerk told her.

The data, recorded in a dizzying array of 0s and 1s, shot through fiber optic relays, flashed into Tharkad's central computer, then shot toward the Monopole corporate computer. There it triggered a program that immediately billed Joana Barker's life savings (leaving her 5,000 Kroner to spend on the trip). It kicked 850 Kroner to the Meier-Star Agency, then sped Joana's data to the Flight Engineering Section.

Flight Engineering sifted Joana Barker's data to determine her physical needs and possible stresses on the journey. It sent off her medical history to anticipate possible needs for medicine so that the appropriate drugs could be added to the ship's pharmacy. Meanwhile, the history of food purchases she'd made from local stores and a catalog of meals she'd recently eaten in restaurants sailed into the Culinary Division. Her preferences for food and any possible religious taboos on certain foods were checked against the planned menu. The results of these calculations were added to the mass of data that slowly shaped the trip's final menus.

Joana Barker's height, weight, social status, and age landed in the

196

Housing database. Her mass determined whether her room would be toward the DropShip's core or out on the fringes, to keep the ship properly balanced for transfer from one JumpShip to the next. Because of her relative youth—which the computer believed to be 25 years—she was berthed on one of the more active decks.

Her known interests, club affiliations, and education influenced the selections available in the ship's library. Her dining partners for the first couple of meals were selected easily. It seemed that Joana Barker was bland enough to fit well with anyone. Her tastes even colored the selection of activities aboard the ship, and reservations were made in her name for those activities she was most likely to attend.

The computer wove all these threads back together into a profile of Joana Barker, then pumped the data to the Lyran Intelligence Corps computer. Though Joana Barker had been born within the LIC computer, the machine subjected the information to all the routine and rigorous searches for possible crime detection. Given the physical data, Joana Barker's name vanished into a Top Secret file of possible candidates to act as a double for Melissa Steiner. Beyond that, however, the LIC computer took no notice and sent the profile to Immigration.

The Immigration computer quickly rifled Joana Barker's medical history and determined that she'd had all the necessary innoculations for the worlds she'd be visiting. Then, while doublechecking her medical history against the disease list for Skye, something odd occurred. A complete duplicate of the Joana Barker profile split off and traveled into a RAM trap while the original wandered merrily on its way. Immigration returned the file to the Monopole computer complete with visas and a note wishing Joana Barker a pleasant journey.

Joana Barker remained in her RAM cell for three hours. Then an electronic inquiry freed the data and dragged it along to another massive computer, which broke down the profile into all its component parts. Immediately and simultaneously, a massive bank of parallel processors tapped the computer's near infinite store of knowledge. Augmented by a hidden trapdoor into the Royal Tharkad Library system, the computer verified each and every bit of data.

Everything checked perfectly. All the records of her education confirmed Joana's personal profile. Computers confirmed the length of her current residence. Her credit history and her medical history matched, item for item, the masters that had produced them. Everything checked. Everything was in order.

Though all the little details of her life fell neatly together, Joana Barker's name actually taxed the computer. First, the computer checked the name against all the generations available for the Barker family. No one on mother Lucy or father Benjamin's sides had been named Joana, though a Joan showed up as a possible match. Eliminating the obvious link, and bearing in mind Joana's listed Catholicism, a quick check against a list of saints only produced another Joan.

Unsatisfied, the program jumped to the largest list it contained. Cross-indexing her year of birth, 3002, with her location of birth on Tharkad, it then organized, by order of popularity, holovid and music stars of that era. Most matches, while close, produced such low probability scores as to be discarded easily. Even so, Yohanna—a female porn queen—joined both Joans as a possible candidate.

Still unrequited, the program sorted through numerous other lists of famous people. Politicians and sports figures produced nothing noteworthy. Historical figures produced the same Joan as the saint list, but otherwise proved unsatisfactory. The names of famous ships and 'Mechs failed to offer any ready matches.

Finally, the program reached the most recently added database. Greedily, it devoured the complete survey of 18th-, 19th-, and 20th-century fiction and compared Joana Barker to a myriad of names. It found one perfect match for her first name: Joana, but that character had no last name. The program immediately traced back along the information tree concerning the mythical Joana. It was then that something else suddenly matched.

Father Benjamin and mother Lucy fitted exactly into Joana Barker's profile. The computer checked Benjamin and discovered that his last name had been Barker, though he was better known as Sweeny Todd. Joana, his daughter, had been lost to him as an infant, and thus had never known or taken the last name of "Barker". In the works that popularized the legend, the girl remained Joana, just Joana.

The program double- and triple-checked the data. The match satisfied all criteria for a perfect pairing. That tripped another piece of programming burrowed deep within the Monopole computer. It coaxed the entire passenger list for the *Silver Eagle* from the computer and retreated without leaving evidence that it had ever been there.

The computer bundled all the information, including statements about probabilities and error disclaimers, and sent it out. The data package coursed through a series of computers. Once the information had passed all along the chain, the machines erased all traces of the data. Twice the information had to be moved physically from one machine to another before it could continue its journey.

Finally, the report scrolled across the viewscreen built into a desktop. It paused at the end of each page so that the reader could catch up with it. Then, as the reader punched a button, a whole new page of text materialized. The overview, only three pages in length, contained all the pertinent information the reader would need.

Duke Aldo Lestrade sat back in his chair. He smiled coldly and licked his lips. "So, the Archon-Designate *is* bound out of the Commonwealth. Having her kidnapped from a Davion world ought to put a stop to this alliance nonsense." He smiled to himself.

Hunting and pecking with his right hand, Duke Lestrade edited the passenger list and itinerary from the document. Using an encryption program, he then scrambled the data. Packaging the data bundle once more, he started it off on its journey from Tharkad to Enrico Lestrade on Solaris.

Duke Lestrade dumped the file from the computer's buffer. "Bon Voyage, Melissa Steiner. Don't forget to write."

Andrew Redburn reached across the candlelit table and took Misha Auburn's hand. She smiled at him, and he returned the smile, but said nothing until the servant had finished stacking the dishes on a cart and left the suite. "Thank you for dining with me tonight."

Misha squeezed his hand. "Thank you for arranging it. Everything was perfect." She stood without relinquishing his hand and led Andrew to the sofa.

Simultaneously, both began to speak. "I..." each one began to say as they settled against the cushions. Embarrassment washed over the faces of the two young people and then they laughed. Andrew nodded to Misha, but she shook her head. "You first, Andrew."

Andrew hesitated, then smiled sheepishly. "You must know how much I've enjoyed being with you here. So much so that I don't look forward to leaving. Tomorrow's all filled up with making arrangements and briefings and another damned reception tomorrow night." Andrew's voice dropped off. "But I didn't want to leave without letting you know how I feel."

Misha smiled, and caressed the side of Andrew's face. "I've enjoyed our time together, too." Her hand drifted down to cover his.

Andrew shook his head sadly. "It feels so good to be with you that I don't want to leave." He shrugged. "But I have no choice. I know I don't like the idea of being on Kittery, which is over two hundred light years from you."

Misha laughed. "241.24 light years from here." She glanced down at their intertwined hands, then back up at him. "I checked when I learned you were leaving on the *Silver Eagle*."

Andrew opened his arms to enfold her, and they kissed deeply. She matched his passion, then broke their kiss and clung to him tightly. "I know how you feel, Andrew Redburn, because I feel the same way," she whispered. "But all we can do is enjoy what we've got *now*...while we still can."

34

26 April 3027

Ardan Sortek shook Andrew Redburn's hand heartily. "Good luck, Andrew. Enjoy your trip home." The Colonel retreated back alongside the Archon-Designate. Melissa linked her arm with Ardan's as they left the VIP lounge to give Andrew and Misha some time alone.

Andrew forced a self-conscious chuckle, but the strong emotions he felt choked it off before it could be convincing. Misha came to him and he hugged her as fiercely as her heavy, gray woolen cloak would allow. As though his arms were a refuge, she lay her head against his chest, then kissed his throat. "I will miss you very much, Andrew."

"I know, Misha. I know." He kissed her lips and forehead, then held her close again. "I'll be back." He smiled gently. "I can't promise I'll record a holotape each week, or write a letter each month, but I won't forget you and I *will* return."

Misha smiled so beatifically that even the tears slowly running down her cheeks could not mar her loveliness. "And I'll be here waiting," she said softly.

Andrew took her hands and held her at arm's-length for one last, long look. Then he released her and stepped onto *Silver Eagle*'s gantry. He turned to wave once to Misha before vanishing into the DropShip's dark interior. Down below, in the lobby for commericial passengers, Andrew imagined that he saw Joana Barker standing in line, waiting to board the ship.

He made his way to his own suite of rooms, and tipped the porter twenty Kroner for delivering his luggage. *Rather different from the DropShips I'm used to,* Andrew thought, surveying the suite with wide eyes.

Compared to his rooms on Tharkad, the *Silver Eagle*'s accommodations were cramped, but they were decorated almost as finely as those in the palace. Gilded fixtures, mirrors, and cut-crystal lamps combined with satin bunting and wooden trim made the suite an exact imitation of the ships plying Terra's oceans millennia before. The quilted fabric on the walls and ceiling did betray the differences, but Andrew knew the ship needed them for safety. *If the transit drive ever cuts out while we're outside a planet's gravitational grasp, we'll be weightless.*

The living room boasted a pair of leather sofas arranged at right angles, one facing the suite hatch and the other the hatch to his bedroom. Between them was a low, glass-topped table. In the corner, immediately to the left of the entry hatchway, two wing-backed leather chairs bracketed a wooden table. A small, unobtrusive holoviewer sat on the table. Beside it, standing neatly in a rack, were holodiscs emblazoned with the logos of several magazines.

Andrew shook his head. He remembered mentioning to Simon Johnson that he read those magazines whenever he had a chance. For Simon to remember…Andrew shuddered. *That's one man I wouldn't want as an enemy.*

A closed hatch next to the bedroom hatchway opened onto his cleaner. Between that hatch and the one to the bedroom stood a wooden cabinet. Andrew crossed to it and opened its upper doors. Within was a holovision monitor and another, larger disc/tape playback unit. In the lower compartment of the cabinet, he found an array of liquors racked and secured against loss of gravity.

Shaking his head in amazement, Andrew passed into the bedroom. It was small, though the chest of drawers built right into the bulkhead did save room. Two comfortable chairs and a round wooden table were opposite his bed, which pressed almost against the exterior bulkhead. Reminiscent of an older age, gauzy curtains and a canopy hung over the bed from four massive posts.

Andrew smiled. The gauzy fabric resembled mosquito netting, but he knew, from similarly equipped—though scarcely as luxurious—berths aboard military DropShips, that the netting would keep the bed's occupant from floating away while asleep. If the ship lost gravity, a simple catch would release and shoot the netting over the open side of the bed. Electromagnets would secure the netting to keep the passenger from drifting away from bed. It would be a rude awakening, Andrew supposed, to float away from the bed and then suddenly to have gravity return.

Andrew turned back to the living room and flopped down on a couch. He laughed aloud. "Yes, Colonel Sortek, I think I'll enjoy this trip."

Melissa scowled as the porter dropped her bags inside the door. She smiled at him but got no response until she pressed a Kroner imprinted with her mother's profile into his moist palm. The porter frowned and withdrew as though afraid of catching a disease. The hatch squeaked as he pulled it shut.

"Great!" Melissa shook her head and surveyed the wood-paneled room. She reached out and tapped a finger against the paneling. "Plastic with pseudo-cellulose veneer." She stalked across the cabin, which took three short strides, and poked the sofa facing the entrance. "Folds out into a bed—manually."

She folded her arms across her chest and sat down hard on the sofa. The cabin, which she guessed was twice as wide as it was deep, reminded her of nothing so much as the barracks she'd heard about on some of the less civilized worlds in the Commonwealth. The room's furnishings were serviceable, and certainly more than Joana Barker had ever owned. It was obvious, however, that they had been moved to this lower deck from the true luxury decks because of their slightly worn condition. The holovision monitor, bracketed to a table next to the hatchway to the cleaner she shared with the cabin inboard from hers, had a minute screen.

Melissa felt the slight vibration of the ship as the crew began the ignition sequence for the launch rockets. Lights dimmed as the engines sucked power from the system, and suddenly a great emptiness opened up in Melissa. A lump rose in her throat and her lower lip quivered. Tears washed the room out of focus.

Stop it! Melissa slammed her balled right fist down on her thigh. *Joana Barker would not be crying right now. This is her "great adventure."*

She shook her head, then massaged her leg. *But I'm not Joana Barker. I'm Melissa Arthur Steiner, Archon-Designate. I don't have to live in a rathole. I deserve better.*

From somewhere in her mind, a sinister voice stirred her most hidden fears. *Deserve? Deserve, little Princess? Deserving means you've earned something. What have you earned, child of plenty?* Harsh laughter seemed to echo through her soul. *Here, Melissa Arthur Steiner, you will begin to earn what you so arrogantly believe that you deserve. See how your people live. Endure the same indignities to spirit and body. Then, and only then, will you begin to deserve.*

202

"So, Leftenant Redburn, that's the basic layout of the *Silve Eagle*." Captain Stefan von Breunig pointed to the illuminated chart at the back of the cockpit-style bridge. "We differ from other *Monarch* Class ships because we ripped out two cargo bays and added more passenger decks. We carry 350 passengers, more or less, and have expanded all facilities to handle that increased population."

Andrew nodded and tapped the image of the large dining facility in the center of the wall chart. "I notice you have one dining facility. I thought the *Monarch* split dining up by passenger class."

Von Breunig laughed and raked a hand through his short, white-blond hair. "When Monopole refitted the *Silver Eagle*, they decided to do away with class distinctions. The dining room bridges two decks." He pointed to the thicker bulkheads and hatches indicated on the chart by wide lines. "Though it's in the center of the ship, we've reinforced it against disaster. We've found that the ordinary passengers enjoy a chance to catch a glimpse of celebrities like yourself." The Captain pointed to a smaller area on the deck where Andrew's suite was located. "Though the *Silver Eagle* is egalitarian in its facilities, which saves costly duplication, we do have a private area for dining and recreation if you wish to escape the steerage passengers."

Andrew looked shocked, then laughed. "Captain, if my government were not covering my bills, I'd be down in steerage myself. In fact, as I told the Purser earlier, I expect to get tossed into the general population at meals." Andrew shrugged. "After all, why would I want to be stuck rubbing elbows with folks who'd have nothing to do with me if I were paying my own freight?"

Captain von Breunig smiled warmly and offered Andrew his hand. "Once again, Leftenant, let me heartily welcome you aboard the *Silver Eagle*."

35

5 May 3027

Justin shook his head. "He's lying, Gray."

The Capellan translator's head jerked around to stare at the MechWarrior. Justin had slipped into the Cathay tenement through an open window in the rear. He kept his hands in the pockets of his gray canvas jacket, and nodded to the elder Capellan seated between the translator and Gray Noton. "The old man says he does remember where the ammo shipment was hidden."

Noton reached out and grabbed the translator's tunic. "Going to come back and sell me the information later, Shih?" Noton shoved him back into his chair, which then tottered over and smashed the man flat on the floor. "Justin, tell the old man I'll give him 15,000 C-bills if he'll tell me where his unit stashed the ammo, and another 15,000 if the information is confirmed by the discovery."

Justin walked over to the old man and knelt at his feet. He smiled warmly at the elder Capellan and bowed his head. Slowly, lyrically, he translated what Gray had offered.

The older man, the last surviving veteran of an ill-fated Liao offensive against House Marik half a century before, considered the offer, then nodded. Carefully and precisely, he explained to Justin the exact location of the weapons cache. As his recall continued, he added information about the booby traps his people had organized before they were shipped offplanet. Whenever the older man paused to remember, Justin translated faithfully for Noton.

Satisfied, Noton stood and gave the old man a silver wager ticket. Justin frowned, but Noton shook his head. "The bet was placed on your last fight, Justin. You won, remember?"

Justin's face closed. *Won the fight, perhaps, but lost as well.* He nodded slowly. "So I did." He turned and stared at the Capellan translator. "If you harass this man, if anyone steals his money, I'll come after you myself with *Yen-lo-wang.*"

"*Wo dong.* I understand."

Justin jerked his head to the side. The translator scrambled to his feet and left the dilapidated apartment. Noton and Justin bowed reverently to the old man, who spoke once more as they slipped out the door. Justin replied to him, then joined Noton in the darkened hallway.

"What did he say, Justin?" Noton flattened himself against the cracked, plaster wall as three small children ran screaming through the corridor.

Justin smiled as he sidestepped the children. "He invited us back again whenever you felt even more generous."

"And you replied?"

"I told him 'Large in the purse is not soft in the head.'"

Noton laughed. The two men left the tenement and walked back down the cobbled back street to where Noton had parked the Typhoon. Two young tongsmen moved away from the car and nodded to Justin. Noton dug into his pocket to pay the boys for watching his aircar, but Justin's steel hand pressed his arm to stop him.

"Don't, Gray. They watched it because of *Yen-lo-wang* and the respect we showed the old man." Justin returned the tongsmen's salutes. "Money would cheapen you in their eyes."

Noton said nothing until they had both entered the vehicle and the gullwing doors had locked down in position. "You know much about the Capellan ways, but it can't all be blood. I'm half-Marik, half-Steiner, but I know virtually nothing about Marik customs."

Justin settled back against the Typhoon's plush seat. "I left the Confederation with my father when I was five, but I already spoke both English and Capellan without accent. Though my parents had divorced, my Capellan grandparents still considered me a member of their family. I visited them on two occasions—both times when my father had to attend a conference. Ever since graduating from Sakhara, I've been posted on the Liao frontier. There've been plenty of chances to brush up on my skills."

Noton nodded thoughtfully. "Listen, Justin, you know I work as an information broker." Noton jerked a thumb back toward the old man's home. "Finding someone who knows about a cache of lostech is pure luck. Most of the other stuff I do is headwork that requires putting together deals, and usually calls for a lot of organizational skill. It's the kind of thing I know you'd be good at, too."

Justin nodded slightly, but said nothing.

"You must have concluded by now that I have ties into the intelligence networks on this planet. They're all here—Maskirovka, LIC, ISF, and MIIO." Noton laughed, "I think even Marik's SAFE maintains a presence here, though the last contingent split and killed itself off during their last civil war."

Noton turned to look at Justin. "I make a very good living doing what I do, and I could use someone with your talents to coordinate matters for me." Noton steered the Typhoon into the underground garage of the building where he maintained an office. "I'd like you to consider becoming my partner."

Both men swung from the vehicle, and Noton waved Justin toward the escalator up to the street level. There, he produced a magkey and opened the back door. Justin preceded Noton into the dark room crowded with cabinets and shelves. The only open space, a doorway in the wall opposite the exit, led to Noton's office.

Justin followed Noton into the office and sank into a chair upon a gesture from the larger man. "What would you want of me?" he asked finally.

Noton sat back in his chair and steepled his fingers. "I'd not ask you to betray your father…"

Justin spat on the floor. "To hell with my father, and the whole Federated Suns. What sort of father would put a whore in his own son's bed to spy on him?"

Noton nodded. "Good," he said, unable to keep the pleasure from showing on his face. "Quite simply, Justin, this is the way things shape up. Marik, Liao, and Kurita will pay devilishly well for information concerning Steiner or Davion. In addition, elements within Steiner and Davion will also pay good money for information about themselves."

Justin frowned. "You mean Michael Hasek-Davion wants information about Hanse?"

Noton smiled. "Not inconceivable, but that was not exactly what I had in mind. Elements in Steiner are working on other elements in Steiner." Noton turned and pulled a file from a stack on his desk. "In January, Baron Enrico Lestrade asked me to bid on the diversion of a DropShip from its intended course. The same night you first fought here, back in February, he paid me the first installment, and I sent preliminary information to the people I needed to alert."

Noton flipped the file open. "Less than a week ago, I received an itinerary from Lestrade. Fool that he is, he also included the passenger list. In any event, I have relayed the information to my people to be ready near Fomalhaut to take the ship. They will capture whoever it is that Lestrade's people—meaning Duke Frederick Steiner and Duke Aldo Lestrade—want, and the Dukes will make their play for power at that point."

Justin nodded slowly. "It seems like a neat package to me, Gray. I can see what you mean about organization, too. What do you make on a deal like this?"

Noton laughed. "Normally, I'd clear 100,000 C-bills, but Lestrade paid me in a wager ticket on Fuh Teng's fight against Billy Wolfson." The information broker frowned. "You cost me a great deal of money, Justin, but I'm not one to hold a grudge."

Justin smiled and lied at the same time. "Neither am I." He narrowed his eyes. "Why don't you just demand more from Lestrade?"

Noton shook his head. "Not good for business. However, he's more than made up for it. The passenger list is worth at least that much to other customers."

Justin held out his hand out to take the folder, while Noton continued to speak. "I've been asked to discover information about others, from time to time, and a name or two appear on that list. My people will deliver the ship to whoever pays the most for it, and I'm the one who'll decide who the buyer's to be. Once that list circulates, the bidding war should start."

Justin nodded, then started as he read the name "Leftenant Andrew Redburn" on the list. The MechWarrior grinned easily. "Hmmm. I can see a few folks here who would be worth some nice ransoms."

Noton nodded. "So I told Lestrade even before seeing the list. His people balked at the fee, which exceeded his budget."

Justin stood and stretched. He took a second look at the passenger list, then closed the folder and handed it back to Noton. "And so, have others bought in?"

Noton glanced at his chronometer. "Well, Tsen Shang will be here in an hour. He'll offer 10,000, but I'll get him up to 25,000. Later I'll nail him on the ship's location." He smiled up at Justin. "What do you think? Are we partners?"

Justin smiled and gave Noton his good hand. "Till death do us part."

36

New Avalon
Crucis March, Federated Suns

5 May 3027

Hanse Davion looked up as Quintus Allard entered the office. The Minister glanced at the other man in the room, hesitated, then set a holodisc down on a table. "Forgive me, my Prince, I did not realize you were occupied."

The Prince stood and moved from behind his desk. "Not at all. Have you two met? Quintus Allard, Count of Kestrel and Minister of Intelligence Information and Operations, this is Baron Robere Gruizot. He's been sent by Duke Michael to ensure closer coordination of efforts between the Capellan March and the rest of the Federated Suns.

Quintus Allard had to force a smile as he shook hands with the noble from New Syrtis. Hanse saw it and understood, for it was truly difficult to look at Gruizot. Swarthiness and corpulence were often a problem of genetics, but this unkempt man's lack of personal hygiene were enough to make the Prince wish for Count Vitios in his place.

The Baron, his hand free of social duties, picked at his teeth. "Pleased to meet you, Quintus. I've heard much about you. Made sure I had my Kentares flu shots before I started out from home."

"So I gathered from your file." Quintus recovered the disc and stooped down before the Prince's playback unit. As Quintus straightened up slowly after loading the holodisc, Hanse thought he looked gray and haggard.

"How bad is it, Quintus?"

Quintus shook his head. "Things begin to unravel, my Prince." He moved to the chair that Hanse indicated for him, but swung it around for a view of both the holovid monitor and the Prince.

"Should I be leaving?" the Baron asked reluctantly.

Hanse Davion frowned. "Why would you leave? I have no secrets from Michael. You, as his representative, are due the same courtesy. We are, after all, nobles of the Federated Suns." The Prince pointed Gruizot to another chair, where the Baron seated himself like an obedient child. "Please, Quintus, continue with your briefing."

"Let me take it from the top." Quintus said wearily, and it almost seemed to Hanse that the man had deflated some.

"On 20 April, Justin Xiang killed Billy Wolfson in a challenge match. After that match, Justin made a statement. It took twenty days for it to get here." Quintus punched a button on the holovid deck's remote control. "Brace yourself, your Highness. This isn't pretty."

Justin, sweaty and still clad in cooling vest, stared out from the holoviewer's screen. The announcer's voice finished a question, and Justin smiled coldly. "What do I think of my opponents? I think Billy Wolfson is a prime specimen of the caliber of all Federats. He was a short-sighted bigot who assumed, naturally, that his racial stock was superior to my mixed blood. He forgot that I had defeated him easily before. Or else he blamed that and my other victories on trickery. He could not admit that I was the superior MechWarrior, and that is what cost him his life."

The announcer's voice interjected. "But what about the Fed contingent's dominance of the fights here, especially in the Open Class."

Justin snorted derisively. "I know what you really mean to ask. Your real question is what do I think of Philip Capet?" Justin laughed humorlessly to cut off the announcer's weak denial. "Well, I'll tell you. Philip Capet is the perfect ape of Prince Hanse Davion. Davion is a coward who sends surrogates to do what he is not man enough to do himself. He plans campaigns, like the Galtor debacle, to kill valiant men, then conveniently forgets so that even more men die because of his inattentiveness. And that is just how Capet killed both Billy Wolfson and Peter Armstrong. He taught them what he believed it is to be a man, but did not remind them that the rules were different when they faced off with me."

"What do you mean, Justin?"

Justin's face hardened into a granite mask. "He told them that real men fight without enabling their ejection seats. He maintains that anyone who can punch out of a 'Mech will leave too early. He taught that to earnest young soldiers and got them killed in war. Likewise, he has preached that to MechWarriors here, and they have died trying to

209

conform to his idea of manhood. Yes, Capet and his master, Hanse Davion, are fearful men hiding behind anyone who will execute their orders—and the consequences be damned."

Quintus hit a button and the screen went black. Hanse Davion sat back in his chair. His steepled fingers masked the expression on his face, but nothing could conceal the fury in his eyes. Gruizot sputtered irate nonsense and glanced from the screen to Hanse and back again.

Quintus cleared his throat quietly. "Forgive me, my Prince. I know the message is vile, but it is not out of line with the usual drivel MechWarriors spout after their battles."

Hanse nodded slowly. "Justin has killed six pilots now?"

Quintus nodded. "All from the Federated Suns. Granted, they were scum and we are well rid of them."

Gruizot waggled his finger and perched himself on the edge of his seat. "But they were *our* nationals, Quintus."

Hanse saw Quintus frown impatiently at Gruizot, and spoke up quickly. "I fear Baron Gruizot is correct. We cannot have our nationals murdered just because they are from the Federated Suns. Could we have one of our agents terminate him?"

Quintus swallowed hard. "There is more, your Highness, and it will answer your question." Hanse nodded as Quintus continued. "According to a debriefing and report directly from our agent closest to Justin, it has been learned that Gray Noton was the pilot who wounded Justin on Kittery. She overheard Noton say something that indicated he was present at the battle. So present was he that our agent believes that Noton was piloting a *Rifleman* on Kittery."

Hanse's eyes narrowed. "I always thought an *UrbanMech* was a poor choice to ambush a *Stinger* company…"

Gruizot nodded emphatically. "My sentiments exactly, your Highness."

Quintus nodded his head toward the Baron. "Following the report from our agent, I had Analysis run a check on Gray Noton. The preliminary workup places him off Solaris within a window that would allow him to be on Kittery. Furthermore, I had them run a check of Justin's story concerning the battle against Noton's available battles. Not only is Noton good, but he used a *Rifleman* almost exclusively. On several occasions, he battled groups of *Stinger*s using the tactic exactly as Justin described."

Hanse nodded slowly. "Well, well…Let us recall your son. I will pardon him—a big public ceremony—and then I'll break Count Vitios."

Baron Gruizot looked horrified, but Quintus Allard did not allow him to comment. "I'm afraid Justin would not return for all the K-F

210

drives in the Inner Sphere."

Gruizot frowned. "You say he's innocent, yet he wouldn't want to return?"

Hanse suppressed a smile. "Yes, Quintus. Explain yourself. This time, you're even losing me."

Quintus exhaled loudly. "After our agent made her report on Noton, she was ambushed. Noton had tumbled onto her activities some time before, but had kept quiet. I believe he realized that she'd reported his slip of the tongue, and had to get rid of her before she could let Justin in on it, too."

Hanse nodded. "Noton exposed her as our agent and killed her…"

Gruizot sniffed. "Pity to lose—"

"No, your Highness, she was not killed." Quintus fished a small sheet of paper from a pocket. "She was about to tell Justin what Noton had done to him, but Justin cut her off with a slap." Quintus raised his left hand and the Prince winced. "The blow broke her jaw. One of Noton's men meant to shoot her, but Justin stopped him. He gave her the following message for us both.

"'You have driven me from you, yet you seek to maintain your hold upon me. I am not yours. I have never been yours. I will never be yours. Spare me your lies and plots and false information. You refused to call me friend. Now know me to be your worst enemy.'"

"Damn his insolence!" Hanse slammed his palm against the desk. "Every time we hope to offer him our hand in friendship, he makes it impossible." Hanse stared at his Minister. "Have we other agents in place to kill him?"

Quintus hesitated, then shook his head. "No. He has made inroads into the tongs in Cathay. He is the Capellan champion on Solaris, and many watch out for him. He's moved from the villa into Cathay itself. We cannot touch him there."

Hanse growled in frustration. "Who will he fight next?"

"He wants Philip Capet," Quintus said, "but Capet may not accept Justin's challenge. Capet fights in the Open Class, but Justin's modified *Centurion* is too small for that class. Capet is not a total fool. He is not likely to leap at a chance to fight Justin."

Hanse smiled. "Send a message, Priority Alpha, via ComStar. It goes to Philip Capet. Tell him this: If he delivers the head of Justin Xiang, I will buy him his own 'Mech regiment and give him a world."

"Brilliant planning, my Prince. Simply brilliant," cooed Baron Gruizot.

Hanse never heard the Baron's words of praise. He saw Quintus hesitate, then nod reluctantly. The fire slowly died in Hanse's eyes. "Forgive me, Quintus, for passing that order through you. I know

211

Justin is your son, and this cannot be easy."

Quintus shook his head. "I helped give him life, and I hoped he would serve House Davion as I have." Quintus glanced toward the dark holovid screen. "If he had not betrayed us before, he has done so now. As you said that day, I no longer have a son named Justin."

Hanse nodded in agreement. "What of our agent on Solaris?"

The MIIO Minister shook his head. "She has been exposed. Because of Noton's ties, I would guess that her identity is known to all our enemies."

Hanse paused for a second, then nodded slowly. "Recall her to New Avalon. I have another duty for her to perform. Let me know when she returns."

"Yes, Highness."

"Is there anything else, Quintus?"

The Minister managed a weak smile. "I do have some good news."

Hanse raised one eyebrow. "Does it balance the bad?"

Quintus nodded. "I think so. The *Silver Eagle* left Tharkad on the 26th of April. It should enter Federated Suns space at Fomalhaut on or about the 20th of this month. We expect it to arrive on New Avalon by the middle of June."

Gruizot, whose ears had pricked up at the mention of a ship from the Lyran Commonwealth, frowned. "Why the interest in a commercial liner?"

Quintus looked at the Baron quizzically. "Didn't you know? Leftenant Andrew Redburn is returning on that ship. I thought that certainly *you* would have monitored the travels of the Capellan March's newest hero."

Gruizot stammered nervously. "Well, you know, so many duties…"

Quintus nodded. "Indeed."

"This is welcome news," Hanse said, smiling broadly. "It does indeed balance the bad."

37

Andrew Redburn held out Joana Barker's chair for her as they joined Hauptmann Erik Mahler, Ret., and his wife Hilda at their table. Mahler stood until Joana had taken her seat, then waved Andrew to his chair. "I have looked forward to this meal since I saw the schedule this morning." Mahler glanced up at the balcony where most of the celebrities took their meals. "I could hardly believe you would be dining with the *untermensch*."

Andrew smiled broadly. "Well, Hauptmann, you must know well from your own days in the harness that no MechWarrior could resist the charms of your wife and Joana here."

The gray-haired MechWarrior smiled and laid a hand over that of his blushing wife. "True enough, Leftenant." Mahler gave Andrew the wine list. "You will share some wine with us? And you, Ms. Barker? We tried the white from Nekkar last evening, and found it quite satisfactory."

Joana nodded her agreement, while Andrew said with a smile, "I agree, but only if we order two bottles and apply the cost to my bill. Consider it a gift of friendship from Prince Hanse Davion."

Mahler clapped his hands. "Done."

Joana shot Andrew a sidelong glance. "Generous with your leader's money, aren't you?"

Andrew unfolded his cloth napkin and spread it over his lap. "Indeed, Joana, did you not know that Prince Hanse Davion is a

213

confirmed bachelor with no wife to spend all the Davion money for him?" Andrew hesitated and coughed lightly into his right fist. "Besides, the Prince shares 'Mech technology with the Lyran Commonwealth. Could he fault me for sharing wine with the three of you?"

Hilda smiled and toyed with her long braid of white-blond hair. "We appreciate the gesture, Leftenant, and we have some love for your leader. We think, as do most Lyrans"—she looked to Joana, who gave an approving nod—"that the accords signed by the Archon and your Prince will mean good things to both our nations."

"Thank you. I share your hope for a prosperous and peaceful future."

The waiter arrived to serve the meals, while the wine steward poured a small amount of wine into Andrew's glass. After Andrew declared the vintage to be excellent, the steward also filled his companions' glasses. The dinner conversation wound its way pleasantly but lightly through the amusing chatter of strangers getting to know one another, but took a turn toward the serious as the waiter cleared the plates to serve brandy.

Mahler frowned as he stared into the golden liquid in his snifter. "As I recall, Leftenant, you were on Kittery. What do you think of this Justin Xiang?"

Andrew stiffened. "Justin Allard was my commander. I knew the man and liked him very much."

"Ja, but is he not a traitor?"

Andrew frowned. "Forgive me, Hauptmann Mahler, but I do not think so. I was present at that trial and it was more like a witch-hunt sponsored by Michael Hasek-Davion. It was a travesty, not a fair trial."

Mahler pursed his lips thoughtfully. "You say Allard's not a traitor, but what about his tirades against the Federated Suns? He has singlehandedly eliminated almost every Fed fighter on Solaris. It is nothing short of a vendetta, one even a Draconian might be proud of."

Andrew carefully folded his napkin and set it down on the table. "I can understand Justin's anger and resentment. I can understand how a true MechWarrior might hate those sham warriors on the Game World, and I can see how he could easily end up killing every one he faces..."

Joana leaned forward. "Forgive me, Andrew, but I do not think Hauptmann Mahler was impugning Xiang's skill as a MechWarrior. Even here in the Commonwealth, we saw holovids of his outburst in the courtroom. Hanse Davion offered him life. He even agreed that the execrable trial should never have been held. He directed that the verdict be "Innocent", and it should all have ended right there."

Andrew's nostrils flared. "Excuse me, Miss Barker, but I would not expect you, a teacher, to understand what it is to be a MechWarrior." Andrew turned quickly to Mahler. "You, sir, retired after years of valiant service. How would you have taken to being a desk-jockey for the rest of your career? How would you have taken to being known as 'the one Hanse Davion saved from justice?' Could you have tolerated living with the doubt you'd surely see in people's eyes, or with the knowledge that the leader you loved and served so well did not believe in you?"

Mahler shook his head without a word, but Joana was not satisfied. "If Xiang loved his leader so much, how could he villify him? In the ship's holovid theatre, I saw Xiang's most recent battle and heard his remarks about Hanse Davion. The man spews pure venom. If there ever was any love in him for his Prince, it has long since died."

Andrew stood abruptly. "If it died, Miss Barker, it died on a political altar. I hope that no one—be they Archon or Periphery Bandit King—believes that he has the right to do that to another human."

Andrew bowed his head to the Mahlers. "If you will excuse me…"

38

Solaris VII (The Game World)
Rahneshire, Lyran Commonwealth

5 May 3027

Tsen Shang cautiously pushed open the door to Gray Noton's office. He kept his right hand parallel to the floor and pressed against his stomach. Shang had earlier applied neurotoxin to the last three razor-sharp fingernails of each hand, and the weak light from Noton's office reflected off the gold leaf also applied to the nails.

Shang closed the door and latched it. He quickly studied the file room, but touched nothing. It was much as he recalled it. Blowing a thin layer of dust from a stack of papers, he satisfied himself that nothing seemed out of the ordinary. *Nothing but Noton's failure to greet me.*

The Maskirovka agent half-crouched as he moved across the storeroom like a shadow. Padding his way down the short hallway to Noton's office, he caught his first glimpse of the former MechWarrior. At that, he straightened up and walked boldly into the room.

Noton sat at his desk with his feet up and his head resting chin-on-chest as though he'd just fallen asleep. Shang pressed one finger to Noton's carotid artery, but the lack of a pulse and the slight coolness of the flesh confirmed what his eyes had told him. Gray Noton was dead.

Shang grabbed Noton's chin between the thumb and forefinger of his left hand. He tipped the head up, but the moment he moved it, Noton's head slumped unceremoniously over onto his right shoulder. *Hmmm, neck's broken.* Shang eyed the thickness of Noton's bull neck. *Hard blow. Well-placed.*

Shang turned his attention to the desk. He searched its clutter of files and papers, but found nothing of interest. Then he slipped behind the body to get at the shelves built over the desk. Reaching up, he pulled down a trophy that Noton had won in Marik's Factory years before.

Damn! So he found this, too. Shang traced the melted crescent where someone had expertly carved the lock from Noton's wallsafe with a laser. Shang swung the round door open, and the cylindrical safe yawned like an empty mouth. The Maskirovka agent shook his head.

He stared down at Noton's body. *What did you do, Gray, to set him off?* Shang shrugged. *Even if you could speak, I doubt that you could have answered that question. So now I must learn the answer, and if necessary, avenge you.*

From a shadowed doorway across the street, Justin watched Tsen Shang leave Noton's office. He waited until Shang had climbed into his Feicui model aircar and passed down the road before moving from his hiding place into the dark alley. As the car vanished around a corner, Justin drew in a deep breath and exhaled it slowly.

Crouching down, Justin once again turned his attention to the lockbox he had removed from Noton's safe. He set it down on the alley floor, then curled the fingers of his metal left hand into a fist. With one quick blow, he shattered the lock. Justin tugged the latch open and whistled at the contents of the box. "Noton, you were full of surprises, weren't you?"

Nestled on a bed of crisp C-bills were various traveling papers issued to a half-dozen individuals who all shared Gray Noton's description, picture, and thumbprint. He also found two small books: one with names and addresses, and the other in a code. *Not a tough code, but it will take time. Looks like a diary of his business transactions.*

Justin turned the left pocket of his coat inside out and carefully tore the fabric apart at the seam. He transferred money and documents through the hole and stashed them in the coat's lining. Finally, he pulled a ring of magkeys from the box. He stuffed them into his trouser pocket and tossed the strongbox back amid the debris strewn behind him.

Justin picked up and flipped open the folder Noton had showed him. In the dusky half-light, he studied the passenger list for the *Silver Eagle*, smiling unconsciously at the sight of Leftenant Andrew Redburn's name. After closing the file, he visually guided his left hand to the fire capsule worked into the folder itself. He concentrated and crushed the lump flat. Smoke drifted up from beneath his synthetic thumb, then flames licked at his metal hand. Justin tossed the folder aside and watched it burn. When the flames died, he smashed the ashes with one foot and scattered them with a light kick.

For your faith in me, Andrew, I deny this file to the Maskirovka. It is all I can do. Now you're on your own. Good luck, my friend.

39

Summer
Isle of Skye, Lyran Commonwealth

6 May 3027

"Just a second!" Melissa Steiner pressed the other brown contact against her right eye, then turned away from the mirror. She opened the hatch to her room, then tried to shut it almost as quickly when she saw who it was. "What do you want?"

Blushing mightily, Andrew Redburn looked down at his shoes. "A truce. A truce—and to apologize."

Melissa stepped back and allowed Andrew to enter the room. "Please, Leftenant, be seated." Her frosty tone mocked the invitation of her words. The door clicked shut behind the MechWarrior.

Melissa pointed to a small refrigerator. "May I offer you something?"

Andrew shook his head. "No, thank you." Looking up, he met her hard stare. "I realize that you did not like what I said last night, and I apologize for any embarassment I caused by walking out. I have already apologized to the Mahlers."

Melissa snorted and narrowed her eyes. "I'm glad to see that you have *some* manners, Leftenant!" Her tone scourged him with his rank, and he recoiled unconsciously. "I assume that Federated Suns officers do not become irredeemably insolent until they reach their Captaincy."

Muscles bunched at Andrew's jaws. "Yes, I suppose I have that coming, but I don't like the veiled suggestion that I will never have my chance at a Captaincy, Miss Barker. You may think that I treated you in a manner not appropriate to your station, and you may resent it, but

219

I'll not be punished for it."

He threw his hands up in the air and growled, "I came here to apologize, and you make it impossible!"

Despite the contact lenses, Melissa's eyes blazed. "Impossible? *You* are impossible. How do you expect me to react when you lecture me on how a ruler should deal with subjects! Such arrogance! You used the fact that Miss Barker could not defend against or refute such an attack. Yes, I resent that."

Andrew closed his eyes and nodded. He forced his body to relax. "Yes, you're right." He shook his head and wandered over to her couch. Sitting down heavily, he then leaned forward with elbows on his knees and hands clasped together. "You just don't know how it feels."

"How what feels, Andrew?" Melissa crossed to the sofa and sat beside him. She heard the pain in his voice and it melted her own anger.

Andrew's adam's apple bobbed as he swallowed. "I revered Justin Allard. I could not have hoped for a better commanding officer, and I did my best to break through the prejudice the Kittery cadets had toward a man with Capellan blood in him. Even when he discharged Sergeant Capet, I defended him against all comers."

Andrew turned and Melissa saw tears gathering in his eyes. "When the Capellans ambushed us, I didn't know what to do. I wanted to relinquish control to Justin, but he gave me command. He didn't say anything, but I heard the confidence in voice. He knew I'd not let him down, and I fought desperately to be worthy of that trust. I pushed my men and organized them. Somehow, we got out of a very nasty situation much better than we should have." Redburn turned away and stared at his clenched hands.

Melissa reached out and touched him on the shoulder, and she could feel the tension rippling through him. She bit her lower lip, but could do nothing but listen.

Andrew never noticed her touch. "I remember seeing the ruins of his *Valkyrie* and how torn I felt when I found out that he'd lost his arm. I knew, right then…I had a feeling…that his life would be different. Then the trial, and all that viciousness. Somehow it got to him."

"I watched a video of Justin's fight against Wolfson just after we jumped to Summer," Andrew said softly. "I heard him denounce Hanse Davion. I…I couldn't believe it, but now I think I understand it all better. I'm sorry."

He shook his head. "I wonder if I ever knew Justin at all…"

Melissa rubbed her hands across Andrew's neck. "It sounds as though you knew him well. But that trial left its mark on him. People can change, you know." She bit off the words as though they were bitter in her mouth. "I just hope it doesn't always have to be a change for the

220

worse."

Andrew, frowning, looked at her. "I don't understand."

Melissa moved to the center of her cabin, which put her back to him. She hugged her own arms around herself as that same mocking laughter seemed to echo at her from the void. "There was once a time when I would have challenged my elders to justify how they'd wielded their power, much as you did the other night. Some considered me foolish, and others thought I was merely an argumentative child. The worst, like Aldo Lestrade, patronized me, which I hated. I vowed to bend him and those like him to my will because I was destined to be Archon."

She turned slowly. "Ruling, you see, was presented to me much as a game. Yes, they gave me lessons to study and Thelos Auburn steeped me in history. I know more boring facts about the Lyran Commonwealth than anyone should be cursed to remember. Yet, despite all that, I *am* the Archon-Designate."

She smiled at Andrew's puzzlement. "I could get away with anything. Courtiers I could not charm were courtiers I could terrorize. I learned, as a wee child, to win with smiles, or to take with an imperious demand. In short, I learned that the Archon-Designate always wins—only sometimes the tactics must be brutal."

Andrew shook his head. "You must have outgrown that, though."

Melissa shrugged, still holding her shoulders with arms crossed over her chest. "Have I? Perhaps…It's true that on an intellectual level, I have learned what it means to rule. Even so, my lessons in power have been rather academic. I cannot fault my teachers, for there is really no good way to teach the use of power. Let's take an example. Your company, perhaps, is being pursued by an overwhelming force. You can outdistance them, but the leg actuator on one of your unit's 'Mechs goes out. Both the pilot and his machine will die unless you turn your command around to defend him. You might be able to draw pursuit away from one warrior, but others in your command will die. What should you do?"

Andrew considered the question for a moment, then nodded. "I would have to leave the one man behind and save my command."

Melissa smiled. "The greatest good for the greatest number." She shook her head sadly and looked down. "We comfort ourselves that the man will die painlessly and perhaps even sell himself dearly to earn you extra time. The fact is, though, that he will not die painlessly. Your Justin Xiang did not."

She raised a hand to forestall Andrew's comment. "Just as you came to apologize for what you had said, I, too, must apologize. You correctly protest against the pain that your friend suffered, and I tried to defend his suffering as a necessary action. Neither of us can alleviate his anguish, and we feel the guilt of that." She smiled sheepishly. "If I thought a pardon would make him whole again, I would ask the Prince to do it."

Andrew nodded, then paused as he thought deeply about all that had happened since that day on Kittery. "I appreciate that, your Highness, but after seeing that tape, I fear that Justin is now lost to us forever."

BOOK
3

40

The click of the pistol's hammer being eared back was loud enough to rouse Justin from his slumber. Turning over groggily, he lifted his head to squint at Tsen Shang. Silhouetted against the light of the desk lamp, the Maskirovka agent looked as dark as his clothes. The only light glinted off the pistol's long barrel.

Justin tipped a pillow up and eased himself into a sitting position against the headboard. He raised his left hand to shield his eyes from the lamp's strong stare, and smiled. "You can put the gun away."

Tsen Shang leaned his head slightly to the right. "Can I? You murdered Gray Noton—quite nicely I might add—so why should I trust you?"

Justin shrugged.

Shang tipped the pistol up. "Noton had a document that was meant for me. We had agreed on a price. I will pay you the same amount to turn it over to me."

"No sale."

The pistol again aligned itself with Justin's head. "I will not negotiate with you, Xiang. All I need do is shoot you and ransack this place to find it."

Justin shook his head. "You won't find it. I destroyed it, and you should be thankful I did."

Shang did not move the gun. "Explain," he said.

Justin smiled and nodded graciously. "Simply put, Noton was

225

working with the CID to set up the Maskirovka. The document he had would have tempted you to commit men, 'Mechs, and money to an operation that would have cost you all of it."

Shang lowered the gun but did not holster it. "Go on." He reached back and turned the lamp away so that it no longer blinded Justin.

"That document was the passenger list for a ship known as the *Silver Eagle*. I recognized the pseudonyms of two passengers as the names given to my father and his wife when they travel. The Maskirovka, within a day or two, would have cracked those identities. You can see what sort of valuable cargo that is."

When Shang nodded, Justin continued. "The *Silver Eagle*, according to Noton, was to be hijacked and taken to a world—whose name you would have purchased from him—where the passengers would be held for ransom. Surely, the Capellan Confederation would not pass up the chance to snatch the head of Davion security, especially upon his return from a covert mission in the Lyran Commonwealth."

"No, that would be too great a prize to let slip through our grasp." Shang lowered himself to the foot of Justin's bed. "How did you discover the deception?"

Justin smiled. "Superstition. My father and his wife never traveled on the same JumpShip in order to protect their children from being orphaned in case a K-F drive malfunctioned." Justin leaned forward. "What made me even more suspicious was that while I was in the hospital, I saw a man who looked exactly like Hanse Davion and one who looked exactly like my father. The doubles had apparently been prepared to deceive someone. I know that Davion wants revenge against Liao, but I don't know what for."

Justin watched Shang's eyes grow distant. *Two parts hospital rumor, one part pure nonsense, and a dash of family anecdote. That ought to allay Shang's suspicions long enough to keep Andrew safe for the moment. Now for the clincher.* "Reach into my jacket pocket."

Shang slashed the pocket open with the sharpened nails of his left hand and pulled out some folded sheets. As he unfolded the document, he saw that they were Federated Suns indentification papers containing Noton's image and description. He studied it and grunted. "They've provided him with a new identity."

Justin nodded. "I tried to reason with him, to get him to refrain from selling the list. He seemed to think you'd only lose a regiment trying to capture the ship. I said you'd be angry and he said he'd apologize from his villa on Verde. Then he offered to sell the scraps of his operation here on Solaris."

Justin lifted his left fist in the air and let it drop to the bed with a thump. "I declined his offer."

Shang slipped the identification document into his own pocket. "Interesting." He bowed his head, then backed toward the door of Justin's spartan quarters. "We will speak again, Justin Xiang. For now, let me express the gratitude of the Maskirovka for all you have done."

Justin nodded easily. "Goring Hanse Davion's ox is a distinct pleasure." Justin narrowed his eyes and tapped his chin with his right index finger. "I wonder how the Prince will take the death of Philip Capet?"

41

11 May 3027

William Pfister, Captain of the JumpShip *Meridian*, shivered with as much anger as his portly body could contain. "My God, Danica," he said, "If this is true, why, it would be a disaster!"

Danica Holstein nodded sympathetically and leaned back in the deeply padded leather chair opposite Pfister's desk. "That's the reason I brought this to you, Bill. My head K-F drive technician, Stephen Leigh, says that he shipped one of his early training cruises with Kevin Mori. He told me that the Mori on your *Meridian* is not the same individual, even though he claims the same credentials…"

Pfister shrugged. "I can't thank you enough, Danica, for letting me know." Pfister glanced over to a corner of the room where Danica's son sat hunched over a computer console. "Do you think he can prove it?"

Before his mother could answer, Clovis raised a hand. The stubby, childlike appearance of the limb did not match the normally sized head or the deep voice booming from his throat. "Console him, mother. My being a dwarf means nothing to Monopole's computer. The codes that the good Captain has supplied me have been most useful …Aha!"

"What? What?" Pfister shot from his chair and darted toward the corner.

Clovis swiveled his chair around and smiled as he pointed to the computer display with his left hand. "Here it is, Captain. Monopole's

228

files include an LIC advisory that Mori is suspected of being an ISF agent. They point out that old and current identification pictures do not computer-scan as having the same Bertillon measurements for the bone structure in the skull or long bones. You have a spy in your crew."

Pfister bent over to read the report. His sharp, shocked breaths were audible across the room, and his thick lips quivered as they formed each word he read. Finally, he straightened up and shook his head. "Blake's Blood!"

Clovis spun back to the keyboard and typed in another request for information. "That's not all, Captain Pfister. Did you know that the seals on your third helium tank are suffering from molecular deterioration? I don't suppose Mori informed you about that, did he?"

Pfister's jaw dropped open as the data scrolled up the screen. "My seals are degenerating? My God!"

Danica stood and brushed her long auburn hair back over both shoulders. "That could be devastating," she said. "If you lose the liquid helium, you can't jump."

Pfister wilted. "What can I do?" I can't trust my chief Tech and I've got this hauling job for Monopole on the twenty-first. Gotta jump the *Silver Eagle* to Errai. If I lose those seals, Monopole might jerk their contract, and then I'll be sunk!"

Danica smiled and rested her right hand gently on Pfister's left shoulder. "Take it easy, Bill. I'll radio the *Bifrost* and have Leigh shuttle over to your ship. If those seals can be salvaged, Leigh's the one who can put them right."

Pfister rose out of his self-pity long enough to look warily at Danica. "You'd do that for me? Why?"

Danica gave him her warmest smile. "Bill, you're too suspicious. Just call it insurance. I know that someday you'll return the favor if I ever need it."

Pfister flushed, then nodded. "Thank you, Danica. And you, too, Clovis."

The dwarf dropped from the chair. "Don't thank us yet, Captain. Wait until Leigh saves those seals."

Pfister looked hopefully at Danica. "You'll send him to the *Meridian* immediately?"

Danica nodded solemnly. "You radio clearance for him to board and inspect, but try to keep Mori from knowing he's there or that you're on to Mori's secret. I'll radio Leigh the second our little shuttle leaves planetary orbit."

"Thank you, Fomalhaut Control. This is *Bifrost* shuttle *Mistletoe* leaving your control on return vector to our home ship. Out." Danica switched the shuttle's radio over to the scramble frequency she'd designated for covert communictions. "*Mistletoe* to *Bifrost.*"

"Leigh here, Danica. How did it go?"

Danica smiled. "Pfister bought it. Take the *Hemlock* over to the *Meridian* and blow the helium seals."

"What about Mori?"

Danica paused for a moment. "As we discussed, make the blow-out look like sabotage and implicate Mori."

Leigh's voice droped to a grim bass roar and rumbled through the shuttle's cabin. "Dead men deny no charges."

Danica nodded. "If you see an opportunity to catch him when the helium tank goes, do it."

"Roger. Out."

Danica removed her headset and swiveled the chair around to face her son. "You did manage to get the *Bifrost* designated as the alternate carrier for the *Silver Eagle* while rampaging around in the Monopole computer, didn't you?"

Clovis nodded sullenly. "You kept Pfister busy enough for me to have reconstructed Monopole's entire corporate structure."

Danica frowned at her son's glum expression. "What is it, Clovis? I know something is bothering you. You can't hide it from me." She narrowed her brown eyes. "Is it killing Mori?"

Clovis brushed his long black hair back from his face and snorted. "Killing an ISF agent? Don't you think I knew that telling you about his ISF connection was his death warrant...? No, that's no concern of mine."

Danica frowned. "What is it, then?"

Clovis sighed heavily. "It's this whole mission, mother. The things Gray Noton has paid us to do in the past have been simpler— running 'Mech parts to insurgents in the Combine, or moving some documents from the Federated Suns to the Free Worlds League. That kind of job doesn't bother me, but hijacking a DropShip to sour relations between the Commonwealth and the Federated Suns...Well that doesn't seem like the kind of thing Heimdall should be involved in..."

Danica shook her head emphatically. "Don't confuse things, Clovis. Performing this job for Gray has nothing to do with Heimdall. Gray is paying us good money—money we need to keep the Styx base functioning—to divert a DropShip. It's a job. Nothing more..."

Clovis crossed his arms and hugged them to his chest. "How can you say that? You speak as though you can divorce Heimdall from what you and I are. Sure, our base in the Styx system harbors refugees who have fled the Combine, but it's mostly peopled by other Heimdall refugees who have fled the Commonwealth. We've refused other missions that would have directly damaged the Commonwealth, but you accepted this one. Why, mother? Why?"

Danica turned and stared out the large viewing-port on the shuttle's nose. "For 700 years, Loki has existed in the Commonwealth. For most of that time, it has been a godsend. Answerable only to the Archon and the head of the Lyran Intelligence Corps, it has searched out spies and carried out operations that have blunted attacks by the enemies of our people.

"From time to time, though, the Archon has turned Loki loose on his own people. During one of those times, a number of loyal nobles and citizens banded together to form Heimdall. They worked passively and covertly, for the most part, to prevent Loki from depriving Commonwealth citizens of their rights. The attack on the spaceport on Poulso twenty years ago was the most public display of our power ever, yet only those within Heimdall even suspect we had anything to do with the raid."

Clovis ground his teeth. "I know all this, mother. Small I may be, but I am not a child who needs to be lectured about the history of Heimdall. You avoid answering my question."

Danica shook her head. "It's not a lecture I'm giving you, Clovis, but you don't know all there is to know. You, my dear, were born into Heimdall and have lived within it all your life. I came to Heimdall while I still carried you…Had someone not rescued me, you and I would be nothing more than casualties blamed upon a raid by House Kurita. Even as Heimdall saved Katrina Steiner from her uncle's plots, it also extracted us from a dangerous situation. Yet, for all that I now owe Heimdall, at that time, I'd only heard it mentioned in whispers— dark whispers. For most citizens of the Commonwealth, Heimdall is as much a fiction as Saint Nicholas or the sanctity of ComStar."

Danica smiled at her son. "The Heimdall you've grown up with is an organization far more public than ever before. Our base is the latest in a series of 'openly' Heimdall centers hidden in the forgotten recesses of the universe."

Clovis shook his head. "I'd hardly call it 'openly' Heimdall, mother. We never admit it to the refugees we take in."

"True, Clovis, but we all *know* what we are. That's just one of the changes in Heimdall that forces me to look at things like this job differently. With Arthur Luvon's marriage to Katrina Steiner, he sent out a signal to all of us that he endorsed her as an Archon who would deserve our full support. She curbed Loki's operations within the Commonwealth, and while that has given Heimdall room to breathe, it has also weakened Katrina's ability to uncover the treasonous plots of her internal enemies. Heimdall has accepted some of that responsibility, but we still must act in a subtle and covert manner to accomplish our ends."

Clovis stared hard at his mother. "This is where you confuse me, mother. In one breath, you say we should be quietly loyal to the Archon. In another, though, you order an operation—at the behest of a political mercenary who is only out to enrich himself—to hijack a ship. In that one motion, you will damage the relations between the Commonwealth and the Federated Suns—hardly the subtle kind of action you claim to favor. How can you, while professing to be loyal to the Archon, undertake an action that will jeopardize a policy that Katrina Steiner supports completely and utterly?"

Danica turned back and smiled at her son. "Congratulations, Clovis. You've asked the question I've wrestled with since the day Gray Noton offered us this job. Had I a chance, I would have taken counsel with the person above me in the chain of command, but I had no time to do so. I weighed the positive and negative points, then made a difficult decision."

Danica clasped her hands together, leaned forward, and rested her elbows on her knees. "It's true that this plot is undoubtly sponsored by the Archon's enemies, and could be very damanging to her. That's why I decided Katrina could afford to have no one else undertake this mission."

Clovis narrowed his eyes, then slowly nodded. "So," he said thoughtfully, "by accepting the mission, you're in control of how it turns out. You can decide whether or not to turn the DropShip over to Noton's people..."

Danica crossed to Clovis and hugged her son. "Exactly, Clovis. With your work, Monopole will let the *Silver Eagle* know that they're to link up with us. We won't jump to Errai, as they expect, or Sirius, as Noton intends. We'll jump back to Styx, and from there, Heimdall will be the one to decide who exactly is to profit from this enterprise."

42

Andrew smiled as he watched over Melissa's shoulder from the back of the cockpit. Captain von Breunig, never dreaming that the young woman was anyone more special than Joana Barker, pointed the long silver cylinder hanging in space. "That is the *Bifrost*, Barker. That circular collar on the side of the Kearny-Fuchida core is where the *Silver Eagle* will dock with the JumpShip."

Andrew glanced at a chart on the wall, then frowned. "Captain, the assignment board says that the *Meridian* was to be our transport from Fomalhaut to Errai."

Von Breunig did not turn, and so did not catch the glance Melissa gave Andrew. "The *Meridian* suffered a helium failure," the Captain said. "You see, Miss Barker, the Kearny-Fuchida jump drive requires liquid helium to stay cold enough to conduct all the energy needed to rip a hole in space and to propel us up to nine parsecs from here. The *Meridian* lost some seals, and so the *Bifrost* came in to keep the trip on schedule."

Melissa smiled. "The name, 'Bifrost'...Why does that sound familiar?"

Von Breunig smiled easily as the JumpShip slowly filled the forward screen. "Mythology, Miss Barker. Bifrost was the rainbow bridge that Heimdall guarded. In many ways, I find it a comfort to find a JumpShip named after a mythical bridge or ship or fantastic beast."

Andrew laughed. "You black-ocean sailors are all the same—superstitious."

233

The Captain took Andrew's remark for the good-natured ribbing that it was. "True," he said, "but you mud-marchers would be out of business if not for the likes of me."

The pilot half-turned in her chair. "Captain, the *Bifrost* signals that she'll be ready to go as soon as we hitch up."

"Good. Signal the passengers that we are fifteen minutes to jump." A soft, pulsing tone filled the air, then a computer-generated voice began to instruct passengers on their options during the upcoming jump through hyperspace. The Captain smiled at his guests. "If neither of you requires dralaxine to combat the travel sickness, you are welcome to join me in my cabin during the jump."

Melissa and Andrew nodded their pleasure at his invitation, then followed Captain von Breunig from the bridge down through the narrow, dark corridor to his quarters. Though the cabin was small, von Breunig had filled it with a galaxy of nautical charts and artifacts. Despite the abundance of sealife samples from across the Inner Sphere, Andrew and Melissa noticed only one thing about the cabin.

Hanging high above them, burning like an opal disk, the clouded face of Fomalhaut V shone through the cabin's transparent ceiling. Surrounding it, stars burned diamond-white and sapphire-blue. Without atmosphere to mute and warp their light, they neither winked nor wavered. Rather, the suns stared down harshly at the people watching from the *Silver Eagle*.

The Captain spoke softly. "It often affects me that way."

A smile spread across Andrew's face. "Those stars are like watchful eyes...Almost as though the universe were alive." He reached up a hand toward the ceiling as though to grab a star and hold it in his hand.

Melissa shivered. "It looks so cold and unforgiving."

Von Breunig nodded. "Space is an anvil upon which the meek are broken. The mariners on old Earth both feared and loved the sea. I feel the same way about space."

A second warning tone sounded through the ship. In compliance, the Captain waved his guests to chairs and then buckled himself into one, too. "I hope, Leftenant, that your Prince Davion and his New Avalon Institute of Science will find a way to manufacture gravity. Going weightless when we shut down our acceleration drive is bothersome."

The Captain punched several buttons on his desk and a viewscreen raised itself from a compartment hidden in the deck. It was clear that the image flickering to life on the screen came from a camera mounted in the bridge. The trio watched as the pilot expertly docked the *Silver Eagle* with the *Bifrost*. The computers spun and contracted the various interlocking rings on the docking collars, then the pilot

234

extended the K-F drive boom and locked it into position on the *Bifrost*.

Her voice echoed from a small speaker on the Captain's desk. "Request permission to jump, sir."

"Granted."

Melissa gripped the arms of her seat. A final warning tone—this one more urgent and insistent—rang one minute before jump. Melissa felt the perspiration trickling down her neck and between her breasts. She forced herself to breathe normally and to keep from screwing her eyes shut. *No, you won't do that this time.*

They jumped.

The stars above them blurred, then flared and filled Melissa's eyes with a flash of light. *Is the universe screaming in pain? Can it feel us pierce its flesh and rend its soul?* The fabric of the ship crushed in on her in one instant, then everything seemed to draw away and to stretch out like the distorted reflection in a carnival mirror.

Just as suddenly, everything snapped back into focus with a nearly physical impact. Melissa shook her head to clear away the dizziness, and fought back against the nausea. More sweat wrapped her in a cold, clammy blanket. She closed her eyes and immediately tasted bile in her throat. Still battling the nausea, she leaned back and looked up.

A planetoid larger than Tharkad City filled the overhead view-screen. Blue lights blinked on high towers. She picked out an obviously man-made dome among the pockmarked cliffsides and canyons on the surface of the tan-colored rock. Then, as the rock rotated, she spotted the lighted square dug into the planetoid's stony skin.

Something caught in her throat. She barely heard the urgency in the pilot's voice, or the worry in Captain von Breunig's hastily snapped orders. Melissa knew, instinctively, that something was very, very wrong.

43

23 May 3027

Subhash Indrahar bowed deeply to Takashi Kurita. The black kimono swathing his barrel chest and broad shoulders seemed somber for a man whom others had named "the Smiling One" for his gregariousness. The somberness was appropriate, however, to the great seriousness of Indrahar's mission.

Takashi Kurita, Coordinator of the Draconis Combine, returned the bow of the Director of the Draconis Combine's Internal Security Forces. With an elegant gesture, he indicated that Indrahar should seat himself on the pillow to the Coordinator's right—a place of honor. As the ISF Director crossed to that pillow, Kurita gathered up the sheets of rice paper that he had filled with calligraphy and set them aside.

Indrahar knelt on the pillow. *"Domo arigato,* Kurita Takashi-sama."* Indrahar allowed a smile to tighten his lips for an instant, then the gravity of his mission smashed it flat. "I have information that might best be described in terms of the Liao curse: 'May you live in interesting times.'"

Kurita nodded slowly. *"Hai?"*

Indrahar straightened his kimono, then looked up at the Coordinator. "We may have in our grasp the means to force incredible concessions from the Lyran Commonwealth. I have reason to believe that Melissa Steiner, the Archon-Designate, is currently in the Draconis Combine."

Kurita's head snapped up and Indrahar felt the extent of the

Coordinator's shock. "How do you know this?"

Indrahar composed his face. "The initial information came from a chance comment made by Precentor Myndo Waterly to one of my people on Dieron, but we have worked to confirm the rumor."

The Coordinator nodded slowly. "Where?"

Indrahar allowed himself the hint of a smile. "My sources suggest that she is being held in the system known as Styx."

Kurita's eyes narrowed. "The system that once belonged to Viscount Robert Monahan?"

Before replying, Indrahar hesitated slightly to show the Coordinator that he had not been completely correct in his recollection. "Monahan owned the Styx Mining Corporation but he sold it to Wayland Smith late in 3025. As you will recall, Smith managed to obtain a large number of investors for his new Styx Mining Corporation by letting them believe that their spies had cracked the security on his computers. The investors saw what they believed were genuine geological reports indicating that the Styx system was not played out, despite the four hundred years of mining done there."

Kurita frowned. He dipped his brush into the pot of black ink on the low table before him and quickly slashed a stroke onto a sheet of rice paper. His irritation flashed in his blue eyes, then died. "You still have not caught this Wayland Smith?"

Indrahar shook his head. "No, though Monahan and his board of directors were executed, as per your orders. We believe that Smith is somewhere in the Lyran Commonwealth now. Ever since he absconded with the 25,000,000 C-bills, malcontents have been using the Styx system as a safe haven."

Kurita nodded. "Better they hide themselves in safety than force us to expend energy hunting them down."

The Smiling One chewed his lower lip thoughtfully. "We have learned that the current contingent has made a contract with Frederick Steiner, a contract negotiated by Gray Noton on Solaris. According to its terms, they have hijacked a Monopole DropShip, the *Silver Eagle*. The *Silver Eagle* jumped from Fomalhaut aboard the JumpShip *Bifrost*. Styx is within range."

Kurita's eyes became azure slivers as he listened to this news. "Why do you believe Melissa Steiner is on board?"

Indrahar opened his hands, then brushed his right hand across his partially bald pate. "Our agents ran all the usual programs on Lyran shipping and came up with several interesting names on the passenger list. Aside from a Davion war hero and a couple of holovid stars, everyone else is normal. In fact, several names and profiles came up as almost *too* normal."

The ISF Director closed his eyes. He felt the Coordinator's penetrating gaze upon him, but he ignored it. Indrahar sank inside himself for a moment and touched the argent pillar of energy he visualized as pulsing up and down his spine. His mind caressed his *ki* and he drew strength from it.

"One person—Joana Barker—matches Melissa Steiner in certain physical characteristics such as height, weight, and proportional limb measurements. Medical histories also match in crucial items such as medical allergies." Indrahar opened his eyes and stared at Kurita. "In addition, I *know* Joana Barker to be Melissa Steiner."

Kurita met Indrahar's gaze, and the ISF Director recognized that look. He'd seen it many times before as the two of them stood patiently for minutes at a time, facing one another in *kendo* contests. Kurita's eyes probed for any weakness, any opening, any lie.

The Coordinator nodded. "I respect your judgement, Subhash. And I'm sure you already have a plan."

Indrahar smiled more openly. "I have an elite ISF unit of jump infantry on Dieron. Many of them participated in the unsuccessful raid on Styx when we attempted to capture Smith. They will get Joana Barker and bring her to us."

Subhash Indrahar expected Kurita to dismiss him then, but the Coordinator stared down at a blank sheet of paper. He dipped his brush gently into the ink, then in a few quick strokes, he had painted an eye with a strange bird in the center of it. The Coordinator smiled and looked up at his visitor.

"Styx is within range of Nashira, is it not?"

"*Hai!*"

"Excellent." Kurita stared at the brush painting he had just completed. "Alert your unit and send it to Styx. But also send the *Genyosha*. They will succeed in capturing the Archon's daughter if your people fail."

238

44

22 May 3027

Philip Capet froze as Justin Xiang's voice lashed him. The other MechWarriors in Valhalla watched breathlessly as Justin and Tsen Shang waded into the room and confronted Capet. Behind the Capellan MechWarrior, there followed a crowd of Battle Commission officials.

Justin stabbed a finger at Noton's alcove. "Get your hands off that shield, Capet. The alcove is not yours."

Capet turned slowly. The confidence and power he tried to project through his easy, casual movement did not match his red-faced embarrassment. "And who are you, Xiang, to tell me that this alcove is not mine?" Capet blustered. "What claim have you to it? Have you come to take it yourself?"

Very good, Philip. Strike out. Play right into my hands... Justin slowly shook his head. "No, I've come here with these officials to prevent a coward like you from desecrating my friend's memory. Neither one of us has a claim to that alcove. Neither one of us defeated Noton and earned the alcove." Justin looked around at the other MechWarriors, many of whom nodded in agreement.

Justin pointed at the "Legend-killer" shield. "Noton did not lose his skill at piloting a 'Mech. In a battle, he could have—and would have—ripped either one of us apart, and we both know it. Just because he lost out in another arena is no reason to betray the memory of his honor." Justin paused and narrowed his eyes. "Perhaps, Capet, you could not bear the thought of challenging him for the right to this

239

alcove."

Capet stiffened, then snarled furiously. "Don't try to lay that murder on me, Xiang..."

"Why not, Capet? There's been murder enough by your hand here. You gave Wolfson a tongue lashing after he bailed out during our first fight. You told him, and all the other members of your 'Capellan Mafia,' that a real man does not fight with his ejection seat enabled. They believed you, trusted you, and you killed all of them as surely as if you pulled the trigger on my weapons." Justin spat on the floor at Capet's feet.

Capet stabbed a finger at Justin. "I've had enough of your chatter, Xiang. I'm not the one who betrayed my country."

Justin laughed in Capet's face. "Bravo, Philip. This from the man who destroyed his command on Uravan. This from the man who preached nonsense to MechWarriors foolish enough to believe him. Face it, Capet. If not for your rash decision to protect your home village—so that you could be hailed as a war hero by your own people—the Capellan forces would never have torn the village apart. If you hadn't moved to defend it, they would never even have noticed it. In your quest for personal glory, Philip Capet, you murdered your own family!"

An enraged scream burst from Capet's throat. He wrenched the shield from Noton's alcove. Knuckles bone-white, he raised it in both hands and lunged toward Xiang. With murderous intent, Capet brought the metal disk crashing down.

Justin dodged to the left, then smashed his right fist into Capet's exposed ribs. Though a bit short, the powerful, pistonlike blow knocked Capet to the side. The MechWarrior collided heavily with the long table to his left and grunted in pain. As he stumbled over one of the benches and dropped to the floor, the shield flew from his hands.

His right fist still cocked and ready, Justin stared down at him. "If you're not a coward, then you'll accept my challenge to do battle." Justin looked up at the other MechWarriors who had gathered around to watch. "If the others think it proper, I suggest we battle for the right to Noton's alcove."

Capet smiled easily and pulled himself to his feet. "Is that all you want, Xiang, a fair fight? Will you use your *Centurion* against my *Rifleman?* I assure you that I will not make Billy Wolfson's mistake."

Justin smiled cruelly. "Which error is that, Capet? Exposing his back to me, or accepting your advice? I am touched at your concern that I will not be able to match your *Rifleman*, but I suggest that you not lose any sleep over it."

Justin turned and began to walk away, then stopped. Resting a hand on the shoulder of the Maskirovka agent accompanying him, he faced Capet again and smiled. "Oh, and don't count on getting that 'Mech regiment Prince Davion has promised for my head. He may hate me, but he's not stupid enough to actually grant you a command. When you die, it will be here…right here on Solaris."

45

Styx
Dieron Military District, Draconis Combine

23 May 3027

Captain Stefan von Breunig turned as Leftenant Andrew Redburn and Joana Barker entered the command center of the mine complex. Beyond him, through the glass wall, the *Bifrost* and the *Silver Eagle* hung suspended by invisible magnetic fields in the cavernous docking bay. Silvery cables, as slender as threads from this distance, fed power from the base's generators to the *Bifrost*'s jump coils. Melissa marveled at the beauty, then shivered at the danger.

"This is Leftenant Andrew Redburn and Miss Joana Barker. As you have requested, I have assembled a number of the passengers here to discuss the problem you outlined to me earlier." The Captain smiled as he introduced the last two of the passengers summoned to this meeting, though Melissa easily read the fatigue and frustration in the dark circles under his eyes. *I'll wager he hasn't slept a wink in the two days since they captured us.*

Melissa nodded to the auburn-haired woman standing across the room from them, and assessed her as she'd learned to do during her military training days. Though shorter and stockier than Melissa, the woman appeared very fit. As their gazes met and Melissa stared into those brown eyes, she realized that the woman was assessing her, too.

"I am Danica Holstein," the woman told her, smiling with impatience in her voice. "I command this little outpost we have usurped from the Draconis Combine." She turned and indicated the young man behind her. "This is my son, Clovis."

242

Though she knew it was impolite, Melissa could not avoid staring at him. Born a dwarf, Clovis wore meter-long stilts so that he could reach the computer controls with which he fiddled. He was apparently well-accustomed to the Styx planetoid's reduced gravity, for the dwarf moved with incredible agility. Like a master musician in concert, he let his stubby fingers drift over the half-dozen keyboards. He turned just long enough to nod at them in profile, then brushed his long, black hair from his face and again attacked the computers.

Danica addressed herself to the group of *Silver Eagle* passengers. "Clovis informed me earlier today that a Combine ship has appeared at the nadir jump point. It has already sent one DropShip in our direction. According to its acceleration vector, we estimate that it will arrive on the twenty-fifth, only forty-eight hours from now. I've brought you together so we may discuss our options."

Erik Mahler stepped forward. "Do you think it represents more than a routine patrol?"

Clovis answered in a voice far deeper than it seemed his small chest could contain. "Patrols use *Scout* Class ships. This is an *Invader* Class JumpShip and it's sent a *Fury* Class DropShip toward us." As he cocked his head, the dwarf's eyes revealed their hint of blue. "The acceleration vector says that they're probably carrying somewhere between thirty and fifty jump troopers."

Melissa heard those words and slowly sank back through the crowd. *To take a base this size would require a company of light 'Mechs.* She stared down at her fingers and quickly went through the guidelines she'd been taught for an assault on such a base. *Yes, they'd certainly need a company of light 'Mechs to subdue this base. So why were they sending jump troops?*

Melissa wormed her way through the crowd and found Andrew. She pulled him to the back, then clapped a hand over his mouth. "Andrew, the jump troops on that ship must be elite ISF troopers."

Andrew's eyebrows shot up, but her hand stifled his outcry. He hesitated, then pulled her hand away. Cupping his hands around her ear, he whispered softly. "How do you know that?"

Melissa shrugged. "A *Fury* is built for hauling infantry, not 'Mechs. It can hold more than a hundred comfortably, so why would they send less? In fact, why would they send anything but 'Mechs? The only answer I can see is that they have troopers who they believe can accomplish the job. That means ISF troops."

"Damn!" Andrew's eyes narrowed. "That also means something else. Clovis said Kurita patrols use *Scout* ships, which means Kurita knows about this outpost. Curious, isn't it, that they decide to clean it up now, yet they chose such a discreet force to do it."

243

Melissa felt her insides coil. *Somehow, by some means, they've learned who I am!* She looked up at Andrew and his curt nod confirmed her fears. She leaned back against the wall, overwhelmed by doubt and anxiety, yet some of the discussion around her registered, albeit dimly, on her brain.

Andrew Redburn pushed his way to the front of the crowd. "Excuse me, but doesn't it seem foolish that the Combine would waste fifty soldiers assaulting this base?"

Danica Holstein shifted her attention to the Leftenant. "Perhaps, but then we have seen governments do so many foolish things. That is why my son and I fled Summer when we did. What is your point?"

"My point is this. From what little I saw of this base, it would take a company of 'Mechs to conquer it." Around him, the few MechWarriors in the group nodded in cautious agreement. "I would suggest that the troops aboard that Kurita ship are tough enough to accomplish the job they've been sent to do."

Danica considered his statement silently, but Clovis immediately spoke up. "ISF, that would be. It's too much of a coincidence to think that they've finally decided to blow us out of here. In fact, all they'd need for that is a bomb. No...it must be that they want someone."

"Be that as it may," Andrew said, taking the floor again. "We have to plan a defense to hold them off. If we don't, many people could die."

Back against the cold wall, Melissa hugged herself tightly and winced at the clawing fear in her stomach. The sinister voice crawled again from the black pit of her self-doubts and whispered in its evil way. *The ISF want you. Kurita's elite troops are coming for you, little Princess. Perhaps this is what you deserve....*

Melissa looked up as Clovis produced a schematic view of the entire base on a holovid screen set high in the far wall. *This whole asteroid is a deathtrap, Melissa, and here you will die.*

Danica turned to face the screen. "As you can see, Leftenant Redburn, it would be it difficult—at best—to defend this maze of mining tunnels and the company-town complex. I concede that there are hard points, but those were meant to seal off the complex in case the outside were breached. This was not built as a military complex, and we can be certain that the ISF troops have extremely up-to-date charts on our set-up."

Captain von Breunig frowned. "But we must do something. I will not turn even one of my passengers over to the Draconis Combine."

Danica laughed coldly. "Why not, Captain? Is the ISF any less brutal than our own Loki? Let's be practical and leave these moral discussions to the philosophers. Those of us here who are not from the Combine have come from the Commonwealth, and we know well the

244

excesses of power." Unconsciously, Danica reached out and rested her hand on Clovis's shoulder. When he hugged her hand between his shoulder and large head, her expression brightened momentarily.

Danica let her hand drop away. "Let us be pragmatic, Captain. If the ISF wants someone, we'll find out who it is and negotiate. If the ISF attacks, we know that many of us, including some of your passengers, will die. If, on the other hand, we sacrifice one person to save the rest, who can say it would not be the right choice?"

Hear that, Melissa? the voice echoed in her mind. *People are going to die because of you. You'll not pass from this life alone. How many will go with you, little Princess? How many of them must die because of you?*

Andrew held up both hands. "Wait a minute!" He pointed out toward the *Bifrost*. "Why don't we just jump out of here?"

Von Breunig shook his head savagely. "Even if we ran the *Bifrost* out to an alternate jump point, the Kuritans are only twelve hours from here, and we'd not have enough of a charge to jump. The ISF troops would catch us in space."

Andrew frowned. "But the generators are recharging the jump drive. Surely they can power it faster than the solar collector."

The Captain again shook his head. "You don't understand, Leftenant. It's not the amount of energy needed to charge the coils that matters. It's the length of time required to do the job. Energy fed in too fast can damage the K-F drive. A speedy loading would probably rupture storage cells or blow the liquid helium seals. The latter would render the ship inoperable. Worse yet, the former could result in a misjump." Von Breunig looked down. "Only an idiot, or a very desperate man, would jump after having spent less then a week recharging his drive."

Danica nodded. "There, Captain, you have eliminated the only other logical choice. Either you surrender any passenger the Draconians want, or we will all die."

See, Melissa. They will all die. You've doomed them all, and you'll finally get what you deserve...

Andrew slowly nodded his head. "Let's talk with them. If it's me they want, I'm willing to trade."

Danica smiled, but von Breunig snarled harshly. "No, Leftenant. The welfare of the *Silver Eagle*'s passengers is my responsibility." He shook his head wearily. "We'll never surrender a single passenger to them. Never."

"I remove that responsibility from you, Captain von Breunig." The woman's voice, strong and clear, reached out from the back of the room and demanded the attention of all assembled. The crowd parted and she whom they had known as Joana Barker came slowly forward. Pulling the brown wig from her head, she shook free the famous gold of her hair.

Fighting back the tears, she spoke without a tremor. "I am the one they want. I am Melissa Arthur Steiner, and no one must die because of me." She lifted her head as everyone in the room, including Danica Holstein and Andrew Redburn, dropped to one knee.

Only the dwarf Clovis remained standing and dared break the reverent silence. "Oh, this makes it very interesting, indeed." He turned and rubbed his hands together. "Now *we* have a Princess, and the Kuritans' second *Invader*, hauling an *Overlord*, has just arrived."

46

Master Sergeant Nicholas Jones nearly jumped out of his skin as the lights came on in the recreation room. All the Kell Hounds surrounded their Lyran Commonwealth Tech Liaison and cheered deliriously. Jones staggered back toward the door of the crowded room, his hands clutched to his chest as he feigned a heart attack, but Rob Kirk caught him and prevented his escape.

Lieutenant Colonel Patrick Kell stepped forward. "Master Sergeant Nicholas Jones?" Kell's features sharpened, and the Master Sergeant snapped to attention. He gave a salute, which Kell returned smartly. "At ease, Sergeant. We're all friends here."

Another round of yells erupted as a smile blossomed on Jones's face. Kell raised his hand, and his people grew more quiet. "In honor of your thirty years of service, Sergeant, we wish to present you with some tokens of our esteem."

Cat Wilson stepped from the crowd and draped a brown leather jacket over Jones's shoulders. As the Sergeant looked down, he saw the Kell Hound insignia on the jacket's left breast and the Captain's bars on the shoulders. "Sir? I don't understand..."

Kell smiled and laughter rippled through the throng. "It's simple, Captain Jones. You've been elevated in rank, breveted, in fact. Now we'll confirm that in the computer and it will travel out with you. I hope no one finds out what happened so that you'll get the higher pension, but that may not work out. At the very least, however, you'll travel in luxury back to Tharkad."

247

"But, sir, I won't be leaving for another six months because the *Intrepid* leaves tomorrow and I've still not been cleared to board her." Jones's appreciation for the gift fought with his desire to avoid abusing it on Pacifica.

Kell laughed and Salome Ward brought the Sergeant a mug of stout. "Captain, would we let such a thing happen?" She waved Jones to a table in the back of the recreation room. "We have everything under control."

Two floors above, Meg Lang's fingers danced across the keyboard on Pacifica's central computer. Austin Brand stood behind her, hands on her shoulders, just barely within the circle of light coming from Dan's flashlight. He looked over at Dan and smiled happily.

Leaning against the computer itself, Dan smiled benevolently and kept the light centered on Meg. *Glad to see you've worked things out, Meg.* She gasped slightly and Dan leaned forward. "Have you got it?" he asked.

She nodded and Brand gently squeezed the muscles at the back of her neck. Meg looked over at Dan. "Got it, Captain. Now, you just want me to move the day ahead by one?"

Dan nodded. "Yes, as soon as the clock passes midnight. On Pacifica, the 25th becomes the 26th. It'll confuse a few folks, but it'll get Jones out of here on the *Intrepid*." Dan laughed to himself. "It'll also cause the jump troopies a bit of trouble, but I'm sure O'Cieran won't mind that."

Chu-i Oguchi could not conceal his agitation. *Sho-sa* Kamekura frowned at his subordinate. *Can you not comport yourself in a more orderly manner, Oguchi?* Staring at the man through the half-light, Kamekura nodded his head curtly. "*Hai*, what is it?"

Oguchi swallowed hard. "It is the 26th, Kamekura-san!"

"What!" Kamekura's roar filled the cavern and caused several soldiers to freeze suddenly before they scurried out of sight. "How is this possible?"

"I do not know, Kamekura-san. I set an alarm on my computer terminal for five minutes past midnight on the 26th and it just started beeping at me. I checked, and it is the 26th!" The *Chu-i* stared blankly at his commander. "What do we do now?"

As Kamakura stood abruptly, he smacked his head on the low ceiling. With a smothered curse, he felt his scalp for any traces of blood, but his hand came away clean and dry. "It is obvious, Oguchi-kun. We attack. Our ninja infantry will get there by four in the morning and blow up the jump troop barracks. Others will slip into the main

248

building and kill the officers. The rest will kill whatever MechWarriors they can find, and then our *Panthers* will destroy any further resistance they offer."

Dan Allard held his autoloading shotgun by the pistol grip and walked over to the Comcenter window. He brushed back the blinds and laughed as he looked out. "Come see this, Cat. Half of O'Cieran's folks are drunk and the other half are asleep."

Cat levered himself up from the desk. "Three-thirty in the morning. They ought to be asleep." He tossed a rag down over the assault rifle he'd broken down and had just completed cleaning. Joining Allard at the window, the big black man laughed deeply. "Rick will have them going full steam momentarily, and will turn this into an exercise in preparedness."

Dan nodded and returned to his chair. He glanced at the seven monitors informing him about the various perimeter alarms around the base. He punched some information in on one keyboard and frowned as the computer spit more data at him. "Damn! It looks like we have a bad IR sensor out in the northern sector."

Cat frowned and started to reassemble the rifle. "The jumpers didn't head out that way? They might have fixed it just to get us out there in revenge for our plan to get Jones shipped out."

Dan shook his head. "No. O'Cieran's got them heading out south, away from Branson's Swamp. He said his men knew it so well that they were getting careless." Dan typed quickly. "Nuts. The wind coming in off the swamp must have knocked down the sensor or wrapped wet leaves around it again because I'm getting nothing."

Cat screwed the rifle barrel back on to complete the weapon. He slammed a clip home. "Want me to go check?"

Dan frowned. "Safety in numbers, remember? I'll call Salome and get her to take over for us here while we recon the sensor. Only take a couple of minutes for her to get down here."

Salome arrived by the time Cat and Dan had pulled on body armor suits from the security locker beside the door. After zipping up the front of his ablative jacket, Dan pointed at the monitor. "The number four north sensor got strange about fifteen minutes ago. Crosschecks with other scanners report nothing but…"

Salome nodded and set her SMG down on the table. "Go peel the leaves off it and I'll have some hot coffee waiting when you return."

"Yeah," Cat laughed as he patted the redhead on the shoulder. "Sounds good."

Something just doesn't feel right, Dan thought as he led the way down the corridor to the stairs. Cautiously, he leveled his shotgun and pointed it down the stairwell. He nodded to Cat and the larger man swung around to cover the stairway as Dan descended. Once Dan reached the base of the stairs, he covered the corridor and signalled Cat to come down behind him.

The two men worked down the corridor to the 'Mech hangar cautiously. They saw nothing, though Dan jumped at even the slightest sound. Cat, as always, maintained an outward air of calmness, but Dan noticed the darting glances that the black man flicked at every shadow.

Dan eased himself up to the door and peered through the narrow window. He ducked back quickly, then looked again. "Someone's in there. Over by my *Val*."

Cat sneaked a glance through the window and nodded confirmation. With his left hand, he pointed to Dan and made a circling motion to the left. Then he pointed to himself and made a circle right. Dan nodded, placed his hand on the doorknob, and slowly twisted it. He nodded at Cat again and shoved the door open.

Cat burst through the door and cut right. Dan cleared the door and cut left. Running blindly, he ducked between two crates of parts. Popping up suddenly, he leaned across the larger crate to steady his aim. His finger tightened on the trigger.

Abruptly, Dan eased off the trigger and pointed the gun toward the ceiling. "My God, Jonesy, what are you doing here?" Swallowing hard, Dan stared at the wide-eyed man standing before him.

Sergeant Jones looked even more surprised than he had earlier in the evening. "I'm sorry, sir, but I couldn't sleep. I came down here... Well, I came..." He looked sheepishly up at the 'Mechs towering silently above him.

Cat stepped from between the legs of his *Marauder*. "You came to say goodbye." Though he kept his face expressionless, Cat's words carried an air of respect.

Jones nodded slowly. "Hell, you work on these things so long, you begin to think of them as friends." He smiled and pointed at the *Jenner* that Eddie Baker piloted. "I used to call that one 'Widowmaker' because of the pilots it lost. Then you gave Eddie, a man I had trained, a shot in it. Now I call it the 'Invincible.'"

The two MechWarriors exchanged glances and smiled. "Hell, Jones, you almost said goodbye big-time." He pointed to Cat and himself. "We're out to check the north sensor. Wet leaves again."

Jones shook his head. "Can't be. I put a screen sphere around it to hold the leaves out."

Dan turned to Cat, but had no chance to speak. Outside the 'Mech bay, a fiery red explosion wreathed the jump troops barracks in flame and crushed it like a Poulsbo python. The shockwave blasted through the same 'Mech bay windows that the explosion had filled with white light only seconds before. Glass fragments whirled through the bay and exploded into sparkling dust against 'Mech legs. The ground heaved and hurled the three men to the ferrocrete floor.

A roar thundered through the 'Mech bay and all but swallowed the secondary explosion that blasted a door from its hinges and sent it cartwheeling into the hangar. Quick figures dressed in black poured through the smoke and fire around the doorway and slipped into the jagged, wavering shadows rippling throughout the bay.

Cat rolled to his feet first. He triggered a long, murderous burst at the Draconians. One ninja, bracketed in the doorway, virtually exploded and flew back outside. Two others, both to the right of the door, smashed back into the bay wall. They slid to the ground like ragdolls, their blood streaking the wall as they dropped.

Jones drew a pistol, but Dan shook his head and gave him a shove toward the rear entrance. "Go to ComCen. Tell Ward." As the Sergeant crawled back along the route Dan had used to enter the 'Mech bay, Dan crawled toward his *Valkyrie*. As one ninja came around between the legs of Kell's *Thunderbolt*, he raised his submachine gun to shoot Cat. Before he could do that, Dan's shotgun blast cut him in two.

Bullets whistled and whined as they ricocheted from the 'Mechs. One slug smashed Dan in the stomach and spun him over to the left. He doubled over, then crashed back breathless into a wooden crate. Somehow he managed to get one knee under him before he hit the floor. Biting back a cry of pain, he saw his assailant run from cover. One-handed, Dan poked his shotgun at the man and triggered two clouds of pellets. The first hit the man in the right shoulder and knocked him sideways. The second cut his legs from beneath him and toppled him to the floor.

Dan probed the impact site with his left hand, and pried the shell loose from his body armor. He crossed quickly back to where Cat was snapping off several shots at the advancing ninjas. "Must be a dozen of them, and every one of them with those damned circle-vision visors."

Cat coughed. "Eleven." Dan heard the gun bark once. A strangled, wet cry answered it, and the clatter of a weapon punctuated the sound. "You hit?"

"Bruised." Dan patted the vest. "Stopped the bullet, but I still feel like I've been kicked by a *Rifleman*."

Cat snorted, then pointed back toward Ward's *Wolverine*. "See there, past the *Panthers* we've rebuilt?"

"Yeah. Looks like they're grouping up." Dan frowned. "Suicide charge?"

251

Cat shrugged. "No figuring Kuritans. Damn! Here they come."

Dodging from shadow to shadow, the Kurita infantry came in with swords drawn. Dan stood up, thrust his shotgun into a ninja's chest, and jerked the trigger. The gun belched a cloud of hot metal and fire that tossed the black-garbed figure backward in a tangle of limbs.

The Kurita commando behind him closed too quickly for Dan to shift his aim. Whipping his shotgun around, the MechWarrior caught the ninja's sword slash on the gun's barrel. The sword bit deeply into the metal and Dan twisted the gun around. In one smooth motion, he tore the blade from the commando's grip and drove the gun's pistol grip into the ninja's circlevision visor. The device shattered, driving shards of metal and glass into the ninja's face. Screaming in his own tongue, the Kuritan clawed at his eyes and reeled away in agony.

Cat stood and fired his autorifle from the hip. He opened a ragged line of holes in one man's chest, knocking him back against Dan's *Valkyrie*. A second ninja wheeled back into the shadows as the bullets ripped him open from hip to shoulder, while a third pitched over backward as the shells blew through his throat and chest.

Off to the right, Dan saw motion at the doorway as someone shouted, "Kell Hounds, down!" He threw his useless shotgun at the nearest ninjas, then tackled Cat and brought them both down to the ferrocrete floor.

Another explosion ripped through the 'Mech bay as brevet Captain Nicholas Jones triggered the inferno launcher balanced on his shoulder. The twin missiles shot from the launcher on a tongue of scarlet flame, then burst into a searing golden firecloud. Flaming tendrils shot down, covered the open 'Mech bay floor with a carpet of fire, and filled the air with thick black smoke.

Though never intended to be anything but an anti-'Mech weapon, the inferno rockets devastated the remaining Kurita warriors. The explosion killed half the ninjas outright, and ignited most others. Screaming, the burning warriors ran blindly through the bay, careening off 'Mechs and walls until they collapsed and died.

Dan scrambled up and looked out over the burning crates that had sheltered him and Cat from the inferno's fury. The 'Mechs, illuminated by just enough flickering light to make their heads visible, seemed to look down and mock the fire. *Those machines have nothing to fear from the flames, but the men who pilot them do.* Dan looked over at his *Valkyrie* and shuddered. *Caught by an inferno, I'd punch out.*

Both men retreated to the doorway. Beyond Jones, Salome Ward came running down the hallway. "It's bad, gentlemen. They had assassins targeted for us. We got them all, but one hit Patrick." She pressed her right hand just below her left breast. "Lung is collapsed."

"Assassins?" Dan turned to Cat. "What the hell is going on here?"

Cat narrowed his dark eyes to shards of obsidian. "Payback. The Dragon never forgets."

Dan's jaw dropped open. "That means..."

Salome nodded. "The *Panthers* are three klicks out and coming strong."

47

Styx
Dieron Military District, Draconis Combine

25 May 3027

Melissa adjusted the headset and brought the microphone into line with her mouth. She reached out over the computer-generated holograph of the mining facility and touched a glowing spot burning in the northern end of the third level above the command center. "Report, Able three."

"The seismic records remain constant. Looks like a drilling decoy. We'll report if anything changes. Able three, out."

Melissa nodded, then glanced over at Clovis. "Able three is negative." When she turned to look up at Andrew, some strands of her golden hair drifted through the laser construct of the base. "What do you think?"

Andrew stared down at the holographic model. The command core rose from top to bottom of the planetoid like an axle. Each of the six levels had corridors radiating out like the spokes of a wheel from the command core. Each of the spokes dissolved into a tangle of smaller tunnels drawn in green to indicate that they were approximations of what existed.

Andrew pointed down at the green mazes. "These maps make no sense."

Clovis turned to him and growled, "They make sense if you're tunneling after a vein of ore."

"Well, they look like Medusa-hair to me." Andrew sighed heavily. "We know where they're likely to have the decoys, which means they'll probably try two or three sites, like the private docking bay down on Echo level." He frowned. "'Mechs would assault the large docking bay and come right in here. I don't know where else to suggest."

Melissa slammed her fist into the table. "Dammit, Andrew! Don't give me that. You may not be a jump infantry commander, but you went to a damned military academy. I know what they teach our men in the Commonwealth. Now you use what you learned at the Warriors Hall!"

Andrew whirled, his face a study in anger and frustration. "That's the problem, your Highness. I'm a MechWarrior. I think like a MechWarrior. Give me a 'Mech, even just a *Locust*, and I'll deal with those ISF troops myself. Arrggghhh…" Andrew's hands bunched into fists and he looked around for something to punch.

Melissa shivered. "You're a warrior, with or without a machine, Andrew. Be true to yourself, and share your thoughts with me."

Andrew closed his eyes and forcefully uncurled his fists. "I apologize. You're right." He even made himself chuckle. "I guess the difference between MechWarriors and Jumpboys is just in the size of their toys."

He returned to the diagram and pointed out two other spots. "There—by the galley on Baker, and here on this level, just down the hall at the recreation center."

Melissa turned and watched as Clovis used his computers to search out information to confirm or deny Andrew's guesses. Looking back at Captain von Breunig and Erik Mahler standing by the door, she wondered, *How can these people trust me so much? Those two appointed themselves my bodyguards as soon as I told them my real name.*

When she'd confessed her real identity, Melissa had expected the hijackers to immediately radio the incoming ISF ship so that they could barter her life for theirs. She'd realized, as she listened to the discussion, that she would die, no matter what. Her sacrifice, she hoped, would save the others.

Danica Holstein had immediately begged Melissa's forgiveness for what they'd almost done. "We are Heimdall, your Highness. We could never harm you."

With that admission, and the plethora of data Clovis coaxed from his computer, Danica, Andrew, Captain von Breunig, and Melissa had managed to puzzle out the reasoning behind the kidnapping. "Having you vanish from a Davion world would sour the relations between our realms," Andrew concluded. "I can only assume that there are factions on both sides who would gain from such a turn of events."

Danica Holstein agreed with a curt nod. "Lestrade," she whispered in a razor-sharp voice. "Aldo Lestrade."

Those present when Melissa had made herself known were sworn to secrecy. The rest of the passengers received vague rumors of an important Steiner envoy among their number. The Heimdall members living in the planetoid were informed of the truth, however, which served to heighten their fervor to fight. Clovis said it best: "Your father was Heimdall. So are you."

A voice buzzing in Melissa's ear shocked her out of remembrances. "Yes, Echo One," she said. "Go ahead."

"Sensors indicate a slow leak of atmosphere from the small bay. Shall we seal the tunnel?"

Melissa looked at the diagram glowing in front of her. "Don't blow it. Back to Echo Two's checkpoint and get that trap ready. After it fires, blow the explosives and seal the tunnel."

"Roger. Echo One out."

Melissa smiled at the dwarf. "Evacuate all non-essential personnel into the *Silver Eagle*." He nodded and complied with the order. Everyone present knew that the Kurita forces would not willingly harm either a JumpShip or DropShip, and so they moved all bystanders into them. *Machines are more valuable than people*, Melissa realized with a start. *It makes no sense.*

Just then, Andrew and Mahler began to strap a pistol belt around her waist. Melissa straightened up and protested. "No, I won't have it."

"Ja, you will." Mahler tugged the belt snug around her waist. "All commanders must wear a weapon. It is the only way."

Andrew picked up an autorifle and a satchel full of clips. "See you later, your Highness."

Melissa froze him with an icy gray stare. "Where are you going?"

Andrew shrugged. "You're going to be moving your fire teams into position soon. You said it yourself—I'm a warrior, and I've got to be true to myself. I thought I'd go down and add my firepower to one of the teams. Team Tiger is light one gun."

"You can't leave me here…" *Dammit, Andrew, I need you.* She looked at him and swallowed hard. "I need your thinking."

Andrew shook his head and ran a hand through his short brown hair. "Between you, Clovis, and Erik, everything will be under control."

Melissa shook her head. *How can you leave me in charge? I've never commanded anything before. You make me responsible for over 750 people on a rock in the middle of hostile space.* She narrowed her eyes and pleaded silently with the MechWarrior.

Andrew set down his rifle and crossed back to her. He rested his

256

hands on her shoulders and squeezed gently but firmly. "Remember what we spoke about that night of the reception on Tharkad? This is what responsibility feels like. These people believe in you, and they're willing to die for you. You can't question why they're doing that. You just have to accept their sacrifice."

Andrew pointed to the holograph. "Use what you know so that their sacrifice can mean something. If you do nothing, if you fall apart, they'll die for nothing." He tipped her face up with his right hand. "I know you can do it. Just the organization of the defense was brilliant."

Melissa shook her head. "But that was like an intellectual exercise. It was just a game."

Andrew nodded. "As this will be—between you and the ISF commander leading the troops."

Melissa grabbed the lapels of Andrew's dark jacket. "But people will die…"

Andrew disengaged himself and picked up the rifle again. "Just make sure it's more of them than it is of us." Andrew smiled and nodded at Mahler and von Breunig. "They won't let anything happen to you. You're a leader, Melissa Arthur Steiner. Now it's time for you to be true to yourself as well. Luck…" He slipped through the doorway and vanished.

Clovis turned as Melissa flicked tears from her face with a shake of her head. "Highness," he said, "we have contact on Echo level."

Melissa pressed her hand to the earphone. "Yes, Echo Two."

"I see them through the viewport. Do I hit them now!"

"Yes, Echo Two." Melissa looked at the holograph and saw some computer-generated figures marching up the corridor toward Echo Two's position. "Fire now!"

Melissa heard the stuttering of an autorifle, but it ceased before she could find out what had happened. A new voice cut in urgently. "Baker Four to Delta Base."

Melissa glanced at the galley two levels over her head. "Go, Baker Four."

"Big breech. They're pouring through. Baker One reports ISF in as well. We need support."

"Roger." Melissa reached down to the radio control on her belt and switched over to a reserve channel. "Teams Panther and Leopard, assist Baker Four." She watched as Clovis moved the icons representing the *Panther* and *Leopard* fire teams into position on the holographic projection.

She switched the radio back to the tactical frequency. "Echo Two, report."

Dead air greeted her. Melissa frowned and fiddled with her radio.

257

"Echo One, report."

Nothing.

"Echo One, detonate the tunnel!"

Clovis whirled. "Radios are dead."

The bright lights marking Echo One and Two winked out. Melissa stared at the holograph and watched Clovis's little Kurita dragon icons inch their way along the tunnel. Above them, as the dragon icons rolled over their position, Baker Four and One died. The panther and leopard images opposed the dragons. Each image flickered, and then some vanished as Clovis's program correlated data and estimated casualties.

Pain shot through Melissa's heart.

They're dying. They're dying because of me.

"Baker Two here, we're being…"

The static that swallowed Baker Two's report shocked Melissa from the vortex of guilt and fear threatening to drown her reason. She shook her head to clear it, then swallowed hard.

'She glanced at the icons representing her reserve fire teams. "Jaguar, Puma, Bobcat to Baker level." They winked from existence on the sidelines and then reappeared to oppose the advancing dragons. Below them, more dragons pressed forward on Echo level.

Melissa bit her lower lip and studied her last unit icon. "Tiger, report to Echo level." *You better live, Andrew Redburn.* Suddenly, she flashed on a memory of Misha Auburn dancing with Andrew back in Tharkad and the image struck her like a blow. *My God, what have I done?*

Redburn dove to the side and sprayed slugs down the narrow corridor. He saw one ISF ninja spin as the bullets picked him up and smashed him further down the hallway. Two other ISF agents returned Andrew's fire. Their bullets blew great chunks of plaster and stone from the walls, but failed to hit the rolling MechWarrior.

Two other Tigers followed Andrew down the corridor. One managed to duck into the natural alcove that shielded him. The other stopped dead as though he'd run full-tilt into a brick wall. A shot snapped the trooper's head back. Before he could fall, a burst of bullets ripped through his chest and whirled him back out of sight.

The other man in the alcove clawed at Andrew's shoulder. As the MechWarrior turned, warm blood spurted at him from the huge gash in the man's neck. He looked at Andrew with unadulterated terror in his eyes. When the man opened his mouth to scream, only blood gushed out.

Andrew shoved the soldier away as two ISF ninjas stepped from cover to advance toward his position. Lying prone, he triggered two bursts. One jackknifed the first agent and dropped him where he stood. The second burst missed its target, but forced him back nonetheless.

Through the explosions of gunfire and the whine of ricocheting bullets, a voice full of panic rang out clearly. "Tigers, pull back!"

Andrew heard the call to retreat. He tried to scramble to his feet, but the dying man clung to him and trapped his legs. Andrew kicked his mortally wounded companion savagely, but the man would not let go. "Damn you! Don't make me die with you!"

Andrew looked up and saw a satchel full of explosives arcing through the air in pitifully slow motion. *Is this how it all ends?* He kicked hard again. He freed one foot, but the dying man had managed to fling himself onto the other leg and it was trapped beneath his body. His dead weight knocked Andrew down.

As he fell, Andrew aimed his autorifle down the corridor at the ISF ninjas. He squeezed the trigger tightly and watched as smoking shells geysered from the chamber. As the world exploded around him, one thought filled Andrew's `mind. *I love you, Misha.*

Melissa felt the tremor and her heart skipped a beat. Clovis glanced over at one screen, then punched information into the computer. Before he hit the "Enter" key, he turned to her.

"Explosion, Echo level. I'm sorry."

As he punched a key, the Tiger icons vanished without a trace.

48

Pacifica (Chara III)
Isle of Skye, Lyran Commonwealth

25 May 3027

Sho-sa Akiie Kamekura did not even try to suppress a smile as his *Panther* came within visual distance of the Kell Hound complex. The fires of the burning barracks illuminated the whole area and seemed to hold Pacifica's dark clouds at bay. Long, dark shadows twisted and snapped like flags in a windstorm while the flames raged uncontrolled. The absence of bodies around the building confirmed in Kamekura's mind that none of the jump infantry had survived the surprise attack.

His smile grew as *Chu-i* Oguchi, in the forward position with Ichi lance, radioed a message to him. "*Sumimasen, Sho-sa.*" The Lieutenant failed to keep the excitement from his voice. "There is a fire in the 'Mech bay. Request permission to investigate."

Kamekura nodded slowly. "*Hai.*" He watched as Oguchi led his lance of four *Panthers* across the ferrocrete to the large hangar doors of the Kell Hound 'Mech bay. Even at this distance, he could see the flames through the open doors. He signaled *Chu-i* Ujisato Gamo to take *Ni* lance over to the west side of the building, while he would lead *San* lance in behind Oguchi. "Be sure to use visual scanners," Kamekura warned. "The fire will render infrared inoperable, and magscan is useless with the 'Mech bay so full of equipment."

Oguchi's *Panther* reached the 'Mech bay doors, while his personnel positioned themselves to cover him. Reaching with the *Panther*'s free left hand, the *Chu-i* grasped one edge of a 'Mech bay door and slid it open.

260

His triumphant cry melted into a wail of terror. A *Marauder* stepped into the breech and shoved both its lobster-claw appendages into the *Panther*'s chest. Twin forks of PPC lightning wrapped the *Panther* in a cocoon of turquoise fire. It lifted the *Panther* like a leaf trapped by a dust devil, then contemptuously dumped the broken 'Mech onto the ferrocrete.

Explosions shredded the bay doors, blasting great holes into them, and finally tearing them from their overhead runners. The doors tottered like playing cards balanced on their edges, then fell outward as *Panther*s scrambled to escape. One's jump jets ignited, but the pilot miscalculated his trajectory. That *Panther* ended up smashing into the door it had sought to avoid. Decapitated by the collision, the 'Mech's torso spun off wildly into the night.

Sho-sa Akiie Kamekura gasped for breath. Flanking the *Marauder* among the flames, the entire Kell Hound 'Mech company stood ready for battle. Kamekura froze for an instant, then issued an order that tasted like ashes in his mouth. "All *Panther*s, withdraw."

From his position on the edge of the 'Mech bay, Daniel Allard saw the Command Lance pull back, but he noticed remnants of the *Ichi* lance pressed in to attack. One *Panther* raised its PPC and triggered a burst of azure energy that struck Brand's *Commando* full in the chest. The blue fire melted armor and sparks flew from within the *Commando*'s chest, but Lieutenant Brand neither panicked nor retreated.

Dan opened his mouth and cleared a direct line to the *Commando*. "Austin, status, immediately."

"Fine, sir." A low growl rumbled through the radio link. "Be better in a minute."

The *Commando* launched two flights of SRMs back at the *Panther*. Two missiles blasted into the *Panther*'s head, peeling off armor and shattering one of the 'Mech's two viewports. The other missiles peppered the left side of the *Panther*'s torso. Their blasts flayed the armor from the 'Mech's body, leaving its skeleton exposed. Brand brought the *Commando*'s left arm up and fired the laser at the *Panther*. The corruscating beam sizzled as it scalped the enemy 'Mech and left its head utterly without armor.

Eddie Baker's awkward and ungainly *Jenner* traded shots with *Ichi* Lance's other unmolested *Panther*. The *Panther*'s PPC shot missed the birdlike 'Mech as the *Jenner* stepped out and away from the 'Mech bay. The *Panther*'s flight of SRMs scattered explosions across the *Jenner*'s hull, but did little more than dent armor.

The *Jenner* pilot then spun his 'Mech about to face the *Panther* head-on. All four medium lasers flashed coherent light at the enemy machine. Two bracketed the Kurita 'Mech, slicing armor from the left and right arms. The other two stabbed into the 'Mech's torso. They melted great canals across the 'Mech's chest and splashed hot ceramic armor to the ferrocrete. The *Jenner*'s flight of four SRMs blasted the *Panther*, with the missile hitting the humanoid 'Mech above the heart doing the most damage. There was a muffled explosion from within the *Panther*'s chest, and then the shuddering 'Mech stumbled and fell to the ground.

Off to Dan's left, by the far side of the 'Mech bay, *Ni* Lance had started to withdraw, but a murderous hail of LRMs from Lieutenant Fitzhugh's *Catapult* cut short the flight of one 'Mech. Half the LRMs chopped off the *Panther*'s legs at the knees and spun the 'Mech to the ground, while the second flight of fifteen opened the *Panther*'s back. Another missile exploded in the *Panther*'s SRM magazine, detonating the store of missiles and ripping the 'Mech into a fiery shower of shrapnel.

Mary Lasker's *Trebuchet* also engulfed a fleeing *Panther* in a deadly rain. Dan shivered as her LRMs hung a collar of fire around the 'Mech's shoulders, and consumed its head in a sheet of golden flame. As the fire boiled upward into an angry mushroom cloud of black smoke and red flashes, the headless *Panther* stumbled blindly into the night.

Dan jetted the *Valkyrie* from the 'Mech bay, targeting the *Panther* that had shot Brand's *Commando*. With the gold crosshairs of his missile targeting system on the *Panther*'s open left flank, he stabbed the launch button with the thumb of his left hand. "Flight away!"

The ten LRMs spiraled directly in on target, their explosions eating through the *Panther*'s chest like a cancer. They shredded armor surrounding the fusion engine and crushed the gyro. Short-circuited relays fired the *Panther*'s jump jets. The 'Mech rose one hundred meters on an ion cloud, then exploded and released the fusion engine's artificial sun to dispel Pacifica's dark night.

Dan dropped his jaw and opened a radio link to Salome Ward. "They're running, Major. Time to close the back door."

"Roger." Her voice dropped a dozen degrees. "O'Cieran, take them."

O'Cieran, hidden with his men in the jungle behind the *Panthers*, silently acknowledged the command. He sighted his inferno launcher on the back of Kamekura's *Panther*. "This one's for you, Patrick," he breathed, then pulled the trigger and filled the night with burning 'Mechs.

* * *

The dawn's light, seeping through a narrow rift in the clouds, brought some warmth to the nightmare scene of broken 'Mechs and charred buildings. Dan shuddered. *Just because we don't see any more of them doesn't mean they aren't out there. If not for that damned prank...*

He pointed the *Valkyrie*'s left hand at the *Overlord* Class Drop-Ship, the *Lugh*. "Jackson, all spare parts for the non-jumpers go in the *Lugh*. Everything for the jumpers goes in the *Nuada Argetlan*. Standard Procedure for combat jumps."

The Tech waved his hands, then turned to direct his astechs. Dan looked over at the *Union* Class DropShip, the *Nuada Argetlan*, and opened a radio frequency to it. "What's the word, Major?"

Frustration threaded Salome's voice. "Janos confirmed the appearance of a JumpShip at the nadir point. He's bringing the *Cu* in, so we'll only need six hours to reach it. He'll keep *Pacifica* between their incoming DropShips and his pirate point so we won't have interference. He says he'll be ready to jump as soon as we hook up."

"Good." Dan squinted against the sting of sweat. "What about loading some of these *Panthers* on board? Has O'Brien figured out what that will do to the *Lugh*'s flight profile?"

"Hang on." Dan heard Salome relaying his question to the *Lugh*'s flight officer. "He says we can pack two or three of them. I'd suggest we take three of the ones O'Cieran burned. No real damage to them."

"Roger." Dan looked up and spotted Brand, Lang, and Baker helping to load some equipment cases into the *Nuada*. "I'll get my lance moving three *Panthers*. What's the latest on Patrick?"

"Fitzpatrick's flyboys have the *Mac* halfway to the *Cu* with no interference. Patrick's lost blood, but the doctor has reinflated the lung. Says the Colonel will be fine if he'll rest."

"Best news I've had all day." Dan closed the link and flicked on his external speakers. "Lieutenant Brand, take your lancemates and see if you can march three of the burned *Panthers* into the *Nuada*." He glanced at the clock ticking down on the right side of his viewplate. "Hurry it up, though. We've only got two hours before we have to blast off this rock."

Choking back his nausea, Dan pulled himself through the Jump-Ship right behind Salome. He pushed off hard from the bulkhead and floated up through the corridor running along the K-F drive. Red signs warning of the liquid helium tanks surrounding the jump drives flashed as he floated past with Cat and Salome toward the *Cucamulus*'s bridge. *God, I hate zero-gravity,* he thought testily.

Deep in the heart of the *Cucamulus*, the three MechWarriors floated into the ship's Command Center. Instruments and tactical readouts filled the dark, spherical walls with flickering monitor screens and flashing data displays. Work stations occupied every centimeter of the circular walls, with crew members laboring at almost every one of them. The MechWarriors drifted in through a hatch in the spherical roof and grabbed onto the hatch's edge just long enough to cancel their freefall.

Dan smiled. *Every time I come into this place, I feel as though I've been shrunk and dropped into the middle of a computer.*

Floating exactly in the center of the room, Captain Janos Vandermeer sat in his command chair. Supported by nothing but the invisible lines of magnetic fields, the chair spun and swirled as he pressed buttons on the two arms. At their entry, a light flashed at the Captain's right hand, and the chair turned him around.

Dan carefully joined Salome and Cat in saluting. "Permission to come aboard."

"Granted." Vandermeer smiled warmly, then frowned and pointed to a tactical display of the Chara system. A dotted yellow line showed the trajectory of the Kurita DropShips coming in toward Pacifica. The line split off and slowly curved toward where the *Cucamulus* glowed on the chart like a green arrow.

"We have company, my friends. You must have made someone very angry."

Dan nodded. "That we did."

Behind him, Lieutenant Brand entered the command center and drifted over to a scanner station beside the one where Cat had settled in. Brand adjusted the controls and punched information into the computer. He pulled back and whispered something to Cat. The big, black man nodded silently, then Brand turned.

He frowned. "I make it eight *Slayer*s coming in hot."

Vandermeer turned his chair. "Branson, does that match your estimate?"

The petite, raven-haired scantech turned and nodded. "On the mark, sir. ETA, two hours."

Vandermeer steepled his fingers. "Shall we scramble your fighters, or…"

Salome shook her head vehemently. "Negative on the fighters. O'Cieran recovered information from the *Panther* base camp that indicated the operation was meant to destroy the Kell Hounds. That's the only purpose for it. It would have worked, too, if the *Panther Shosa* hadn't been early off the mark."

Vandermeer nodded at Dan. "The day you spared for Jones is what surprised them?"

264

Dan nodded. "Better them than us." He watched the line depicting the fighters grow closer. "You're planning to jump out before they get here, aren't you?"

The Captain nodded, then turned his glance up at Salome. "If they intend to destroy you, wouldn't it be safe to assume that they've made plans against our escape? They could easily have covered all the Steiner worlds within range."

Salome nodded slowly. "That's a fair assumption. What do you have in mind, you old fox?"

Vandermeer ran a hand over his head, patting the white hair back into place. "Just a little trick, my dear, to make them think we misjumped." His chair spun quickly, then locked in, facing away and down from Salome and Dan.

"Mr. Harker, load Jump Plan Four into the computer. Jump countdown of 10 on my mark." He spun the chair again and shouted at a large blond man hunched over a console. "Mr. Garrison, jettison the spare helium, the oxygen in Tank 3, and the debris from the agro-domes."

"Aye, sir."

Dan found Vandermeer smiling at him again. "Mark, Mr. Harker." The Captain opened his hands like a conjurer innocently suggesting he had nothing up his sleeves. "In ten seconds, they will believe the Kell Hounds are no more."

Dan smiled. "The helium, oxygen, and debris will make them think that the ship destroyed itself?"

Vandermeer nodded enthusiastically.

Salome frowned. "But won't the Kurita ships waiting at other stars—"

The jump rippled and melted all reality. The muted lights within the command center flared to life with the intensity of strobes. The colors melted together into a kaleidoscopic vortex of hue and abnormal shapes. Dan's stomach roiled in sympathy with the visual display, but something in Salome's half-asked question worried him more than the physical discomfort.

"—see us arriving and know we're still alive?" she said, a moment later.

Vandermeer laughed aloud. "They would, but we've not jumped into a Steiner system." He opened his hands broadly. "Welcome, my friends, to Kurita space!"

49

Styx
Dieron Military District, Draconis Combine

25 May 3027

With an encouraging nod from Yorinaga Kurita, *Sho-sa* Tarukito Niiro strode to the forefront of the amphitheatre-style briefing room aboard the *Shori*, an *Overlord* Class DropShip. Clad only in a cooling vest, shorts, and headband, he felt slightly self-conscious, but all the others gathered in the room were similarly attired. The *Sho-sa* cleared his throat as the lights dimmed and the holographic representation of the Styx base rose in intensity.

"This, as you all know, is the planetoid toward which we are currently en route." He flicked a laser pointer to life and touched its white dome to the uppermost deck. "As usual, we have designated the decks according to the military alphabet: *Ishi, Roji, Hata, Torii, Chi,* and *Wa*. The ISF warriors have entered the base through the galley on *Roji* level and the small docking bay on *Chi* level. They have met stiff resistance on these levels, but they are pushing the defenders back."

Tarukito flicked the pointer at a light-sensitive panel on the wall. In an instant, the computer-generated projection of the Styx base expanded. The decks above and below *Torii* and *Chi* levels evaporated. Those levels expanded to take up the space used by the previous model and more. When the structure ceased its growth, the computer added a vector-graphic image of the *Bifrost* and the *Silver Eagle* in their locations within the ship bay.

Tarukito's pointer caressed the *Silver Eagle*. "It is believed that the person we seek will be aboard the *Silver Eagle*. The vessel has no

266

weaponry and should surrender without a fight. The company that owns it, Monopole, is being informed by ComStar that the ship will be impounded until its illegal jump into the Combine can be explained."

He shifted the pointer's spotlight to the base command center on *Torii* deck. "This is the central office on the base. As you can see from the diagram, it overlooks the hangar area. The ISF troops at the base believe that defense of the planetoid is being coordinated from that point."

The pointer flicked to the smaller docking bay on the far side of *Styx*. "The ISF troops who entered through this bay on *Chi* level are assigned to neutralize the command center. Those coming down from *Roji* level expect to isolate the *Silver Eagle* and to extract the prisoner."

Tarukito nodded sagely as rough laughter rumbled from the shadowed audience. "I know you intend no disrespect to our brethren in the ISF, but you will agree that neutralization of such a large base is not a matter to be left to a handful of jump troopers."

Tarukito turned again to the diagram and used the pointer to summon back the first model. "Our objective is to capture the *Silver Eagle*, not just a single person. Toward this end, we will drop toward the hangar opening." Indicating a location on the planetoid's surface just north of the hangar mouth, Tarukito added, "The *Shori* will land here and wait for our return. *Hai, Tai-i*, what is your question?"

The pointer's white dot quivered on the cooling vest that *Tai-i* Kagetora Asai wore. "*Sumimasen*, Tarukito-san. I wish to know the estimates of the 'Mech strength we will face." No fear rang through the warrior's words; his question was merely a request for relevent information.

Tarukito nodded solemnly. "A good question. To the best of our knowledge, and according to the reports we continue to intercept from the ISF troops on site, there are no 'Mechs in enemy hands on the planetoid. The *Panther*s we will take in should be more than enough to handle anything we must face." He smiled and turned toward where both Yorinaga and Narimasa sat. "*Tai-sa* Kurita-sama and *Chu-sa* Asano will both unlimber their 'Mechs—a *Warhammer* and a *Crusader*—and use jump packs to drop into the base with us."

Another *Tai-i*, Norihide Kiso, stood up behind Kagetora. "Forgive me, Tarukito-san, but I must ask this. Why are we being dropped in if the ISF has already secured the base? It has been rumored that their twelve-hour headstart came about through a delay in the ISF channels transmitting the alert to us. Will we not lose face to appear after they have accomplished our mission?"

Tarukito stared at Norihide for a second, but *Chu-sa* Narimasa Asano usurped any answer he might have given. Narimasa walked around the table to a point where the green and blue computer-construct could illuminate him. Though he smiled easily, it put no one at ease. "This rumor you have heard is not wholly true," he began. "Yes, there was some delay in transmitting the message to Nashira. This ensured that the ISF contingent from Dieron got first pass at this target. Is it not right that they have this honor? Did not their organization pierce the veil of deception that told us of the base's location and also the identity of the person we seek? Could we shame them by demanding the right to capture the prize they had located?"

Narimasa shook his head slowly and Tarukito felt shame for his resentment against the ISF forces. Narimasa laughed lightly. "Of course, we all chafed beneath the gaze of the *Taishi*—not because we are anything less than utterly devoted to the Dragon, but because the *Taishi* did not think us worthy of the responsibility we had assumed. We must not let our feelings about the late Shinzei Abe color our thinking about the rest of the ISF."

Narimasa waved a hand at the holograph. "You must recall that the Coordinator himself ordered us into battle. He could not tell Subhash Indrahar that he believed the ISF could not conquer the base, could he? There would have been a loss of face. No, he merely suggested that we should have our chance to help the ISF take the base."

Narimasa turned and nodded toward Yorinaga. "Nor could Yorinaga-sama allow our arrival to shame the ISF. If we arrived too quickly, we could have robbed them of their victory. With this thought in mind, Yorinaga-sama delayed our departure from Nashira by two hours, just so the ISF would have ample opportunity to win this battle on their own."

Tarukito turned to hide the smile beginning to tug at his mouth. By the time Narimasa had returned to his seat beside Yorinaga, Tarukito had regained control of himself. He faced the assembled soldiers of the *Genyosha* and directed their attention to the base's model.

"*Sho-sa* Nobuyori Kinoshita and I will lead the main assault. In addition to our lances, we will have *Tai-i* Kagetora Asai's lance and *Tai-i* Norihide Kiso's lance. *Tai-i* Masanori Shoni and his lance will have the honor of entering the base through the small bay on *Chi* level. In this way, we may trap the defenders between our superior forces and crush them."

With hands on hips, Tarukito surveyed his audience from one side to the other before adding a final cautionary note. "We must take care to avoid over-confidence, however, for this assault may not be as simple as it seems. Keep in mind that the planetoid's gravity will be

268

only one-ninth that of Nashira. Never forget that the stupid man is his own greatest enemy, for he defeats himself." Then Tarukito used the pointer to bring up the lights in the room. "You are dismissed. Report to your 'Mechs and prepare for a full combat drop."

As the crowd dispersed, a courier fought through the tide of bodies and presented a slip of yellow paper to Yorinaga. The *Genyosha* commander read it carefully. Then he dismissed the courier with a solemn bow and reread the message. He passed it to Narimasa as Tarukito approached them.

Narimasa frowned as he read the message. Reluctantly, he handed the paper to Tarukito. "I am sorry, Tarukito-san. Your planning has been flawless."

Tarukito took the slip of paper in trembling fingers. He read it once, and then again. Bile washed up into his throat to choke him, but he forced it down and then willed himself to ignore the fire that had begun to burn in his belly. *Damn them. They spoil my assault!*

He whirled and stared at the red outline burning on *Torii* deck. He glanced back down at the message. *Is it treason to hope that this message is false? Can they truly be that close to taking the command center?* He faced his superiors again. "Do you think it is possible?"

Narimasa and Yorinaga exchanged a look that made both of them seem ancient. Narimasa nodded. "I believe the ISF agents are earnest in their reports."

Tarukito held out the message in one hand. "But do you think they will take the command center within the hour?"

Narimasa shrugged. "Let us go to our 'Mechs. Until we jump in, we'll not learn the answer to that question."

50

Captain von Breunig spun carelessly away from the doorway. The bullet holes in his chest traced an uneven red line from breastbone to his left shoulder. His autorifle flew from nerveless fingers and clattered against the far wall as the Captain smashed hard onto the ferrocrete floor.

Melissa jerked away from his twitching body, but the cable connecting her radio headset with the holograph console snagged. Her head snapped back, and then she, too, stumbled to the floor. The headset ripped free as Melissa fell on her right hip, crying out in pain as the holstered pistol dug sharply into her flesh.

Erik Mahler half-rose from behind the makeshift barricade securing the command post's doorway. He triggered a long blast from his autorifle, then glanced back at Melissa. "Are you hit?"

"No!"

Erik looked back as Melissa screamed and stabbed a finger at the doorway. An ISF ninja had leaped atop the barricade and now raised his *katana* to strike. Mahler fired at point-blank range even as the sword's blade chopped into his left shoulder. The retired Hauptmann reeled away to the right as his burst opened the ninja from navel to throat, blasting the lifeless body back over the barricade.

Another ninja, dressed in shadow and smelling of death, sprang over the barricade. He slammed the hilt of his sword into Mahler's temple. The short, sharp blow dropped Mahler to the deck and left his moaning body in a slowly growing pool of blood. The ninja grunted with satisfaction, then turned his attention to Melissa.

He tilted his circlevision visor up and smiled with a mouth full of uneven teeth. "Ah, we find you here instead of on the *Silver Eagle*. That makes it so much more pleasing." He advanced and straddled her. Reaching for her long, golden hair, he smiled again. "I am so glad to meet you, Melissa Steiner. I bring you the greetings of our Coordinator."

Melissa twisted and rolled to her back. Her right hand surrounded the butt of the pistol she had not wanted to wear. She tipped the holster up and tightened her trigger-finger.

Fire and metal ate through the holster with volcanic fury. The first bullet slammed into the ninja's stomach and lifted him from his crouch. The next two shots lanced through his chest. He whirled away, seeming to brandish his *katana* even as his body met its death. The ninja sat abruptly against the glass wall overlooking the *Silver Eagle*. His *katana* clattered to the ferrocrete beside him.

Trembling and tearful, Melissa stared at the man she had killed. The sharp scent of gunsmoke nearly masked the sticky-sweet odor of blood. Her left hand idly tried to brush blood from her sweat-soaked trousers. *My God, I've killed a man.*

Clovis's stinging slap across her face brought her back. "He's dead," the dwarf said grimly. "We aren't. Move it."

Shivering, Melissa looked up at him. He pointed a stubby finger at an open panel beneath the computer consoles where he worked. "Computer needs venting, Melissa, and we can escape through the tunnels. Let's go."

Melissa numbly crawled into the darkness. Clovis shoved two autorifles in after her, then—having shed his stilts—dropped to his knees and followed her into the passage. He swung around and pulled the panel shut behind them.

Melissa gave Clovis no conscious sign that she had heard his directions, but she crawled on in accordance with them. *All this death and destruction because of me. Andrew and Captain von Breunig, dead because of me. Hilda Mahler is a widow because of me. The people in the fire teams—whose names I never learned—dead because of me. I haven't earned this sort of loyalty. Why?*

Clovis grabbed Melissa's ankle and brought her to a stop. She turned back and looked at him. It took a moment, but she finally interpreted his wild gesturing. Together, they slid the panel above them aside.

Clovis jerked the pistol from her holster. Holding it unsteadily in his two tiny hands, the dwarf slowly stood and surveyed the room.

Confident of no immediate danger, he tugged Melissa to her feet. "Clear, Archon. Don't forget the rifles."

Melissa whirled. "No. I've seen enough killing. I won't carry them."

Fury twisted the little of Clovis's face revealed in the half-light. "What in hell do you think is going on here? This isn't a holovid. This is a war!"

"Dammit, I know that." Melissa bit her lower lip to stop it from trembling, but the tremors merely transferred themselves to her whole body. Tears streaked through the dust that the short crawl had caked onto her face. "I know it's real, and I know Andrew will never be back." She turned from the dwarf. "I don't want more killing."

With more strength than Melissa could have imagined possible, Clovis gripped the shoulder of her shirt and turned her around. "I don't care what you want, and I'm fairly certain a bunch of mad Kuritans share my feelings. I'd grab the guns, but I can't even hold this damned pistol." He shook his head and looked with disgust at his stubby-fingered hands. "Great! The dream of a lifetime—a dwarf at court. And I get stuck with a pampered princess who figures us peasants owe her their lives."

Melissa grabbed the front of Clovis's shirt in a deathgrip. "Don't ever say that! I don't deserve any of this!" She released him and covered her tear-streaked face with both hands. "Why must people die for me?"

She felt Clovis's hand on her shoulder again, but it did not pull her around. His voice became softer. "I forget. You're just a kid. Listen, the reason we're fighting, the reason von Breunig and Redburn and the others died for you is not because of what you are. Nobody, outside of fairy tales, puts his life on the line for blond locks and long legs. That's not why we're fighting."

Melissa's hands fell from her face. She turned back and looked into Clovis's brown eyes. "Why, then? Why are you fighting?"

The dwarf shrugged. "We're fighting for the future. Everyone has to hope, somehow, that his life will change things for the better. Granted that the Kuritans view that a lot differently than we do, but those ninjas and the 'Mechs coming in want to change things, too.

"You represent the future. We're not fighting for, over, or about you, really. We're fighting so that our vision of the future, of which you are a part, will win out over their vision of the future. If you die here, lots of dreams will die with you."

Melissa glanced down at the guns lying on the tunnel floor. "But I don't know if I could shoot anyone ever again."

Clovis flipped her pistol around and offered it to her. "If you're not willing to fight for the future, who will be?" Clovis stared ahead while he spoke, as though gazing light years into the distance. "Besides, you and I have a duty to protect the Commonwealth. The Draconians are after us here, but it was someone inside the Commonwealth who arranged your kidnapping. We've got to get out of here to prevent them from gaining any benefit from this little bit of treachery."

Though tears streamed from her eyes and her face wore a stricken expression, Melissa reached down to pick up the autorifles. Standing aside slightly, she let the dwarf take the lead.

Clovis climbed from the hole and crossed to the doorway. Melissa followed. Cautiously, they crept from the room and worked their way down the hall. Traveling away from the command center, they quickly reached an engineering stairwell leading down to Echo level.

Clovis smiled. "As I remember it, Viscount Monahan used to berth his small boat back by the small docking bay. He used it to travel to some of the other asteroids that the company mined in this system. Unless the ISF ninjas have destroyed it, we can use the boat to hide on another of the asteroids."

Melissa nodded and made her way down the stairs. Then she covered Clovis as he worked his way down. Finally, at the bottom of the stairwell, Melissa checked the outside corridor, then signaled all-clear.

As she stepped from the doorway, all she caught was a slight blur of motion as a ninja clinging to the wall above the doorway dropped onto her. He encircled her neck with a thick arm and kicked her rifle away. Though she made to grab the pistol on her right hip, the commando numbed her arm with a chop from his right hand, then flipped her roughly against the wall. Stars exploded before Melissa's eyes as her head smacked into the ferrocrete. Through the flashing lights, she saw the ninja scissor his legs and spill Clovis to the ground. In one smooth motion, the ninja drew his *katana*. He raised it up beside his right ear, as Clovis raised one hand to ward off the coming blow.

"No!" she said sharply, with all the power and authority she could summon. "I am Melissa Steiner. Do not kill him." The ninja, used to taking orders, stiffened, then turned. He lowered the blade, then bowed deeply. "I am honored, Archon-Designate." He pointed back to the stairwell. "You will follow me to my Commander."

She saw something tug at the commando's left shoulder and begin to spin him about even before she heard the shot. Without conscious thought, her right hand reached for and drew her pistol. As the commando looked back down the hallway and clawed for the carbine hanging down at his hip, Melissa shoved the automatic pistol into his stomach and jerked the trigger.

273

The ninja danced backward into a twisted heap of blood and limbs. The dying man's hands clutched at his stomach and he cried out, but Melissa felt no pity or remorse. A cold rage, a rage directed against the people and events that had forced her to kill him, filled her. *Perhaps now I have begun to earn what will become mine. Before I can accept responsibility for others, I must take responsibility for myself.* This time, no mocking laughter taunted her from the depths of her being.

Keeping her pistol trained on the dead ninja, Melissa glanced back in the direction from which the original shot had come. Slumped, tattered and torn, against a wall, Leftenant Andrew Redburn slowly lowered his rifle. His dark green tunic had been all but torn from the left side of his body, with only a ragged strip of bloodsoaked cloth linking cuff and shoulder on his left arm. His trousers had fared better, and some of the burned patches still smoldered. Redburn coughed wetly, and dropped to one knee.

Taking one last look at the ISF commando, Melissa dashed down the hallway, with Clovis close behind. "Andrew! You're alive! Thank God!" She reached out and touched the side of his face. Her hand came away wet from the blood trickling from his ears.

Andrew coughed again and winced. A droplet of blood leaked from the right corner of his mouth. "Yeah, well, that's the idea, isn't it."

Clovis stared at him. "How badly are you hit?"

Andrew shrugged. "Busted some ribs and popped my eardrums in an explosion. I can't hear too well, and I think my right lung is punctured. It only hurts when I breathe. Of course, this beats what happened to the guy sitting on my legs at the time. He shielded me from the blast."

Melissa forced herself to smile. "Clovis knows of a boat back by the small docking bay. Can you walk?"

Andrew nodded and levered himself to his feet. "Hell, for a chance to escape this rock, I'll dance if I have to!" Melissa tried to put his left arm around her shoulder to help support him, but he shook his head. "You need your hands free to handle one of the rifles. With any luck, the guy you shot was the only man posted on this level." Andrew pointed at the dead ninja. "Clovis, grab his little pig-sticker. You need something."

The dwarf grabbed the *tanto* and led the way down the hall. The trio proceeded carefully. Despite the fact that Melissa had fallen prey to the ninja's earlier trap, both men looked to her for direction. Honoring their trust, she studied each stretch of the corridor and silently pointed out what she saw as hazards.

The trio picked their way cautiously through the remnants of a

274

long, running battle. When they reached the spot where Andrew's fire team had died in an explosion, the stench of blood and burning flesh overwhelmed Melissa. She fell to her knees and vomited, but refused help when both men tried to lift her to her feet. *I will redeem the sacrifice of these lives,* she vowed silently. *I will make the plotters pay...*

As they moved further down the battle-scarred corridors, nothing further interfered with their swift progress. Melissa even found herself smiling as they reached the corridor to the smaller docking bay. "This is it, gentlemen." She signaled Andrew to assume her position, and started to sprint across the corridor. Halfway there, she slowed, then stopped.

Andrew stepped out beside her, and his rifle clattered to the ferrocrete floor as soon as hers did. Clovis peeked around the corner, then sagged against the wall. He shook his oversized head. "So close...so close."

The trio raised their hands in the universal sign of capitulation.

A *Panther* filled the path before them. With a gracious bow from the waist, the 'Mech and its pilot accepted their unconditional surrender.

BOOK
4

51

Dan threw up his hands. "Am I the only one who sees this thing as insane?" He looked around the oval conference table, but none of the Kell Hound executive staff would meet his gaze. "Yes, jumping us into Kurita space was a brilliant bit of planning. They'd never expect it. Do you know why? It's utterly mad, that's why." *Why can't the rest of you see that?*

The hatch into the narrow, dimly lit conference room hissed open. Pale and drawn, Patrick Kell strode uneasily into the room and gently lowered himself into a chair at Dan's left. Because Patrick was not wearing a shirt, everyone could see the massive bandages covering the puncture wound on his left side. The faintest hint of pink in the center of a bandage indicated that the wound still leaked.

Patrick smiled, then nodded his head to Captain Vandermeer at the far end of the table. "Well done, Janos."

Dan twitched as though the praise for the Captain had stung him. He shook his head and Patrick Kell reached over with his right hand to pat the MechWarrior on the arm. "Calm yourself, Dan. There is method in our madness." Kell winced with pain, then raised his left hand to quiet concerned inquiries. "It hurt more when they shaved my chest to tape these bandages on. Thank God the Kuritans use sharp swords."

He looked around the room and met the combined gaze of his subordinates. "Janos and I hatched this plan after the physicians sewed me up. Desperate situations require desperate measures. What I will

279

reveal to you now must be held in strictest confidence." Kell waited for everyone to nod agreement before he continued.

"Janos's people intercepted messages from the incoming Kurita ships to their forces on the ground. When the incoming attackers learned of the action around our base, they demanded confirmation of our destruction." He narrowed his eyes for emphasis. "They didn't want troop positions or strength estimates. They just wanted to know we were dead!"

"Payback," Cat mumbled.

Kell nodded solemnly. "That's it exactly."

Richard O'Cieran frowned. "If they want us dead, this little trick isn't going to do anything. They'll backtrack and find us here. Hell, we're close enough to Dieron for scout ships to flood this and any other uncolonized star in the area." The jump troop commander nodded at Dan. "Dan's right, we've dodged lasers and waltzed into PPC fire."

Salome Ward nodded sympathetically. "It'll take a week for us to recharge the K-F drive…"

Dan shook his head. "This is a K8 star, not a G. It'll take just over 199 hours, but we're not at the optimum recharging point, and we've not unfurled the solar collector yet. That adds another five hours to deploy and recover."

Major Fitzpatrick looked at Janos, who nodded slowly. With a frown, Fitzpatrick turned to Kell. "Forgive me, Patrick, but spending a week and a half here will get us killed."

"I know." Patrick leaned back and another wave of pain twisted his features. "We're going to try something dangerous. It's as likely to kill us as all the Kuritans who are after us, but it's also got a higher margin of success. Janos, please explain."

The *Cucamulus*'s Captain stood and pressed a button to dim the lights. He slid a panel at his end of the table toward himself, then flipped it to reveal a computer keyboard. He slid the keyboard back into place and typed in a command. Hovering above the center of the table, a holographic diagram of the *Cucamulus* glowed to life.

"You all know that it is the Kearny-Fuchida drive that allows us to travel so rapidly between stars. And you know, too, that the K-F drive can translocate us up to thirty light years from our current location. Those drives require an incredible amount of power to rip a hole in the fabric of space, and then project the ship through to its destination."

Janos typed another command into the computer linked to the keyboard, and the image shifted. A chart appeared and slowly rotated so that everyone at the table could read it easily. "As Dan has pointed out—doubtless because he had to memorize such material while at the

New Avalon Military Academy—A2341CA is a K Class star. Were we positioned at the optimum charging point, it would take us just over 195 hours to power the drives. Adding two hours to deploy and three to recover the solar collector, we would be here more than eight days."

Dan shook his head. *Eight days if we were in the right position, which we're not.* He swallowed but said nothing aloud. *I haven't had such a feeling of doom since Morgan Kell broke up the regiment eleven years ago. Hell, the Defection was a simulator battle compared to this mess.*

Janos smiled uneasily. "The reason it takes so long to charge a Kearny-Fuchida drive is not because of the amount of energy needed to fuel the equipment." His fingers flew across the keys and a series of equations flashed up. "We could actually do it in sixteen hours."

Fitzpatrick laughed. "Now we're cooking with magnetic induction."

Janos shook his head. "Not exactly, Seamus. The K-F drive is a delicate instrument. The charge must be fed into it slowly. 'Hot-loading' an engine causes damage on the molecular level, or so some whiz kids at the New Avalon Institute of Science believe."

Dan frowned. "They don't know?"

Janos shook his head quickly. "No. A couple of people have reported successfully 'hot-loading' their engines, but no one can prove it. Other attempts have, apparently, been utter failures."

Salome shivered. "What happened to the ships?"

"We don't know," Janos said with a shrug.

Patrick Kell leaned forward. "We do know, however, that it's possible to use our in-system engine to power up the K-F drive."

Cat smiled slyly. "So we'll jump-start our K-F drive and leave here before it is 'theoretically' possible for us to be gone. The Draconians will be left assuming we died in a misjump."

Patrick nodded slowly. "There it is."

Dan shook his head. "I don't like it. If we try this, we *are* likely to die in a misjump." He turned to Janos. "What happens if the K-F drive just quits? Can we fix it?"

"I doubt it." The Captain sat down. "The *Cucamulus* is more than 300 years old, and has worked—if the translations of the early Kurita logs are correct—like a charm since its maiden voyage. All the while this ship has been hopping between stars, no one has rediscovered what makes the K-F drive tick. If it goes, we stay here."

Fitzpatrick leaned back. "Until Kurita comes for us."

Patrick nodded. "Right again. What I want is for all of you to put your people to work. Seamus, your Techs and aerojocks are to make sure our fighters are ready to deploy at a moment's notice. If a Kurita ship arrives—and if they've got Janos's knowledge of non-standard jump points—we'll need them ready to go. Salome, I want all 'Mechs fully operational, and as many of those captured *Panthers* working as possible. I want anyone without a jump-capable 'Mech checked out on a *Panther*."

Patrick turned to the jump troop commander. "Rick, I need your troops looking sharp. Have them check out all their equipment, especially anything they need to go outside a ship."

Dan narrowed his eyes. "It sounds as though you expect trouble."

Patrick pursed his lips. "First of all, Dan, I don't want a bunch of people running around thinking they're going to die when we jump out of here. No one is to know about our plan to leave quickly. Granted, few folks know enough about the K-F drives to be worried, but I don't want an undercurrent of fatalism sapping morale. Giving everyone something to do will keep them too busy to speculate about our plans. All they'll know is that we're getting out of here."

Salome cleared her voice. "I don't think that was Dan's question, Patrick. Have you and Janos decided where we're going, and do you expect trouble when we get there?"

Kell nodded. He looked toward Janos, but the Captain shook his head and pointed at a blue light flashing on his keyboard. "I must report to the bridge. I'll let you know what is happening."

"Very well." Patrick waited for the hatch to slide shut behind Vandermeer before he continued. "We're going to appear in a system that is little more than an asteroid belt. It was home to a mining company until the firm collapsed a year ago. Wayland Smith, whom some of you may remember from his time with us before the…Well, he conned a great deal of money from the Kurita authorities using this played-out system as collateral. Since then, certain people have moved in…"

Dan smiled. "From the way you say 'certain people,' I hear echoes of the word Heimdall." Dan shook his head as the other officers nodded or smiled. Because he'd grown up in the Federated Suns, and because of his father's work as a Rat-catcher, he had never understood this romantic attachment that the others felt for this outlaw group. He shook his head. "I should have known."

"We'll make a good Lyran out of you yet, Dan," Salome said with a laugh.

"Janos says that one of his 'pirate points' is near the main base, which will put us at one gravity hour out from the base. I expect no trouble, but I want everyone ready."

The officers nodded in unison. "How long do we have to recharge?" O'Cieran's question focused everyone's attention on Patrick.

"Janos said we'd run a 28 percent failure risk if we took twenty-five hours to power, and we've already got three under our belts." He winced and opened his hands. "The odds get better if we wait longer. Worse, if we don't."

The image of Janos's head and torso replaced the holographic image of formulae and tables. "Patrick."

Kell punched the button on a small commlink at his position on the table. "Go ahead."

"A Kurita ship has arrived at the nadir point. She's released one *Invader* Class DropShip, and it's coming fast."

"ETA?"

"Twenty-one hours."

Kell nodded sagely. "That gives us nineteen hours to power the K-F drive. What does that make our odds?"

Janos grimaced. "Worse, Patrick. Much worse."

Lieutenant Austin Brand disengaged his hands from Meg Lang's as they both snapped to attention and saluted. "Afternoon, Captain."

Dan's head came up, and his vision cleared. They'd been sitting beneath an apple tree on the *Cucamulus*'s starboard agrodome. Locked deep in thought, Dan had not noticed Meg and Brand as he approached. He smiled now to see them together, then his brows furrowed. "Why aren't you down on the *Nuada* getting your 'Mechs ready?"

Meg smiled. "My *Wasp* is perfectly checked out, and Austin's *Commando* is on the *Lugh*."

Dan frowned at Austin Brand. "Lieutenant, I thought I ordered you checked out on one of the *Panther*s."

Brand nodded. "Done, Dan. Jackson gave me the *Panther* I walked into the *Nuada*, and so I needed only a fraction of the time others took to 'imprint.' Don't forget, the *Panther* is a simpler machine than my *Commando*, even with the jump jets. My 'Mech is nestled in the *Nuada*'s drop bays between your *Val* and Meg's *Wasp*."

Dan nodded distractedly. "All twelve bays are filled?"

Brand nodded and ticked the 'Mechs off on his fingers as he spoke. "You, Meg, Eddie, and I make one lance. Major Ward's *Wolverine* and Fitzhugh's *Catapult* are there. McWilliams and Lasker have been assigned to *Panther*s to even that lance out."

Dan wrinkled his nose with distaste and turned away. He grasped the thick branch of a gapel tree, then turned to face his people again. "That only gives us eight 'Mechs for the drop. I don't like it."

Meg looked at Austin, concern on her face. "Jackson and Jones have two more *Panther*s operational. Bethany Connor and Cat are being imprinted on them. That gives us ten."

283

Dan looked up. "What about the *Victor*?"

Austin shook his head. "It's still on the *Mac*, and still imprinted for Colonel Kell. No one else here could pilot it anyway."

Dan nodded. "Well, get back to your 'Mechs. We'll be leaving soon, and Patrick wants us ready to drop when we arrive."

Meg frowned. "Hot zone?"

Dan chuckled. "This *is* Kurita space."

Meg nodded. "Silly question."

"Yeah," said Brand. "Well, I have one that's not so silly." His eyes narrowed. "How can we charge a JumpShip so quickly, especially when the solar collector hasn't even been deployed?"

Dan's head came up, and anger frosted his words. "Don't think about it, Lieutenant. You're not being paid to think. When you get to be a Captain, then you can think. Dismissed."

As his two subordinates left, Dan ground his teeth. "And when they pay you to think," he murmured to himself, "that's when you wish you didn't have to..."

52

Fuh Teng and his mechanic, Tung Yuan, glanced nervously at the black shadows surrounding the cone of light where they stood. "Justin, do you really think it's wise for us to be in Montenegro at this time of night?" He glanced out into the darkness and watched for roving bands of hoodlums.

The MechWarrior chuckled softly. He turned his back to the warehouse wall and shook his head. "We don't have to worry. Gray Noton himself arranged the security for this place."

Yuan grunted and shoved his fists deeper into the pockets of his quilted black jacket. "In that case, his death does nothing to inspire confidence."

Justin laughed, then turned his attention back to the door beneath the sole streetlight. He pulled a key from his pocket and inserted it into the lock. As it clicked, he opened the door and ushered his two companions into the warehouse's dark interior. As Justin shut the door behind them, the utter blackness seemed to swallow them whole.

Justin flicked on the fluorescent lights, which sputtered to life. As their pale pink glow allowed Yuan a first glimpse, what he saw took his breath away. The Tech staggered forward as though drunk or in shock.

Fuh Teng wheeled and stared at Justin through slitted eyes. "You don't mean to use this, do you?"

Justin nodded, a vulpine grin tightening his lips. "I want you and Yuan to go over it. No modifications. Just check all the circuits and

285

make sure it's fully operational for tonight."

Yuan turned. "What about the insignia?"

Justin smiled. "I can think of no better. Let it stand."

Justin squinted against the glare of the searing studio lights. A buxom blonde leaned over him, gracing him with an intimate view of her ample assets while she patted makeup onto his face. "There, Mr. Xiang," she cooed. "That'll make you look as calm and fearless as I know you are."

God, she's wearing enough perfume to be a Class 3 atrocity under the Ares Convention. Justin forced himself to smile at her. "Perhaps I should just find a power connection for my cooling vest."

She stared cow-eyed at him for a second, then laughed shrilly. "Oh, yeah, the lights are hot, aren't they?" She slowly straightened up. "Well, if you need anything, just let me know." She tucked a slip of paper down the front of his cooling vest. "Any time."

Justin nodded as she walked away, then glanced over at Philip Capet. *He looks suitably nervous. Good.* Justin shook his head slowly.

Capet's head came up. "What are you looking at, Xiang?"

"A man who is about to die."

Capet parried the attack with a laugh. "I don't see any mirrors, Xiang."

Justin smiled easily. "I hope you open a radio channel to me during the fight. I want to know what you see when your life flashes before your eyes. I want to hear you whimper."

Capet shot to his feet, but the arrival of the program's host forestalled any battle. The heavy-set man looked like a bumblebee in his yellow blazer and black pants. "Whoa, boys, we don't want a fight before the cameras start running." He rested his hands on Capet's shoulders and slowly pressed the champion down into his seat.

The host seated himself between the two combatants, clipped a microphone to his lapel, and smiled directly into the holovision camera as the red light above its muzzle flashed to life. "Welcome, sports fans, to 'Pregame Palaver,' the program that brings you the combatants before the battle. I'm your host, Kevin Johnson, and we have quite a show for you tonight."

The host turned toward Philip Capet. "On my left is Philip Capet, the current reigning champion in the Open Class of warfare here on Solaris. You've all seen him fight many times before. He's got a double-dozen kills to his credit in the arenas, and even more in his military career. Glad to have you here, Philip."

"My pleasure, Kevin."

Johnson turned toward Justin. "And here we have Justin Xiang

He's a newcomer, but his rise has been impressive, to say the least. He's fought seven times and killed every opponent he's faced. Those of you keeping track know that those have all been kills of warriors from the Federated Suns. None have escaped him or his *Centurion*, the *Yen-lo-wang*. Welcome aboard, Justin."

"*Zao*, Kevin. I am honored."

Kevin smiled again at the camera. "We'll continue with these two warriors in a minute, but first a word from your LCAF recruiter."

The red light on the camera faded, and Johnson's smile went with it. "O.K., you two. Let's make this entertaining. Got it?" He glanced down at his clipboard. "When we come back, we do a taped piece on Capet's background, and then one on you, Justin. After a brief piece about the Kurita arena, I'll go into the live interview. Watch the language."

He turned toward Justin. "As our final question, I'll ask what you're fighting in tonight."

Justin shook his head. "My contract does not require that I reveal the identity of my machine."

Johnson shrugged, seeing the show's producer wave at him. "On the mark, Kevin," the man said. "Bring the Ishiyama construct up."

Johnson levered himself out of his seat and crossed to where a black "X" had been painted on the floor. A camera closed in on him and a holographic image of the Kurita arena, Ishiyama—or Stone Mountain—materialized in front of Johnson. "Built twenty years ago, this arena in the center of the Kobe District of Solaris City is one of the most popular with fight fans. Its 'Mech-scale tunnels twist and turn through multiple levels. Though all the maps for the arena were destroyed after its construction, there are rumors of hidden passages and movable walls that literally alter the battlefield as war rages within the mountain."

Johnson turned to Capet. "Philip, you've fought inside Ishiyama before."

Capet nodded. "That's right, Kevin. Eight months back, I faced two *Stingers* and a *Panther* in the labyrinth. It was a long battle, but they made a classic mistake. Instead of working together, they split up. I picked them off one at a time."

Johnson nodded, then turned to Justin. "Justin, what are your thoughts about fighting in the Ishiyama for the first time?"

Justin smiled. "I feel quite confident. The labyrinth benefits a tactician, which no one has ever accused Capet of being…"

"I've got a surprise or two for you, Xiang!" Capet stood quickly and thrust a finger at his foe. "You may believe yourself my superior in combat, but I've learned many things here on Solaris…"

Justin steepled his fingers and sat back. "Have you learned not to blunder into ambushes, Philip?"

Capet shook his head. A camera swung around to get a better shot of his face. "What you did to Armstrong, you will not do to me."

Justin looked up. "I was hardly thinking of that incident, Philip. I referred to Uravan."

A cry of inarticulate rage bubbled from Capet's throat, but Johnson crossed back quickly and interposed himself between the two MechWarriors. He shoved Capet roughly back, then made the mistake of turning to smile at the camera. Capet's punch caught him in the jaw and snapped his head around. Johnson sank to the studio floor without a sound.

Capet straddled the unconscious commentator, but he stared at Justin. "You will be dead, Xiang. Not because I will win the fight, not because my nation demands your death, but because I want to see you dead!" Capet ripped the microphone free of his cooling vest and stalked off the set.

Justin let the announcer's voice-over fill his neurohelmet as he doublechecked the 'Mech's equipment. "Well, Kevin," the announcer was saying, "that was the most explosive interview you've ever had."

"Yeah."

"How's the jaw?"

Kevin's voice dropped to a low growl. "Hard to describe, Karl, but if you really want to know, maybe we can get Philip Capet to hit you after the fight."

Justin laughed as the announcer carefully nudged the conversation in another direction. The status monitor on his command console confirmed that both large lasers were operational. The autocannons appeared to be in fine working order, as were the twin, torso-mounted medium lasers. *I must remember to use the cannons sparingly, as I don't have that much ammo for them. I'll only use them when the lasers need to cool down.*

The green light on his command console flared to life. Justin smiled as the doors before him slid open and the holovision camera across the tunnel focused on his 'Mech. He instantly brought up both of his 'Mech's arms and stepped forward.

Kevin Johnson's voice filled the cockpit. "Well, Karl, do you see that? Xiang's using a *Rifleman*, just like Capet. This will make for an interesting match. Let's see if we can focus in on the crest there on the 'Mech's chest."

Yes, Kevin, do that. I'm sure your viewers will love it.

"Blake's Blood," Johnson blurted.

"What is it, Kevin?" Karl gasped. "The logo looks like a cartoon ghost to me, with a set of crosshairs surrounding it."

"That *Rifleman* belonged to Gray Noton," Johnson replied in a low tone. "Xiang chose it specially for its name."

"Which is?"

Johnson laughed coldly. "*Legend-killer.*"

Justin killed the commentary and stepped the *Rifleman* out into the corridor. He turned the ponderous 'Mech to the left and headed up the slight incline. The naturally smooth surfaces of the tunnel walls arced up to meet in a stalactite-festooned roof. Stalagmites and piles of debris from partially collapsed walls or ceiling dotted the tunnel floor, but did not impede the *Rifleman*'s progress.

As Justin reached the far end of the tunnel and prepared to follow it around into the switchback on the right, he turned his 'Mech's vulnerable back to the wall. Sliding the 'Mech sideways, he let the tip of his left-hand guns peek into the corridor. When that drew no fire, Justin worked along until he had a clear view of the new tunnel.

It led up into darkness. As Justin switched over to infrared scanners, he saw a few heat pockets set along the walls ahead, but dismissed them as holovision cameras. Ascending slowly, he reached the crest of the tunnel.

At that point, Justin paused. He saw that the whole left side of this level section of the tunnel was gapped. *The pillars formed where stalactites and stalagmites that have flowed together are large enough to hide a 'Mech in profile, but the spaces between them are too narrow to let this monster pass. That means I have to march all the way through this shooting gallery in one burst. I don't like it.*

Justin looked up as the IR display revealed red tendrils coiling lazily up through the air at the tunnel's far end. *Hello.* He snapped both arms forward and waited. The second the swirling communications mount of the Garret T11-A com system came into view, Justin centered his crosshairs. He let them drift down as the other *Rifleman*'s silhouette grew like a sailing ship emerging over the horizon. When Capet's canopy bobbed up, Justin let loose.

Cascades of white heat swirled around the ruby shafts of laser fire from the *Legend-killer*'s arms. One large beam shucked armor from the other *Rifleman*'s right shoulder. The other beam stitched a series of small explosions across the 'Mech's left shoulder, blasting chips and chunks of armor into the air. The *Legend-killer*'s medium lasers also scored the same targets as their larger cousins, spitting more half-melted ceramics onto the tunnel floor. One of the two autocannon bursts tore holes in Ishiyama behind Capet's *Rifleman*, while the other smashed armor from the 'Mech's right shoulder.

289

"Damn!" A wave of heat washed over Justin. The 'Mech's heat indicators spiked high into the red zone. *This isn't an efficient machine. It vents heat poorly.* Justin slapped the manual "shutdown" override with his right hand, then cursed again as Capet backed his *Rifleman* down the far slope.

Sweat coursed down Justin's face, leaving one droplet suspended from the tip of his nose. He shook his head to flick it off, then studied his heat monitors again. As the *Legend-killer*'s ten heat sinks vented the excess heat that his firing had created, the monitors slowly sank back down through the red and yellow zones to what MechWarriors often referred to as "green fields."

Justin centered his attention on the far end of the tunnel, but watched for heat or movement through the columns. Seeing nothing, he marched the *Legend-killer* into the tunnel. At each of the gray stone pillars, he stopped to wait, but there was no sign of Capet. Though that tunnel was only three hundred meters long, it took Justin fifteen minutes to journey through it.

He smiled as the producer's green light on his console began to blink urgently. Cautiously beginning his descent at the far end of the tunnel, he did his best to ignore it. *I don't care if I'm moving too slowly. Just put more advertisements into the program.*

The tunnel ended on a ledge midway up the side of a vast crevasse. Its steep sides sloped down for three levels, and were dotted with tunnel mouths on different levels. Justin saw burn marks on a number of them and realized that light, jump-capable 'Mechs could easily cross the opening. *Not so, a heavy machine like this.*

Above him the stalactite ceiling rose into darkness. Behind and to the left, he saw the pillars of the gallery he'd just traversed. On the opposite side, up above him, he saw a similarly designed tunnel. The crevasse curved back out of sight on the left, but extended straight on the right.

Justin kept the *Legend-killer*'s back to the tunnel wall and moved laterally along the ledge. Suddenly, Capet's *Rifleman* appeared in an opening on the opposite wall. Justin smiled as he brought his weapons into line with the *Rifleman*, and opened a radio line to Capet. "It's over, Philip."

"Is it, Xiang?" Capet's laughter filled Justin's cockpit. "Here's your surprise, Capellan. How do you like these tactics?"

Infrared images filled Justin's sight. The computer painted the silhouette of a 'Mech to his right, and another one to his left. Justin glanced left and saw a handless, humanoid *Firestarter* emerging from the tunnel mouth. An *UrbanMech* shuffled into view on his right. *That's why the director's light was flashing. They wanted to warn me...*

290

A high, keening wail echoed within his neurohelmet as the computer warned that each foe had a weapons lock on the *Legend-killer*.

"One more thing, Justin." Capet's voice was triumphant. "It seems I *will* command the regiment the Prince has offered for your head. It's time for you to die."

53

Patrick Kell's voice filled the steel womb of Daniel Allard's *Valkyrie*. "So that's it, ladies and gentlemen. Because we have Kurita forces incoming, we're going to jump out of here ahead of them. Let me stress that the Kearny-Fuchida drive is fully charged, through we did not deploy the solar collector. Everything reports out at 100 percent effectiveness."

Just from the sound of his voice, I know he's not lying. If there were trouble, he'd tell us, Dan thought. Though all the equipment had checked out, none of the instruments could measure damage on the "molecular" level. Dan knew that Patrick believed every confident word he spoke, and that heartened him. *From your lips to God's ears, Patrick.*

The Kell Hound CO continued his video briefing. "Once we enter the Styx system, the *Nuada* will be launched. We expect our reception to be friendly and well-negotiated by radio before the *Nuada* arrives. But we'll have an ace already played if things get nasty. The *Nuada* will drop its two reinforced lances over a small docking bay on the dark side of the mining planetoid. It's on the side opposite the main bay entrance, but has a direct link to the docking bay."

"Our aero wing will deploy to cover the *Cu*. Captain Vandermeer will keep us at his pirate point, and we'll begin to use our engines to recharge, much as we have done here. If things look friendly, we'll move the *Cu* in and draw power directly from the planetoid."

Kell's image furrowed its brows. "I'll not kid you. All of this is dangerous. It could be the end of the Kell Hounds if we have a drive failure here or if someone anticipates our arrival at Styx." Patrick shook his head. "We'll make it, though, and that'll irritate Takashi Kurita more than bad sushi. There's no one in the Inner Sphere who deserves it more. Luck to you all."

And to you, Patrick. I wouldn't wait behind for all the beer in the Free Worlds League. Dan flicked switches on his command console. The on-board computer executed thousands of checks in mere seconds, then reported the results on the screen previously occupied by Patrick Kell. Dan opened a commlink. "Alpha Leader is at 100 percent," he said.

"Likewise, Captain," reported Austin Brand.

"Alpha Three is green all the way." Following Meg's report, Eddie Baker added, "Alpha Four is aces up."

Dan smiled to himself. "How about you, Cat?"

"All systems go." The man who normally piloted a *Marauder* quickly amended his statement. "The machine is ready, but I think my left hand will wither for lack of something to do."

"Yeah." Dan switched his radio over to the command frequency. "Salome, Alpha Lance is operational."

"Good. Beta is all green as well. You're the Tactical Commander on this drop, Dan. My *Wolverine* and Mike's *Catapult* are here for support because you've got the superior grasp of light 'Mech tactics. Let us know where you need us."

"Roger." Dan glanced at the timer ticking down on his console. He switched his radio over to the battle frequency for the whole assault team. "Ten seconds and counting. Brace, because we'll be in-system and away almost immediately."

Following his own advice, Dan slipped his hands from the joysticks down to the arms of the command chair itself as the clock revealed three seconds to jump. He felt the familiar, yet unsettling thrum of the K-F drive engaging. *What was that? Is something wrong?* Questions ripped through his brain as he sought to match his current feelings to the faded memories of all the other jumps he'd made.

Lights flared and twisted as always, but instead of the mosaic of soft, melting pastels, hard, crystalline daggers of intense color stabbed at his eyes. Glittering fragments of reality raked across his consciousness like nettles. They caught and tore, then shattered as he cried out in pain. Spinning away, they winked out of existence like fairy dust.

Dan snapped his eyes open. He felt the lurch and vibration as the *Nuada* disengaged itself from the *Cucumulus*. He floated up in his seat for a half-second, then his restraining straps caught him. From beneath

293

his feet, he felt a strong tremor, then the gravity induced by the *Nuada*'s engine thrust smashed him back down into his command chair.

Almost instantly, Patrick Kell's voice filled his neurohelmet. "Bad news, Dan. We've got two Kurita JumpShips at the zenith point. One DropShip is on a return vector for the JumpShips, but a scan reports traces of an ion trail heading in toward the planetoid. The ship must be on the sunside."

"Roger, Patrick. Thanks." Dan opened the battle frequency. "Heads up, campers. We'll have playmates when we hit solid ground." Dan reached out and flipped a switch. "Captain Helmer? Dan Allard here. What do you show on the planetoid?"

Captain Thomas Helmer of the *Nuada Argetlan* answered carefully. Dan could almost see the man studying a sensor screen as he selected his words for accuracy. When he spoke, however, there was not a trace of fear or anxiety in the Captain's voice. "The surface is full of pitted valleys and canyons. It's got enough metal in it to make the magscanners useless. Because we're coming in on the dark side, IR should work, but I'm getting nothing at this range."

"I understand. Have you located our target?"

"Affirmative. It actually has an active homing beacon. Wait! What's this?" Dan heard Helmer snap an order at someone on the bridge. "Patching visual through to you, Dan."

Dan watched as computer-generated topography filled an auxiliary monitor. A grid of green lines formed themselves into rolling hills and jagged mountains. In the distance, winking occasionally from between two particularly sharp mountains, Dan spotted the yellow rectangle designating their drop target. The computer added five yellow asterisks bouncing along on a direct course for the bay.

"What are those?"

Helmer coughed lightly. "I'm not sure. Mass marks them as thirty-five tons, give or take. Probably *Panthers*."

"They haven't seen us, have they?"

Helmer laughed. "No, and it wouldn't make any difference if they had."

Dan frowned. "I don't understand."

"No Comsats, Dan. They're on the dark side. Until they get into the mining facilities, they can't communicate with the DropShip or anyone else."

Dan nodded. "I see. We better beat them in. Would you mind goosing this baby?"

"My pleasure. Speed to 2.5 Gs. Twelve minutes to drop, Dan. Happy hunting."

* * *

Dan watched Cat Wilson's *Panther* streak planetward. The *Valkyrie*'s jump jets stabbed flame from the bottoms of both feet and from the rocket pack on the 'Mech's back. The ion streams slowed the *Valkyrie*'s descent, then lifted it and arced it forward. Cat's *Panther*, riding similar leg jets, floated up beside him and followed him into battle.

Fitzhugh's *Catapult* launched twin LRM volleys at the lead Kurita *Panther*. Five missiles tore armor from the *Panther*'s head, and another quintet savaged its left leg. Eight more missiles zeroed in on the *Panther*'s right arm, blasting every shred of armor from that limb, but failed to cripple it.

The *Panther* raised its PPC and triggered a blast at the *Catapult*. As the PPC beam whipped across the birdlike *Catapult*'s right leg, it melted armor and sent droplets of molten ceramics streaming to the planetoid's surface.

The *Catapult* answered the *Panther* with all four of its medium lasers. Two scarlet laser beams slashed ugly, bubbling scars across the *Panther*'s torso. Armor exploded away from the 'Mech's left arm as a third beam burned across its surface. The fourth beam sizzled into the *Panther*'s damaged right arm, melting the last of the armor and eating hungrily into the tattered limb. In a bright burst of sparks, the charging coils on the *Panther*'s PPC went black.

Salome's *Wolverine* descended at the rear of the Kurita lance. Targeting a *Panther* that was tracking Meg Lang's *Wasp*, Salome unleashed her 'Mech's full fury upon it. The shoulder launcher belched a full SRM flight, and four of them hit. Two missiles blasted armor from the *Panther*'s left arm and leg. Two others, as though homing in on the *Panther*'s weakness, blasted thin armor from the center and left portion of the 'Mech's back.

Realizing his predicament too late, the *Panther* pilot hit his jump jets. As he rose on columns of ions, the fire from Salome's autocannon punched through the broken armor on the left side of the torso. Meanwhile, the *Wolverine*'s medium laser melted through the *Panther*'s spine. Hot shards of armor rained to the ground, and a flash of heat spilled from the 'Mech's infrared silhouette on Dan's battle screens.

"Meg, one's on you, to your right." Dan watched as she reacted. She boosted power to the jump jets, then drew up the knees on her *Wasp*. The *Wasp* twisted wildly and arced back as the PPC beams and flights of SRMs released by two *Panther*s sailed wide of their careening target.

Flashing beneath the *Wasp*, Austin Brand's *Panther* tracked the *Panther* that Salome had already savaged. The PPC in the right hand of Brand's *Panther* released an azure energy bolt, and the SRM launcher over the 'Mech's heart sent its flight of four missiles up and away. Three of the missiles found their target and exploded armor from the enemy *Panther*'s chest and right leg. The PPC beam struck the other *Panther* full in the chest, and sent all but the last layer of armor flaking away in a turquoise explosion.

Cat Wilson's PPC stabbed out. It drenched the planetoid's surface in cerulean highlights and lashed a third *Panther* across the chest. 'Mech armor boiled up, cracked loose, and dropped away in glowing plates. Cat's quartet of SRMs smashed into the same *Panther*. They blasted armor from either side of the torso, and cratered the armor on the *Panther*'s right leg. Staggered, the *Panther* twisted to target Cat with its return volley of SRMs.

"Break wide, Cat!" The MechWarrior rolled his *Panther* as the SRMs twisted toward him. Two burst against his 'Mech's right arm and crushed armor with fiery explosions. The only other missile to hit blasted armor from the *Panther*'s chest.

The confidence in Cat's voice rang through clearly. "Thanks for the warning. It's all yours."

Dan dropped the gold crosshairs of his weapons systems on the third *Panther* and tightened his triggers. The medium laser mounted in the right arm of his 'Mech gouged chunks of armor from the ragged right side of the *Panther*'s chest.

Six of the *Valkyrie*'s LRMs spiraled down into the *Panther* with hideous effect. Like flies to an open wound, the missiles blasted through the weakened torso armor and on into the 'Mech's core. An explosion brought a wave of white heat from the *Panther*'s chest as the missiles shattered shielding on the fusion reactor.

Baker's *Jenner* landed in a crouch, facing an undamaged *Panther*. The 'Mechs exchanged SRM volleys, but the *Jenner*'s lower profile let the *Panther*'s SRMs fly overhead, where they exploded against a barren hillside. Half the *Jenner*'s SRMs hit their target, drawing first blood and shattering armor on the *Panther*'s torso.

Four lasers stabbed out from the *Jenner*'s wings. One carved more armor from the Kurita 'Mech's torso, while another burned an uneven line through the armor on the *Panther*'s left leg. The final two beams lanced through the *Panther*'s left arm, stripping it of every scrap of armor and exposing the myomer muscles.

The Kurita *Panther*'s right arm came up and triggered a blast with its PPC. The blue bolt jerked and writhed as it scourged *Jenner*'s chest. Gobs of molten armor flew away from the *Jenner* on vapor jets. As the debris cloud evaporated, it left the *Jenner*'s chest naked and vulnerable.

296

Bethany Connor's *Panther* swung about and targeted the Kurita *Panther* attacking Baker's *Jenner*. Her PPC spat blue fire in a direct line at the enemy *Panther*'s wounded chest, bursting through the remaining armor as though it were paper. The beam melted all it touched, then ignited the SRMs stored in the *Panther*'s chest.

The SRMs exploded in a staccato string of bright flashes. Like a fountain of fire, bursts of light lanced from the 'Mech's torso. A pair of brilliant detonations sent the 'Mech's naked left arm spinning past Connor's *Panther*. Fire roiled and swirled within the Kurita 'Mech's heart, then grew in a series of explosions that the *Panther* could no longer contain. In a flash of platinum fire hot enough to momentarily overwhelm Dan's scanner, the 'Mech disintegrated.

Diane McWilliams and Mary Lasker bracketed the remaining *Panther* and concentrated their fire upon it. As their PPC beams both savaged the 'Mech's right leg, its armor melted away like wax. Muscles snapped apart and titanium bones glowed white-hot before they dissolved into tiny droplets.

As the Kurita *Panther* wavered and began to fall, the paired SRM volleys from the Kell Hound's captured *Panthers* battered the crippled 'Mech. Explosions blossomed across its chest like a necklace of fiery flowers, twisting the big machine and knocking it to the ground.

The Kurita *Panthers* moved to withdraw. "We have to stop them, Kell Hounds." Dan hated the sound of his voice as he issued the order, but he knew that there was no other choice. *If they get to where they can radio for help, we're finished.*

Fitzhugh's *Catapult* launched two more flights of LRMs at the *Panther* it had first attacked. Over a score of missiles hammered that 'Mech, shrouding it in a cloak of fire. The broken right arm snapped clean off after a series of hideous detonations. Several missiles shredded what little armor remained on the *Panther*'s head. Even more LRM missiles blasted away the fragments of armor shielding the 'Mech's chest, then crushed the *Panther*'s gyro system and SRM launcher. The broken machine spun to the planet's surface.

The Kurita *Panther* that Salome had first attacked turned in midflight to face her *Wolverine*. The two 'Mechs exchanged flights of SRMs like duelists settling a vendetta. Three missiles launched from the *Panther* exploded against the *Wolverine*'s left flank. Though they blasted away armor, the wounds appeared to be trivial.

Four of the SRMs arcing from the *Wolverine*'s shoulder launcher struck their flying target. One exploded within the confines of the enemy *Panther*'s chest, while the other three blasted armor from the left side of the chest, left leg, and right arm. The last missile, though it did little more than superficial damage, exploded against the PPC on the *Panther*'s right arm. The blast forced the fearsome weapon wide of its intended target so that the blue beam it had released burned harmlessly over the *Wolverine*'s head.

Salome's return fire struck home savagely. The autocannon's burst hit the *Panther* in the face, snapping its head back like a fighter hit by a punch. As the Kurita 'Mech began to roll over slowly, the *Wolverine*'s head-mounted medium laser stabbed deep into its front torso. Oily smoke burst from the *Panther* as the laser melted yet more shielding from its fusion engine.

The energy beam also destroyed the *Panther*'s gyrostablizer. The gyro's destruction accentuated the roll begun earlier, and the 'Mech went spinning helplessly out of control. It spiraled around on ion jets as the pilot fought to control it, then slammed against a mountainside in a brilliant explosion.

Cat and Brand caught the third *Panther* in a withering PPC crossfire, the turquoise energy beams slashing through the stricken 'Mech like scalpels. Cat's beam sliced all the armor from the *Panther*'s right arm. Steaming vaporized metal, the smoking carapace dropped to the planet's ochre surface.

Ignoring the damage done by Cat's attack, Brand impaled the enemy *Panther* with his PPC's artificial lightning. It spitted the fusion engine and split open the remaining shielding like the shell of a nut. Fire blossomed in the *Panther*'s stomach, then exploded outward. It bisected the 'Mech, then greedily gobbled the upper half before the plasma ball imploded and vanished in a golden flash.

"Dan, what the hell are they doing?" The urgency in Meg Lang's voice filled Dan with dread. "The other two pilots have activated their eject mechanisms. Their canopies are blown!"

Dan punched magnification and Starlight onto his forward scanner. He focused on the face of the *Panther* with one leg missing. He shivered and nearly vomited. *Why do they do that? Damned Kurita sense of honor! What a waste.*

The Kurita pilot had opened his cockpit to the outside vacuum without the benefit of a sealed suit. Dan could barely make out the blood dribbling from the warrior's nose through the viewplate on the neurohelmet. He glanced at his own scanners and they told him that the warrior's body was rapidly cooling.

Dan swallowed hard. "They're dead. Let's move on. We don't want to get caught in the open if their DropShip cruises back to find out what happened to them."

298

54

Three kilometers further on, through craters blasted into the planetoid's surface by meteors, the Kell Hounds reached the small locking bay. Set flush into the red-rock surface, the 100-meter wide square glowed yellow in the backglare of blinking directional lights. Dan's magscanner confirmed that the interlocking metal doors were structurally sound, and that energy flowed to the circuits needed to open them.

"Dan."

Dan turned his *Valkyrie* toward where Brand's *Panther* knelt beside the smaller airlock meant for personnel. Though the titanium doorway appeared plainly on Dan's magscan, he could see some sort of plastic cover shrouding it on the visual scanner. "What have you got, Austin?"

The *Panther* raised its head. "It looks as though jump troops came through here," Brand said. "The instructions on the seal are in Japanese. With two Kurita ships in-system, that must mean that the foot soldiers were Draconian."

Dan could almost see the frown on Cat's face that would match the rumble in the MechWarrior's voice. "Jump troops sent in before Mechs? That means one thing."

Dan nodded. "ISF." *I hope like hell the folks inside knew that they were coming. If not, we probably won't find anything alive in there.*

Salome broke into the conversation. "Dan, did you notice the

299

crest on those 'Mechs?"

Dan tried to visualize it, but could not. He punched up a replay of his combat footage, and froze the display when a crest popped into view. He magnified it and studied the simple design in the standard Kurita red circle. "I make it a black wave with stars in it. If that little boat carried up almost under the crest of the wave is to scale, that is a massive tidalwave."

"Right, that's what I have too." A nervous edge crept into Salome's voice. "I've crosschecked it against all unit designations in the Successor States. It's a blank."

That's impossible. Icy fingers traced a line down Dan's spine. "A unit that doesn't exist and ISF troops. This is strange." He switched to the battle frequency. "Let's be careful, people. This could be nasty. There must be something inside this rock that the Draconis Combine wants very badly."

Meg Lang's *Wasp* knelt beside the large bay doors. She attached the radio landline to a small panel at one edge of the bay. "Dan, I've set up our remote relay so that we can communicate with the *Cu* from inside this rock. I've also got full operational control of the airlock and this small docking bay. Both doors work. Everything is set for us to pretend we're an incoming ship."

"Good. Salome, I'd like your *Wolverine* to shield Meg's *Wasp* and Baker's *Jenner*. Meg, Eddie, you two will go in last and hang back because the *Panther*s will eat your 'Mechs alive. Brand, I want you and Connor up front. Your *Panther*s may confuse the Draconians for a moment or two."

Meg keyed in a standard access code, and the massive doors slowly slid apart. The thin layer of red dust from the planetoid's surface drifted up as traces of atmosphere burst free of the airlock. The Kell Hound 'Mechs quickly stepped onto the elevator platform that had risen from the interior to the surface.

Meg detached the landline from the exterior access port and snapped it into a similar connection on the elevator floor. She started the elevator moving downward, then closed the doors over their heads. In the darkness and silence of the airlock's vacuum, the Kell Hounds descended.

Dan shivered unconsciously. "Meg, how about some lights?"

"No can do, Dan. Styx Mining was a frugal company. Why waste them in an elevator shaft? I am bringing the atmosphere back up, though." The elevator began to slow and Meg laughed. "Ground floor. Lamps, lingerie, and angry Kuritans."

Bethany Connor laughed, too. "Lamps? Now I know what to do with the next *Panther* I see."

300

Dan swallowed as the elevator stopped. "O.K. Can the chatter. Connor and Brand are point. Fitzhugh, Baker, and Lang are rearguard. Open the doors, Meg."

The interior airlock doors opened slowly. Connor and Brand dropped their *Panther*s into low crouches, thrusting the snouts of their PPCs through the widening crack. Not a word passed between the two MechWarriors, but each covered a different arc of the room.

"Clear, Dan."

"Roger. Head out and secure the hallway."

In response to the order, Brand slipped through the half-opened doors. He covered the large, 'Mech-scale doorway in the wall to the right. Bethany Connor trotted her 'Mech behind Brand's, then took up position where she could cover the doorway more fully. Brand closed the doorway and peeked his *Panther*'s head around the corner.

"Clear again, Dan."

Dan stepped his *Valkyrie* from the elevator. "Go down the corridor no more than two hundred meters. You do remember enough Japanese to answer some basic questions if you meet a force before we can come up, don't you?"

"*Hai*, Allard-sama."

"Cute. Get going."

Brand's *Panther* vanished into the corridor, with Connor's 'Mech following closely. Cat Wilson took up Brand's old position next to the door, and Salome's *Wolverine* backed him up. The other *Panther*s, piloted by Diane McWilliams and Mary Lasker, formed up behind Dan's *Valkyrie*. The *Catapult*, *Jenner*, and *Wasp* still stood in the elevator.

Dan waved Cat and Salome forward with his 'Mech's left hand, then started to follow them. McWilliams and Lasker took up defensive positions near the doorway, then drifted into the corridor behind the *Valkyrie*.

Brand's voice exploded into Dan's neurohelmet. "Son of a bitch! Dan, get down here. Fast!"

"Austin, what is it?"

The Lieutenant's laugh carried utter disbelief. "This you've got to see."

Dan frowned. "This is not the place for jokes, Lieutenant. What is it."

"I'm not joking, sir. The Captain wouldn't believe me if I told him."

This better be good, or your ass is in a sling, Brand. Dan squeezed his *Valkyrie* past the *Wolverine* and quickly marched to where Brand's *Panther* had dropped to one knee. Further up the corridor, crouched

301

just this side of an intersection, Connor covered the converging hallways. Dan waved his left hand, and Cat brought his *Panther* up to match Connor's at the other side of the corridor.

Dan caught his first glimpse of them over Brand's shoulder. "Oh my God!" he muttered, switching over to the command frequency. "Salome, we have trouble."

"What?"

"Not what. *Who.*" Dan now understood the disbelief in Brand's radio message. "We've just found a dwarf, a MechWarrior, and the Archon-Designate of the Lyran Commonwealth!"

Dan shifted his radio from Tac-2 to the battle channel that all the Kell Hounds shared. "O.K., this is the plan." Dan swallowed hard as he looked at the different 'Mechs standing around the docking bay. He turned his *Valkyrie*'s head toward the *Wasp* and *Jenner*.

"Meg, you and Eddie will take the Archon-Designate, Leftenant Redburn, and Clovis to the surface. Stay hidden. The *Mac* is coming in for you. After the rest of us leave here, switch over to Tac-2 and Patrick will give you instructions for pickup."

Both 'Mech pilots acknowledged the instructions, then Dan continued with the briefing. "The rest of us are going to buy the *Mac* the time it needs to get away with Melissa Steiner. The *Cucamulus* has already started moving away as fast as she can, and the *Mac* will catch up once it takes our passengers aboard. The *Cu* will have worked up two days' worth of charge—which is more than we had getting here—and will jump our guests out to some Fed star."

Cat Wilson's bass voice thundered through Dan's neurohelmet. "The aero wing will screen the *Mac*, right?"

"Correct. That keeps it safe from any Kurita *Panthers* roaming the surface. The DropShip heading back to the Kurita jumpers can't turn around in time to reach the *Cu* before it jumps. The only interference comes from the ship that dropped the *Panthers* we destroyed on the surface."

Austin Brand spoke with chilling finality. "And it won't take the *Cu* unless it has some military forces—the *Panthers* Clovis says it dropped into the big bay."

Dan shrugged and sighed. "That's it, folks. We've got to hold the Kuritans long enough for the Archon-Designate's escape to become a mathematical certainty." *Which means that the Kurita force will pour us into plum sauce, if Clovis's computer projection is correct.* Dan realized that the same thought would also be occurring to the others in his command, but no one voiced the gloomy prediction.

"Captain Allard, this is Leftenant Redburn." Pain and anger

readed Redburn's words, but his utter fatigue dominated them. "Let e out of this *Jenner*. I've got some fighting left to do."

Dan laughed. "Sorry, Leftenant. I've got my orders. Kell Hound ompany policy. No pilots at less than 100 percent allowed into ombat." Dan focused on the *Wasp*. "And if you're listening, your ighness, we will not leave you or Clovis here, either. Colonel Kell as quite clear in his orders."

Dan walked his *Valkyrie* toward the doorway. Because the battle anners gave him full, 360-degree vision, he saw Brand's *Panther* ach out and touch hands with Meg Lang's *Wasp*. *For your sake, Meg, ope that your grandmother was wrong in making you promise never love a MechWarrior. I have a feeling this battle is going to be ugher on the survivors than it is on those who die.*

Dan's *Valkyrie* led the remaining Kell Hounds deeper into the anetoid. Cat Wilson formed himself up as Dan's partner. Diane cWilliams and Mary Lasker hung together right behind the *Valkyrie*. rand and Salome Ward, with their vastly different 'Mechs, formed e third fire team. Fitzhugh in his *Catapult* and Bethany Connor in a *nther* formed the column's rearguard.

Dan studied a schematic that Clovis had pulled from the base's omputer and pumped into the *Valkyrie*. It showed the docking bay here the *Silver Eagle* and the *Bifrost* hung suspended by invisible agnetic threads. The massive area extended two levels and featured er two dozen 'Mech-sized corridors converging on it. The Kell ounds would have ample holes from which to attack, and an equal umber through which to retreat. Dan smiled. *We can do some damage fore—*

A loud, screeching signal howled into his neurohelmet for a cond or two before the computer cleaned it up. "Hello! Hello!" The ice, which Dan had never heard before, hesitated with the words and most succumbed to converting the Ls into Rs. *A Kuritan!*

Dan did not reply. With the *Valkyrie*'s arms, he motioned to his ople to spread, and they quickly moved into the positions he signated. Dan marched his *Valkyrie* past Cat's crouching *Panther*, d continued a bit further on down the corridor. On ahead, through a ightly lit archway, he knew he'd see the large docking bay.

Again the voice burst into his ears. "Hello? We know you are out ere. I am *Sho-sa*...So sorry, that's Major Tarukito Niiro. I am the ctical commander for this operation. You will reply. Yes, please?"

Dan typed furiously on his console keyboard. He shot a ghtbeamed message back to Cat, with instructions to pass it on to the her Kell Hounds. The messages designated the points where he anted each Kell Hound stationed, and the amount of time he allowed for each one to obtain his firestation. *Now to buy us that time.*

"*Hai, Sho-sa* Niiro Tarukito-san. *Konnichi wa.*" Dan smiled
himself. "I and my regiment are here. What can I do for you?"

"Excuse me, but to whom am I speaking?"

"Captain Daniel Allard."

Tarukito's voice came back, almost apologetic. "And your reg
ment is…?"

"Unimportant, *Sho-sa,* but large enough to destroy any comma
you have." Dan inched the *Valkyrie* a bit further down the corridor. "/
I asked before, what can I do for you?"

"You can surrender to us the Archon-Designate, Melissa Arth
Steiner."

Dan felt chills down his spine. He forced levity into his voice
put off the Kurita *Sho-sa.* "I am afraid that I haven't the least idea wh
you're talking about."

"That is a pity." The Draconian sounded truly sorry. "Pleas
Captain Allard, continue down the corridor. Consider yourself und
a flag of truce. You have my word." Tarukito's voice lightened. "I c
your bluff, Captain."

Dan advanced far enough to see the ship bay. The *Bifrost* float
freely above the bay deck. Supported by a forest of landi
staunchions, the *Silver Eagle* rested beneath it on the bay deck itse
Surrounding the elegant DropShip, Dan saw a ring of *Panthers.* At t
Silver Eagle's nose, a *Warhammer* and a *Crusader* supplemented t
smaller Kurita 'Mech force.

Dan froze. *Something about that* Warhammer. *It just feels
familiar?* A feeling of dread clawed at his mind. *There've got to
twenty* Panthers *out there, and then those two heavies. Outnumber
and outgunned. Melissa better escape cleanly.*

Dan narrowed his eyes. "I see your force, Major. Very admirab
I trust they will die as well as the *Panthers* we destroyed on our w
in."

The Kurita voice took on an air of superiority. "Perhaps, Capt
Allard. As I can see from the markings on your *Valkyrie,* you are
member of the Kell Hounds. You have lied. You have no regimen

Dan stiffened. "What I don't have is the Archon-Designate."

"That is unfortunate." A *Panther* raised an empty hand and pat
the *Silver Eagle*'s hull. "If you do not deliver Melissa Steiner to
within one hour, we will destroy the *Silver Eagle* and every pers
aboard."

55

Trapped on a ledge, with a *Firestarter* at his left hand, an *UrbanMech* on the right, and a *Rifleman* facing him across a crevasse, Justin knew what Philip Capet expected from him. *If caught in the same position, you'd give up, wouldn't you, Capet? You'd surrender and die. You'd make it easy for me, wouldn't you? And now you expect the same from me.*

Justin laughed defiantly. "You're still no tactician, Capet!" He snapped his *Rifleman* forward, and dropped into the crevasse.

The *Rifleman* shot down like a streaking meteorite for twenty meters. The impact of metal feet hitting the slightly inclined crevasse wall slammed Justin down into his command chair and crushed the heavy neurohelmet into his shoulders. His jaw smashed shut, and Justin felt tiny tooth chips grind beneath his molars.

He fought to control his balance and, with it, the balance of the sixty-ton monster encasing him. The 'Mech's left toe caught in a narrow crack. The *Legend-killer* slowly began to twist toward the right, but Justin arched his back and wrenched his shoulders around to the left. The *Rifleman* tipped backward and crashed flat against the stony slope.

Damn! he thought. *I feel as though I'm wrestling an entire mountain!*

Dust and debris shrouded the sliding 'Mech in a gray cloud. The sharp, keening sound of metal scraping against stone and the trail of

sparks and armor chips eloquently informed him of the damage bein[g]
done to his 'Mech's already-inadequate rear armor. Justin scanned hi[s]
monitors for any other problems, then flinched as a piece of ston[e]
kicked up by the 'Mech's feet ricocheted off his viewscreen.

All too quickly, the ground stopped the *Legend-killer*'s sled-lik[e]
descent. The collision with the crevasse floor threw Justin forward i[n]
his safety harness. It burned and pinched as it restrained him, then flun[g]
him back into his command chair. The dust cloud swirled around an[d]
settled over the *Rifleman*.

Justin scanned the 'Mech's monitors and cursed. By sliding dow[n]
on the 'Mech's back, he had totally shredded the rear armor. *Damn[it]
all to hell. Tsen Shang could cut through that armor with his finge[r]
nails. I can't let any of them get behind me.*

Proximity alarms filled the cockpit with screamed warning[s.]
Justin looked up. From above, the *Firestarter* was descending on a j[et]
of ion flame. Justin shook his head. *Idiot. Battered and bruised I m[ay]
be, but tinder for a pyre I'm not.*

Twin laser beams from the *Legend-killer*'s arms lanced u[p]
between the legs of the other 'Mech. The beams liquified the armo[r]
covering the *Firestarter*'s groin, then pulsed on up into the 'Mech['s]
torso. There, they punctured the fuel cells of the two torso flamethrow[-]
ers like needles bursting overfilled balloons. Fire spurted in ragged je[ts]
from the *Firestarter*'s shoulder joints and neck, then a fireball ripp[ed]
the 'Mech apart and sprayed Ishiyama with flaming debris.

Justin heaved the *Legend-killer* to its feet and marched the 'Me[ch]
forward amid the burning blizzard. Apparently damaged during th[e]
long slide, the left knee joint froze up and sent the *Legend-kill[er]*
stumbling forward. Justin regained his balance just in time to keep th[e]
'Mech from falling on its face.

He frowned and executed a diagnostic program. The auxilia[ry]
monitor flashed to life with a schematic of the *Legend-killer*'s le[ft]
knee. It showed a chunk of ferrocrete lodged in the joint. *If this 'Me[ch]
had hands, I could pull it free,* Justin grumbled inwardly. Unable [to]
repair the damage, he jammed the left leg against the crevasse flo[or,]
then pivoted forward on it. Limping badly, he jogged the 'Mech in[to]
a tunnel mouth.

A hail of autocannon shells swept the valley floor behind him, b[ut]
only succeeded in blasting *Firestarter* detritus into even smaller scra[ps]
of waste metal. Fragments of ferrocrete peppered the rear of Justin['s]
Rifleman, but did no real damage. After a short pause, another lo[ng]
burst of fire rattled through the artificial valley.

That's the UrbanMech. *He's got a ten-shot-burst autocannon,*
opposed to the five-shot popguns our Riflemen *carry.* Justin narrow[ed]

his eyes. *They have to assume my back armor is in sad shape. Given Capet's rudimentary cunning, that means they'll try to trap me between them so that one of them can get a shot at me. The* UrbanMech *has the jump jets to get it down here. How stupid is that pilot?*

Justin opened a radio channel to Capet. "Find some spot with ample camera coverage, Capet, because I'm coming up to kill you." He closed the line before Capet could answer, then allowed himself a quiet laugh.

Justin limped his 'Mech deeper into the tunnel. While still in view of the crevasse, the tunnel opened onto a passage running parallel to the crevasse. He swung the *Rifleman* right, just barely around the corner, and turned it so that its back pressed against the corridor wall parallel-ing the crevasse. *I'll give him ten minutes. If he's not down here by then, I'll just have to take my chances up above.*

Justin heard the echoed report of jump jets as the *UrbanMech* landed in the crevasse. A tiny laser beam—the *UrbanMech*'s other weapon system—splashed against the opposite wall of the corridor. *He's cautious, but not cautious enough,* Justin thought grimly.

He pivoted the *Legend-killer* on its frozen left leg. The huge 'Mech swung around and filled the tunnel mouth, its guns snapping into line with the smaller *UrbanMech*. Then Justin let loose with every weapon the *Rifleman* had.

The large lasers cored through the *UrbanMech*'s heart like ruby drills. Shards of hot armor careened off the tunnel walls and whirled through the air. Fire and steam flared from the huge hole in the 'Mech's chest as one of the medium lasers stabbed through and destroyed everything it touched. White heat erased the 'Mech's midsection on Justin's infrared display as engine shielding evaporated.

Autocannon fire smashed armor on the 'Mech's dwarfed left arm, and shredded armor on the right side of the *UrbanMech*'s torso. The other medium laser in the *Legend-killer*'s chest slashed into the torn armor on the *UrbanMech*'s right side. It blasted away what little armor remained, then shot needles of fragmented ruby light into the 'Mech's chest, which ignited everything they touched.

One light spear hit the autocannon magazine, and detonated the first of the caseless explosive shells waiting to be fed into the *Urban-Mech*'s Imperator-B autocannon. When that shell burst, it sowed white-hot slivers of metal throughout the magazine.

The uneven flashes of light popping from within the *Urban-Mech*'s chest spat metal and fire. One explosion tore the autocannon off and sent it skittering back into the crevasse on a jet of ochre flame. More explosions dented the *UrbanMech*'s torso armor from the inside, then punched out to freedom. The whole top half of the 'Mech snapped open like the lid on a jack-in-the-box, and a column of flame shot up to engulf the tunnel roof.

The explosion's shockwave rocked Justin's unsteady *Rifleman*. Pieces of debris sizzled through the air and hammered the *Legend-killer* with a fury that suggested the *UrbanMech* wanted revenge for its death. Justin, shaken by the explosion and stifled by the volcanic heat-vortex swirling in his cockpit, struggled to keep the *Rifleman* standing. He stumbled the 'Mech backward and came to rest with its back to the corridor wall.

The diagnostic program redrew the knee joint and beeped urgently at Justin. *Well now,* he thought. *There is a silver lining in this whole sordid cloud.* Something—the shockwave or a piece of *Urban-Mech*—had dislodged whatever had previously jammed the *Rifleman's* left knee. Waiting for his heat levels to drop to acceptable levels, Justin chuckled silently to himself. *Even when you cheat, Capet, you can't get it right.*

Justin spun the *Rifleman* and sent it lumbering off to the left. Taking the first ramp leading up, he mounted it at a nearly reckless pace. He sped on through intersections after only the most cursory examination. He altered his course almost at random, but always continued upward.

Slow down, Justin, he told himself. *Haste will get you killed. Capet will want to hit you from behind. You must take more care.* Justin smiled slowly as an idea blossomed in his mind. *Perhaps you can turn his desires against him.*

Justin opened a radio channel to his foe. "Come out, Philip. Stop hiding."

"Hiding? I anxiously await your arrival."

Justin narrowed his eyes. "I found myself unavoidably detained a bit earlier. I felt compelled to watch the *UrbanMech* explode. It is a pity you were not there."

Capet's laughter sounded hollow. "I'll catch it on the replay. I warned him that you Capellan bastards are sneaky."

Justin nodded. "That we are, Capet, but you'll never understand the true depth of our brilliance in that department."

Justin turned his 'Mech to the left and entered a narrow tunnel that gradually sloped upward through the shadows. As he started into it, the darkness shrouded his 'Mech. Inching along slowly and laboriously, Justin became uncomfortable, for the tunnel was too narrow. He had no room to turn.

As though Capet had read Justin's mind, he suddenly stepped his *Rifleman* up to block the *Legend-killer's* line of retreat. "It's all over, Justin Xiang. Good riddance."

Even as Justin brought the *Legend-killer*'s guns up and over to cover Capet's 'Mech, the other man's *Rifleman* blazed away with everything he had. Before his weapons could blast into their target, however, Capet's inhuman scream of rage echoed throughout Ishiyama. In the laser's backlight, the ghost painted into the logo on the *Legend-killer*'s breast seemed to mock Capet's ambush with a fool's grin.

Capet's two large laser beams hammered into the *Legend-killer*'s right side. Chunks of armor shot away on vapor jets as the energy beams instantly converted ceramics and metal to gas. One of the *Rifleman*'s medium lasers pierced the gray, swirling cloud and destroyed a medium laser on the *Legend-killer*'s chest. Capet's other medium laser boiled armor from the *Legend-killer*'s left breast, while the autocannons puckered and chipped armor on the left arm and leg of Justin's 'Mech.

"That's right, Phillip," Justin said with a laugh, "I marched the *Legend-killer* into this little trap *backward*. Just like a treacherous Capellan to pull a trick like that, eh? And so like a stupid Federat to fall for it."

Justin ignored the dozen warning lights flashing for his attention. He concentrated on his phantom left arm and watched the golden crosshairs that it controlled drop onto the box of glass and metal jutting out from between the *Rifleman*'s shoulders. The gold cross drifted down into place, then flashed in syncopation with Justin's racing heartbeat.

"Philip, in your last moment, try not to dwell on the thought of failure…"

Justin commanded his left arm to fire its weapons.

The large laser washed over the *Rifleman*'s head like a tidal wave devouring a sand castle. Its scarlet cylinder blasted armor from the head of Capet's 'Mech, and the pilot's canopy exploded into a million fragments that melted to the ground in a burning rain of glass.

The medium laser in the *Legend-killer*'s left breast hissed through the air and blasted again into the other 'Mech's head. More armor and internal structures sailed into the air. For the first time, Capet's *Rifleman* shuddered, as though stunned by the impact. With that, Justin knew that Capet had been knocked unconscious.

With no regrets, Justin watched the autocannon shells career through the *Rifleman*'s head. What little had survived the energy weapons now fell to the autocannon's projectiles. The final shells continued their flight through to where the *Rifleman*'s head had been and ricocheted deeper into Ishiyama.

Justin nodded slowly as the headless *Rifleman* wavered, then crashed to the ground on its back. "So falls the Prince's champion," he said, being sure the broadcasters would pick up his words. "Can his master's fall be far behind?"

Justin stared at himself in the glass. The gold and black silk robe delivered to his locker room after the fight fit him perfectly. Cut to just below his waist and tied with a gold sash, the robe felt comfortable and yet looked formally proper. The gold embroidery over the shoulders and down the sleeves hinted at tiger-stripes, which echoed the stylized tigers on each breast and the larger tiger sewn around the midsection.

He read the card once again. *Your actions bring honor to us all.* Though unsigned, Justin easily recognized the holographic "chop" sealed to the card as that of Tsen Shang.

Justin opened the locker room door and hesitated. Two lean, lupine-looking Capellan youths in leather tunics stood by the door. One smiled courteously as he restrained some unruly fans, while the second one bowed. "*Zao,* Justin Xiang. I have been sent to conduct you to a friend." The youth's gaze flickered over the robe and silently revealed the "friend's" identity.

Justin nodded his head graciously. He followed the tongsman through the underground maze of tunnels honeycombing the foundation of Ishiyama. Kurita guards allowed them to pass through several limited-access doorways before they reached a back entrance to the building. The tongsman opened the door for Justin. Across the rain-slick alley, the MechWarrior recognized Tsen Shang's Feicui.

A rear door slid open and Justin stepped into the aircar's dark interior to join Tsen Shang on the wide leather seat. The tongsman climbed into the driver's seat. At a nod from Shang, the driver engaged the engine, and the car rose on its cusion of air.

"Congratulations, Justin. I am most proud of your efforts. I dare say that sentiment is shared by everyone in Cathay." Tsen Shang smiled. A muffled pop sounded as he carefully worked the cork free from a bottle. "I trust you liked the House Palos vintage I sent to you after the Armstrong fight."

Justin smiled. "I did, indeed." He brushed the fingers of his right hand against the robe. "And I very much appreciate this robe. My mother's family crest also bore a tiger."

Shang carefully poured wine into two glasses, then settled the bottle into an ice-filled bucket built into the bar opposite their seats. "Exactly the reason I specified that design." He handed Justin a glass and brandished the other one himself. "On behalf of the entire Capellan Confederation, I thank you for your efforts."

Justin nodded and they both sipped from their glasses. "What else

310

do you know about me?"

Shang shrugged, but the warm smile on his face never faded. "As a member of the Maskirovka, I know all there is to know about you—at least, all that is important. You would be amused, I think, by our assessment of your part in the battle on Spica in 3016. Had any bookies gotten our agent's report, you would have been a long-odds favorite in all fights. Our agent did not like you at all."

Justin narrowed his eyes. "That is a flaw with the Maskirovka."

Shang nodded and sipped his champagne. "That oversight was corrected in later reports, which are quite flattering concerning your abilities and strengths." Shang reached in to a narrow pocket set in the Feicui's far door. He drew from it an envelope and passed it to Justin.

Justin drained his glass and set it down before accepting the packet. His name had been calligraphed across the front of the envelope. Flipping it over, he saw that it was sealed shut with the chop of the Ministry of Social Education. Justin broke the seal and opened it.

Inside were a host of documents. What caught his eye first was a pair of passports bearing his picture and signature, though one claimed he was a Thomas Yuan, not Justin Xiang. In addition to the passports, he poured two full sets of documents into his lap. There were identification papers, credit chips, and full transcripts of education and societal functions for both himself and this Thomas Yuan.

Justin frowned. "I don't understand..." He shook his head, which suddenly felt as though it was stuffed with cotton. He blinked his eyes twice, then watched everything blur beyond recognition.

He looked up. "What did you do to the drink? Why?"

Tsen Shang chuckled. "The drink was drugged. I took another drug to counteract its effects before you entered the vehicle." Though Shang easily blocked Justin's clumsy punch, the look on his face showed that the speed of Justin's strike in the drugged state surprised him. He pushed the MechWarrior back into the seat as though the other man were weightless.

Justin's world faded from view, though he struggled valiantly to retain consciousness. As he drifted under the anesthetic's influence, Shang's voice came to him like a shout echoing through a very long tunnel.

"Fear not, son of Quintus Allard, I follow the orders of those who believe you much too valuable to kill..."

56

Styx
Dieron Military District, Draconis Combine

26 May 3027

Dan found himself nodding as Patrick Kell finished his radioed explanation of the situation. "Don't worry, Dan. Nor you, either, Salome. The hour the Draconians gave us has gotten the Archon-Designate up and away. We've just got to buy a little more time."

Salome's voice warbled a bit as Dan's computer reconstructed the scrambled transmission. "We still attack?"

"Affirmative." Patrick's voice dropped to a grim bass. "I'll give you a signal when to initiate the attack."

Dan frowned. *I don't like the sound of that.* "What signal?"

"You'll know it. Kell out."

Patrick's voice faded, but Dan's unease did not. *Is it just that Kurita 'Mech you can't identify, or is it something more?*

Dan scowled as he spoke. "What do you think, Salome? I don't like this anonymous signal business." He glanced over and saw a yellow light blinking on his console.

Salome's sigh survived the computer scrambling. "Patrick's the boss. And that gives him the right to be secretive. Time's almost up."

"I know. I think the Kurita commander is trying to reach me. Pass the plan of attack on to the others while I stall him."

"Roger."

Dan switched his radio over to the frequency that the Kuritans had used before. "*Sho-sa* Niiro, you wished to reach me?"

The Draconian voice was almost apologetic. "*Hai*, Captain Al-

312

lard. You realize the time is almost up."

Dan moved his *Valkyrie* to where he could see Tarukito's *Panther*. A slight bow of the 'Mech's head acknowledged Dan, who returned the gesture before answering. "I am afraid my people have not found the Archon-Designate in the hour you gave us. This was no surprise, for we believe she is safely on Tharkad. But if you wish to give us more time…"

Tarukito selected his words carefully before answering. "I would have thought, given the reputation of the Kell Hounds, that you would not let all these people die just to play word games. I…"

Tarukito's words died in a hiss of ion-static. One of the *Panther*s nearest the magnetically warded bay opening jerked and danced as though trapped in an invisible cyclone. Autocannon shells snapped the *Panther*'s back like a dry stick, then touched off the SRMs housed in its breast. The thunderous explosion blasted *Panther* parts throughout the ship bay. Limbs whirled through the air to batter other *Panther*s, and an orange fireball curled up from the empty space that the destroyed 'Mech had occupied.

The brilliant flames curled in upon themselves, then suddenly evaporated, as though by some magic. Standing where the *Panther* had stood, a *Victor* materialized from within the fire and smoke. It pointed its stubby right arm at another *Panther* as its autocannon consumed a second Kurita 'Mech with a voracious storm of metal.

"You are right, *Sho-sa Niiro*," Patrick Kell growled over the radio. "The Kell Hounds would never let these people die. The Archon-Designate is already offworld and headed for our JumpShip. We're here to cut off your retreat."

Patrick, what the hell are you doing? Fighting the shock of Patrick's appearance, Dan snapped his radio over to the tactical frequency. "Move it, Kell Hounds! Hit them hard! Patrick's in the *Victor*." Dan dropped the crosshairs of his LRM battery onto a *Panther*, then stabbed the fire control with furious vengeance.

The missiles arced away and blasted into the target, tattooing the *Panther*'s right arm with fiery explosions. As the missiles peeled off sheets of molten ceramics, the arm was laid bare. The *Valkyrie*'s medium laser lanced out and stabbed through the same arm. The blood-red beam sawed the limb off at the elbow, sending the PPC crashing to the ferrocrete deck.

"Dan, I've got an equipment malfunction!" Austin Brand's voice filled Dan's neurohelmet. "Targeting computer is screwy!"

"Cat, cover Brand. Austin, what's wrong?"

Fear rode through Brand's reply. "I get no read on the *Victor*."

Dan glanced at the *Victor*. He watched a half-dozen PPC bolts

313

streak from *Panthers* all around the massive assault 'Mech, but none of them hit their target. *They're too close. That's why they're missing.* Even as the logical side of his brain offered that explanation, he rejected it immediately. *I've got no thermal image of that monster,* he realized suddenly. *It's just like Morgan on Mallory's World!*

Dan swept his crosshairs past the *Victor* as he sighted another *Panther.* He ignored the queasy feeling rising in him—for the crosshairs had not acknowledged the *Victor* as a target—and triggered another flight of missiles at a *Panther.* These caught the Kurita 'Mech in the knees and forced it to stumble forward.

Two more flights of missiles slammed into that *Panther* from Fitzhugh's *Catapult,* cloaking the enemy 'Mech in red, orange, and yellow smoke and fire. As the fire collapsed into a dense black smoke, it drifted away like a ghost, leaving a broken, lifeless *Panther* in its wake.

Other *Panthers* now turned from the *Victor* to face the attacking Kell Hounds. Dan dodged a quartet of incoming SRMs, then spotted the *Warhammer* stalking back toward the *Victor.* It moved with a fluid grace that only one in a thousand MechWarriors could impart to such a massive machine. *I know I've seen that 'Mech before. But where?*

Cat Wilson's *Panther* appeared at Dan's right. He triggered a shot that lanced out and smashed into a Kurita 'Mech's head. The azure energy lance blasted armor from the *Panther* like a storm tearing shingles from a house. The *Panther* shuddered, then stumbled. The MechWarrior in it, exhibiting incredible skill, twisted the 'Mech so that it would fall on its back, then punched out.

Dan turned and shouted a warning. "Lasker, *Panther* at nine o'clock!"

As Lasker's *Panther* spun back, it caught the PPC blast on its left arm instead of the weak back armor, but that did little good. The PPC bolt rippled up the arm and dropped melted armor in steaming clumps onto the ferrocrete deck. Lasker launched a flight of SRMs at the enemy *Panther,* but her haste had sent them wide of their target.

Beyond her, Diane McWilliams's *Panther* reeled beneath the impact of enemy LRM barrages. Two sets of five missiles each plowed furrows through her 'Mech's breast armor. Eight more missiles scythed into the metal left leg and shattered the armor on its thigh.

Twisted around by the blasts, McWilliams faced the *Crusader* that had attacked her *Panther.* She sent a bolt of blue lightning slicing into its chest, but it barely dented the thick armor over the 'Mech's heart. In reply, the *Crusader* sent two more flights of LRMs.

"No, Diane, no! You're not in your *Rifleman.* Punch out." Helplessly, Dan watched the missiles smash into McWilliams's *Panther* as

314

the hollow feeling in the pit of his stomach told him what his sensors calmly presented as damage factors. The LRMs had ripped off the 'Mech's left arm and sent it skittering across the ferrocrete deck. More missiles then exploited the gaps previously blasted into the *Panther*'s chest. They scattered the remaining armor, then crushed the *Panther*'s heart. The 'Mech exploded like a supernova.

"Fitzhugh, take that *Crusader*! Now!" Dan swung his missile crosshairs beyond the *Crusader* and slid them over toward the *Warhammer*'s back. *Let's open you up!*

Suddenly Dan's mouth went dry. *The way it moves...It's stalking the* Victor. *It couldn't be...* Dan raked his targeting joystick hard to the right, but the crosshairs refused to acknowledge the *Warhammer*'s existence. *Oh, my God! No! NO!* He stabbed the radio switch. "Patrick, look out! The* Warhammer, *it belongs to Yorinaga Kurita!*"

The *Victor*'s head came up and turned to acknowledge the approaching *Warhammer*. Contemptuously, Patrick pressed the autocannon's muzzle to the chest of a nearby *Panther*. Spear points of flame vomited from the gun, cleaving the target from left shoulder to right hip.

The *Warhammer* raised its twin PPCs to send blue spears of incandescent fire stabbing at Kell's *Victor*. One beam scarified the armor over the *Victor*'s right breast, obliterating the unit crest painted there. The second beam drilled through the armor on the *Victor*'s middle. Armor chips blasted free on vapor jets, and rained down on the broken *Panther*s lying at the *Victor*'s feet.

Dan saw a thermal image flicker over the *Victor* for a half-second. Even that brief glimpse told him the true damage the bolt had done. Flashing through a chink in the *Victor*'s armor—probably a weak plate over the wound Ardan Sortek had suffered in it—the PPC had blasted shielding from the 'Mech's fusion engine.

The *Victor* was slowly cooking its pilot.

"No!" Dan set his *Valkyrie* off at a dead run. *Patrick, I won't let him do this to you!*

Dan watched with horror as the *Victor* ignored the *Warhammer*. It blasted another *Panther* into spare parts with its autocannon, then used its SRMs to finish off a wounded *Panther*. Its medium lasers stabbed out at the *Crusader* and carved armor from it even as the Draconian 'Mech reeled under an LRM volley from the *Catapult*.

Four SRMs blasted into the *Valkyrie* as Dan streaked across the ferrocrete bay. The missiles exploded against his right arm and twisted his 'Mech around with the sheer violence of their assault. Fragments of armor trailed behind him, but a quick glance at the control console told Dan that his medium laser was still working. He used the spin the

315

missile hits had given his 'Mech, and kept on running.

The *Warhammer* again fired at the *Victor*, sending both beams lashing across the *Victor*'s chest. Chunks of armor rode jagged blue spikes of lightning out and away from the assault 'Mech. They crashed smoking to the ferrocrete deck as though the humanoid 'Mech were a medieval knight shedding his breastplate. As the armor fell away, it left the *Victor*'s chest, already burned by the first bolt, open and vulnerable.

Dan saw the PPC bolt out of the corner of his eye, but it was too late to do anything. The turquoise shaft of man-made lightning vaporized the *Valkyrie*'s right arm. Unbalanced, the *Valkyrie* began to fall, but Dan pushed off the ferrocrete floor with the 'Mech's left hand and righted himself. *Nothing will stop me.*

Dan flipped the cover off a switch on his command console. He snapped the silvery toggle to the left, then punched the round red button glowing to life beneath it.

"Ten seconds to abort sequence," the computer informed him.

"Negative!" Dan slid his left hand down and armed his command chair's eject option. "Ejection on verbal."

The thunder of blood pumping against his ears drowned out the computer's acknowledgement of his command. "No, Patrick! No!" he screamed in rage. "You have to fight it!"

As though to prove what might have been, the *Victor*'s autocannon mauled a *Panther* huddled in the *Warhammer*'s shadow. The *Warhammer*, unimpressed with such bravado, again fired its PPCs at Kell's assault 'Mech. The forked bolts stabbed deep into the *Victor*, filling its belly with blue fire, and crushing its heart.

Released from slavery, the dwarf star that had powered the *Victor* gnawed at its master's vitals. The radiation detectors on Dan's command console shot into the red zone immediately, and a heat silhouette whitewashed the *Victor*. The SRMs stored in its left shoulder ignited in the heat and were soon joined by a rolling series of explosions from what little autocannon ammo still lurked in the *Victor*.

The *Victor*'s faceplate exploded outward, but Dan cheered when he saw Patrick's command chair blast free of his doomed 'Mech. The chair righted itself on tiny jets, but did not rise quickly enough away from the *Victor*. A horrendous explosion shuddered the assault 'Mech and vomited a gout of fire and shrapnel through the *Victor*'s open face. It caught the command chair and swatted it down.

No! Dan looked away from the dying *Victor*, and despite the tears of anger and pain blurring his vision, he centered the *Warhammer*'s broad back in his viewplate. *You son of a bitch! I'll give you payback!* Dan hit his jump jets and rolled the *Valkyrie*'s head 180 degrees. "Eject!"

316

Explosive bolts blasted the *Valkyrie*'s canopy away. Unbearable heat filled the cockpit as rockets ignited behind the command chair. G forces smashed Dan back against his command chair as the rockets catapulted him out of the 'Mech. The computer reported "All systems go," but because of the *Valkyrie*'s angle of flight, the command chair's foot clipped the 'Mech's chin and sent Dan spinning out of control.

The one-armed light 'Mech crashed into the *Warhammer*'s broad back amid a din of screaming metal and snapping ceramic armor plates. The *Warhammer* stumbled forward two steps and dropped to one knee as it tried to shake itself free of the *Valkyrie*. It twisted to the right, but the effort proved fruitless. The *Valkyrie*'s left arm had hooked over the *Warhammer*'s left shoulder and was now jammed between the 'Mech's head and the spotlight on its shoulder.

Suddenly, the destruct mechanism that Dan had armed exploded deep within the *Valkyrie*, touching off a chain reaction in the LRM magazine. Pressed chest to back against the *Warhammer*, the *Valkyrie*'s missiles blew through the light 'Mech's thinly armored chest and clawed explosively into the *Warhammer*'s spine. The *Warhammer* arched its back as though in agony, then burst at the waist.

The gyrojets on Dan's command chair flared to life and whirled the *Warhammer* out of his vision. They straightened his flight and propelled him toward a safe landing zone at the far end of the battlefield. As the chair jetted along, however, the magnetic fields holding the *Bifrost* aloft knocked the gyros out of phase.

Dan's chair crashed hard to the deck. It skipped and rolled along, still aided by the chair's jets, then smashed into a ferrocrete wall. Rebounding once, it then headed in toward the wall again. Half-torn out of the chair's protective grasp, Dan screamed as his shoulder slammed into the wall. He heard something grind and snap, then a wave of black pain washed over him and dragged Dan down into unconsciousness.

As a doctor from the *Silver Eagle* tightened the sling strap running around Dan's chest, pain shot through his left arm. "Dammit, doctor," he said angrily, ignoring the pain. "Let me go see him!"

The doctor frowned. "There's nothing you can do."

Dan swallowed against the lump in his throat. "I don't care, you bastard. Let me go." Dan jerked away and stood. A wave of vertigo hammered him, but he fought against it. He stalked over to where they had cordoned off a small cubicle with rope and sheets hung between two Kell Hound *Panther*s. Dan pushed his way through the opening and bit back tears.

Patrick Kell smiled at him weakly, his face ashen. Salome and Cat stood on the other side of the cot. "Glad to see you up, Dan." Kell's words were punctuated by pain-induced gasps and grimaces. "Knew they'd not keep you down long."

Dan jerked his head back in the direction from which he'd come. "They're ready for you now, Patrick."

The leader of the Kell Hounds shook his head, but forced a smile to his cracked lips. "Triage," he said. "I'm too messed up inside to survive, Dan. I can feel it. Let them save others." Agony molded Kell's face into a mask of torment, but he choked back the moans of pain. Patrick looked toward Salome. "Continue your report."

"The Kurita forces retreated to their DropShip and returned to their JumpShips. They knew that they could not catch the *Mac* or the *Cucamulus* before they jumped out, which our ships will do in twenty hours."

Dan turned as the curtains behind him shot open. Melissa Steiner dashed through and dropped to her knees beside the cot. She grabbed Patrick's left hand in hers and squeezed hard. *"You can't die!"* she whispered hoarsely. Following close behind her was Clovis, who stopped at the foot of the cot. Andrew Redburn, bandages wrapped around his chest and arms, closed the curtains and stood guard at the opening.

Patrick lifted his right hand away from the bloody chest wound, which had reopened during the battle, and brushed away Melissa's tears. "No crying now, cousin. Can't have the Archon-Designate crying for a mercenary, can we? Don't want Takashi thinking you've got a soft spot." Patrick gritted his teeth as pain seized him.

Melissa distractedly touched the bloody streak that Patrick's fingers had left on her cheek, then she narrowed her steel gray eyes. She looked up at the three standing Kell Hounds and Clovis, then down at Patrick Kell. "I want you to be first to know, Patrick Kell. I'm going to marry him. I'm going to marry Hanse Davion."

Patrick smiled broadly, his pain momentarily forgotten, and squeezed Melissa's hands. "It'll be a grand wedding, Mel. Tell him he's a lucky man." He shook his head. "That'll be a big day. I wish I could be there."

Melissa clutched his hands tightly. "You will, Patrick. You *will* be there."

Kell nodded slowly. "In spirit, Mel, in spirit…"

Pain contracted every muscle in Patrick Kell's body and bowed his back. He slammed back down onto the cot, then turned and stared through Dan. "Dan, tell him…tell Morgan I understand. Tell him I finally understand." Patrick Kell stared straight up at the 'Mech standing above him. "Is it supposed to hurt this much?" he gasped.

painfully. He turned to Salome and with great effort made his voice clear and firm, lifting it somehow beyond the pain. "The command is yours, Major."

His body contracted once more, then Patrick Kell fell into the sleep from which there is no waking.

57

Northwind
Draconis March, Federated Suns

5 June 3027

Quintus Allard shook his head as Dan slipped his left arm from the sling. "I don't think that's a wise idea, Dan."

Dan gritted his teeth against the sharp pain in his shoulder, then stared straight at his father and grinned. "Father, I've only broken my collarbone. It's almost healed." He raised his right hand to the spider-like electrode taped just below his left shoulder at the clavicle. "This little NAIS gem hurts more than the break."

"Yes, but the electrical impulses speed the bone's knitting-together." Quintus took Dan's dress jacket from the valet and dismissed the man. He stepped behind Dan and held up the jacket so that his son could slip in his arms. "Colonel Kell's plan worked admirably."

Dan nodded and let his father carefully slide the left side of his jacket up over his left arm. "Yes. Patrick realized he could not be certain that the passengers would make it to the *Cu* at all, but he also knew that the Kuritans would never leave the base unless they believed their quarry had fled. Patrick only told those of us inside the rock that the passengers would be loaded up to the *Mac* and headed out to the *Cu*. Because we were supposed to buy them time, the hour the Draconian commander gave us was a godsend."

Quintus eased the red jacket up onto Dan's shoulders, then came around to help him button up the front. "But Kell also refused to trust the lives of the passengers to a JumpShip that was making a second 'hot' jump in a row. He told Lang and Baker to hide the passengers

320

somewhere back inside the base while the *Mac* made a phantom pick-up run."

Dan nodded, then grimaced as his father fastened the dress jacket's tight collar. "Patrick jumped the *Victor* out of the *Mac* and into the docking bay as the Kurita time limit ran out. He told the Draconians that the passengers were already up and away. He also told them we were there to cut off their retreat."

Quintus helped Dan snap the jacket's unique double-breast into place. The black layer of cloth had been cut in the shape of the wolf's-head design that was central to the Kell Hound crest. The pointed ears snapped up at the shoulders and the snout fastened down at the waist. The fiery scarlet eyes matched the rest of the jacket's color. The inverted black chevron imposed over a blood-red triangle on Dan's collar mimicked the Lyran insignia for a Hauptmann, though the Kell Hounds called the rank Captain.

Dan's voice dropped lower as he painfully worked a black armband up past his left elbow. "Patrick kept shooting and destroying *Panthers* as the *Warhammer* attacked him. He wanted to whittle down the Kurita numbers so that we could drive out the remainder of their force after he died. He drew the *Warhammer* to himself, and in doing so, saved the rest of us."

Quintus backed away to better study his son's uniform, then nodded with satisfaction. "You look good."

"Thanks. Not every day I get to meet the Prince."

"Indeed." A frown creased Quintus's brow. "Dan, are you certain that the *Warhammer*'s pilot was Yorinaga Kurita?"

Dan smiled. "That, and questions about the unit's designation, have been really popular with your debriefers, father."

The Minister nodded solemnly. "We have no record of any Kurita unit known as the *Genyosha*. As for Yorinaga Kurita, the last we knew, he had retreated to a Zen monastery on Echo Five."

Dan shrugged, then winced. "I watched Yorinaga stalk Morgan eleven years ago. When you see a MechWarrior that good, you don't forget him. You'll remember his moves no matter how long it's been. I'm just sorry that Cat saw him punch out after my *Val* hit him."

Quintus shook his head. "You shouldn't be. All our reports suggest that when he ejected, the tactical commander, *Sho-sa* Niiro, panicked. He ordered the retreat that Patrick had bluffed him into believing had been cut off."

Dan flicked a white thread from his black trousers. "The *Cu* jumped out here to Northwind when the *Mac* reached it. The threat of our aerofighters kept the Kurita DropShips at bay, and so they returned to their JumpShips. We loaded all our spare equipment and the

321

refugees onto the *Silver Eagle* and used the *Bifrost* to reach North-wind."

The valet knocked gently at the door, then opened it a crack. "Excuse me, Count Quintus...Lord Daniel...but the Prince has requested your presence in his office before the ceremony."

Quintus led his son through the corridors of the government building Hanse Davion had converted into his headquarters on North-wind. "The Prince assembled his staff and brought us all here to Northwind when the first message from Vandermeer reached New Avalon. Your mother and your sister Riva will arrive on the next run up from New Avalon."

Dan shook his head. "They didn't have to..."

Quintus winked at his son. "Truth be told, I think they're coming as much to meet the passenger you rescued as they are to be sure you survived this battle in one piece."

The two CID guards at the office door snapped to attention. Quintus nodded to them and preceded his son into the room Prince Davion had appropriated for his makeshift office on Northwind. The whitewashed walls contrasted sharply with the wooden pillars supporting the ceiling.

Hanse Davion stood up behind an unfinished wooden desk. "Welcome, Quintus and Daniel. May I offer you both a drink?" Before either man could reply, the Prince had crossed behind where Melissa sat swathed in a silver-gray robe of native snow-fox furs. He poured an amethyst liquid into two crystal goblets, then held both goblets out to Quintus, who passed one to his son.

Dan shot a quick glance over at Cat Wilson. Clad in his dress uniform, Cat looked uneasy for the first time since Dan had known him. He held his glass of wine carefully, as though the goblet might somehow shatter at any moment.

Beyond him, Salome caught Dan's eyes and they shared a smile at Cat's apparent discomfort. Salome's dress uniform differed only in the rank insignia at the collar and in the cut of her trousers. While Dan's were tucked into the tops of his cavalry-style boots, Salome's trousers hung loose and square to just below her knees. Like both Dan and Cat, she wore a black armband on her left sleeve.

Seated between the standing Kell Hounds and the Prince's desk, Andrew Redburn and Clovis Holstein turned to acknowledge Dan's arrival. To Dan's eyes, Andrew looked only slightly less comfortable than Cat. He also noticed that the right shoulder of his golden Sunburst Vest now featured a narrow white band across the base. Dan smiled. *That man certainly deserved a promotion. Captain Redburn...That's got a nice ring.*

As Clovis gently set his wine glass on the table between him and Redburn, Dan thought that the outfit they had given him looked very much like a Royal Brigade uniform. Cut perfectly to his diminutive form, the military uniform lent Clovis an air of nobility.

The Prince seated himself at the desk. "As you know, in a few minutes, I will honor the Kell Hounds and the other defenders who held off the Kurita forces on Styx. I will speak about how you protected a hijacked DropShip, and how you drove off superior forces. I will speak about those who gave their lives: Captain von Breunig, Diane McWilliams, Bethany Connor, and Mary Lasker. I will especially mention the supreme sacrifice made by Patrick Kell."

The Prince paused and looked toward Melissa. Taking up a position behind her, he rested his hands upon her shoulders. She reached her left hand up to touch him, but her right hand brushed away tears.

A lump rose to Dan's throat. *Patrick would have been happy to see them together. I'm glad she told him.*

The Prince looked up. "I have already spoken with the other members of the Kell Hounds and those Heimdall survivors who know that Melissa was on the *Silver Eagle*. Quintus Allard, meanwhile, has his CID people spreading the rumor that the *Silver Eagle* was carrying an important Lyran official coming secretly to New Avalon for medical treatments at the NAIS."

The Prince hesitated, seeming unsure of himself for a moment. "I asked the five of you here because you were present when Melissa told Patrick Kell of our engagement." He smiled down at Melissa and squeezed her shoulders. "I am not sorry she did so, for perhaps the news helped to eased his passing."

Cat raised his glass. "To Patrick Kell, and the dreams he died to protect."

Everyone in the room nodded silently and drank.

Hanse was studying each of their faces. "You all realize, of course, that no word, no rumor, of this engagement must yet slip out. If it were to become common knowledge, chaos would reign. Neither of our realms is ready for such a revelation. Critics of the alliance within both the Federated Suns and the Lyran Commonwealth would attempt to stir up controversy."

Melissa leaned forward. "Knowledge of our bethrothal could do even worse than that. It would make Kurita and Marik feel trapped. It could unite our enemies, and that would create serious problems for stability in the Successor States."

Salome nodded solemnly. "I speak for the Kell Hounds, High-

323

nesses, when I say that our lips have been sealed by the blood of our dead comrades. If we were to betray this secret, we would be betraying the sacrifice that they made."

Clovis also nodded agreement. "I'll share this information with no one, inside Heimdall or out. Not even my mother shall learn of it from me." He glanced down at his boots and added in a tense whisper, "And never my father."

Prince Hanse nodded solemnly. "Captain Redburn has already given me his oath, and he has been duly rewarded for his efforts on Melissa's behalf." The Prince indicated Clovis with a quick nod and grin. "Clovis has also bargained for a reward. He and his people have been pardoned for the hijacking. We have offered them whatever medical treatment they require, and are providing for them on Northwind until they can return to the Lyran Commonwealth."

The Prince looked up at the three mercenaries and shrugged helplessly. "Had I the chance right now, I would gladly give the Kell Hounds titles and land. I would make you heroes in the Federated Suns. When the day comes that all this can be revealed, I will induct you into the Order of Davion. I have already issued the Dragon Slayer's Ribbon for the Kell Hounds as a unit. I have also prepared a document to be opened after the wedding, that awards, posthumously, each of your slain comrades the Medal Excalibur. I will have a monument built to them on New Avalon."

The Prince paused and swallowed hard. "But what can I do for you now? I know medals and titles mean nothing when you have lost comrades. How can I reward your bravery?"

Dan cleared his throat and inched forward. "I'll speak for myself. What I did was foolish and desperate, but it's now considered brave because of the result. I did what I felt I had to do, and I still didn't save Patrick. Now Patrick…well…he knew exactly what he was doing. He continued to kill *Panther*s so that the rest of us could live. He goaded the Kuritans into attacking the *Victor* so that we would survive. He knew, from the moment he hatched that plan, that he'd never walk away alive. But he hoped that Melissa and some of the rest of us would. That's bravery and courage."

Dan opened his hands and winced at the pain shooting through his shoulder. "The best reward for me would be something that would keep Patrick's memory alive. I don't mean a statue or a medal." Dan swallowed past the lump in his throat. "Maybe a scholarship…one that would give potential MechWarriors with the same sort of 'heart' as Patrick the chance to get the training they could never have otherwise. That would be reward enough for me."

Dan felt Cat's hand on his shoulder. "I agree with Captain Allard.

324

your Highness." Salome nodded her approval as well.

Prince Hanse smiled genuinely. "It shall be done."

Melissa leaned forward earnestly once more. "It shall be done here, and in the Lyran Commonwealth," she said. "Patrick Kell shall never be forgotten."

Epilogue

Sian
Sian Commonality, Capellan Confederation

10 June 3027

Justin glared at Tsen Shang as two servants knelt at his feet, carefully tucking the silken trousers into the ankles of the black court slippers. Then he looked back at the mirror, which reflected him dressed in a full-length silken coat of gold cloth embroidered with black tigers and with riding slits in front and back. When Shang merely smiled back amiably, Justin said, "If you find this so amusing, I'll trade places with you."

Shang shook his head. He wore a robe of similar length and cut though his was deep blue with a design of yellow dragons worked into it. "That would not help you, Justin. We are bound for the same place." Shang clapped his hands sharply and the servants withdrew. "Follow me."

Justin snorted. "If you'd said that on Solaris, I would have…"

Shang shrugged. "I do as I am told, Justin. This way."

Justin walked behind Shang as they passed quietly through carpeted hallways. Muted lights glowed from within stone lanterns and cast just enough light for Justin to make out a few of the mythological designs in the carpet. The MechWarrior also marveled at all the exquisite teak latticework as Shang led him deeper into the building.

What Justin did not like was the fuzziness of his narcotic hangover. His muscles ached as though he'd caught the flu, though he knew that to be a residue of the jumps through hyperspace. *How far have they taken me*? he wondered.

Shang stopped before two massive bronze doors and motioned for Justin to stand beside him. From beyond the doors, Justin heard the muffled thunder of a gong. As the doors slowly opened, the gong's dying echoes bled out into the corridor. Justin felt Shang's hand on his elbow and allowed himself to be steered into the room.

Longer than it was wide and rising up to another level, the cavernous room dwarfed Justin. In the soft, indirect lighting, the walls of the main floor glowed a dull red that lent a feeling of warmth to the chamber. The upper section, with its balconies latticed in intricate teakwork, gave Justin the impression that he had been invited into a viewing gallery.

At the far end of the room was a dais holding a huge throne. The throne's back had been carved from a single piece of mahogany. Even from the doorway, Justin recognized the carven symbols and images as from Capellan mythology. The throne, quite literally, was backed by the universe. Seated there, with his hands clasped before him, was Maximilian Liao.

With the deliberation of a spider, the Capellan Chancellor rose slowly from his seat. He, too, wore a formal robe extending to the ankles. All black except for the silver of the Liao crest embroidered over his heart, the garment fell in straight lines that emphasized Liao's tall, slender frame. As the Chancellor stared at Justin with steely eyes and a stony expression, Justin felt as though he were being mechanically scanned, digitized, and analyzed.

"*Zao*, Justin Xiang." The Chancellor bowed slightly in the MechWarrior's direction, then waved him forward. "I have anticipated this meeting with great pleasure."

Justin bowed deeply, then advanced, feeling Shang follow several steps behind. By the time Justin had reached the dais, Liao was seated once more, his fingers steepled together in a sinister fashion. The thin wisps of moustache trailing down beside his mouth made Liao's masklike face appear even more inhuman.

"You have kindled pride in my heart with your victories." Liao then looked past Justin. "And Tsen Shang has reported your great contribution toward frustrating the trap that Hanse Davion had set us."

Maximilian handed a sealed document to Justin, who accepted it with a bow. "Open it, Xiang. The contents should please you."

Justin slid his thumb beneath the red wax seal and broke it. As he unrolled the rice paper and quickly scanned the lettering, a frown creased his brow. "I don't understand."

The barest hint of a smile twisted Liao's lips and put life in his eyes. "As well you know, Justin Xiang, the fact that you were born in the Confederation to a Capellan woman does not guarantee you citizenship. In our realm, each person must first contribute to the society in a way that makes it grow and makes it proud. That is the lifeblood of the Confederation—service of the individual to the whole of society. As a youth, you never completed an activity that would have earned your citizenship." Liao smiled more fully. "Your battles on Solaris, however, have made you more than worthy of the citizenship that document confers upon you."

Justin's heart caught in his throat. "I don't know what to say…"

Liao nodded sagely. "You need say nothing. You have earned it, and I trust that you will continue to offer your worthy services in the future."

Justin bowed. "I would be honored to battle in the games you sponsor here in the Confederation."

Liao shook his head. "No, Justin Xiang. Unlike other rulers in the Successor States, I see with a clear vision. I know your true worth. We are all aware that you fight like a demon in the arenas and that many spectators would rejoice to see you compete in the next quarterly games. In fact, *Yen-lo-wang* has been brought here to Sian for your use."

The Chancellor stood abruptly and towered over the MechWarrior. "Though your skill is great, it would be a needless risk to let you step into the arena again," Liao said, producing another cruel smile. "More valuable to me than your reflexes and your tactical skill is your mind. You know how Hanse Davion thinks and plans, having taken part in so many Federated Suns actions. You also know your father well enough to guess how he may react in a certain situation. Best of all, you know fellow graduates from Sakhara, and have served with other key Davion commanders. All the intelligence training I give my people could never duplicate your close knowledge of the ways of House Davion."

Liao paused as he looked hard at Justin for a moment. "I watched with outrage as Davion justice spat you out like so much chaff. I nearly ordered my people to deny that you were an agent, but I knew Count Vitios would have taken that to be even greater proof of your guilt.

grieved for you as everyone turned against and abandoned you." Liao pointed to Tsen Shang. "When I learned that you had gone to Solaris, I ordered Shang to help you in any way he could."

Justin nodded. "What would you have me do, Chancellor?"

Again Liao smiled like a predator. "It is not what I would have you do, but the opportunity I will make for you. Because of Tsen Shang's excellent performance, I have recalled him here to Sian to serve as a Maskirovka analyst. I offer you this same chance to put your knowledge of the Federated Suns to use. You will sift through reports to help determine the truth about Hanse Davion's plans and intentions. These analyses will help me to one day destroy our mutual enemy, Hanse Davion."

Justin nodded solemnly. "And if I accept this commission, how will you know to trust me?"

The Chancellor threw back his head and laughed heartily. It was not a pleasant sound. "Ah, Justin, I can read you like a book. I know, despite what they have put you through, that you will not betray your family to harm. That I admire, and so I will not ask such things of you. But in the work of breaking Hanse Davion as he tried to break you, in this I know you can be trusted."

Justin nodded. "You are correct. I willingly accept your offer."

Liao smiled broadly. "Excellent." At a single clap of his hands, a wall panel slid up into the ceiling. Liao descended from the throne and led the way toward the opening. "Come. It is time for us to celebrate your arrival, and to dine with yet another ally."

Justin followed the Chancellor, then jerked to a halt in the doorway. The only other guest was already seated in the dining room, his bright green uniform clashing violently with the rich artistry of the embroidered silk screens surrounding the table on three sides. The petulant look on the man's face disturbed the sense of peace that the arrangement of cherry blossoms on the dark walnut table was meant to create.

Liao glanced back over his shoulder and noted Justin's astonishment. "I thought you knew our other guest," he said.

Justin nodded slowly and lurched forward with a stiff-legged gait. "We have met." Justin forced a smile to his lips, but his eyes showed no warmth. "Politics makes for strange bedfellows," he said, extending his hand to the man seated to the right of Liao's place of honor.

"Indeed," murmured Duke Michael Hasek-Davion as he took Justin's proferred hand. "And that is because the end always justifies the means."

Liao lifted a glass of plum wine. "Let us drink, then, to the one end upon which we can all agree—to the destruction of Hanse Davion—his line and his House!"

329

Glossary

AUTOCANNON

The autocannon is a rapid-firing autoloading weapon. Light vehicle autocannon range from 30 to 90 mm caliber, while heavy 'Mech autocannon may be 80 to 120 mm or more. The weapon fires high-speed streams of high-explosive, armor-piercing shells. Because of the limitations of 'Mech targeting technology, the autocannon' effective anti-'Mech range is limited to less then 600 meters.

BATTLEMECH

BattleMechs are the most powerful war machines ever built. First developed by Terran scientists and engineers more than 500 years ago, these huge, man-shaped vehicles are faster, more mobile, better armored, and more heavily armed then any 20th-century tank. Ten t twelve meters tall and equipped with particle projection cannons, lasers, rapid-fire autocannon, and missiles, they pack enough fire power to flatten anything but another BattleMech. A small fusion reactor provides virtually unlimited power, and BattleMechs can b adapted to fight in environments ranging from sun-baked deserts t subzero arctic icefields.

COMSTAR

ComStar, the interstellar communications network, was the brainchild of Jerome Blake, formerly Minister of Communications during the latter years of the Star League. After the League's fall, Blake seized Terra and reorganized what was left of the League's communications network into a private organization that sold its services to the five Successor Houses for a profit. Since that time, ComStar has also developed into a powerful, secret society steeped in mysticism and ritual. Initiates to the ComStar Order commit themselves to lifelong service.

JUMPSHIPS AND DROPSHIPS
JumpShip

Interstellar travel is accomplished via JumpShips, first developed in the 22nd century. Named for their ability to "jump" instantaneously from one point to another, the vessels consist of a long, thin drive core and an enormous sail. The sail is constructed from a specially coated polymer that absorbs vast quantities of electromagnetic energy from the nearest star. Energy collected by the sail is slowly transfered to the drive core, which converts it into a space-twisting field. After making its jump, the ship cannot travel again until it has recharged its drive with solar energy at its new location. Safe recharge times range from six to eight days.

JumpShips travel instantaneously across vast interstellar distances by means of the Kearny-Fuchida hyperdrive. The K-F drive generates a field around the JumpShip, then opens a hole into hyperspace. In moments, the JumpShip is transported through to its new destination, across distances of up to 30 light years.

Jump points are the locations within a star system where the system's gravity is next to nothing, the prime prerequisite for operation of the K-F drive. The distance away from the system's star is dependant on that star's mass, and is usually many tens of millions of kilometers away. Every star has two principal jump points, one at the zenith point at the star's north pole, and one at the nadir point at the south pole. An infinite number of other jump points also exist, but they are used only rarely.

JumpShips never land on planets, and only rarely travel into the inner parts of a star system. Interplanetary travel is carried out by DropShips, vessels that attach themselves to the JumpShip until arrival at the jump point. Most of the JumpShips currently in service are already centuries old, because the Successor Lords are unable to construct many new ones each year. For this reason, there is an unspoken agreement among even these bitter enemies to leave one another's JumpShips alone.

331

DropShip

Because JumpShips generally remain at a considerable distance from a star system's inhabited worlds, DropShips were developed for interplanetary travel. A DropShip attaches to hard points on the JumpShip, and will later be dropped from the parent vessel after entry into a system. DropShips are highly maneuverable, well-armed, and sufficiently aerodynamic to take off from and land on a planetary surface.

LRM

LRM is an abbreviation for "Long-Range Missile," an indirect-fire missile with a high-explosive warhead. LRMs have a maximum extreme range of several kilometers, but are accurate only between about 150 and 700 meters.

NEW AVALON INSTITUTE OF SCIENCE (NAIS)

In 3015, Prince Hanse Davion decreed the construction of a new university on New Avalon, planetary capitol of the Federated Suns. Known as the New Avalon Institute of Science (NAIS), its purpose is to recover the lost technologies and knowledge of the past. Both House Kurita and House Marik have followed with their own universities, but neither is as well bankrolled or staffed as the NAIS.

PPC

PPC is the abbreviation for "Particle Projection Cannon," a magnetic accelerator firing high-energy proton or ion bolts, causing damage both through impact and high temperature. PPCs are among the most effective weapons available to BattleMechs. Though they have a theoretical range limited only by line-of-sight considerations, the technology available for focusing and aiming the bolt limits effective range to less then 600 meters.

SRM

SRM is the abbreviation for "Short-Range Missiles," direct trajectory missiles with high-explosive or armor-piercing explosive warheads. They have a range of less than one kilometer, and are accurate only at ranges of less than 300 meters. They are more powerful, however, than LRMs.

STAR LEAGUE

In 2571, the Star League was formed in an attempt to peacefully ally the major star systems inhabited by the human race after it had taken to stars. The League continued and prospered for almost 200 years, until the Succession Wars broke out in the late 28th century. The League was eventually destroyed when the ruling body known as the High Council disbanded in the midst of a struggle for power. Each of the Council Lords then declared himself First Lord of the Star League, and within months, war had engulfed the Inner Sphere. These centuries of continuous war are now known simply as the Succession Wars, and continue to the present day. As a result, much of the technology that had brought mankind to its highest level of advancement has been destroyed, lost, or forgotten.

SUCCESSOR LORDS

Each of the five Successor States is ruled by a family descended from one of the original Council Lords of the old Star League. All five royal House Lords claim the title of First Lord, and they have been at each other's throats since the beginning of the Succession Wars in the late 28th century. Their battleground is the vast Inner Sphere, which is composed of all the star systems once occupied by the Star League member-states.

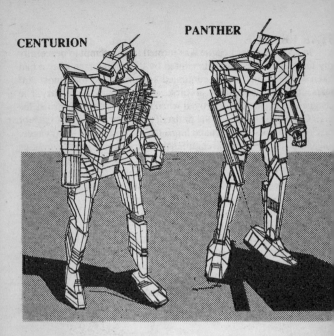

CENTURION

PANTHER

CENTURION

The 50-ton *Centurion* is best known for its ability to make slo~
steady advances. With its right-arm autocannon and torso-mount~
medium lasers, the CN9 prefers to attack at close range, where it c~
do the most damage. Equipped with 8.5 tons of armor and enough he~
sinks to prevent overheating, the *Centurion* is tough enough to abso~
a considerable amount of damage. In smaller encounters, t~
Centurion's left-torso LRM is also effective. With its maximum spe~
of 64.8 kph and ability to fire without overheating, the *Centurion*~
often used as part of a raiding lance.

PANTHER

The *Panther* is a 35-ton, jump-capable 'Mech with a maximu~
speed of 64.8 kph. Its main function is as fire support for light and fa~
moving 'Mech units. Its right-arm PPC is an unusual weapon for~
'Mech of its size. For close-in work, the *Panther*'s center-torso SR~
has also proved to be a reliable weapon. This nimble 'Mech~
especially suited to the dirty tactics of city street fighting, where~
PPC gives it the chance to disable all but the heaviest 'Mechs with a f~
well-aimed shots.

334

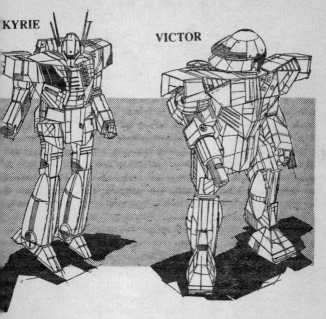

KYRIE

VICTOR

ALKYRIE

A 'Mech design seen only among the forces of House Davion, the *alkyrie* is a highly regarded light 'Mech.. Its six tons of armor, top eed of 86.4 kph, and 150-meter jump capacity allow it to outmaneu- r heavier units in battle and to absorb a fair amount of damage. Its ft-torso LRM is unusual in a light 'Mech, making it a potentially ugh opponent at long range. At close range, its right-arm medium ser and super jump capability can be a potent mix. Though no match r a medium or heavy 'Mech in one-to-one combat, the *Valkyrie* is fective when part of a lance.

ICTOR

This 80-ton Assault 'Mech moves at a maximum speed of 64.8 h, and is the only one of its class with jump capability. The *Victor* ounts an autocannon in its right arm, two medium lasers in the left m, and an SRM 4 in its center torso. In battle, the *Victor* often throws opponents off guard by surprising them with its jump-capability.

WARHAMMER

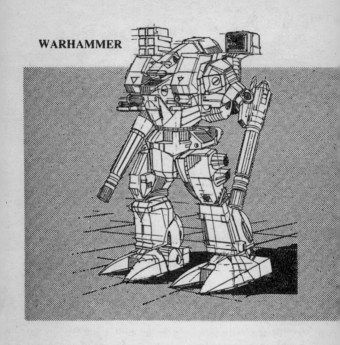

WARHAMMER

Because of its size and weaponry, the 70-ton *Warhammer* is on of the most dangerous and powerful BattleMechs ever placed in th field. With its right- and left-arm PPCs, torso-mounted medium laser and its right-torso SRM 6, this 'Mech has the sheer firepower that first-line fighter needs. The WHM-6R is also equipped with torso mounted small lasers and machine guns, making it a threat to an infantry and support craft foolhardy enough to close in on it. Th *Warhammer*'s maximum speed is 64.8 kph, and it is not jump capabl All *Warhammer*s are equipped with a special searchlight that ti directly into their targeting and tracking systems, making the 'Mech formidable night fighter. Mounted on the 'Mech's left torso, th system can function either as a simple searchlight or as part of th targeting system.

336

MONARCH

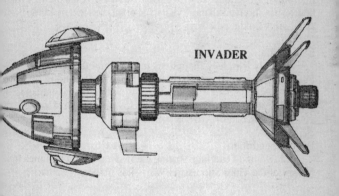

INVADER

MONARCH CLASS DROPSHIP

The *Monarch* is one of the few civilian liners still in service in the Successor States. The 5,000-ton vessel can carry over 266 passengers plus 900 tons of cargo.

INVADER CLASS JUMPSHIP

The *Invader* is the most common JumpShip operating in the Successor States today. Capable of transporting up to three of the DropShips, the *Invader* is well-suited for both commercial and military purposes.

337

Subject: Michael A. Stackpole

Observation:

Subject continues to cling to his delusional belief that he was born 27 November 1957. He has fabricated a complete history, in which he reports to have taken a degree in history from the University of Vermont in 1979. Though our documents contraindicate it, he claims to have moved from Vermont to Arizona in 1979, and amassed a list of publishing credits from late 20th-century game companies, including Flying Buffalo, FASA, TSR Inc., Mayfair Games, Hero Games, Interplay Productions, and Electronic Arts. He is unable to explain how he has survived all these years, but points to a text by Mark Twain as possibly holding the key.

Evaluation:

Probably harmless, though his insights into the workings of the Successor States are interesting. Of all that he has said in our interviews, the only detail with any veracity is that he has modeled his portrayal of Maximilian Liao after Governor Evan Mecham (an obscure 20th-century Arizona politician).

Recommendation:

Allow him to continue writing the two remaining volumes in his history of the Third Succession War—it is obviously cathartic.